THE CHANGEFUL
MAP

SALLY STOUT

Sally Stout

STORY WEAVER PRESS • FRANKFORT, MICHIGAN

Story Weaver Press
155 Beech St.
Frankfort, MI   49635
Orders: storyweaverpress@yahoo.com

ISBN 13: 978-0-9795580-0-9

*For
Doug, Adam and Emily*

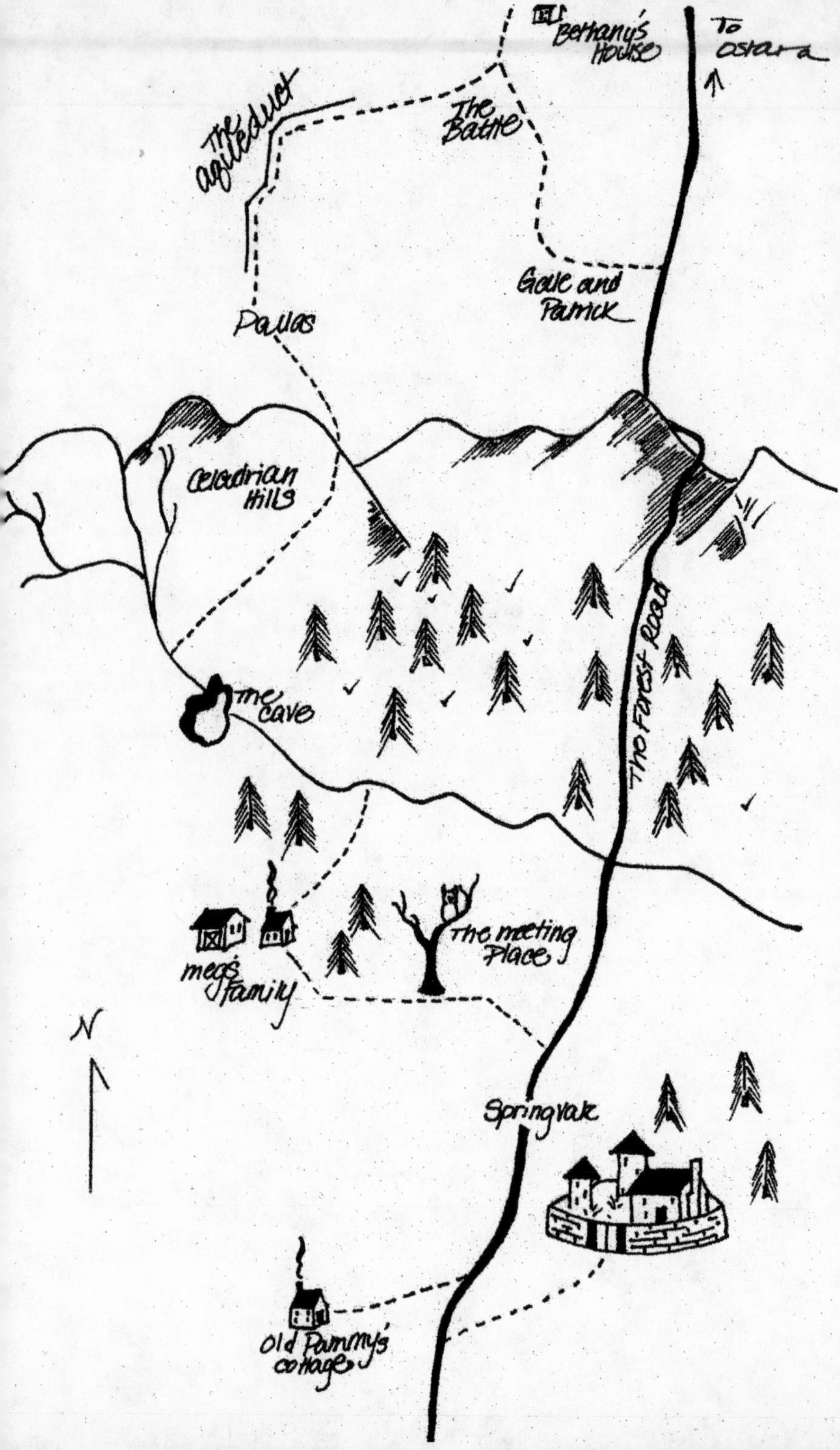
Bethany's House
To ostara
The aqueduct
The Battle
Gale and Patrick
Dallas
Celadrian Hills
The Forest Road
The cave
The meeting Place
meg's Family
N
Springvale
Old Pammy's cottage

PROLOGUE

THE YOUNG MAN'S BLADE sliced through a shaft of sunlight, never touching his opponent, who danced away mockingly. The wound to his forearm was slight, but it stung, and now his sleeve was soaked in blood. It was making his sword hand slippery.

His master had tried to tell him what it would be like, but as soon as the fighting began, the apprentice saw that parrying his master's blows or engaging in hand-to-hand combat with the sawdust-filled dummy hung from the workshop ceiling had given him false confidence. He had actually enjoyed the lessons – enjoyed showing off for the young women who leaned on the windowsills and watched him. Once he thought it would be impossible to lose with this sword in his hand; now doubt lurked at the edges of his mind, slowing his reactions.

All around him, the men and boys of the city fought for their lives. A moment before, the apprentice heard John Daine grunt in surprise when a thrust took him, but he could do nothing to comfort or save his friend. He mechanically blocked the blows of his own opponent and tried not to stumble over the childhood companion who lay unmoving just behind him.

The Ostaran danced out of range again. Out of the corner of his eye, the young man caught movement. He and John had been fighting back to back. Now that John was gone, of course the one who had slaughtered him would move on.

Tightening his grip on Mabus's hilt, the young man spun around, slicing deep into the neck of the Ostaran. It was his first kill, but again there was no time. He didn't even watch the man fall. Continuing full-circle, he met the blade of the one who had wounded his arm and would have struck him down from behind. The clang echoed above all the other noises of battle.

This is what it had come to. When the militia marched out from Pallas, weapons shining, the people shouted encouragement. *You show 'em boys. Send 'em running.* But none of the men were thinking of their pride now. Each was engaged in a simple struggle for his own life.

The young man's work with the trees had strengthened him, and his master's patient tutelage had made him a good swordsman, but he was weakening. He didn't notice the moment when he began to favor his right arm. The decision to draw his short knife and begin fighting with his left hand was also unconscious, but it did not confuse his opponent. The man seemed to have been expecting it.

The sounds of battle seemed to come from far away as he warded off blow after blow. He was only twenty-three, without wife or child. The people at home reckoned him the best wood-worker in the city since his master came twenty years before and moved into the big house by the city gate. All the life he had not yet lived seemed unbearably sweet now that he was about to lose it.

In the end, he wasn't the one who stumbled over John. The Ostaran rushed forward, forcing him to leap back. As the foreigner tripped and began to fall, the young man raised his arm to strike, but it had been a trick. The foreigner thrust upward, into the unprotected place under his arm.

As soon as the Ostaran was sure the boy was mortally wounded, he turned away. The apprentice stood curiously alone, his left hand pressed to the place where his life's blood was escaping. He sank to his knees. Fell onto his side.

The watcher pivoted his head, amber eyes wide, uneasy above the sunlit clearing. After a moment's hesitation, he swept down from the tree and brushed the young man gently with the edge of his wing. Then he flew towards the Celadrian hills with blood on his feathers.

By the time the runners came, darkness was falling. In the end, the men of the city had routed the Ostarans, but it had been at great loss. The few raiders who survived the fight had fled, but the level place by the stream was no circle of victory. Most of the forest folk leaned back against trees at the edges of the clearing with their eyes closed, or they gazed dully into the distance.

A group of three men from the city militia, staying close together, moved haltingly from one body to the next and paused. Was it someone they knew from home, or an Ostaran, his face defenseless and no longer frightful in death? When they knew the face, they called a name softly and knelt in a tight circle, listening for a groan or a breath, ready to offer comfort when it came. It never did.

No one went near the apprentice. His body sprawled awkwardly near the brook that sang over small stones, oblivious to human drama. When the runners cautiously entered the clearing at dusk and looked down at him, they shook their heads. But the Lady had told them to bring this one to her, so they lifted him as gently as they could and carried him without notice to the litter they had left within the forest. His fingertips trailed along the ground as they carried him away. Had his comrades noticed that trace, they might have followed, but in the morning they found only his bloodied sword, with no sign on the trampled ground to tell them where his body had gone.

The butcher mirrored the actions of the others, looking fearfully over his shoulder into the forest. "The woodworker's apprentice was dead. I'm sure of it." He lifted the sword with its glittering gems and tried to wipe away some of the blood on his filthy tunic, but it had dried. Then he removed his own simple blade from its scabbard and slipped the young man's into its place. "His master will be wantin' this back, I expect. I never understood why he gave it to the boy in the first place. Even if he did come from up the hill. A fancy sword can't save you if you lack the skill to use it." He held his own sword up boastingly and looked at it with satisfaction.

"Hush that," snapped the wheelwright. "The boy was like a son to him and that good with his hands. Last summer he took a piece of wood I brought him and shaped it into a chair so silky smooth and restful that when I'm working I think about the moment when I will ease into it. When I am at home, I see people go out of their way to stroke the grain of it. I don't want to see the old man's face when you tell him."

"Me?"

"Well, you're carrying the sword, and there's no one here who will take it from you now." He looked into the faces of the other men for the agreement he knew he would find there.

Far from their voices, the boy lay still and white on the litter. It rested in a meadow full of asters and goldenrod where the land began to rise into the Hills. The four runners shifted restlessly from one foot to the other, wishing the Lady would tell them what she wanted them to do next or, better yet, release them.

They agreed. It was too bad. They had all liked him. The woodworker's apprentice had been more decent to them than most of the people of the town, and now he was dead. They had carried him far enough to know that. The bouncing and jolting of the litter had not elicited a single groan from him, and they had seen the Lady touch his throat where the life-drum should have been beating. She looked grave, but she still packed the wound with the herbs from her bag. That was hours ago; they had seen no change.

She looked up at them with a weary smile, as if she could read their thoughts.

"He lingers close to the border between the worlds. I cannot call him back. His healing is beyond me…"

She trailed off and continued softly, as if to herself. "There is a place where time may do its work. Poor boy." She stroked his hair.

"This is not the future we chose for you, your master and I, yet neither is it quite the end…"

1

AT THE GATES

THE TWO STOOD A little apart from one another. They did not call or knock at the wooden gate but settled themselves to wait at one side of the frozen, rutted path. Dawn would come soon enough, and then the manor gates would open. Beyond the high wall, smoke from the chimneys of the tower house hung like earthbound clouds in the cold air. After so many days hastening toward this destination, they had arrived too early. They were silent, and their deep hoods hid their faces.

Because of the snow, it had taken thirteen days to walk the forest path. This meant Abel had been too long away from Ostara; Katherine knew his return would be rapid once this business at Springvale was finished. But he had been kind enough. He would have made one more camp. It had been her idea to walk through the night and bring the journey to an end.

During that final night, Kathe mostly wrapped herself deep in her thoughts, only half surfacing to listen to Abel's monologue. His theme was always the same – to convince her that she was doing the right thing. That the right thing was to run away and to hide in a place no one would think to look for her.

"Only for a month, or maybe two," Abel had said. "Greystone sits in your father's place. He barely had to lift his sword. But he still seeks the blood tie. He has promised to marry the daughter of Ostara's lord."

"You, Sparrow," he said lightly, using her childhood name.

Katherine nodded. In truth, she had no wish to be a pawn. Even though her bones ached with cold, she still believed it was right to be taking the forest path. If she had remained within the Hills as a prisoner or worse, what plan could her brother and father have made to chase the Claymon back to their frozen land?

As they walked under the naked, arching branches, Abel continued to argue aloud, more for his own sake, she thought, than for hers. "The people of Springvale will accept you easily. After these days of travel..." He paused, but she caught his glance and knew what he had been about to say.

After almost two weeks in the forest, her hair was no longer in shining plaits. She had chosen a plain, blue gown for the journey, and her cloak was ragged along its finely embroidered hem. Lord Stefan would see her strong hands and clear eyes, but he would not care to hear too many details about her past. He would accept Abel's tale of a family that lost its head and home and was now scattered and seeking refuge. After all, it was the simple truth. It made sense that the daughter of such a house should seek a roof over her head, even if it meant servitude, when there was no uncle or friend to protect her.

After a pause, Abel continued, "This way you'll be safe, and as important, so will the Elder family line."

Katherine always snorted when Abel came to that part of the plan, as he did with annoying frequency. She squinted to see his face in the moonlight, wondering if he really believed in the importance of a family line...people who hadn't been born yet and might never be born. Even though she knew the rules of her world very well, Katherine planned to make her own way. She would never be a prize for some warrior to win, like a piglet at the village fair. She forced her exhausted legs to keep walking in order to avoid just that fate.

There were not so subtle differences between her own point of view and Abel's, but she kept silent. This had been an important and early part of her training. She could still hear her mother's voice telling her, "Think thrice, child, before uttering a word. Watch the waters well before you make a ripple."

Katherine knew the only reason Abel could bear to absent himself from his beloved city was his strong belief that, by protecting her, he was protecting Ostara. Despite his youth, he was a favorite among her father's counselors even though he was so often far away. All the things he quietly observed as he indulged in wanderlust made him useful to a landlocked city like Ostara.

He had begged a single night's shelter in Springvale Manor years ago. Then, he found its lord and lady kind, old fashioned, and completely uninterested in affairs beyond their own fields. While hospitable, they had not asked a single question about the politics or customs of the Three Hills. He filled some of the dinner silences with descriptions of Ostara clinging stubbornly to the flanks of the hills and of his brushes with beauty and danger in the forest, but their polite expressions betrayed no particular interest.

The custom in Ostara was to linger over wine and tell stories after eating, but on the night of Abel's visit, the Lord and Lady of Springvale retired early. At that time, he was amused by their country manners, but later, in need, he remembered Springvale and its incurious master and mistress.

Abel passed the hour before dawn pacing the length of the wall and walking a short distance back the way they had come. As if he had not walked enough. As if he would not soon be retracing all their steps. Katherine huddled miserably within her cloak and watched him.

But when the gate creaked open, he was by her side again, ready to play the part of a kind neighbor delivering the manor's newest kitchen maid. After more waiting in the stone paved courtyard, Lord Stefan approached stiffly, bulky in a woolen cloak.

"Is she of good character?" he asked, showing no sign of recognition when he looked at Abel. "Is she strong?" Stefan listened while Abel told the story, and he paid a few silver coins – all without a single word to Katherine.

The time for her interview came later, after the family's dishes had been cleared away that night, when the servants sat around the kitchen fire. As they slowly ate stew from wooden bowls, they did their best to crack this delectable nut that had dropped into a dull day.

Cook sat nearest the fire. Despite the bright flames, the room was chill two steps away from the hearth. Snow still lingered in shady places in the garden, and the wind crept through the cracks around the door. Because she was new, Katherine sat next to the old woman on the same bench.

"I can remember when my own father brought me here," Meg began kindly. She was the youngest of the girls, a year or two younger than Kathe. "I had just turned nine. Oh, I cried to leave the little ones. For a whole week, that's all I did. Cry. It was my job to fetch buckets of water for the washing. That week, we washed the clothes and dishes in my tears."

"I remember," interrupted Cook. "Such sobbing and moping. Like a puppy taken from its dam too soon. I was about ready to drown you before you quieted. This one," she said, turning toward Kathe, "seems glad to have left the rest of the litter behind. Maybe life was cruel there and she looks for kinder treatment here. Or maybe she's just too simple to know she's been sold."

Kathe had been studying her own hands holding her bowl, but now she glanced into Cook's face.

"Never mind that," said Mole. He worked the kennels; three dogs sprawled at his feet. "There's no one beholden to Lord Stefan to the north, so the man and her must've come from the forest – maybe even by way of the Three Hills, I don't know how many days' walk beyond the trees. Do you remember the tinker from Ostara, a week or two after the new year? He said it looked to him like a fight was brewing there."

. "Girl," he said, addressing himself to Katherine. "What do you know of war?"

Katherine closed her eyes and was once again in her dark chamber, waking from uneasy sleep to Abel's pounding at her bedroom door. Again she felt the panic in her gut and the trembling of her hands as she pulled a cloak around her shoulders, and the two of them moved like shadows through the darkened halls of her home.

"Yes, there is war," she whispered. Against her will, springing from exhaustion and fear, tears threatened to fall. She brushed them away.

Meg said, "You don't have to tell it." She had come to the manor so young that the dangers outside its walls had grown in her imagination until she scarcely dared to go in search of the cattle in the evening. Now sixteen, she didn't want to hear about war, especially war within a fortnight's journey of Springvale.

Impatiently, Mole leaned forward. "What do you know?" he demanded, his expression hungry. "This manor at the edge of the world receives few visitors."

Kathe recognized his expression. She had seen it on the faces of her father's own men, after word of the Claymon advance began to circulate through their ranks. For Mole, who spent each day in numbing sameness tending to his master's hounds, and his master, moreover, too old to stray often from his fire, the hunger would be greater. How could a servant broaden his world? War might end his life or give him a chance to win his freedom.

When she looked around the circle, Kathe saw the same intent expression in the other men's faces. The women and girls sat with their eyes downcast or looked at each other nervously, as if trying to find a way to ease the sudden tension in the kitchen.

Katherine turned further toward the fire and leaned forward so that her hair fell forward to screen her expression. "Ostara is no more," she said. "The Claymon rule the North. They have taken the city, and now they hold it by their great strength." She looked into Mole's face. "Perhaps they will move south when they grow hungry for more land."

Seeing his eager expression, she added, "The man who brought me here has warned your master. Perhaps you will be soldiering soon."

Cook elbowed Katherine hard in the side, sending her bowl clattering to the floor. "Your master? Your master? You had best get used to the idea that Lord Stefan is your own master too. The plain truth is there's no reason any army would waste its time to fight for a poor, out-of-the-way place like Springvale."

As she spoke, she glared at Meg, who had turned pale and seemed about to burst into tears. When the girl looked away, Cook turned her angry attention toward the others in the circle. "War hasn't got anything to do with people like us, especially when it's way on the other side of the forest. Who among you has journeyed one day into it, let alone seen the other side? Bah!" she spat into the fire, "We might as well be getting all worked up about a war on that moon up there." She stood and pulled Kathe roughly to her feet. "Now clean up that mess, girl. Then you and Meg do the rest of the washing before you sleep."

2

THE KITCHEN GIRL

AS SHE PUSHED THROUGH the blackberry thicket into the woods, Kathe felt the sun chasing her. Through the morning, the heat at the edge of the field had pressed and melted her until she thought she would disappear into the parched ground, leaving nothing but a half-filled basket of berries and an old, blue dress. In the woods, shaded by leaves, she moved lightly, like a wild cat. *Or a wild Kathe*, she thought ruefully. *Despite the way I spend my days, I'm not domestic any more.* She lifted the thick braid of damp, red hair and savored the breeze on her neck.

When she looked back toward the edge of the forest, she saw the shapes of other household servants scattered along the margin of the brushy trees, intent on collecting berries for pies that would appear on the long table that night. She knew they were just as intent on resisting a taste of the juicy, sun-warmed fruit. Though their hands were stained purple, as hers were, each knew better than to return to the manor house with a stained mouth.

Cook would be looking for them in late afternoon with enough extra fruit to dry for a taste of summer next winter, but the bread they had eaten as they passed through the gate early that morning was a distant memory. Now, nearing mid-day, it was hard to remember far-off winter through the thirst for berries. It was a thirst the water from the skin bag hanging in the shade could not touch.

Kathe crouched behind an oak and reached into her basket for a handful of purple-black fruit. She crushed several berries in her mouth and savored their juice as it trickled down her throat. She closed her eyes, relaxing against the broad trunk of the tree until the sharp rapping of a blue jay on a limb just above her called her back to her duty. She stood and stretched, arching her back and startling the bird. It flew deeper into the forest, screaming an alarm.

Her eyes followed the flight of the bird until it disappeared among the trees. With all her heart, she longed to follow it.

For the past five months, she had watched the moon. Every time it reached full, she lay awake under the blanket she shared with Meg, listening to straw rustle as sleepers tried to find warmth and comfort. When all was still, she crept to the door, silently placing a spell of quiet on it. Since she had little trust in her own magic, she also kept the hinges greased with bits of fat from the kitchen, working it into the leather as she passed by.

On those full-moon nights, Kathe always stayed in the shadows at the base of the wall before climbing to the byre roof and jumping down into the bushes below. It was easy; the wall was made to keep animals and strangers out, not in. Then she hurried to the lightening struck tree, just off the path into Springvale, before the track entered the fields. There, she searched for the arrow Abel said he would leave where the tree forked. It was to be his sign that he would meet her that night.

It was never there.

Not the first time in the cold moonlight of early spring or the second, when clouds hid the moon, and she spent the night huddled in the rain under a cedar tree. It wasn't there the third time, when the biting insects swarmed around her nor the fourth, when she sat under the tree and wept until the stars turned toward morning.

A great-horned owl stayed near the marked tree. Perhaps it even lived in the hollowed trunk. After so many months, Kathe had come to expect its call. Even though it sounded far away, she had come to understand this was only a trick of the creature's voice. Once, she saw it land lightly on the jagged trunk. It had become her companion through those long nights.

Kathe could never find a way to climb back over the wall into the manor, and anyway, she was unwilling to return before dawn. What if Abel should come and not find her? She always waited until the gates were opened at daybreak. She watched the boys driving the cattle and sheep through, and her stomach growled at the scent of the meat pies they were carrying. Then she entered as innocently as if she had just returned from delivering an early morning message to one of the nearby tenants, or with a skirtful of vegetables, as if Cook had sent her out to the gardens.

The full moon would rise again this midsummer night, and Kathe had decided that, if no arrow awaited her, she must leave Springvale. So far, no one had asked about her wet clothing, her arms covered with insect bites, or her face streaked with tears, but soon they would. It was lucky Meg slept so deeply.

She couldn't wait any longer for Abel to return for her. In fact, she couldn't believe she had waited this long. How could she have stayed here, chopping vegetables and hoeing gardens instead of returning home to look after those who surely needed her?

Maybe the plan Abel devised had been wrong. Perhaps she could have hidden near the Three Hills, even ridden with her brother. But of one thing she was sure. Abel was faithful.

If he could have come on the first full moon, he would have. If he could not have come then, he would have been there on one of the others or, more likely, he would have come during the day and pounded on the manor door, demanded to talk to her. But he had not come. That meant he could not come.

For weeks she had swallowed her fears. Now they all roared into her mind at once. She could not dam them. She leaned against the oak and closed her eyes until the noise faded.

When she opened them, a dark-headed girl stood in front of her, with one hand on her sleeve.

3

MEG

"I DIDN'T MEAN TO scare you. I saw you go into the trees, and when you didn't come back, I worried." Meg glanced uneasily about her, as if she were deep in the forest instead of just inside the brushy edge, within shouting distance of her companions. "To tell the truth, though, the shade does feel good. Did you fall asleep?"

Kathe managed a smile and shook her head. If she really intended to leave Springvale, she must start to pay better attention to the here and now, not linger in daydreams.

Meg spoke again, looking intently over Kathe's shoulder. "Or are you thinking about tonight?" Kathe took an involuntary step away from the girl. "It is the night of the full moon, isn't it?" Meg asked softly.

After a long silence, Kathe sighed, took Meg's hand, and pulled her down to sit beside her under the tree. "I'm sorry. I should have told you, since we share a blanket each night." She paused, reading Meg's expression.

Meg was carefully studying a green acorn lying by her foot. "I've no wish to pry. You don't have to tell your secret. It's only... well, since you came to Springvale I feel happier. I like listening to your stories. Sometimes, when you sing at a task, I sing too.

Though I have a voice like a frog." Meg smiled tentatively. "It's no business of mine why you slip away every month, but I do not sleep after I feel you go and am not content even after you return early in the morning. You look so sad. I am sure — soon you will not return at all."

Kathe laughed out loud, startling Meg. "No, I'm not mad, and I am laughing because it will be pure relief to tell you the tale, though you will likely think I am just making up another story. For that matter, many of the stories I told you over the washing and in the garden were true, from memory, not imagining." Then her eye again fell upon her half filled basket.

Meg saw the direction of her glance and said, "I'll share my berries with you. My basket is about to overflow. And we can help each other to have two full baskets for Cook."

Kathe wondered why she had never appreciated the intelligence that lay, along with kindness, in Meg's character. She gave her head a little shake; she had looked only inward for too long.

"I am Katherine Elder, of Ostara. My father ruled there, until mid-winter, and I lived in a big house high on the slope of Mara, the gentlest of the Three Hills. It is no palace, just a comfortable, old manor house, cold in winter but cool in summer because of thick walls and narrow windows." She paused, remembering again the way the late summer sun slanted through those windows, illuminating the web on her mother's loom.

"You may envy my easy life. But have you noticed that Irene, Stefan's lady, is dead tired at the end of every day? I was willing enough to learn the women's arts of managing the household and sewing, and even showed some promise at the loom, but it was really my brother's world I loved. Boys seem to spend most of their time outdoors, under the sky. Bard's world of horses and dogs called me much more loudly than did the world of servants, kitchens, and cloth growing on the looms. When I listened to his tutor's lessons, they seemed much more fascinating than my own. Isn't it funny that I should end up as a kitchen servant? And these days I would gladly spend an afternoon weaving even plain linen."

She took a deep breath so she could say the next words calmly. "My brother is two years older than me, twenty..." She knew he still lived. Surely she would feel empty if Bard had been killed.

"Luckily for me, he was often willing to take his pesky little sister along, into the forest and sometimes even further, to the foothills of the eastern mountains. So long as he was with me, my mother and father were content to indulge me — if I did my own work as well. Abel was often with us. He is the one who brought me here."

She paused, seeking words to explain Abel. At last she said, "Abel has greater freedom because he is not noble. I think he has seen the whole world. At least, he seems to have friends everywhere."

Meg had some ideas about Kathe's nights outside, that there was an unhappy love affair, or maybe Kathe left the compound to worship some northern goddess under the full moon each month. Mostly she had thought Kathe was homesick, as Meg had been when she first came to the manor.

"What happened?"

"At midwinter our eyes were opened to what should have been seen seasons before." Kathe's face and voice became carefully matter-of-fact. Her fingers braided long stems of grass growing within reach. "My uncle has long been counselor to my father, who trusted and valued his advice, but my father has other advisors and always thought...thinks... for himself. My uncle grew tired of so often seeing his wishes ignored. With his confused vision, he saw an opportunity to rule in my father's place — through the Claymon. I do not know what has happened to him, but if he holds any position of power, it is with the trappings of authority, as a puppet to calm the people of the city. To them he is a familiar face. I wonder if they know he is a traitor."

"And your father?" Meg asked.

"By the time the proof of my uncle's treachery was clear, it was late. By the time my father could bring himself to act, there was little he could do. The city was lost."

She looked at Meg and managed a smile. "It seems so long ago and so far away. Sometimes my life there and even the Three Hills themselves seem to be a dream, but it has eased my heart to tell the dream to you." Kathe once again rose to her feet and picked up her basket. "Abel told me he would meet me at the full moon by the lightening struck tree, to take me home or at least to bring news. Four moons have come and gone. Tonight is the fifth. I am still here, and I do not know what has happened to my mother or my father, or to Bard." She moved to take Meg's hand, pulled her to her feet, and turned to make her way back to the briars.

"But the story isn't finished!" Meg said. Kathe stopped but did not turn around. "Tonight is the full moon, and you will climb the wall again. But this time, I think, you won't return."

Kathe waited to hear Meg's next words. After keeping the secret for so many months, surely she wouldn't tell Cook to bar the door! Kathe turned and lifted her eyes to Meg's face. She saw only open friendship there.

"You will leave all alone." Meg spoke softly, almost to herself. "In these parts, some say the forest goes on forever – that if you wander too far into it, you will lose your way and never see the open sky again. And yet here you are, a visitor from the other side of the forest, from a city that is legend to us. It's enough to make me wonder…" She swallowed hard. "I won't deny it – the thought of the journey scares me. But I'm not about to let you go such a way all alone. I'll go with you!"

Kathe stared. Whatever she had been expecting, it wasn't this. The girl's face was still friendly, but it also looked stubborn. Here was still another side to Meg's character.

"Don't look so surprised," Meg pleaded. "I know I jump when I see my own shadow, but I want to be brave. I have to try sometime. Besides, if there are two of us, then each of us will only have to be half as brave," she joked. She picked up her own basket, tipped some of the berries into Kathe's, and turned back toward the sunny field as if the matter was settled.

Kathe shook her head. When she imagined a journey back through the forest to Ostara, she was always alone. She was used to living out of doors, and she liked sleeping under leaves or stars. This was a soft season for travel. She knew she would be able to find food.

At the same time, she would be afraid. She might lose the path – or lose her way entirely. And there were other things too. Once, on the journey to Springvale, when they were camping within a circle of beeches, a panther screamed above them. When Abel snatched a burning branch from their small fire and held it high, they saw eyes shining before the big cat disappeared.

Could a person choose to be brave? Especially a girl who had not been farther than the water meadow since her ninth year? Could she go back to sleep after hearing the panther scream or after awakening to the howling of wolves? More likely she would regret her kindness and forget why she wanted to find out, with her own eyes, what the wide world holds.

If Meg came with her...Kathe rejected the possibility, though she recognized the part of herself that longed for a companion. Meg *would* be afraid. Kathe would be able to offer neither safety nor comfort. Besides, this is where Meg belonged. Her home was here in Springvale, just as Kathe's was far away in Ostara.

As they rejoined the other servants bending over the bushes in the shade that was now creeping out from the edge of the forest, both girls fell silent. Kathe could not imagine what Meg might be thinking. Her own thoughts were so many that she thought they must show. She wondered why the other workers did not surround her to ask her where all these thoughts were coming from, spilling into the sultry air and disturbing their own daydreams. A part of her mind was busy making plans for the journey that would begin that night after moon-rise. How would Meg react when Kathe told her, as she must, that she would be leaving Springvale alone?

Kathe sighed in frustration. Meg's dark head was bent over her task as if she did not have any other care beyond filling a basket with fruit. Just as Kathe was about to touch her hand, ready to whisper that Springvale was Meg's home, where she must stay, and that Kathe would climb the wall alone that night, as she had for the past many months...and no, there was no point in discussing or arguing further, Meg glanced up and smiled. There was so much affection and trust in that look that the words stuck in Kathe's throat. She would find a few minutes to talk with Meg later. It would be easier to tell her and to answer all her arguments if they were alone.

4

A Red Standard

At Mid-Day, the Workers had paused to eat more bread and some cheese and to cool themselves with water from the skin. Kathe had dreamed that time away, but Meg had saved a bit of food for her. Now their baskets were both overflowing with berries, and the whole group rested before beginning the walk back to the manor.

Meg lay back in the tall grass of the field and looked at the clouds while Kathe sat cross-legged nearby and savored the cheese that had melted into the bread, softening and flavoring it. From this spot, they could see down the hill and across the valley of the little river running through Lord Stefan's land.

The manor house looked like a doll's house from here. The animals in the pastures and people moving about in the fields reminded her of the animals and people her mother used to make out of bits of wool to inhabit her own doll's house at home when she was small. She smiled at the memory.

They were all real to her. The children in her doll-house family were mischievous, always running away or letting the pigs out to root up crops or invade the kitchen. She remembered when Bard took her woolen family and rubbed them in cat-mint. It had taken her days to find them all, and after that she always had to make sure the door to the room was tightly shut. She was angry enough to bite, and she knew Bard's forced apology was insincere.

She laughed as she pictured the schoolroom and how it had looked then, full of the household cats, all in ecstasy because of the mint, batting her poor people around the room and peering through the windows of the doll's house.

Meg woke from her doze at the sound of laughter and struggled up to her elbows. She saw Kathe's smile fade.

Meg looked toward the north, the direction in which Kathe was now gazing with such a serious expression. Her eyes searched the line of the narrow track from the spot where it left the forest. The valley looked peaceful from so far away, though she knew it was really bustling with end of day chores and preparations for supper. The children who had stayed behind to help Cook would now be going out to the meadow to collect the cloth that had been left to dry in the sun. If she squinted she could see movement there and the bright white of the sun-bleached cloth, though she had to use her imagination to see the girls gathering and folding the linen.

Meg's legs and back ached from standing and bending over the blackberries. She wished they did not have to walk the long way home, though it was downhill almost all the way, and it would give them time to talk and plan for tonight.

Nearby, the other workers were beginning to sit up, stretch, and cover their baskets. Meg glanced at Kathe again. She was still, tensed like a rabbit that has seen a hawk. Meg looked back at the scene below. Nothing seemed amiss. She wanted to make Kathe smile and was just about to make some joke about how she looked as if she had seen a ghost, and would she introduce her to it, when she noticed a small cloud of dust on the stretch of road near where it passed the manor gates.

It was too far away to see much, but she could tell there were men on horseback. Several, by the amount of dust they were raising. She looked at Kathe inquiringly. Visitors to Springvale were unusual, but not unheard of.

"What? Who do you think it is?" she whispered. Most of the other workers were now standing, and a few had already begun the walk down the hill toward the fields.

"Can you see the color on their standard?" Kathe answered.

Meg shaded her eyes and looked again at the horsemen. "Red, I think."

"Yes, that's what I see. I saw them come from the forest. They must be northerners." She turned to Meg, looking fierce. "I wish it were not true, but I think they may be — must be — Claymon raiders."

Meg felt sick. She remembered how Kathe had looked in the firelight that first night, when she had told of the war in the north. The day she came, the women watched her – they noticed how she was willing, but awkward, at the tasks she was given; how her dress, though plain and stained, was of fine stuff; how her feet, bare until a pair of felt slippers could be found for her, were white and smooth. Again she heard the low voice from behind the curtain of red hair, "Yes, there is war."

"It is time for us to return now," said Kathe. "Look. We will be the last ones unless we hurry and overtake old Cluny." She pointed towards the farm hand, already several minutes ahead of them on the path. "You know what Cook will say if we trail far behind a lame old man."

Meg took several steps down the hill, carried along by the sound of Kathe's voice before she really understood her words. Then she stopped and turned around, amazed. "You cannot be thinking of returning! If you are right, and these are some of the same as drove you from your home, how can you go back?"

Kathe did not answer. She kept walking quickly, intent upon the house in the distance. Meg trotted after her, forming her thoughts as she spoke. "It is possible that they know you are hidden here. And if that is so, it will be easy for them to find you. If the master does not recall which of us came here in the last of the snow, any one of the servants will point you out and think no harm in it. You are as out of place in Springvale as a swan hiding in a flock of ducks."

Kathe did not answer at once. Then she said, "All you say makes good sense, Meg," She turned with a shadow of a smile, "except that I believe I fit into the kitchen better than you think. Yet, I will return. Perhaps the Claymon have heard of this small holding and are here to demand loyalty only."

Meg looked doubtful.

"Even if they have learned of a chance to find the daughter of the house of Elder," Kathe added, choking on the words. "I still have to return. Don't you see? Only a few people know I am hiding here. If the soldiers are looking for me, the knowledge could only have come from my parents, or my brother, or from Abel." Kathe quickened her steps.

Meg once again stopped, and this time she pulled hard on Kathe's arm, swinging her around until she was facing back up the hill. Kathe stumbled. "Let me go," she said angrily, sounding for the first time like a noblewoman. Meg heard the command in her voice and ordered herself to disobey. She kept her grip on Kathe's wrist.

"I cannot," she said urgently. "Maybe the Claymon are here by chance. But if they know you are here, even I can imagine a way or two they may have discovered it, leaving your loved ones out of it. Neither you nor I wish to think of torture, but supposing that's the way it was. Supposing someone was hurt or even died before giving away your secret. It seems to me it would be wrong to just walk down the hill, maybe into a trap. You wouldn't be able to help them at all, then."

She could tell that Kathe had heard her. She was no longer pulling away. Both girls had stopped walking, looking toward the manor house that was already much closer.

"Yet, how can I not return and learn what I may? I have to take this chance. I will be careful, and then tonight I will be gone."

"Listen to me!" Meg could not believe the idea that was forming in her mind. "I will be your mouse in the corner. I will listen, and then, when the moon has risen, I will meet you at the lightening-struck tree."

"I can't hide any more, it isn't safe!" Kathe protested.

Meg flung her answer over her shoulder as she began to run down the hill. "When I come, I will bring you news, and I will also bring the bag that makes such a lump in the straw of our bed. You know this is how it must be." Kathe stood watching, her fists clenched at her side, until her friend caught up with Cluny. After a few moments, she watched Meg take the old man's basket and carry it, along with her own, toward the manor, where the horsemen had already been admitted into the courtyard.

5

IN THE COOL WATER

A S SOON AS SHE walked through the manor gate, without hearing
a word or asking a single question, Meg knew something was
wrong. On an ordinary day, she could predict what each person
of the household would be doing at this particular moment
in late afternoon, but today Springvale's residents were rushing
about with worried faces.

Lord Stefan had just one son, but even when Gale was
at home, which was not often, the family was content with
simple fare. Their servants were always busy, but rarely hurried,
especially in these sleepy days of summer before harvest. And
young Gale was now away doing who knows what in the newly
cleared lands to the east, where some of the younger sons of the
manor's tenants were tending the fields. Or, for all she or even
his parents knew, he might be wandering within the forest itself.
She had seen him return more than once, looking shaggy, with
clay jars of honey or fragrant herbs for his mother. It had been a
few weeks since she saw him at the first cutting of the hay, when
she and Kathe had helped to fill the byres.

No, Cook wasn't preparing an ordinary family supper this
afternoon. The fowl were running around in panic and flying
short distances, chased by boys with sticks and rope hoops. Some

birds were already slaughtered. A drift of feathers littered one corner of the yard where two girls worked grimly at the task of scalding and plucking the birds.

Mole had been called from the kennels and pressed into service. He emerged from the cellar with half a ham in his arms. By his narrowed eyes, he set himself apart from any festival for these guests. He looked as if he wanted to fight, not feed, the visitors.

Cook met Meg at the kitchen door. She seized both of the baskets. Her face was flushed, and her apron, usually a crisp symbol of authority, hung limp in the heat. Judging by its purple stains, the first berries to arrive at the manor had already made their way into pastry.

"Where have you been, girl? No!" she shouted at a boy who was hurrying across the courtyard carrying a bucket of milk. "I want to save some of the cream; cool it in the well until I call for it."

She turned again to Meg, gripping her by the shoulder. "Find Kathe and the two of you get yourselves down to the stream. I want watercress and some of that sweet fern if you can find young fiddleheads. It is late in the season," she fretted. "And hurry!" Before she finished her instructions, she had already turned away, back to the darkness and heat of the kitchen.

Meg had been ready to seek a task that would take her to wait upon the manor's visitors, but after a moment of surprise at her new orders, Meg did hurry – back through the gate and down the lane toward the stream.

It would have been worse than worthless to argue with Cook. It was cool here in the shade under the arching branches of the young sycamores bordering the lane. The silence calmed her. Nothing bad was likely to happen for the next little while, at least. And no one would miss Kathe if she was supposed to be with Meg, picking watercress in the stream.

When she reached the churned place where the cattle drank,

she turned and made her way upstream to where the water ran clear. She tied her skirt above her knees, waded into the stream and began to collect the green leaves of the cress. Not until both hands were full did she realize she had brought nothing in which to carry them, so she made her way to the stream bank where she quickly broke cattail reeds and began to weave them into a crude basket.

She was grateful for a few moments of solitude, but she knew it could last only until she finished this basket and filled it with as many greens as two girls could pick in the time.

When she heard the jingle of tack and the voices of men, she froze. Standing close to the stream bank as she was, she couldn't see the place where the cattle crossed. She didn't move even when she heard the voice directly behind her, but stood still among the reeds that rustled and swayed around her.

"The summer sky is a welcome sight after riding through that cursed forest," said one male voice.

"And to what purpose did we ride?" answered his companion. "If the captain is as anxious as he seems to get the loyalty of this manor's lord, then there must be a great shortage of southern allies. This is little more than a great farm. Did you notice how the people look at us?"

"Yes, as if we walked out of a minstrel's song. But I could have wished for a better welcome. After the riding we've done in the past days, we should be taking our ease, not watering our own beasts."

Meg heard one of the men spit. A horse whinnied. The men had not seen her yet, but horses are smart in their own ways. She risked a look, turning around smoothly and slightly parting the reeds. Sure enough, one of the horses, a chestnut, stood in the center of the stream, the rope trailing from its halter. Its intelligent eyes met hers. She held its gaze as she slowly sank down into the water until she was kneeling in the silty streambed.

"That's the truth, but when I asked for the loan of a boy or two, that shrew of a cook spoke to me like I was one of the boys myself, 'With all the unexpected visitors, I can't spare a one,' she said. And when I complained to the captain, he told me to water 'em myself."

Several minutes of silence followed, but Meg could still see the horse's legs in the stream. It lowered its head to drink.

"The captain isn't likely to tell the likes of us what he's thinking, but it doesn't take a scholar to see something is going on. The lord of this place was so scared when he came out to meet us that it looked like his lady was holding him up," he snorted. "He would have pledged his loyalty then and there, without any further threat of force. No, the captain wants something else, and he's taking it easy until he's sure he can get it."

Meg waited, barely breathing, until she heard the men leading the horses back up the path away from the stream. When she was sure they would not be able to see her if they looked back, she quickly filled her basket with cress. Then, skirt dripping, she ran up the path herself, careful not to overtake them.

She wasn't sure how long she knelt there with the water flowing around her legs, but she was pretty sure it was longer than it should have been, at least in Cook's eyes. As she tried to think of a story to explain the delay, her mind was also sorting the possible meanings of the conversation she had overheard. If the horseman was right, and the captain was looking for something at Springvale, then she knew what it must be. What other treasure did the place hold than Kathe?

Dashing through the gate, she nearly collided with Mole. He caught her by the arms so that she did not spill the wet cress leaves onto the dusty ground. He looked over her shoulder. "Where's Kathe? Cook is impatient for her greens, and she said the two of you were off picking them at the stream. I was to hurry you. But here I have you, and the greens, but no Kathe."

"When Cook asked me to go, I could not find Kathe," Meg stammered. "I think she must have gone into the pasture, to help the boys to drive the cattle home. The cows have been hard to find at the end of a day, going with their calves to the deep shade in the water meadow, and then they are unwilling to come when they hear the horn. Kathe said she would go to help look for them, if she was not needed in the kitchen."

"But she is needed, isn't she?" Mole said. "Well, along with you now. Cook will have your hide, and Kathe can be glad the old woman is too busy to leave her work and look for her now. She would be well off to stay all night in the pasture," he added in a thoughtful tone.

Meg hurried toward the kitchen, and throwing a glance over her shoulder, she saw Mole still standing there, looking after her.

Cook bent next to the fire, taking golden pies from the ovens built into the side of the stone hearth. If it had been hot outdoors, it was a furnace in here, and Meg was momentarily blinded in the darkness of the room.

After she had placed the hot pastries on a table to begin cooling, Cook turned and put her hands on her hips. "So. Here you are with my cress, slowpokes. And no fiddleheads, I see." Cook poked through the greens in the basket. Then, looking behind Meg she asked, "Where's Kathe?"

Meg answered more confidently this time, telling the same tale she had told Mole. She had always been truthful, having no reason to lie, but now she began to think she had a natural gift for it. She found that, if she told a lie as if she wished it were true, it would be believed. And besides, how could anyone suspect that Meg, the most biddable and meek of all the girls, would have any reason to lie?

"Oh, that's grand," Cook said sarcastically. "That's just lovely. Kathe has gone off to herd cattle, and Lord Stefan has asked for her by name to serve his guests tonight. She doesn't know a thing about the proper way to serve nobility, and she has never set foot in the dining hall, except to scrub the table, but that makes no difference to him. No one will suit except Kathe."

Cook paused, leaning against the table for a moment, looking ill at all the unaccustomed demands that had suddenly been placed upon her. She looked speculatively at Meg. "If Lord Stefan wants a pretty young girl serving at his table tonight, instead of Mary, who is plain, but skillful, then you are the best I can provide." She looked at Meg's sodden skirt. "Find Mary quick, and tell her to get you a clean gown and tunic. You'll serve in the hall tonight." She paused, "And while you're at it, ask her to advise you on the serving of this meal I am killing myself to prepare. I want Lord Stefan and his guests to notice the good food, not their servant's clumsiness."

6

A Mouse in the Corner

Buzzing filled Meg's ears, and she looked around for something to hold to keep upright. She felt the blood leave her hands and face and knew she was about to fall, so she sat down hard on the stone floor.

Oblivious to all the bustle in the kitchen, she relived a day before her father brought her to the manor, a day when she was watching her brothers at the edge of the forest. The little boys had made a bird of a large leaf, some sticks, and a bit of string they found, and they took turns throwing it, chasing it wherever the breeze carried it.

Once, when the leaf bird rode the breeze, it did not land in the grass in front of them but soared high above. As the boys stood watching it climb, it lodged itself in the top branches of a fir tree where the trunk was little thicker than Meg's forearm.

When she turned to lead the boys home, expecting to see mournful expressions as they gave their toy up as lost, she found that all three of them were looking at her hopefully, as if they were only waiting to see what she would do. To her surprise, she began to climb.

The branches were sturdy and close together near the bottom. Though the needles poked at her through her thin, summer dress, it was quite simple to climb the ladder of branches, almost like climbing the ladder to the hayloft. When she was about halfway up, the branches thinned, but she was still able to reach up to steady herself. It was just as if some rungs were missing.

After an eternity of climbing, she could see the toy not far above her, and she began to climb more slowly, pausing often to listen to the thumping of her heart. She had felt then as she did now, sitting on the kitchen's stone floor. When the falling feeling came that day long ago, she held onto the trunk tightly and listened to her own breath rising and falling until she could again look up. Finally, she reached for the toy, but at that moment, the wind dislodged it, and it floated down to the boys standing below.

Now she listened intently to her breath again. Off in the distance she thought she heard Cook's voice; people were shaking her by the shoulder; she wished they would stop. She didn't want to open her eyes. She knew, if she did, she would see all the distance she was about to fall.

"Wake up! Get up! Silly girl. I have no time for your nonsense. Get up!"

Now she remembered. She was to find a sober, dark dress and a white tunic. She was to serve Lord Stefan and his guests tonight.

Meg found Mary just outside the kitchen, combing her hair in the shade of the wall. When Meg spoke, Mary stopped in mid-stroke, her hand tightening upon the comb. She was proud of her position, knew herself to be good at her work, and she was affronted that Meg, and not she, would be serving in the hall that night. She turned abruptly with a sharp word on her tongue, but a look at the girl's frightened face told her the story. Clearly Meg had no thought of trying to rise within the ranks of the servants at Mary's expense. She looked like she would rather spend a whole night outside the walls than a single hour serving Lord Stefan and his guests in the hall. Mary took Meg's arm and gently shook it.

"There's no call to be so affrighted. They're just men, like Mole or old Cluny, and when you put the food in front of them, they eat it and hardly notice what it is they're putting into their mouths." Mary looked through the window into the kitchen where Cook was arranging trays on the table. "I don't know why Cook is getting so worked up. The riders didn't even come with any ladies. They'd be harder to please. The only lady there will be our own, who orders the meals but never complains about how they are served – and she'll have other things on her mind. Those blackberry tarts will be wasted on Lord Stefan and Lady Irene tonight."

Meg still felt a shaky core of fear, but it was retreating deeper thanks to Mary's matter-of-fact attitude and unexpected friendliness. She managed a tentative smile up at the older woman. "I've never served, not even when you were ill last winter or on festival days. Cook always put me to work in the kitchen. She said I startle too easily, and she thought I would drop a platter on the floor if someone spoke to me."

Mary led her back through the kitchen to the little room where clean linen was stored. "I'll ask Cook if I can take Ann's place and help you. Surely she doesn't expect you to serve alone! Ann will be happy to rest tonight; her back has been hurting. That way I'll be able to give you a bit of advice as we carry the dishes in and out."

In the privacy of the linen room, Mary hauled a tub from under a shelf. Then Meg took off her muddy dress and stood in the tub while Mary poured a bucket of clean, cold water over her head. As if this were not heaven enough, the older woman then helped her to wash her hair with the lather from a piece of lavender scented soap that Lady Irene had given her. After rinsing with another bucket of clean water, she toweled it dry with a length of cloth.

By the time Meg stood in clean clothes, with her hair freshly braided and shoes on her feet, she felt like a different person. Mary walked around her appraisingly. Satisfied with the results of her work, she gently patted Meg's cheek. "Those young men from the north will notice these bright eyes and black braids more than the freshly cooked birds on their plates, and your quiet way will only attract their attention more strongly. It's a good thing you still sleep in the kitchen." She looked suddenly sober. "I'll be watching you, but Meg...you must begin to look after yourself. Today you look like a grown woman."

Then Meg helped Mary to bathe, standing on a stool to pour water over her, leaning forward to avoid splashing her own clean clothes. The older woman accepted when she offered to comb and braid her blond hair; Meg twisted it into the form of a crown as her mother had taught her, as a way of thanking her for the way she was feeling now, with clean hair and skin, in clean clothing.

When they were both finished, they walked together through the kitchen, down a narrow passage, and up the steep, curving stairs to the hall. Far away, behind and below them, they could hear voices from the kitchen. Before them was the plain room, with a hearth at one end, empty in the heat, a scrubbed wooden floor and three long tables. Lady Irene had brightened the room with woven hangings, and the light of a golden summer evening poured through the windows, making the stones of the walls and the white cloths on the tables glow. Freshly polished candlesticks gleamed, and a young boy bit his lower lip in concentration as he moved down the table, lighting candles and trying hard not to drip wax or ash onto the snowy linen.

Mary whistled low. "These are honored guests indeed. New candles, and that's the damask cloth woven by our Lady's own mother. The last time I saw it on the table was two years ago, when Lady Irene was hopeful that Gale would wed his cousin, Ailis. Do you remember? The girl stayed here for the whole summer. Our lady set such a table when the girl's father and brother came to take her home and didn't really give up hope until the whole party was on their horses and riding away."

Meg said nothing. She tried to picture herself moving around the table, serving all the strangers from the north. As if reading her thoughts, Mary briskly led her into the room, sat her at the head of a table, and played servant to her, showing her how to serve without speaking, indeed, without putting herself forward at all… like the mouse she had promised to be for Kathe.

The light in the room had begun to turn rosy when the Lord and Lady of Springvale and their guests entered and took their places around the tables.

Meg stood by the door, waiting for a signal to begin her duties. She watched Lord Stefan take his place, with Lady Irene at his right hand. They were always quiet, country people, but tonight they seemed positively ill at ease. Meg saw Lady Irene flash a look of worry at her husband, and he took her hand and held it for a moment.

A tall young man with brown hair was taking his place at one of the side tables. She blinked. When had Gale returned? It had been weeks since anyone had seen him in the manor. His life in the fields and forest was such that no one really expected him to appear until autumn. Yet here he was, looking like a farmer in his open necked shirt and rolled sleeves next to the Claymon officers who were seating themselves. They wore red tunics over white shirts with bloused sleeves, and she noticed they looked hot and uncomfortable. One of them, more richly dressed than the others, lowered himself gracefully into the chair at Lady Irene's right hand. Meg stared at him, but quickly looked away when he met her eyes. His gaze made her feel cold in the hot room.

At the Lady's signal, Meg filled each goblet with wine and placed baskets with loaves of warm bread along the table. Then she began to serve Cook's salad, made of the cress she had gathered in the stream. She stayed intent on her work, keeping her eyes downcast, trying not to see the men at the table, but only the plates in front of them.

She had served the head table and the men at one side table when she glanced up and again met the black eyes of the Claymon captain. She saw him whisper to Lord Stefan, who frowned. As she turned back to her task and served Gale, she noticed he seemed to be watching the interactions at his father's table with intense interest.

Without looking away from the head table, he whispered, "I'm glad to see you, Meg."

His voice startled her almost as much as the captain's glance had. Mary had told her that she would not be expected to speak and that even the Lord and Lady would treat her as if she were deaf as well as dumb. She looked at him in confusion, then quickly moved on to serve the other men.

By the time she had finished carrying the platters of meat from the kitchen, serving the other hot dishes, and refilling the goblets, her body no longer felt cool and clean, and her fresh clothing had wilted. By the time she began to clear away the plates, her feet, unaccustomed to shoes, were aching.

As she and Mary carried the still warm, blackberry tarts from the kitchen, Meg began to relax. This was the last course. After this, all she would have to do is carry away dirty dishes and leave the company to their talk, which had seemed of little importance so far. Although she had twice felt the captain's eyes following her, the conversation had been all about the journey through the forest, the crops in the fields, and hunting. She had heard no mention of an expanding Claymon rule, of Ostara, Kathe or her family.

When Meg began to serve the pastry, Mary followed with a pitcher of fresh, thickened cream. As she placed a dish in front of Lady Irene, she allowed herself to notice the beautiful colors of the golden crust and purple berries, with the pale yellow cream running over the edges and pooling in the bowl. She wondered whether there would be any for her and Mary to eat after their work was done. She imagined carrying the good food into the coolness of the courtyard and eating it there. It had been a long time since the bread and cheese she had eaten up on the hill.

"Katherine?"

Meg heard the name and instantly awoke from her reverie, but she didn't realize Lord Stefan was speaking to her until he said again, "Katherine?" and Mary tugged at her sleeve. Then she put a dish in front of him too abruptly so that her suddenly shaking hands would be empty, but she still did not speak.

"Are you Katherine?"

A voice from one of the side tables answered for her. "Father. You must know this is Meg, all but grown. Don't you remember? Her father brought her from his farm on the far side of the water meadow when she was just a curly headed child, and she has been in the kitchen all these years."

Lord Stefan said querulously, "But I asked for Katherine tonight." Meg caught the apologetic glance he gave the Claymon captain. "Where is the girl?"

He looked again at Meg, and she felt herself shrink. Lord Stefan had never paid her the slightest notice. There was no reason he should know one kitchen girl from another. When she opened her mouth, she expected to hear no sound, or only a squeak, but the words emerged soft, but clear.

"I do not know, my Lord." This was true. She knew where she had left Kathe, but had no inkling of where she might be now. Far away, she hoped. Lord Stefan was still looking at her expectantly. "We could not find her, so Cook told me to serve in her place. We thought, perhaps, she had gone to help bring the cows home. She often has done so lately, in this hot weather. We were berrying, and she did not know she would be needed."

Now the Claymon captain turned his eyes to her again. When he spoke, his northern accent was pronounced. "I very much want to see Katherine," he said flatly. "When she returns, you will send her to me." It was not a request. She nodded.

Gale spoke up from the other end of the table. "What's this? Why are you so interested in this girl – Katherine, is it?" Lady Irene whispered to Meg, and she continued serving the pastry, trying to make herself small so that they would stop looking at her.

The Claymon officer ignored Gale's question, took a bite of his tart and stared stonily at Lord Stefan, who sat like a statue.

"I asked a question. This manor is not part of your domain yet, but we know the story of Ostara. Perhaps you can sift the truth from the exaggeration for us."

"Son! Enough!" Lord Stefan's voice rang sharply.

The captain turned slowly toward Gale, who was leaning forward on his elbows. His expression did not change. There was no hint of friendliness in the man's face. "Tonight we have eaten Claymon fowl and meat and drunk good Claymon wine. What makes you think our reach does not extend to insignificant manors such as this one? There is no need to conquer those too weak to fight us. We just take. Life may go on much as it always has here. Or it may not. It is up to you. Of course, we will return each autumn to collect taxes. One of my men," he gestured to a short, swarthy soldier opposite Gale who was leaning back in his chair, listening with his eyes half closed, "will stay behind to keep the peace."

"Your father will be the Lord of Springvale for many years." He lifted his glass to the haggard looking Lord Stefan, "And you will follow him – as long as you both look to our interests."

Meg noticed that Gale's face had paled behind its tan, but he still leaned forward intently, and his eyes glittered. "Why do you want the girl?"

"Why does it matter?" the captain responded wearily. "Surely you can find another kitchen maid, if she is the one we seek."

"Still, I am curious. Why did you ask that she be sent to serve in the hall tonight?"

"Isn't it obvious? I wanted an opportunity to observe her, to find out if she is the one. It would have been an opportunity to," he paused, "rescue her."

"Rescue her?" Gale echoed in an openly skeptical voice.

"She is in need of rescue if she is indeed Lady Katherine Elder of The Three Hills," snapped the captain.

Meg had finished serving the blackberry pastry and again stood in her place by the door. She should have followed Mary down to the kitchen. Their work here was finished, but the attention of the Claymon captain had shifted from her. She felt safe playing the mouse again. She could leave meekly if she was told to, with her ignorance of serving as an excuse.

"Lady Katherine Elder?"

"Is your son simple, Lord Stefan?" the captain asked. "He repeats everything I say."

Gale managed to sound amused, as if he wasn't as frightened as his father was, though Meg saw his foot rapidly tapping under the table. "What would the Lady of Ostara be doing in our kitchen?" He addressed his father, "Is this the same Katherine, a tall, red-haired girl, who came to the fields during the haying? She was as strong and brown as the boys, and unafraid of work. I lifted her onto the wagon with Meg to stamp down the hay. I have always thought you should know all our people, Father, more than just those, like Mole, who serve you every day."

His father seemed not to hear the criticism. He was not looking at the Captain as a servant does not look at his master when he is afraid.

The Captain spoke slowly, "We know Lady Katherine and a companion left Ostara in early spring. Until a few weeks ago, we did not know where she had gone, but then one of her friends, worried by her long absence, sent a message that she had traveled here to pretend servitude until sent for."

He paused. In the stunned silence after his announcement, the flames of the candles wavered. "Now she has been sent for. It is unseemly that my future queen should continue serving in a kitchen. If the kitchen girl Kathe is indeed the Lady Katherine Elder, I will take her back to Ostara, where she will become a bride. The marriage of Lady Katherine to Peter Greystone will ensure the peace of Ostara – so that we may turn our attention elsewhere."

There was another long silence. Judging by the startled looks exchanged among the men of the Claymon party, they had not known they would be escorting their future queen back to the Three Hills. Lord Stefan and Lady Irene looked utterly beaten. She was weeping quietly and dabbing at her eyes with a corner of her linen napkin. Gale stood suddenly and left the room.

The captain glanced out the narrow windows. "We have lingered long at table. The moon is shining. Lady," he spoke firmly to Irene, ignoring her tears. "Go to the kitchen. If Lady Katherine has not returned, you will send a party to search for her."

1

ORO

KATHE SAT UNDER THE lightening struck tree, screened by tall grass. She had wrapped her arms around her legs, and her chin rested on her knees. Night was falling. She felt sleepy with long waiting, but she listened intently and watched the gathering darkness for any sign of movement. She knew it was much too soon to hope for Meg to come.

During the hours since their parting, Kathe had slowly worked her way here, staying just inside the edge of the forest as it made its great circle around the cleared lands.

As the light began to soften, but long before the sun tipped below the horizon, she waded a stream. Further down that same stream, though she did not know it, Meg crouched hidden by reeds while two soldiers watered their horses. Kathe drank deeply and ate more berries from the basket she still carried. Then she began to think seriously about the days ahead.

It did not take long to inventory her assets. She had a strong, young body and the clothes she wore. She had a ring made of gold, set with a green stone, sewn inside the waist of her dress. She had a basket half full of berries. That was all.

Meg might not come. She might be prevented from leaving the manor or, more likely, regret her hasty promise to join Kathe, especially since keeping that promise would mean tracing Kathe's monthly journey over the wall and into the forest. Back in the everyday world of the kitchen, Kathe's story might begin to seem just that, an exciting story spun to while away a hot summer afternoon. In that case, Kathe told herself, she would have to travel back to the Three Hills alone and find all she needed along the way.

At best, if Meg came bringing news and some food for their journey, they could travel together, perhaps with a blanket to share. Despite her decision that Meg need not... must not... come with her, Kathe felt herself wavering. Tonight, for the first time in her life, no place was home. Even on the journey to Springvale, she had felt at home, curled near a fire each night with Abel sleeping nearby. She wasn't lonely now, but she was beginning to know that she soon would be.

A warm breeze played in the treetops and rustled the leaves of the bushes behind her. The sky had gradually deepened to velvety cobalt, but she could still see streaks of pink clouds, tinted by the setting sun, drifting across the sky. The first stars brightened. It would be a good night for travel with the summer moon to light the way.

By now the servants would have cleared away the dinner things from Lord Stefan's table, and they would be making a meal for themselves of the leftovers. At the thought of roast chicken and fresh bread, her mouth watered. She reached into her basket for more berries. She hoped she would be able to recognize the plants Abel and Bard had shown her – the ones that would keep her alive on the journey ahead, even without fire.

After Meg finished her meal, assuming she still planned to slip away from the manor, there would still be washing up to do, and she would not hurry. Kathe knew Meg well enough to expect her to be careful.

Then, even after everyone found his or her pallet, there would be that nerve-wracking hour of lying awake, of whispered conversations, of listening to the household settling into sleep. Meg would lie tensely waiting in the darkness, trying to separate the groans and snores of sleep from the sounds of tired bodies still seeking ease. Only after she was certain that everyone around her was sleeping would Meg rise and chance opening the door.

She wished she had really made up some story instead of telling her true history, something about retreating to the shade of the forest because she was dizzy in the heat. She could have let Meg think that she was sneaking away at night to meet one of the farmhands. But it was too late. She had drawn a friend into danger and trouble rightfully her own.

After a time Kathe lay back on the soft grass and listened to the breeze in the tree-tops. Since there were no plans to make, she made none. Instead, she mentally revisited her old home in Ostara, entering by the heavy front door and walking through each room. She stopped in the library to touch the soft leather binding of a book of poems she had treasured. Opening it, she read:

> The palest dawn,
> The brightest noon,
> The blooming flower of the setting sun
> Illuminate the three hills of Ostara.
> We live in the shadow,
> The shadow of three hills.
> But some of us look up
> And climb from the shadow to the light.

Gently, Kathe closed the book and placed it on the shelf. Half asleep now, she allowed her thoughts to drift into the world of dreams and to carry her deeper within her old home.

In the kitchen, the savory aromas of food simmering and roasting captured her attention. She tasted the sauce bubbling on the stove and heard the cook, old dame Mather, scolding. Even as she chided, she sliced the heel from a loaf of bread, still warm from the ovens, spread it with butter and gave it to Kathe.

But just as Kathe reached for the bread, the dream carried her out of the kitchen and through the Hall where, when she was a little girl, her father sat upon his carved chair. Now the chair was empty, but as she paced the length of the room, she thought she saw ghostly shapes whispering and gesturing. None of them seemed to notice her.

She climbed the narrow stairs to a sunny workroom and paused in the doorway. There was her mother's loom, and before it, a woman with glints of silver in her bright hair. She intently wove colored threads into an ivory warp. Kathe peered over her mother's shoulder. A picture was growing.

Kathe breathed softly, watching her mother's agile fingers. In dream time there was no need for spinning, for gathering the plants needed for making such bright dyes, or for winding the butterflies of thread. The weaving rose like the waters in a stream after a heavy rain, first trickling, then rushing.

She was so fascinated by the swift movements of her mother's hands that she did not at once notice the image being woven, but when she did, she leaned closer. She saw a girl sleeping under a blighted tree and a circle of animals, their eyes reflecting the light of a rising moon.

Kathe, still dreaming, gasped. The weaver stopped her work and turned with a smile of such tenderness that Kathe reached out to touch her mother. But even as she did, she knew she could not really embrace the dream weaver; instead, she felt stems of dry grass between her fingers.

Still, the image of her mother's tapestry stayed with her. She brushed her hair from her face and rubbed tears from her eyes. The lightening struck tree rose above her, and she looked around, half expecting to see the animals of the circle. There had been squirrels, rabbits, a stag with spreading antlers, a panther, a bear, a badger. While she dozed, the moon had risen.

She stood up and stretched, squinting into the shadows. As

she did, she felt the brush of a wing and heard a whisper.

"*Come.*"

She lifted her hand to her cheek.

Again the whisper. "*Come.*"

She turned towards the sound, her heart suddenly beating wildly and strained to hear another word.

"*Come here here here.*"

Kathe crossed the clearing in a few steps, reaching for the sheath at her waist where her knife should have been, if only she had her knife. She paused, straining to see in the darkness.

"*Follow follow me,*" came a voice so soft that Kathe thought it might have been the wind shifting direction. Who was calling? Not Meg. And she was certain it wasn't one of the Claymon. She had observed them well and knew they lacked the subtlety to summon her in such a way. She glanced back over her shoulder at the meeting place, then slipped in among the trees. Again she felt the feathery brush of a wing against her face, and she allowed the breath of a voice to carry her forward, trusting it to lead her until her eyes became used to the deeper darkness.

Later, she had a hard time explaining why she followed the strange invitation. She finally said she followed because, after so many nights of waiting, someone had finally come for her.

She never stumbled as she threaded her way through the trees. The moon cast silvery shadows around her, and the night seemed to grow brighter instead of darker. She walked among giants on a thick carpet of loam. The further she walked, the more clearly she could see the path. It was not a trail beaten by human feet, but seemed to be a secret way. It wasn't until the whisper stopped and left her alone among the giant trees that she tripped and nearly fell.

Where was the person who had called to her? How far had she walked from the meeting place? Kathe felt a flicker of fear. Stepping forward, she saw that she was standing at one edge of a ring of massive oaks. Though many branches reached toward the center of the circle, the sudden brightness of the moonlight streaming into the clearing made her blink. Soft, thick grass grew under her feet, and as she became used to the brightness, she could see small flowers, white or golden, blooming in the opening. Her heart still pounded, but the loveliness of the place eased her heart. She took a step forward.

"*Welcome, Flame Child.*"

The voice came from above her. She peered up into the branches of a grandfather oak and met the round, golden eyes of a magnificent horned owl. She held her breath. The same breeze that whispered through the leaves moved the soft fringe of its feathers. Long moments passed. The owl dropped down to a lower branch as if to emphasize its greeting.

Kath swallowed, suddenly dry mouthed. She was not sure she would be able to speak. Finally she whispered, "Greetings, Spirit of the Night. Every month since I first came to this place, I have listened to owl talk under the moon, but never before have you spoken to me in human words. I am honored."

The owl swiveled its head. "*And I have watched you each of those nights, and as you walked off toward the dwelling of men each dawn.*" Again he fixed his gaze on her. "*Tonight you have been called to the Gathering. The others are here because we have all agreed it is time for you to know us. But talk with man or woman is dangerous.*"

"Dangerous?" Kathe thought of how frightened she had felt when she sat on the hillside that afternoon and saw the Claymon party advance toward the manor gates, how frightened she felt right now. "How could I be a danger to you?"

"*Men and women destroy what they do not understand. Or they call it evil and flee from it.*"

Kathe could not take her eyes from the owl. She noticed the streaks of tawny color on its feathers and the strength of its talons as they curved around the branch. When it spoke, she had to pay very close attention. Instead of words, it seemed to make pictures in her mind. The owl's eyes were mirrors reflecting the entire clearing, and they were not alone. When had the others arrived? She could have sworn the clearing was empty when she stepped into it, but now she stood at the center of an animal circle much like the one in her mother's tapestry.

Still, she was able to contain her fear. She did not run even when she saw the black panther sitting directly behind her licking its paw. Next to it sat a rabbit, scratching behind its ear. It certainly didn't seem nervous. Kathe stood perfectly still, sensing they all were waiting for her to speak.

"Have I been brought here so that you may know me, then?" she said at last, haltingly.

The owl's expression did not change, but laughter echoed through Kathe's mind and rippled around the circle. "No, child. We have brought you here so that you may know us. We already know you, just as you know the poisonous snake, the spider that bites, the brown bear with her cubs."

"I don't understand."

"You are here so that you will know the messengers when they come to you and not fear or hurt them. These are your guides. Look!"

Kathe felt herself released from owl's gaze and slowly pivoted, looking at each of the animals in the circle. Besides the panther and rabbit, there was the badger of her dream, looking as grumpy as every other badger she had ever seen; a trio of squirrels; and yes, the great stag, standing below the owl, next to the tree a few paces in front of her. Next to him was a bear, the one she had been worried about meeting in the briars that afternoon. It hunched half in, half out, of the clearing. Each one returned her gaze. She had never looked into a wild animal's eyes before. They were shining pools, unfathomable.

"Keep looking until you are certain you will know us," the owl said softly.

Kathe turned again, this time noticing the panther's green eyes and the missing tip of its scarred ear. The rabbit was light brown, like all rabbits, but it had a streak of white under its chin.

The stag's antlers were perfect, and broader than her arms could reach. Though she had never seen one so close, she was sure she would know him again. The squirrels rolled and played in the grass. It was hard to get a good look at them. She supposed she would have to look for the three of them together. As she looked at each animal, she allowed it to separate from its kind and become an individual.

Finally she turned back to the owl and said, "I will know all of you." Silence reigned again in the clearing. She still didn't understand why she had been called. Surely this couldn't be the end of the meeting. In an effort to learn more, she said, "I will tell you my name. It is Katherine Elder."

"Names are a human invention, but I have given myself one. It is a human name I heard when I sat one night above a fire. My name is Ordzhonikidze."

Kathe's eyes widened.

The Owl preened its wing and added, *"When we meet again, you may call me Oro. That is also a human name, I think."*

"I thank you," she said gravely, "Since you claim to know me, perhaps you know what has brought me to the lightening struck tree, and of the journey before me. I thank you for the guidance you have promised, though I do not know how I merit it."

When Oro spoke again, stretching his wings, Kathe had the sense that he was testing them for flight. *"You listened, you followed, and you have seen us. Now, before you return, you must understand…"*

He was interrupted by a bat that swooped into the clearing and flew from edge to edge making the shape of a star in the air above them. It finally glided down to hang from a small branch near Oro. As it chittered a message, Kathe was surprised to find that she could understand it too. She was already used to the owl's voice, but it had spoken to her without words. Now she was able to understand the bat's squeaks and clicks, translating them in her mind.

"Small one and another, walking in shadows, close not far, hurry hurry!"

Oro again stretched his wings. Looking around, Kathe saw the other animals had vanished.

"Come, child. This sentinel warns that one is coming, but who is the other?"

Kathe shook her head worriedly. "I don't know."

Had Meg brought a friend? Or had she been forced to bring one of the Claymon to the meeting place?"

"Come," Oro said. Once more she felt the brush of his wing as she turned and left the clearing, stumbling again into darkness after the brightness of the circle. She retraced her steps back to the lightening struck tree, listening for the owl's voice from branches where he paused to wait for her.

"Before you return, you must understand..." swoop...wait... feathers tickling her ear. *"These guides will speak to you when they are needed and when you listen. But if you wish to hear us, you must be alone."* The voice stopped as Oro glided ahead and away. *"Do not betray our trust..."*

He did not speak again, but Kathe recognized her surroundings. She had come to know every bush and tree during the long nights she spent waiting for Abel. Oro had led her back to the meeting place. If she took three steps forward, the lightning struck tree would be a black silhouette in front of her.

Hidden in the shadow behind a honeysuckle bush, she watched the place where she expected Meg to enter the clearing. The pair moved quietly, but Kathe's ears had been tuned by darkness. She heard the whisper of their clothing against the branches crowding the path.

Even after waiting for so long, it was a small shock to see Meg step forward and stand blinking in the moonlight. She was holding Kathe's bag and a bulging bundle of her own. She turned back toward the opening and gestured to her companion.

"This is the place," Kathe heard her whisper.

"What is the signal?"

The cadence of that voice was familiar. It belonged to Springvale.

"We didn't talk about a signal, but then, I was to come alone. Neither of us expected I'd be bringing you." Meg's voice sounded resentful. Kathe decided to listen a little longer before showing herself.

"It's a good thing for you I was sleepless tonight. The forest is no place for two young girls to wander by themselves. Kathe will be glad to see me, you'll see."

Meg was skeptical. "If she is glad to see you, and if she is here, then why hasn't she greeted us?"

The young man stepped into the center of the clearing. Now Kathe could see him clearly. He carried a pack on his back. It looked heavy.

"Katherine!" The man did not shout, but he spoke loudly enough after so much silence. "It is Gale. I want to help."

Gale? Ah, now she knew him. A face smiling up at her where she stood on the packed grasses on the hay wagon. A voice encouraging her to jump, saying he would catch her, steady her. She remembered thinking how little the son resembled his sallow, taciturn father. That day, she had jumped down from the wagon, trusting him. Now she stepped out into the moonlight.

8

HIDING AT HOME

FOR A MOMENT ALL three stood frozen in the silvery light. Then Meg rushed forward to embrace Kathe. As the two of them stepped apart, holding hands, Gale felt his position shifting. Wasn't he Stefan's son, here to protect two of his father's servants? The young women eyed him speculatively. They did not look as if they needed or wanted his help. He had learned one of them was a noblewoman. In fact, she was destined to be Lady of Ostara.

Gale was not vain, but he did consider himself to be unusually level-headed and observant. Now his confidence wavered. How could he have looked up at Kathe on the hay wagon and seen only a red-haired kitchen girl, laughing and flushed with the heat? Was this imperious-looking person really the same woman? Clearly her disheveled appearance did not signify panic or distress. She didn't have to speak. He could sense that she, not he, would be in charge of any journey they might undertake together.

And Meg. He had known her since he was twelve years old, but now he hardly recognized her! She had been part of the furniture of the courtyard and kitchen, a quiet, reliable detail of the manor's life. What was she thinking? With a start, he saw the expressions on the two faces were almost identical. They did not make him feel like a welcomed protector. More like unwanted baggage.

Kathe's face suddenly softened into a smile. "Thank you for bringing Meg. She does not have my experience in moonlight wanderings, and I worried about her safety."

Gale shifted uneasily. Clearly, Kathe expected, or at least hoped, he would accept her thanks and then head back to his warm bed, leaving the two of them to begin their journey without him. He certainly had not imagined having to convince Kathe to let him come along. He had thought she would welcome him, maybe even with grateful tears.

Could he join them if they were unwilling? There was enough of his father in him to make that a repugnant possibility. Though he really did want to help Kathe to reach her home, he was equally anxious to join or, if necessary, organize resistance to the Claymon. There was otherwise little hope that he would someday be the true master of the manor lying behind him at the center of the fields and meadows he loved. There was little hope even if he did join the struggle – none at all if he turned and returned to that house where his father was restlessly trying to get used to his new position as overseer of someone else's land.

The silence was becoming awkward. Finally, Meg broke it. "I don't think you'll rid yourself of Gale so easily, Kathe. I've never known him to take a hint or turn away after he has an idea in his head. I wish you could have heard all the arguments I used to convince him to let me come here by myself tonight. Then you would not have to weary yourself making them again."

Kathe sighed. "It is too late. I have no wish to argue. And though I want to hear the story of how you, how the two of you, came here and what you have learned from the riders, we must sleep, at least for a few hours. I have only one question that will not keep until tomorrow." After a pause, she asked. "What have you heard of my father, of my mother and brother? Do you know whether they live?"

Meg and Gale looked at each other, searching their memories for a scrap of overheard conversation and came up with nothing. At least they had not heard that her family was dead.

"I am sorry," Gale said at last. "I heard no mention of any of your family, for good or ill, save yourself only. The Claymon are seeking a stronger hold in Ostara. Perhaps they still have something to fear. Perhaps your father is still a threat to them. Your mother and brother may be with him, in hiding."

On the night she fled Ostara, Kathe's brother had been riding in the hills outside the city, gathering companions for the struggle ahead. As darkness fell, her father strode angrily out from the house without saying farewell.

Her mother spent the hours before bed calming servants and gazing out the window to the west. Kathe's uncle's house lay just out of sight in that direction. Kathe watched her mother's tense shoulders and thought about her own flight. Perhaps her father had gone to reason with her uncle, making a last effort to draw him back into the family, trying to find a way to avoid the fate that the two of them, one through action and one through inaction, had brought to the city's gates.

When she lay in her bed that last night, her mother had come into the room, had stroked her hair and kissed her. They had not said anything to each other except the usual goodnight. Kathe had not wanted to worry her mother, who would surely have seen the flaws in the plan Abel and Bard had made for her safety. Now she wondered what plan had been made for her mother. How could she have assumed that her father would be able to protect and hide his Lady?

Tears welled in Kathe's eyes. Impatiently, she shook her head to clear the cobweb of memories and reached to take her bag from Meg. She would have turned towards the forest road at once if the girl had not pulled her sleeve.

"Wait," Meg said. "They are already searching for you. The Claymon soldiers, a few of our men, and the dogs. They went to the water meadow first, since I told them you were there, but before long they'll turn to the forest."

Kathe listened. Yes, she could hear the baying of hounds in the distance. That they were the manor dogs she had cosseted did not ease her mind. They were trained for the hunt.

"It's all through the kitchen and farmyard. Who you are, I mean. Mole whispered to me that he would mislead the search party if he could, but it will be unsafe to hide near the road tonight. Even now we are too close."

Were they coming closer? Kathe thought she heard a shout.

"We had an idea." Gale interrupted brusquely. "Well, Meg had one. Her father's fields are further west, maybe a two hour walk from here."

"We can be there before dawn," Meg said, "and sleep through the day in the byre loft. Then tomorrow night, when we are rested, we can begin the journey, not by the forest road, but by the ways Gale knows."

An owl swooped through the clearing, startling all three of them before it flew off to the west. Kathe gazed after it.

"You thought to travel alone, I know," Meg said. "You didn't even ask me to come, but here I am. I can't turn back now."

Kathe nodded, hugged Meg again, and shouldered her bag. "Lead," she whispered to Gale.

As they began to follow a faint trail to the west, she could hear the owl calling. Was it a particular owl named Oro and not some other? She could not understand owl talk now. Indeed, with each step her encounter with the animals of the circle seemed more and more like a dream.

They walked silently, too tired to speak even if it had been safe, listening intently for the baying of dogs or the voices of searchers. The path they followed was little more than a deer trail. Sometimes they lost it entirely and had to push slowly through thick, prickly undergrowth before they picked it up again.

Kathe was already convinced to welcome Gale as a companion. Together she and Meg would have found the croft, but never so surely. And no matter what the hardships of fatigue or hunger, following someone who knows the way is much more comfortable than having to question yourself at every step.

The stars were beginning to fade when the three joined the shadows in the pen where Meg's father kept his cow and a few chickens. They crept along the wall and slowly made their way around the edge of the little farmyard. They couldn't know whether the dog of Meg's childhood, or its successor, still guarded the house.

A cow snorted softly as they entered the byre and climbed the ladder to the loft. They crawled to the back of the nearly full platform; burrowed into the fragrant, dry grass; and, still without speaking, slept.

9

IN THE LOFT

WHEN KATHE AWOKE, DAYLIGHT streamed through cracks in the barn siding, and muffled voices rose from the farmyard below. She heard the squeak of a crank and clink of a pail being lowered into the well. Gale and Meg were still lost in sleep.

The angle of the sunlight told her it must be early afternoon. Her stomach told her it was time to eat. The three of them had finished the rest of her berries as they walked the night before, and the empty basket lay on its side next to her.

She felt herself drifting off into sleep again, but just as she was wondering that her aching body could find release in sleep when she thought it only craved movement, she heard a rustling. Gale was gingerly pulling himself backwards out of the straw, stretching his arms and legs. It looked as if it felt good. Kathe followed his example as quietly as she could, but their movements woke Meg. They soon sat close together, dirty and covered with scratches but so glad to see the day that they grinned and clasped each other's hands. The Claymon must have lost their trail.

Gale opened his haversack and placed a loaf of coarse bread and a knife on the straw in front of him. Reaching further into its recesses, he pulled out a ripe, yellow wheel of cheese wrapped in a square of cloth. It looked and smelled delicious. Kathe

wondered why she had not smelled it through the leather. She
waited to see what other wonders his bag might hold. He added
three bruised early apples and a skin of wine before cutting thick
slices of bread and cheese.

Kathe held her portion in her hands for a moment, noticing
the springiness and deep golden color of the bread crust and the
soft creaminess of the cheese. She forced herself to wait another
moment, remembering what her mother had taught her – always
to give thanks for food. She never had been so thankful as she
was now.

She looked into his face and mouthed, "Thank you." As
answer, he nodded and cut another piece of bread for her.

Meg still looked sleepy. Her hair was full of straw. Kathe
noticed for the first time that she was wearing one of the decent
tunics reserved for Mary and the others who served in the dining
hall. And on her feet were the soft leather shoes that allowed
Mary to move silently around the long table.

Kathe wondered what Meg was thinking. Surely she heard the
activity outside. Was she remembering the lean autumn when
her father took her to serve Lord Stefan? So far as Kathe knew,
she had not seen anyone from this farm since then, though she
often spoke of them, especially her young brothers, with love
in her voice. What connection remained between this refugee
in the hayloft and the young men whose deep voices drifted up
into their hiding place?

After they had finished eating and each had taken a long drink
of the sweet wine, they decided to take stock of their supplies.
Kathe began. She righted her empty berry basket from the straw
and began to transfer her possessions into it from the canvas bag
Meg had retrieved from under their mattress.

Lord Stefan's servants wore felted slippers in winter, but
Kathe had become used to walking on bare feet in the warm
months. Now she pulled her shoes from the bag and put them
on, remembering the feeling of leather fitting snugly around

a foot. After a moment, she took them off again and set them aside, along with the woolen stockings her mother had knitted for her and given her at the new year. Tonight would be soon enough for shoes. She smoothed the wrinkles from her dark blue cloak and folded it. It would serve as blanket or shelter if need be.

Next she took her knife from the bag. Catching Gale's eye, she handed it to him. He removed it from its sheath and balanced it in his hand, holding the jeweled handle to the light and running his finger appreciatively along the edge of the blade. He whistled softly as he handed it back to her.

The food she had hoarded over the past days seemed a poor collection now, after the meal Gale had provided. She was usually so hungry at the end of a day that she ate everything in her bowl before remembering that she was going to save something for the journey. She added to her basket a few heels of dry bread, a morsel of cheese which needed trimming on one side, and an empty water skin she had found hanging from the branch of a tree, abandoned by one of the cowherds in the meadow.

Rummaging deeper in the bag, she found several small cloth bundles. These contained dried oatmeal saved a bit at a time from its destiny in the breakfast pot and mushrooms she had found in spring and dried on a secluded, sunny wall top. A third bundle contained a few handfuls of walnuts and raisins, left from a session of baking during the spring festival.

When Kathe gestured that she had finished, Meg began to untie her bundle. Kathe had run into it several times the night before when she misjudged the distance between herself and Meg. It had hard edges.

Once she loosened the knot on top, all of Meg's possessions lay in a heap on the piece of cloth she had used to carry them. Looking at the collection, Kathe again realized that while she would be running toward her home, Meg was running away from hers. Here were things she could not bear to leave behind.

Reverently, Meg pulled out and carefully inspected a book that lay under the other things in the heap. That must have been one of the corners Kathe bumped in the night. She leaned forward. Seeing her interest, Meg handed it to her. The title on the cover was too worn to read, but the script looked very old. Any book was valuable, but this one was a treasure, with golden letters tooled into the leather, and silky pages. Kathe ran her hands over its smooth binding and opened it to a page near the beginning. Her mouth dropped open. Here was a fantastic bird with impossibly long tail feathers, delicately drawn in ink and illuminated in red and blue. Below it was the shape of an island. Or at least it seemed to be an island. It had the small marks all around it that meant water on the maps in her father's library. Turning to the next page, Kathe found the margins filled with drawings of leaves and fruits. Did these plants grow on the island where the beautiful bird lived? She was aware of Meg's outstretched hand, waiting to reclaim the book, but it was hard to tear her eyes from the page. She reluctantly gave it back with a questioning smile. Meg returned the smile, whispering that she would explain how the book came to be in her keeping later. She placed it gently next to her in the straw before turning back to the rest of her things.

In addition to the book, wrapped in the blanket from the bed they had shared, were a small cooking pot, a ladle, and two spoons. She looked guiltily at Gale as she unpacked them. It was clear she had taken them from the manor kitchen and considered herself a thief confessing to the master's son.

"Good girl," he mouthed silently, and patted her hand. She blushed and lifted the pot so they could see inside it. It contained fifteen or twenty biscuits from the store always heaped on a shelf by the kitchen door. The servants each took one or two to eat if they had to go into the fields for a day. They were dry and crumbly, but very filling.

The rest of the pile consisted of her old dress; a ball of yarn and two knitting needles; and a large piece of smoked bacon. She whispered that Mole had given it to her from the cellar.

Kathe could see a bright red something sticking out from the faded gray folds of Meg's everyday dress. She pointed, raising her eyebrows. Meg pulled a square of cloth free. Its colors glowed, a flowered design in crimson and ivory. Kathe recognized the woven pattern her mother called Summer and Winter. It was made of soft, fine wool to protect neck and shoulders from winter chill but also to delight the eye. Kathe had never seen Meg wear it.

"My mother wove it," Meg mouthed.

Since Meg had so much more to carry than she did, Kathe added the cooking pot to her own bag, then helped to tie the other things back into a tidy bundle. As she did, she reflected gratefully on Meg's practicality. The food and cooking things would keep them alive during the first days of their journey. And although the book was not a practical choice for a journey such as this, she understood why Meg could not leave it behind. She had never seen such fine pictures, even in her father's library in Ostara, and she was sure Stefan owned no book so precious. She was already looking forward to the time when she could look at it again.

After the two girls had repacked their things, they waited for Gale to follow their example. He unceremoniously emptied the contents of his large rucksack onto the straw at the center of their small circle. It made a clatter, and he winced an apology. They all sat completely still for several minutes, waiting for shouts from the farm yard that would herald their discovery.

Then he began to repack his bag, digging through the pile on the straw to find each item. Into the bottom of the pack went a thick hank of rope, a firestone, and knife. This knife was a contrast to Kathe's slender blade, a serviceable tool, scarred by years of use. To these he added a small pouch of dry tinder, and another of leaves for tea.

"But I forgot the pot," he mouthed.

On top of these practical objects, he placed two warm blankets, fruit of his mother's loom, a second cloak, another empty water skin and the food he had brought – the wedge of cheese remaining from their meal, more apples, and a second loaf of bread.

Meg and Kathe both gestured that they would carry some of these things, but he would not lighten his load.

After passing the wineskin one more time, he lashed it to the outside of the pack and tightened the cords holding his bow and a quiver of feathered arrows.

10

SAM

As THE AFTERNOON PASSED, it grew hot in their small space between straw and roof. While Kathe and Gale dozed, Meg watched through a crack in the barn siding for her father and oldest brothers to return from the fields. It was as if she watched her family from the sky, or heaven. When a tall, skinny boy crossed the yard to fetch water, she decided it must be Jack, the littlest one. He had their mother's unruly blonde hair, while all the other children were as dark as Meg. And the age was about right. Jack had just learned to run when her father took her to Springvale.

A woman came to the door, calling after him to keep an eye on the baby while she went to the garden. It was her mother. Meg hugged herself as she watched the familiar, beloved form settle a small child in a grassy patch by the doorstep and disappear around the corner of the house, and she did not breathe until she was out of sight. She closed her eyes tightly

Meg remembered how it once felt to be standing at the well, drawing water. Once she was the one who kept one eye on Jack as he played by the doorstep when her mother was busy in the garden. She watched closely as the little girl collected pebbles and placed them in patterns on a bare patch of earth. She was separating the prettiest, smoothest ones and using them to make her design.

She might have been three years old. Her hair was long, and black, but it was not tangled. Meg knew her mother must have combed it, sternly warning the child to stand still as she worked the wooden comb through wiry snarls. This little one must stand where Meg once stood early each morning, wiggling through this necessary task, feeling the patient fingers in her hair, sometimes hurting herself by pulling against those fingers.

She sighed softly and sat down with her back against the wooden wall. During her years at the Manor, Meg had convinced herself that she had grown up, that all the tears at leaving her family were in the past, but now she was overwhelmed by sadness. Her face twisted. All the fear and anger she felt when her father made his decision returned. She felt as she had on that day when he led her, unwilling and lagging, to the gates of Springvale.

How could he have taken her away from this place, away from her mother, and from the brothers she loved? How had he not heard her pleading? He did not soften at all at her tears; in fact, he became furious. He shouted that he was only thinking of her and that she was only thinking of herself. It had been a poor growing season. Her mother was expecting another child in winter. At Springvale she would have enough to eat…a warm place to sleep. The older boys helped him in the fields, and the youngest ones could take her place in the house. He had made his decision.

Meg did not know if her mother cried when she left. She could not bear to look into her face that morning, and she did not open the bag her mother pressed into her arms as she gave Meg a farewell embrace. It wasn't until a week or more after arriving at Springvale, when the place began to seem a little less foreign and her new duties more familiar, that she knelt in a corner of the courtyard early in the morning and looked inside.

When she did, she found the scarf, soft and bright, and a packet full of honeyed walnuts, her favorite childhood treat. As she held these things from home in her hands, her tears began anew. Though her mother could not write a message, she had told her through these gifts that she was loved, as clearly as if she had written words upon a scrap of paper. She ate the walnuts, one every day, until they were gone, and when they were, her well of tears had run dry.

She never wore the scarf. She kept it in her bed and held it at night when, as she often did, she thought of home.

She glanced at Kathe, sleeping in the slanting light of sunset. Meg had just heard her own mother's voice. Though the space between the two of them could not be crossed, at least it was narrow. She could see her mother, her brothers, and a little sister she had never met. At least she knew they lived. Kathe could not know whether anyone would greet her when she reached her home. And suppose her parents did still wait for her. She would not find them in that old manor house on the hillside above Ostara.

Long awaited yet unexpected, voices a few feet below them interrupted her thoughts and startled Kathe and Gale awake. Meg's father and the boys had returned from the fields. The three fugitives had stayed quiet all day, but now they became even more self-consciously silent, willing themselves not to sneeze as they watched the dust floating in the still air.

"Before you milk, muck out Ammie's pen and give her new bedding. Make it thick. The loft is full of straw for a change." A man's weary voice rose up to them.

As response, he received an adolescent grunt.

Meg looked out over the farmyard again. She saw her father's broad figure walking slowly towards the house with a tall young man. That meant a third brother was still below, given the evening chores of milking and caring for Ammie. But which one? They had changed so much, she couldn't be sure. And surely he could not be milking the same Ammie, the old cow she had helped to tend! This must be one of Ammie's spring calves, saved from market to replace its mother.

Her mother came around the corner of the house again, carrying a basketful of beans and lettuce. She handed it to her tall son before stooping to take the little girl's hand and lead her into the house. Meg's father and brother followed them inside, and the yard was again empty.

Meg shut her eyes tightly, trying to understand how her home came to be occupied by these older, smaller parents; these nearly grown children; and the girl who could have been herself as a little child. From below she heard the sound of a wooden rake as it pulled dirty straw from the cow's pen followed, after a few moments, by the creak of a wheeled cart being pulled outside to the midden, then more raking, and another load taken away. The three fugitives crept as far from the front edge of the loft as they could.

It is possible to stay motionless for a long time in sleep, or when deep in thought, but when one cannot move, when movement could bring danger, then being still becomes a torture or a discipline. Kathe looked the way a rabbit looks when it is caught in the open and is staying still until it knows whether it will have to run. Gale lay back against the straw where he had been sleeping. He might have still been sleeping, except his eyes were half open.

Meg waited for her brother to climb the ladder. A part of her hoped he would discover them. Of course, it would be simpler if they just slipped away when it was dark, leaving nothing but depressions in the straw. If they were found, her father would either hand them over to the Claymon or he would have to lie about seeing them, and she could not be certain which he would choose.

But still she wanted to see them, wanted them to see her before she left Springvale forever. She longed to embrace her mother and to look into her father's face. Would she see any regret there? No, she decided, losing courage at the thought. It would be best to leave the farm as she had come, as a shadow in the night. The news would eventually reach her family from some passing peddler or on market day – how two kitchen girls had run away from the manor. There would be a wild story about how one of the girls was high born, from beyond the forest, but her father was a practical man and he'd disbelieve most of it. Chances are he wouldn't even tell her mother. Why upset her?

Meg felt the shudder of the loft floor as her brother climbed the ladder, but she had made herself small in the straw, and she did not see him when he climbed onto the loft itself and began to kick straw over the edge. The three remained still until the noise suddenly stopped. Without breathing, they waited for the sound of the lad climbing down. When it didn't come. Meg pushed the straw away from her face and opened her eyes to see an 'o' of surprise on the face of her brother. He was staring at the shape of Gale's pack sticking out from the straw against the byre wall. It was only partly uncovered, but it was enough.

With lightening quickness, Gale pulled the youth forward, at the same time clamping his hand over the open mouth so that, when Meg opened her eyes, she saw the struggling form and wide eyes of the middle boy, Sam.

She scrambled forward and captured one of his flailing arms, holding it firmly, and she put a finger to her lips. "Shhhh, Sam," she whispered, "Shhh, we won't hurt you. You must be quiet."

He stopped struggling. After another moment of staring into Gale's stern face and a glance at the shadowed form of Kathe, the boy nodded, and Gale removed his hand from the boy's mouth, keeping a grip on his shoulders.

"How, How'd you know my name?" he blurted too loudly. "Who are you?"

Gale once again silenced him.

Meg took Sam's hand and gave it what she hoped was a

reassuring squeeze. "You must be quiet! Don't you know me? It's sister. Meg. These are my friends. We need help. Will you help us?" She realized she had fallen back into using the simple words she had used so long ago, when this boy was a young child, when she had to make him understand and do as she asked.

His eyes once again widened, and they turned pleadingly to Gale's face.

"Last chance," Gale whispered, before removing his hand.

"Meg? Truly? But you have grown!" The boy said, so softly that Gale relaxed his grip on his shoulders.

"As you have not?" Meg replied, with a chuckle.

"I've got to go tell Mother and the others. They will be so happy!" His voice threatened to rise again.

"Will they?" Meg asked doubtfully. "No. We cannot linger here, and I do not wish to bring trouble." Very softly, speaking almost into his ear, she tried to explain to him about Kathe, how the Claymon had come to Springvale, how she and Kathe, and Gale planned to travel through the Forest, to Ostara where three mountains made a kind of gateway to the rugged lands of the northern plain. Even to her, it sounded fantastic. The boy listened intently.

Kathe stayed almost hidden in the gathering darkness. She, too, knew how the story must sound to this farm boy who had expected another boring night of chores.

"You must finish bedding and milking the cow," Meg said urgently.

"But you said I can help," Sam said stubbornly and too loudly. "Milking the cow isn't helping."

"Father will soon begin to wonder why you are so long at your work," Meg explained patiently. "And you can help by keeping our presence secret until we are able to leave, by doing things the way you would usually do them."

Sam nodded. "Yes, I can do that." He rose and turned to climb back over the straw. He stopped and turned. "I can do more, can't I?"

"Yes," Gale said quickly. "You can fill our water skins with fresh well water."

The boy still looked sulky and confused.

"And you can share some milk with us," Kathe added.

At the sound of her low voice after such a long silence, the boy smiled for the first time. "Yes, I can do that," he said.

Sam shoved more straw over the edge of the loft and disappeared down the ladder; the three could hear him spreading clean bedding in the cow's pen. They kept their bags close at hand, ready to slip away as soon as the household slept. Sam would have to finish his milking by lamplight, but this was not a household to waste oil or candles. After a day of hard work, they would be ready to go to bed soon after the sun did. Sam would finish his milking, eat a supper kept warm in the fireplace, then sleep too. It was what he usually did.

When he had finished, Sam crossed the farmyard to the house, but after a few minutes he returned to climb the ladder one more time, this time bringing a deep wooden bowl filled with milk. He carefully handed it to Kathe who took the first drink, savoring its creamy warmth before passing it to Meg and Gale. "Thank-you," she said. "It is good."

He stammered a response as Gale handed him their two empty water skins. They made a whispered agreement that the boy would leave them leaning against the far side of the north wall.

They passed the bowl of milk around again, draining it before returning it to Sam. He was just about to go when Meg took his hand. "I'm glad you found us, Sam. It would have been too hard to leave home a second time without even speaking to one of my boys."

"Why can't you stay with us?"

Meg saw Sam was growing to look like their father. She was young when she left the farm, but she could not remember her father showing any emotion except impatience. But still there, too, were traces of the little boy she sang to sleep so many nights, and with him the two others, bundled together into one bed.

"I am promised to Springvale," she whispered. "I could not stay here without returning to the manor." But even as she spoke, she knew this was not the whole truth. Despite the uncertainty of the future, she was looking forward to the journey ahead. Even if she chose to stay with her family – and was allowed to stay – the time would be short before she left again, this time as wife to a man her father would choose. She had had only a small taste of freedom, not nearly enough.

She hugged him and felt him stiffen. She wondered whether anyone had hugged him since she went away. She released him and smiled. "Thank you, Sam."

11
Into the Forest

DARKNESS FALLS SLOWLY WHEN there is no fire or candle. After the sunlight faded, there were minute gradations in the twilight until at last they could not see each other in the loft, or finally, their own hands in front of their faces. When they peered through the cracks in the side of the byre, the house looked dark too. The family must be sleeping.

There was not room enough to stand, so the three fugitives stretched their stiff legs as best they could. Then Gale climbed down the ladder, and Kathe lowered all their things to him. Outside, they found the water skins where Sam had promised to leave them. Gale lashed one to the outside of his pack, and Kathe slung the other over her shoulder. Then they skirted the farm and entered the forest.

For a little way there was a narrow, but clear, path, used by the family when they collected firewood. Meg led them. Now that they were outside, it seemed much lighter. The moon was rising; after a few minutes they could see their way easily as mature trees rose on either side. Stars trembled in the spaces between branches arching over the path.

Kathe felt like running. She finally was going home, and it felt wonderful to move freely after a day of enforced stillness.

Even so, she was startled when Meg darted swiftly ahead. Kathe would have run after her if Gale had not placed a hand on her shoulder. Together they stood and watched as Meg raced toward a pale form that had stepped onto the path. The figure stretched its arms, and Meg ran into them, held the shape and was held by it. Kathe and Gale felt a wave of joy pass over them. It made ripples in the deep pools of loneliness within themselves, places they usually tried not to think about.

They walked slowly forward, not wishing to intrude on the reunion, but drawn by the two women who were now holding each other at arm's length, crying and laughing, then pulling each other close again. Meg and her mother created a radiance around themselves. The edges of it seemed to spark in the moonlight, and Kathe and Gale stopped a few steps away, needing an invitation before going any closer.

"Mother," Meg breathed, "This is my mother." She stretched one hand out to Kathe, holding her mother's arm with the other as if she were afraid she was an illusion and might vanish.

Meg's mother took a few steps closer to them. They saw she was wearing a homespun night shift and had a shawl wrapped around her shoulders. A thick plait of blonde hair shot with silver hung over her shoulder.

"Sam knew how I've missed her. So many times he's heard me say our Meg must be a young woman now and how I longed to see her. He could not keep such a secret." She reached to stroke Meg's hair away from her face. "And look at you. Taller than me now, yet I would have known you anywhere." The two embraced again, then turned their glowing, tear-streaked faces toward Kathe and Gale.

"I am Sofie," Meg's mother said warmly, "and Sam told me about you too." She greeted Kathe and Gale, and took their hands. "As soon as he finished the milking, he called me outside into the garden." She paused. "I am thankful it wasn't Gregory doing the chores tonight. He might not have found you, or if he had, he would surely have gone straight to your father, Meg."

Meg looked down at her feet.

"He is a good man, though I can understand why you might not see it. If he discovered you and stopped to think, maybe he would have sent you on your·way, but more likely he would have kept you here."

They stood in a circle, listening to the wind in the leaves above them. Finally Sofie spoke again. "Before you leave again, Meg, forgive me."

"Forgive you?"

"Before you went away, I should have fought to keep you. Your father listens to me if I fight hard enough. But I was weak then, carrying the child I lost soon after you left. Then for many weeks I took to my bed, sickened by grief. By spring I was stronger, but by then it was too late. No amount of arguing could make him go to claim you. I am sorry."

"Oh Mother, I never blamed you." Meg said, raising her face and smiling joyously. "I was sad at first, but the people at the manor are kind, mostly, and I was well cared for. And now I have a friend." She turned to where Kathe stood in the shadows, and seeing Gale there, amended, "Two friends."

"I know," her mother replied. "If it were not for them, I could not let you go again." She picked up a basket she had left by the side of the path. I've packed some things for you: dried meat, some hard rolls, some sewing things and candles – what I could find quietly after Sam told me."

"Don't worry," she said quickly, "Your father pays little attention to the busyness of women. He thought I was just getting ready for tomorrow, if he thought about it at all. But I had better make my way back. He knows I am sometimes restless and wander at night, but if I am gone too long he will come to look for me."

Gale said, "I will escort you back to the farm."

Sofie protested, but Meg and Kathe added their insistence.

Kathe said, "Go ahead, Meg. Spend a few more moments with your mother. I'll wait here with our packs until you return."

Gale almost spoke again, to insist that Kathe should come with them to the farmstead, but he caught himself. Kathe had already spent many nights alone at the edge of the forest; to reach Springvale, she passed through parts of it he had never seen. And she had been ready to journey alone. He put his pack on the ground under the beech tree and offered Sofie his arm.

After the three of them disappeared around a bend in the trail, Kathe sank to the ground and leaned back against the rough trunk of the tree, gazing up through its branches at the stars shining through the leaves.

She whispered, "Oro." She sat still for a few minutes, waiting for the little wind of his wings, or the softness of feathers sweeping her face. She stood up again and called a little more loudly, "Oro."

The owl still did not appear. A light breeze smelled of rain. She listened harder. Maybe the rustling of leaves masked other sounds she was too human to hear. She sat again, leaned back, and closed her eyes, straining to remember how the owl's glowing eyes had looked – was it really only two nights ago?

When she felt warm breath on her cheek, she opened her eyes and quickly closed them again. A hands breadth away was a dark face, feline and intent.

"*Just don't scream,*" a smooth, furry voice said. "*Please. We hate it when you do that.*"

Kathe's heart raced, and her hands clutched at the roots of the tree. She forced herself to look again. The green eyes of the panther met hers. They were eyes she had seen before – in the meeting circle.

"*I am myself, Maraba. Like Oro, I often linger near people, though they do not know it. Like him, I listen to their beautiful words before they sleep. You called Oro. He hunts tonight, but I am here."*

Kathe swallowed, "I called Oro because I wondered if he, if all of you, are real."

The big cat leaned its head to the side, studying her. *"Say more words."*

"I thought I just dreamed the circle when I was sleeping."

"Are you sleeping now?"

"No, of course not."

The panther moved closer and licked her face. She felt the roughness of its tongue and touched the moisture on her cheek.

"Is this real?" Without warning, Maraba struck at her forearm with one huge paw. Kathe gasped in pain, saw a half circle of dark spots appear as blood welled from the places where the big cat's claws had punctured her skin. She shrank away.

"For a few days you will feel those marks, see them. Every time you feel the rough place where I touched, you will remember you were awake and I am real. What will happen when they heal?"

Kathe had shut her eyes again. Now she opened them and steadily met the panther's gaze.

"Will you begin to think that we are a dream again? Perhaps you should learn to pay more attention to your dreams. And when you do, you will meet us in both worlds." Maraba looked away. *"There are paths in this forest I have never walked, but I know the forest has an end. The farmers tend their fields on every side of it, and each season it grows smaller. But the land of dreams has no end."*

The cat licked Kathe's wound, gently this time. She felt its silky side brush her shoulder before it vanished into the trees behind her.

12

First Steps

As soon as Meg and Gale returned, all three of them took up their bundles and began walking north. At first they were guided by the stars; later, when the trees became more massive and the branches hid this map, their intuition led them – that and Gale's knowledge of the forest. In the darkness after moon set, he stopped now and then to run his fingers along the trunks of trees, feeling for the moss that grows most heavily on the north side.

Meg relived her reunion with her mother, each time thinking of something else she wished she had said. She began each of these waking dreams with her first glimpse of the figure on the path ahead and ended it with an embrace of farewell and fresh tears. Finally, she put her memories aside and looked about her. Until she did, she was hardly aware that she was walking through the forest she had feared so much.

Kathe, on the other hand, was very much afraid. She had almost convinced herself that the talking animals had come to her in a dream. It had been a beautiful and interesting dream, and maybe someday she would even figure out what it meant, if dreams really had meanings. Now her arm stung where Maraba clawed her, and every pang reminded her that the messengers were real. They had chosen her – but to what purpose?

She remembered peering through a window on a frosty morning back home in Ostara. She breathed on the bubbly glass and rubbed it with the sleeve of her dress. In the courtyard outside, people were gathering, more arriving as she watched. They looked like bundles of old clothes huddled around the small fire built for them in a sheltered corner near the gate.

Her mother's waiting woman crossed the courtyard. The people crowded around, and presently she led them, one at a time, to the small room built into the courtyard wall where Kathe's mother was already sorting the herbs she had collected that week, hanging them to dry along the rafters, putting the dried plants in neatly labeled jars and bottles.

Mother would have seen the people in the house if Father allowed it. Ellen of Ostara was well known as a healer, and though her father thought it improper that his wife spent so many hours with the ill and injured who gathered in front of his house each day, he found it impossible to forbid it. And so her mother went out to them, choosing remedies according to the need of each but also healing through her touch – and something more.

Kathe winced as she bumped against a low branch and as she recalled her own childhood embarrassment. She had sided with her father. Both of them preferred to see her mother working at the loom or gliding through the house overseeing the work of the servants. Every time her mother crossed the courtyard and stepped through the dark doorway of the room in the wall, it seemed to Kathe that she was crossing an invisible line. On the other side of that line were frightening people – dirty, desperate, even mad.

After her encounters with the animals, Kathe understood that it was really her mother's magic she feared. The idea that just talk with her mother, and a little pouch of the dried herbs from the kitchen garden could make one of these wretched souls leave with a lighter step filled her with confusion. This was probably why her thoughts always wandered from the school room when her mother had tried to teach her the healing arts. Kathe often preferred to avoid what she could not readily explain.

Kathe preferred the teaching Bard had given her in the use of the knife and in living outdoors. She had learned something from her father about the responsibilities that came with leadership. But what had her mother taught her? Could she use it now?

They walked through the night, and just before dawn they found themselves on the brink of a ravine. It was not deep. Even in the grey light, they could see it would be possible to scramble down the bank and wade across the stream they could hear pouring swiftly over stones below them. They had already crossed several similar barriers, though none with flowing water at the bottom.

Gale's voice sounded bone weary. "As soon as there's a little more light, we'll climb down and follow the water further to the west. Sooner or later, the search party will think of Meg's father and his croft, and if they find our trail in the next day, the dogs will be able to follow our path here, but they won't be able to track us through the water."

Meg stepped closer to the edge of the ravine and peered down. "I'll grant you that. But why west? Wouldn't it make more sense to travel east? That's the way to the forest road."

"Yes, and it's the way the Claymon soldiers took to Springvale and the way they will look for us when they are hurrying back to Ostara with the unwelcome news that their prize has escaped. If the dogs follow our trail here, they will see the place where we slid down to the stream. We can fake a trail for a short way on the other side, but it will not confuse them for long. They will return to the stream, and when they do..."

"They will follow it east," Kathe finished. "You are right. We will go west."

13

FIRE

THE CLAYMON CAPTAIN STOOD rigidly next to the well in the farmyard. His face showed his distaste for the task at hand. He had made so many threats that he finally had to accept the defiant protestations of the barrel-chested man lying in the dust before him. It had taken three soldiers to put him there, in a proper posture of submission, but his story didn't change. He hadn't seen his daughter since the day he took her to Springvale, and anyway, if she had turned up here, he knew his duty.

The two sons agreed with their father. They had heard nothing unusual during the night, and if Meg's father chose not to ask his wife why she sent Sam to help the neighbors early that morning, that would be between the two of them later. Sofie sat on a low stool next to the house with the little girl on her lap. When the captain questioned her, she deferred meekly to her husband, but Meg's father knew her well. He saw her expression when the officer's back was turned.

No, the captain decided, the family probably did not assist the runaways, but still, they had been here. He was certain about that. There were signs: a slender footprint in the soft ground next to a wall; the straw in the loft showing the impressions of bodies.

They were careless. He supposed it was the overconfidence of youth. It was an inconvenience, but soon his trackers would have them. Greystone would want to know. The captain rolled a tiny scrap of parchment and slid it into the metal cylinder attached to the pigeon's leg. Then he threw the bird into the air and watched it wing north.

After another strong warning to watch for Kathe and to hold her and her companions if they came, the captain and his horse soldiers followed his trackers into the forest.

A little way into the trees, the captain stopped and ordered five soldiers back to the farmstead. "Burn it," he commanded.

The farmer watched the soldiers returning. They threw the burning brands they carried into the thatching of the house and byre roofs and galloped away. Sofie stood silently next to her husband as their home collapsed in upon itself.

"They would have burned our home whether we helped the young ones or not, but if they knew we helped, they would have killed us," she said.

He walked away from her towards the fields without a look or a word. Sofie looked after him for a long moment until she noticed the little girl was sobbing, her face hidden in her mother's skirts. She picked her up and tried to soothe her.

"Hush now, they're gone. Come. I will find you something good to eat. The red raspberries are ripening."

Their neighbors would have seen the smoke. They would come, and Sam with them. There were weeks left before the first frost, and the cow was in the pasture. They could build again. She had to believe everything could be rebuilt.

14

WHERE THE STREAM LED

THEY FOLLOWED THE STREAM for half the day, adding their shoes to the baskets and bundles they carried. At first the cool water soothed their tired feet, but they soon were bruised by the pebbles lining the creek bed. By mid morning, both Meg and Kathe had fallen many times, stepping into deep holes or tripping on their wet skirts. Kathe was first to hitch all the excess cloth above her knees, tying it at her waist with a strip torn from the hem. Meg followed her example, and then they made better progress. They had eaten a little bread as they waited for the light. Now they perched on a rock in mid-stream, as big as a small island, sharing cheese and apples and dipping to drink the clear water flowing around them.

Tired as they were, they still took pleasure in the lacy fern that grew all along the banks and the flash of fish where the sunlight caught their sides in shallow places. They heard the rattle of a kingfisher nearby, and their eyes hunted the overhanging branches until they saw its bright, iridescent blue.

Meg waded near the shore and brought back water cress to add to their meal. As she did, she tried to remember. How long had it been since she crouched in the stream at the manor, listening to the Claymon soldiers watering their horses? She squeezed her aching eyes shut. Only two days? She stood straighter, stretching her back and shoulders.

The sunny island was large enough for all three of them to stretch out to rest after their meal, but rock is hard even when one is very weary, and water is no barrier to dreams. Less than an hour passed before they roused themselves and prepared to move on.

Whenever he stepped into the forest, Gale felt he had come home. Looking around now, he could name all the trees, and he recognized most of the plants growing along the stream bank. He could follow the traces left by animals. When the supplies they carried were gone, they wouldn't starve, especially at this time of year. Still, he nervously unloaded and reloaded his pack, checking the string of his bow and the tips of his arrows before shouldering it again. Kathe watched him, then glanced back downstream.

"Have you ever been here before?"

He didn't answer right away. Then he shrugged. "No," he replied. "I have followed this stream from the forest trail, wandering a short distance from it to collect plants for my mother, but I have not come so far, and I always traveled by daylight, never moonlight." He tugged the drawstring at the top of his pack tighter. "Truthfully, I have never spent more than two nights in the forest at a stretch, though I have explored most of it within a day's journey of Springvale." When she turned away, he added, "I was rarely at the Manor because I preferred to be on the land, and most of the time I really was working. I didn't spend nearly as much time wandering as rumor claimed – but I do know North from South, and I believe I will be able to read the forest whether I am one day into it, or many days."

Kathe sighed. "You are probably right. Anyway, you have led us this far, and I am grateful. But now I am ready to walk on dry land again. Do you think it is safe to leave the stream?"

Gale had a feeling she had already made up her mind about

this and was only asking his opinion to be polite. "I was just going to suggest that. But let's climb up and down on the south bank and then travel a bit further in the water before we climb out on the North. I don't know how hard the Claymon will try to find you, and away from the forest road, their horses may slow them. Still, we should confuse the trail as much as we can."

About a hundred yards beyond their resting spot, the stream curved sharply north. They paused, considering whether this would be the place to climb out of the ravine and continue overland. Meg cupped her hand behind her ear.

"Do you hear something?"

The others strained to identify the sound.

"What is it?" Kathe asked.

"Let's walk in the water a little farther," Gale suggested.

Kathe and Meg were thoroughly sick of being wet. Even though their feet were hardened by a summer without shoes, the stony streambed had battered their feet. Still, curiosity won. The sound was coming from ahead of them, upstream.

The water began to rush faster around their knees as they made their way toward the distant roaring. The rocks grew from pebbles to boulders until they were finally able to step from one to the next without walking in the water at all. For a time they forgot their tiredness in the child's game of jumping from stone to stone. On each side of them the banks had become walls of rock. Meanwhile, the noise was getting louder.

Kathe and Meg looked up from their footing to see Gale waving his arms. He had been out of sight around the next curve in the stream, but now he reappeared ahead of them, gesturing for them to hurry as if what he had found wouldn't wait. It looked as if he might have been yelling something, but the roar of the water completely drowned his words.

As they neared him, Kathe saw that the water racing around the large boulder where he stood was folding and curling upon itself before it shattered on the stones farther downstream. She and Meg helped each other to follow him around the curve and stared in shock, clinging to one another. Meg sat down abruptly and put her hands on each side of her head as if she was dizzy. Kathe sank to her knees behind her. The stream had narrowed abruptly here, and Gale stood to one side, grinning and steadying himself by holding tightly to a root snaking down the slick rock of the cliff face.

They had become used to being enclosed by green. For many hours they had only been able to see a little way up and downstream and hardly at all into the forest on either side. Now the world opened up into a huge bowl of stone and rushing water. The stream poured through the opening where they stood, fed by a clear pool of water several times larger than the mill pond at Springvale.

But it wasn't the sound of the rapids behind them that made them cling to the rocks and each other. It was the roaring of a mighty waterfall pouring over the rim of the stone bowl, feeding the pool and stream and filling the air with mist and rainbows.

Of the two girls, Kathe was first to tentatively stand again. She offered her hand to Meg, pulling her to her feet. They stood for a moment with their arms around each other's waists before either of them spoke.

"Now what?" Meg shouted. Even standing right next to her, Kathe and Gale could barely hear her, but they shared her question. The stream banks here formed a canyon the height of several tall men and leaning slightly inward near the top. They scanned the edge of the pool, but they couldn't see all of it from their rocky perch. What they could see appeared unclimbable.

It was as if this circle of earth had simply sunk into the ground. Although flooded by late afternoon sunlight, the world ahead of them and around them felt subterranean. Glittering white deposits of minerals on the rock walls added to the illusion. Without waiting for an answer, Meg shrugged her bundle into a more comfortable position on her back and turned to retrace her steps back through the rapids.

Kathe stopped her, placing her hand on Meg's shoulder. Gale was gesturing for them to join him on a large boulder nearer the stream bank. They gathered there with their heads bent into a close triangle. The explorer in Gale had awoken, and he couldn't contain his excitement.

"Let's think. Before, we were just going to climb up the bank back there and travel north, but if we can find a way out of this rock bowl, the Claymon would have to fly to follow our trail."

Meg looked doubtfully, first at him, then at the waterfall thundering into the roiling pool some distance to their right. Even though Gale was not Lord Stephan, he was used to getting his way. He couldn't help it. He had been telling people what to do his whole life. Just as she did what she was told. She felt the tug of habit.

As she tried to decide how best to speak the many good reasons not to try to climb the cliff, Meg heard Kathe's laugh. She saw her plant her bundle on the stone and turn. Then she jumped far forward into the pool – feet first. Meg shrieked and grabbed Gale's arm. They stood staring at the surface, stunned by Kathe's disappearance. After what seemed like eternity, but was really less than a minute, she surfaced some distance to their right, nearer to the waterfall.

After stumbling and splashing through the stream all day, all three of them were wet to the skin, but this wanton immersion momentarily stunned Kathe's two companions. Then Gale carefully leaned his pack next to Kathe's bag and, with a mighty yell, catapulted himself into the water too. He rose to the surface and shook his head like a bear, splashing Meg, who once again lowered herself to sit on the rock, clutching her bundle tightly in her lap.

After a few more minutes of diving and playing in the water, Kathe gracefully swam over to Meg and pulled herself up partway onto the rock, resting her chin on her arms. Her skirt was still tied up above her knees from wading, and her legs floated behind her. "After a whole day of slogging through the water without the pleasure of swimming, I just had to do that," she gasped. "Come in! It's so wonderful, it's a rest!"

Meg shook her head firmly, as if Kathe had suggested that they visit the land of the Mer folk. "I can't swim, and it's no good wishing for the gift. I tried in the mill-pond, but I sank like a stone. Anyway," she scanned the rim of the bowl and looked over her shoulder, back downstream. It doesn't feel safe."

Kathe's smile faded. "You're right. I let myself forget." Then she grinned again, "I have to continue forgetting for just a few more minutes." Seeing the look on Meg's face, she added. "Don't worry. I'll stay close to the edge. This is too turbulent a place to teach you to swim, Meg, but teach you I will – someday."

She turned and pushed off from the rock again, swimming strongly toward Gale. He was treading water, having swum as close to the base of the waterfall as he dared. Now that they were in the pool, they could look all around and see its walls weren't as smooth as they at first seemed. The base was mostly ringed by tumbled stone. Raw scars marked the places where it had fallen from the rim of the basin. Here and there, small trees and other plants had taken root where the rocks had broken away, and the cliff face on both sides of the waterfall looked eroded and ragged. Also, they could now see that there wasn't just one waterfall, but several. Only one of them truly thundered into the pool. The others made veils across the face of the cliff. Trees overhung the top of the bowl. Looking up at them made Kathe feel dizzy, so she dove and swam closer to the edge.

In the stream, the large boulders were smooth, with flat tops and curves like stone clouds. Here they jutted from the water jaggedly, and Kathe soon found a place where she could pull herself out. As the water streamed from her hair and clothing, she allowed herself to remember Bard.

Many years before, when her brother had led her to the pond

for her one and only swimming lesson, she had known his motives were mixed. He had really wanted to share the joy of swimming with her, but he was also looking forward to seeing the look on their parents' faces when they both returned home dripping wet. After her father stalked out of the room, her mother informed her that swimming lessons would form no part of her education as Lady of the Three Hills. Despite the discipline she faced that day, from then on she had slipped away whenever she could to practice and to feel the silky water on her skin. Her mother must have known, but she never chided her – and Kathe took care that her father never saw her until she was completely dry and lady-like again.

Kathe looked across the pool to see Gale further along the edge, on the rocks, working his way back toward Meg and the entrance to the canyon. Kathe pulled her clinging skirt away from her knees and began picking her way toward the waterfall. Even though the footing was slippery, it was easier than she thought it would be. A kind of moss grew in shady cracks in the rock walls, and it cushioned her hands as she steadied herself. There was no such padding on the rocks under her feet, and she knew that a fall and a broken bone would end her journey.

By the time Gale pulled himself onto the rock where Meg sat nervously waiting for them, Kathe was standing in the spray next to the largest waterfall. By the time he realized she was not following him, she had disappeared.

15

The Sleeper

Meg, on the other hand, had not taken her eyes off Kathe from the moment she first plunged into the pool. Whenever her friend was above water, Meg was watching her intently, imagining herself as an anchor that could pull Kathe onto the safety of dry land. So, although she was afraid of the water, she was not afraid for Kathe the way Gale was when he clambered onto the rock and turned around to see no sign of her.

She could tell by the look on his face that he was about to jump back into the water to search, so Meg grabbed his shoulder and pointed at the waterfall. As she did, Kathe emerged from behind the sheet of water, balancing precariously on a rock in the spray next to the falls. They couldn't see the expression on her face, but there could be no doubt about what she wanted them to do. She was gesturing strongly for them to join her.

"Maybe she has found a way up," Gale said doubtfully.

"I just hope she hasn't decided to give me a swimming lesson after all," replied Meg. She picked up her bundle and would have carried Kathe's too if Gale had not taken it from her.

Burdened as they were, they found it very difficult to work their way around the base of the bowl to the spot where Kathe stood with her back pressed against the wet rocks. By the time they stood near Kathe at the base of the falls, the air was so full of mist that Meg checked the sky to make sure it really was not raining. She could not stop thinking about the treasures in her pack. She hoped they were dry, protected by the blankets in which she had wrapped them that morning. If they got wet, the scarlet threads of her mother's weaving would likely run and spoil the book. Despite her preoccupation with keeping these objects safe, she was aware of the irony – a kitchen girl protecting a precious book (which she had no hope of ever reading), while ahead of her stood the Lord of Springvale and the Lady of the Three Hills, soaked to the skin and carrying tools, food, and a battered pot.

There was no hope of communicating even by shouting now, so close to the torrent, so Kathe simply took her bundle from Gale with a nod, and catching their attention with a glance over her shoulder, disappeared once more. They were able to follow her through a cleft in the rock next to the falls. It was just large enough for a slender woman to push through sideways, carrying her bundle in one hand. It was a very tight fit for Gale.

After the bright reflections of light on water, the chamber they entered seemed Stygian at first, but as their eyes adjusted, Meg and Gale could see that it was not a large space, perhaps fifteen paces across and a bit more than that deep. Water seeped down the walls, and they stood in a pool a few inches deep. Behind them, the falls roared. Although there were window-like gaps in the stone through which they could see the flood rushing past, the sound was muted here.

Gale's weary voice echoed in the enclosed space. "This cave is a wonder. I wish we had time to explore it, but the afternoon is dwindling. We have only a few hours until darkness." He let this reminder sink in, looked down at the water around his ankles and added, "This is no fit place to spend the night, nor have I seen any way up and out of the sink hole. We will have to return to the canyon and follow it back until we find a place where we can climb the bank."

Kathe had been standing between Meg and Gale and the back of the cave. She didn't know how to prepare them for what she had found there. She was shaking, and not just because of the cold.

"Wait," she said. "There's something you have to see. She stepped aside and motioned them deeper into the shadows. She took Meg's hand and held it tightly.

Meg gasped.

"I'm sorry. There's nothing to fear – or at least I don't think there is," Kathe soothed, hugging her shaken friend. How could she have forgotten how difficult all this must be for Meg? She should have prepared her better. She must be stupid with fatigue.

For once Gale was speechless.

"Who is he?" Meg breathed.

A shelf had been cut into the back wall of the cave, and a man's body lay on it. They could see the glint of chain mail that protected him during his life. It covered his shoulders and extended almost to his knees. Leather boots covered his feet and lower legs, and a wooden shield lay across his chest. It was plain, bearing no image to help them discover his origin. A dented helm leaned against the wall behind him. He must have been dead. He looked as if he was only sleeping.

Kathe bent toward the knight's face and studied him closely in the cave's twilight. She could not call him handsome. His nose was too large and his mouth too wide. Nor was he particularly tall or strong looking, though it was hard to tell about this, lying as he was on the stone bier.

There was something appealing in his expression. It may have been the slight smile softening the mouth, or the fine web of lines around his eyes. She was certain she had never seen anyone like him among the foreigners visiting Ostara. The design of his armor and the texture of the thick woolen cloak spread beneath him and trailing over the side of the slab was strange to her.

"He may be dead and under a spell which has kept him from decay, or maybe in some deep enchanted sleep," said Gale unnecessarily.

Curiosity and pity drew Meg closer until she stood between Kathe and Gale looking down at the sleeper.

Her voice shaking a little, she asked, "Is there nothing we can do for him?" She wanted nothing more than to squeeze back through the crack, crawl as rapidly as possible over the rocks to the canyon, and make her weary way to any dry place far away from here. Until now she had seen nothing in the forest to really frighten her. The hungry bears and lions of her fantasies had not appeared. Back when she was safe within the walls of Springvale and reciting her litany of forest dangers, magic had been entirely absent from the list.

"Sir," Kathe said loudly, startling them all. They had instinctively been speaking in lowered voices. "Well, it does seem sensible to try the usual ways of waking someone first," she explained. She straightened herself and slowly reached forward to touch the bare hand of the sleeping warrior. Getting no response and growing a little braver, she took his hand in her own and lifted it. She squeezed it and said again, "Sir!"

She turned to Gale and said in a shocked voice, "His hand is so cold…yet tell me what you think."

Gale reluctantly took the knight's limp hand, held it, and examined it. Turning it over, he ran a fingertip over the calluses on the thumb and at the base of the fingers. Gently replacing the hand by the man's side, he said, "He has the calloused hands of a swordsman."

Kathe reached across the body to lift the folds of the cloak. "Here is the scabbard, but no sword."

"He has a kind face," said Meg.

"And that is all we know. His hand is as supple as that of any living man but as cold as death. I fear this mystery is beyond us."

They stood rooted to the cave floor for several more minutes, knowing they must leave, but reluctant to abandon the mysterious sleeper. Then they removed their packs and bags from their shoulders again in order to squeeze back through the opening. Kathe gave Meg a damp hug before she turned to lead the way. Gale followed, and Meg stood waiting for them to clear the opening. She contemplated the warrior. He really did look as if he was sleeping, and Kathe and Gale said he was cold. She knew it was foolish to think it would make any difference, but she lingered to lift the man's cloak that had fallen across the front of his bier and to spread it over him. As she bent to arrange the folds of cloth, a beam of sunlight fractured as it streamed through the waterfall, reflecting from the pool's surface and, illuminating the front of the stone platform.

Meg rushed to the entrance and shouted, "Kathe, my Lord, come back…come back." She waited with one shoulder through the entrance hole, ready to bolt if they had not heard her and did not appear at once. When Gale reached her, she grabbed his hand pulling him back into the cave. "Look," she said, pointing at the stone ledge.

There, carved into the base of the bier in glowing letters were five lines of script. Gale knelt in the shallow water and traced the words with his finger.

16

The Summer Wanderers

KATHE DID NOT HEAR Meg's shout, but after a moment or two she paused in her work of rock-climbing to check the progress of her companions. As soon as she realized they were not following her, she started back toward the falls.

Her knees twinged. She thought that this day had taught her joints about the aches they would know every day when she was an old woman. If she ever got to be an old woman. Right now that did not seem likely.

Just before she reached the cave, she looked up from her feet to search the tumble of rocks for the entrance. She had been lucky to stumble upon it the first time; it just looked like a crack between two boulders that had fallen together.

A deep snarl at shoulder height broke her concentration. She might have fallen or jumped into the pool had it not been for sharp claws hooking into the fabric of her dress. They pulled her roughly back against the rocks and into the flow of one of the small water falls that companioned the cataract. She didn't scream. There was no time, and by the time she caught herself and drew her next shuddering breath, the moment had passed. By then she realized that when she looked up she would meet the green eyes of Maraba, the panther. And indeed, it was so.

"You scared me!" she blurted indignantly.

"*I have been watching you. I choose to help you,*" said the panther.

Kathe couldn't imagine what form this help would take, but she realized that she had hurt the big cat's feelings. "I'm sorry, it's just...you startled me, and I am tired and worried."

"*Yes. When you leave this place, watch for my shadow. Then climb. Follow it to a safe, dry place.*"

"I thank you," Kathe said, feeling the same sense of trust that had carried her into the forest three nights before, "But I wish I knew why ..." She received no answer. Maraba had once again disappeared among the big rocks above the waterfall.

When Kathe entered the cave again, she found there was no need to allow her eyes to adjust. In fact, if anything, the sunlight in the chamber was now brighter than outside as the sun sank toward the rim of the sink hole and streamed through the cracks in the rock.

"Quickly, before the light fades. Look at this inscription."

Kathe sank down beside Gale and began studying the words. "It looks something like the words in my mother's old herbal," she finally said.

"Well, can you make it out? I can't make any sense of it."

Gale had had a tutor when he was a boy and had reluctantly learned to read and write – enough to manage a small estate like Springvale, anyway. He had often thought he would be more skilled at the art if there had been anything in the manor worth reading.

"Maybe." Translating slowly, Kathe pieced the message together. This looked like the oldest part of her mother's book. There were differences in spelling, though. Her mother had told her the herbal once belonged to her grandmother, who had gotten it from the one who taught them both the healing arts. Once again she wished she had paid more attention. "Flowing water will cover...no...heal...your wounds. Lie down here and rest. Something something through the years. Or maybe it means seasons." Kathe paused in frustration, running her fingers over the bottom two lines, which had been partly obscured and discolored as the water level in the cave changed. "Till summer wanderers find the key...to waken you again."

"That's us. We are summer wanderers," Meg said flatly. Having no knowledge of letters, she stood to one side out of the light, but now she spoke up. "We must be part of the enchantment."

"I don't see how we could be," Gale said. "None of us knows this sleeper, and if Kathe is right about the language of the inscription, he's been here since long before any of us were born."

"And we don't have any idea how to wake him up," added Kathe. "Even if we did know the key to waking him, would it make good sense to do so? After sleeping here for who knows how long, *has* he healed? We don't even know what his hurts were. Would we be able to talk with him? I can decipher most of these words, but I have never heard them spoken. If we awaken him, we cannot abandon him, yet how can we take him with us?"

She was about to suggest that they leave once again and for good when she saw something which made her forget all the logical arguments she had just made. She was standing up, gingerly straightening her back, when she caught herself looking again into the warrior's face, so alive in the rosy setting sun. When her eyes wandered to his throat, she was transfixed by the glint of silver. She held her breath and looked more closely. A key rested and gleamed in the hollow there. She didn't know how they had missed it before except that it had blended into the intricate metal work of the chain mail below it. She carefully picked it up and held it for the others to see. It was perhaps as long as her little finger and intricately worked. Its flat edge was embossed with the shape of a honey bee.

"It is not secret knowledge to waking him, not *a* key we are meant to find, but *the* key, *this* key," she said.

"Are you saying we were meant to find this cave at this hour and to break whatever enchantment is here?" Gale asked skeptically. "I say it is chance." The stubborn set to his jaw told Kathe more than his words. Gale thought they had enough troubles – more than enough – without saddling themselves with an ancient, and possibly injured, man. "Who knows what his attitude will be if we wake him up? Will he thank us, or will his first thought be to look for his missing sword?"

Meg spoke up with unaccustomed firmness, "None of us has ever been to this place, and it is not likely we will ever visit it again if we manage to get ourselves out. If we leave without breaking this enchantment, we will never know if we did the right thing, but if we awaken him, at least we will *know.* We won't have to wonder. And maybe it is right to awaken him. Maybe we *are* the summer wanderers. How many others are likely to travel this way, so far from the Forest Road?"

Kathe and Gale stood silently, thinking over Meg's words. Then, in unspoken agreement, they began searching, almost frantically for a keyhole. Gale looked among the folds of the cloak and along the warrior's wide leather belt for a purse. Kathe knelt again and studied the base of the bier more closely, studying the inscription for clues and running her fingers over the surface, looking for indentations which might hide a secret recess. Since these seemed to be the most likely hiding places, Meg walked slowly around the walls of the chamber, looking for more words that could still be hidden in the shadows.

When she reached the stone cracks in the rocks separating the cave from the waterfall, through which the sun still streamed, she stood a little aside so as not to block the light the others were using. She listened to the water rushing by and remembered the cozy feeling of lying on her straw mattress at Springvale, listening to the rain hammering the roof and knowing that she would remain warm and dry, well wrapped in her blanket. Meg knew there was no assurance that she would ever be dry again. Wet all day, and without even the supposed pleasure of a swim!

On impulse, she thrust her arm through the opening nearest her and felt the rush of the waterfall over her arm. With her legs ankle deep in water and her forehead pressed against the seeping wall of the cave, she allowed her fingers to play in the inside edge of the cataract.

"Meg…please…the light," Kathe said.

"Sorry."

As she began to gingerly pull her arm back through the rock opening, her fingers caught an unexpected shape. She said nothing at first, but worked the object back and forth until she was certain.

"Gale…my Lord. Kathe," she stammered. "Here's something."

"What?" asked Kathe, rising from her study of the inscription.

"It feels like a chain. I touched it outside this opening."

Gale straightened and turned. "Let me see."

The two women stood aside as Gale tried to work his arm through the opening. "It's no good. It's too small."

Kathe tried next. Knowing what she was looking for, she quickly found the chain, "Got it," she grunted. She slowly worked it upwards until she found the end. Something seemed to be attached to it, but of course they could not see what it was with her arm stuck in the opening, and it was too large to pull into the cave.

Kathe stood with her shoulder pressed against the wall of the cave. She didn't want to let go of the chain, but this was an impasse. "What do we do now?" Her arm was starting to ache.

A second crack was next to and slightly below the one with

the chain. By bending at an awkward angle, Meg could reach through this opening and up, so that she was supporting the object with one hand. This helped rest Kathe's arm, and since Meg did not have to hold onto the chain at the same time, she could tell that the something had a smooth, flat bottom.

"I'll try to turn it on its side. Maybe it will fit through that way," Meg suggested.

Since he couldn't help, Gale moved away to stand near the bier again. With the two openings blocked, the cavern was once again dim, though some light still entered through smaller breaks in the rock higher up on the wall.

Several more moments of shifting and struggle passed before Kathe surrendered in a strained voice. "It's no good. I can't hold it any longer."

When Kathe dropped the chain, Meg managed to keep her grip on the object and scraped it through her opening. It knocked against the wall below the window, dangling from its chain. She grinned and did a little splashing dance in the water.

At first they thought it was a kind of metal egg, flattened at the bottom, but closer examination showed it to be a bee hive, a perfect, miniature copy of one of the hives made of bound reeds that formed part of the landscape at Springvale. It was even the same golden color. It seemed undamaged by its suspension against the cliff face under the waterfall. They each handled it in turn, admiring its intricate beauty. It was hinged on one side, and where the two halves met, at the base of the hive, there was a keyhole. None of them had any doubt that the silver key would open this golden hive.

When it came to her, Kathe once again held up the key. When she did, it looked as if the embossed bee was flying toward the keyhole. Surely this casket must hold the counter measure for whatever magic held the warrior. They were acutely aware of him lying as still as death behind them. "Should I?" she asked. She pictured herself pushing the hive back through the opening where it would dangle again under the falls, maybe forever. They could replace the key on the chest of the sleeping warrior, follow Maraba up the cliff, and never talk about this adventure again, but she knew she lacked the secret of forgetting. She very much wanted to see what was inside the golden box. The glow of sunset illuminated the bier, warming the sleeper's pale face.

Gale said gruffly, "Oh, go ahead."

Meg didn't speak, but nodded solemnly.

Kathe's hand was shaking, but she managed to fit the key into the lock. That's all she had to do. It turned by itself with a quiet click. The two halves parted. The three of them had set something in motion.

Kathe held the box near a stone window so that the light fell upon its contents. Gale and Meg crowded close, eager to see whatever precious object lay hidden inside it.

They didn't know what they had been expecting. Perhaps the enchantment's antidote would swirl into the room like a wind and be drawn into the sleeping warrior on a breath, awakening him. Perhaps a piece of damp and smeared vellum would give them more words to decipher and chant – though if they were written in the same archaic tongue as the inscription, this would be difficult.

Gale picked the object up between his thumb and forefinger. The casket held only a tiny packet wrapped in green leaves. It could easily be held and hidden in the palm of one hand and was securely tied with a length of rough twine. To Kathe, seeing it recalled the name-day morning when she tore open the package by her plate hoping for a pair of longed-for ice patens only to find a length of linen and colored wools portending endless hours of embroidery. She glanced at the enchanted sleeper to see if anything was happening.

Although the packet looked ordinary, Gale placed it in his cupped palms to keep from dropping it. Meg tentatively tugged at the loose end of one of the knots holding the green leaves together, and they fell apart revealing a tiny bead. It was about the size of a pea, the color and shape of a freshwater pearl.

"Did you notice the green leaves?" she asked "They must have been hidden in the box from the beginning, yet they look as fresh as if picked today."

Gale carried the bead, still cradled in the green leaves and stood by the bier. "So now what?" He asked. "Should we feed it to him, try to crush it and blow it up his nose, place it over his heart?"

"Let's try placing it on his heart first," Kathe said. "We can try the other ideas if that doesn't work."

"Right. Crushing it would be rather final, wouldn't it?"

"Look," Meg whispered.

The crystal was rising from its bed of leaves. It hovered above Gale's outstretched hands, moving in a circular motion, like the wheel of a cart. Not only that, but its pearlescent glow, unnoticed near the stone window, was growing stronger. Outside, in the world above the basin, the world was still lit by a rosy summer sunset, but the light of the pearl eclipsed the outer light. It created a world within a world, making them feel nothing else existed except the three of them and the figure stretched out before them on the stone shelf.

As they watched, the crystal slowly began to move forward, wheeling its way across the warrior's body, continuing to increase in size and light, until it rested in the center of his temple. Its circular motion ceased. It began pulsing. Its rhythm was a heartbeat.

As their mood turned from fear to wonder to calm anticipation, the heartbeat slowed. Gale dropped the leaves onto the warrior's cloak. The three companions didn't notice when they took each other's hands. It was as if the four of them had become one creature with blood and breath in common. For this moment, at least, they had no doubt. They had chosen wisely.

They could never say for certain how long they stayed in this mood, but they all agreed about how it was broken. The light of the pearl diminished. Soon the bead was the size of a seed again, and then it was gone. They dropped each other's hands. Meg hugged herself.

Nothing happened at first. Then the sleeper's eyelids fluttered. His hands slowly flexed. It seemed to them that his breathing, unnoticeable before, had become noisy. He snored slightly. Kathe, Meg and Gale stayed rooted in place. After an eternity of twitching and stretching, with a few snorts thrown in for good measure, the no-longer-sleeping warrior rolled stiffly onto his side and opened two very aware brown eyes.

Four mouths dropped open. At least three hearts began to pound so loudly that it was all they could hear. Meg noticed the warrior's lips moving. "Shhh…" she said, even though none of them was speaking.

They strained to understand the warrior's speech. He seemed to have noticed their stupefied expressions and was patiently repeating the same words over and over again.

Kathe said quietly, "It is the old speech, not the ancient language written on his bier, but of the story poems. No one uses it any more, but if you listen closely, you may begin to understand him."

The warrior watched them during this exchange. Now he pulled himself into a seated position with a groan and spoke again, more slowly. This time Kathe understood better, and the others began to pick out familiar words, though the accent was very strange to them.

"Who are you? How long have I been here?" He seemed to remember something unpleasant because his face closed, and a sudden fierceness clouded the kindness they had seen in his sleeping countenance. Hands unused to movement groped at his side; his eyes narrowed at finding his scabbard empty. "Who are you? Where is Mabus?" His eyes searched the corners of the cave as his hands searched around and behind him on the platform.

"Mabus is the name of his sword," Gale guessed.

Of the three of them, Kathe was obviously best able to serve as their interpreter, at least until the others became more used to the cadence of the stranger's speech. She measured her words carefully. When she spoke at last, she used the formal constructions she remembered from the story poems, hoping to put him at ease.

"My name is Katherine Elder, daughter of Maxim Elder, Keeper of the Three Hills, King of Ostara," she began. She hesitated as the man grimaced and hid his face in his hands as if his head ached.

"Ostara," he muttered. "That is a name I have heard before. Go on."

"These are my companions, Meg…" she paused, realizing that she did not know Meg's surname nor the name of anyone in her lineage except her brothers, "…the strong-hearted, the intrepid summer wanderer, and this man is Lord Gale of Springvale. We are making our way through this forest to my home country, and we found your resting place by accident."

"As to how long you have been sleeping, we think it must have been many, many years." After a pause she added hesitantly, "We are sorry, but we do not know where your sword is."

Gripping the edge of his former bier, the man struggled to his feet and stood swaying in front of them. "I am Patrick, the Unlucky," he said bitterly. "My lineage has been lost in time and would mean as little to you as yours does to me. My freshest memory is of receiving my mortal wound." He felt along the edge of his chain mail below his right arm. He was beginning to shiver uncontrollably. "It seems someone has tried to hide me from Death." There was a trace of amusement as he added resignedly, "I suppose I ought to thank that person – and you. If I have been sleeping as long as you say, this cave must be well-hidden." He closed his eyes, struggling to understand, "I don't know why I am here."

Kathe took his arm and said, "Travel with us for now."

"We have to get him out of here. We all need a dry, warm place." Gale rested his pack on the empty bier and rummaged through it until he found the wineskin. He offered it to Patrick, who took a gulp and choked." Over the coughing Gale continued, "If this day doesn't end soon I'll...well, I don't know what I'll do, but it will be ugly."

"Yes," Kathe said. "Can you walk?"

"I have little choice," said Patrick, looking down at the water lapping around his ankles. The light was now so dim that they could hardly see each other. They wondered whether the illumination outside now came from the moon rather than the sun reflecting on water. If so, how would they ever get out of the basin?

"You say I have spent lifetimes here, but I have no memory of this place." His voice trailed off, "I have lived in the world of dreams..."

Kathe remembered what Maraba had told her about the dream world back at the beginning of the journey. After they rested, she would ask Patrick about that world. He had certainly been there long enough to be called a citizen. The big cat had ordered her to pay better attention, and she was beginning to believe her life might depend on it.

Again, Kathe led the way out of the cavern, waiting for the others just outside the entrance. Gale agreed that Meg would follow, then Patrick, and that he would be last.

"One moment more," said Meg. She walked to where the golden hive and its key were still hanging by the chain against the wall of the cave. She broke it loose with a sharp tug and carefully stowed it in her bundle. "We may want this," she said, "and it is too beautiful to leave behind."

Outside, they found the world suspended in purple twilight. "I forgot to tell you," Kathe shouted above the roar of the falls. "I found a way to climb."

17

Maraba Climbs

KATHE SHOULD HAVE KNOWN they wouldn't believe her. Looking up at the sheer cliff face streaming with water, she didn't believe herself. It was obviously impossible. Even in the poor light, she could easily read the doubt on the faces of her companions. The animals had insisted upon secrecy, but even if it were not so, she could hardly tell her exhausted companions that they would climb out of the basin following Maraba, the black panther. We'll just follow in the shadow of the panther, she practiced.

Instead she said, "No, really. It was much lighter when we were outside the cavern last time, and as I made my way back to you, I had a chance to study the cliff face. Many stones have fallen away, remember. It won't be easy, but I am sure we can do it."

Gale glanced back across the pool towards the entrance to the canyon, now hidden in shadows. It would be a treacherous scramble to reach it across the slick rocks at the base of the cliff. He weighed the chances of one of them breaking a bone under each plan.

Meg stood in the spray with slumped shoulders, and Patrick stared up without saying a word. Gale spoke for them before they could fully understand the task before them or decide that they were not strong enough.

"Ready," he said.

"Stay close. Watch where I put my feet."

Kathe faced the cliff and leaned back a little to better see the big cat's shadow. It took a few moments, but then she caught it moving swiftly down the cliff face at an angle. Maraba stopped above them, about twice as high as Kathe could reach, just beyond an outcropping of jagged rock next to the waterfall.

As she scrambled up, she did not think about anything – not the Claymon who might still be chasing them or the stranger laboring up the cliff behind Meg, or even about falling. It took all her attention to follow Maraba – to step in the places Maraba had stepped – and to find the handholds needed by humans. The cat's shadow was always some distance ahead of her, showing the direction they should climb, but Kathe often had to stop and make her own plan. Once the big cat simply disappeared for long enough that Kathe thought she had abandoned them half-way up. Twice, Maraba forgot that people cannot follow everywhere a panther can go.

The first time this happened, they had to creep across a ledge so narrow that there was no choice but to face the cliff and grope for hand-holds while the weight of their packs and bundles threatened to pull them backward over the edge. Even though this terrifying place could be passed in three steps, the constant spray of the falls had coated it with a slimy layer that made the footing treacherous. As soon as Kathe reached the other side, she stopped to encourage the others.

"Look at me," she told Meg firmly. "Do just as you saw me do."

Kathe reached as far as she could and held Meg's shoulder until she reached safety. Patrick followed. He seemed to be keeping up, but then, Kathe was climbing very slowly.

Gale, the last to cross, had just taken a grip on the final hand hold when the ledge beneath him crumbled. The women screamed at the sickening sound of stone crashing against stone. Patrick spun around and, lightening quick, grabbed Gale's wrist, pulling him forward. One of the water skins tied to Gale's pack scraped loose as the two men struggled for balance. They heard it splash into the water far below.

Gale lay against the cliff face for a long time. "Thank you," he said, testing his bones. "Kathe, if this day ever ends, I want you to explain how you stood on the bottom and could see a way to the top of this. One thing is certain," he added, looking back at the broken ledge behind him, "no one will be following us this way."

"And we will not be turning back," added Meg in a small voice, staring at the raw gap in their trail.

The second time Maraba forgot she was leading people happened when they were almost within reach of the cliff top. Kathe saw Maraba's shadow move at an impossible angle, smoothly scaling the last sheer section of the cliff face. She watched the tip of a black tail disappear over the top and scrambled to stand below it. It was a jump only a panther could make. She watched Gale test the distance. When he stretched his arms over his head, his fingertips barely brushed the edge. And he was tallest.

Kathe rested her palms and forehead against the cool stone. There was no room to maneuver. There was barely enough room for the four of them to stand. Like Gale, she felt the edge of something. It was panic.

Water had been with them during the whole climb. Sometimes they had side-stepped, bellies pressed against the stone under the flow or mist of the smaller side-falls. Now she could feel the droplets of water running around her fingers and down her wrists, dripping from her elbows.

She sent a silent pleading to Maraba, but the cat must have considered her work finished. There was no response.

"I trusted you, Maraba," she muttered.

"What?" asked Meg.

Kathe was saved from answering by sudden activity. By standing on tip-toe, she could barely see the form of Patrick squatting, his back against the rock of the cliff face. Gale was trying to climb onto Patrick's shoulders. When Meg saw what they were doing, she did her best to steady him. For one precarious moment, he struggled for balance himself; then he was scrabbling for a handhold at the top. Slowly, with Meg pushing Gale's legs, Patrick rose, lifting until Gale's upper body disappeared from view over the top and he swung his legs after.

When his grinning face appeared above them he said, "Who's next?"

They decided Patrick would stand between the two girls, and they would help to bear his weight when Gale pulled him up. The most dangerous part of this plan would be changing positions on the narrow ledge. Meg knelt, and Kathe steadied Patrick as he stepped towards her. He was shorter than Gale, but when he reached up, the two men were able to grasp wrists. With the girls' help, he soon disappeared out of sight as well. Meg was next. A boost from Kathe hurried her over the top.

Finally Kathe stood alone on the ledge, arms raised. She gazed upwards and allowed herself to be dazzled by the rising moon. It looked as if her future would hold at least one more meal and a fire after all. As she waited for arms to reach down for her, she spoke again to the watcher in the shadows. "Thank you. I'm sorry I doubted you. I'm sorry I doubted us."

Then she felt strong fingers on her wrists and began scrambling for toe holds. Soon, other hands grasped her shoulders, and then she stood in safety, with a web of arms steadying her.

18

THE WOODS RUNNERS

TWO RUNNERS WATCHED FROM the opposite rim of the sinkhole until the three fugitives emerged from the healing place. They saw the black haired girl take the arm of their boy to steady him on the slippery rocks, and they saw the shadow of the big cat when it came down to meet the red-haired woman. The runners didn't move until Kathe's companions had lifted her up over the edge and all four headed off together into the trees.

Then one of the men whistled low. The sound was lost in the roar of rushing water, but it meant something to the Evening Swifts that were still weaving their nets in the air over the pool. The birds shifted their pattern to encircle the two runners and soon flew off in many directions.

An hour later, six Woods Runners stood shoulder to shoulder in front of the empty bier in the cave behind the waterfall. By now, darkness had completely filled the chamber. Two of the men held torches so that, to the men left outside to guard the entrance, the waterfall seemed eerily illuminated from within. Not that there was much to see inside. Only what was missing.

One of the men noticed the broken chain hanging through a crack in the chamber's wall. He studied it closely in the torch light as if it could explain what had happened here. Neither he

113

nor his fellows had bothered to keep count of the generations that had passed since his people had carried the boy to the cave, dead, or so they thought. They had done so and had hung the golden hive in the flow of the waterfall to please the Lady, and they had looked in on the boy whenever one of them happened to pass this way. They had carried him here through a passage now gaping blackly to one side of the chamber, the rocks that had disguised it pushed aside. It was not an easy way, but easier than the slippery rocks outside.

Now the boy was gone, and based on the witness of the two who had been watching, he was well enough to walk and even to climb. Worse, he was with the others – the ones the Northerners wanted them to find. Badly wanted, based on the amount of gold they had been willing to promise as an advance.

The Runners had gathered silently, and they would remain silent until one of them had something to say. They didn't have a leader but governed themselves by mutual consent. In this case, the silence stretched on until the torches began to die before one of the oldest men spoke. "Our first loyalty is to the Ancients, to the Lady and her Consort. They're the ones who put the boy here, or had us do it, and it may be they're still looking out for him"

A general murmur of agreement passed around the chamber.

The man who had lifted the chain dropped it and stepped forward, "That's right, but what about the Northerners? It looks as if they've come to the forest to stay. They'll never be friends, but do we want them as enemies?"

The first Runner again broke the silence following these questions. "No. But we need time. As far as I know, no one has had a message from the Lady since the exile. We have to find her. In the meantime, we'll keep an eye on those we've been sent to track – and on the boy too."

A slight young Runner, one of the two who had tracked Kathe and her companions as far as the sinkhole, held up a dripping water skin. "We can give this to the Northerners, tell them we found it in the stream. They don't have to know everything. We'll follow the four until they separate from one another – or until the time is right to turn them all over and claim the rest of the prize. There's no hurry. We are still a free people."

When no one objected to this plan, they shared it with the three who waited outside on guard. As soon as they also agreed, seven Runners disappeared up the passageway, leaving two to cover the opening. Then they too slipped away and left the chamber to its emptiness.

The Claymon captain kicked the object his trackers had dropped in front of him. It was soggy; water splashed out of it onto his polished boots. He looked away from them toward the ravine and listened to the creek, willing the sound of the water to soothe his jangled nerves.

He should have caught them by now. They had left a trail a lap-dog could follow. There was no way for horses to ride down into the ravine, especially at night. In the morning, they would have to search for a way to cross up or down stream. Well, Lady Katherine would have to stop too.

"You followed them up the other side, didn't you?" he asked. "How fresh is that trace?"

The tracker's faces were gloomy. Their dark green tunics over grey homespun made them almost disappear into the background of trees. "There's a trail all right. Stone cold. It goes maybe a hundred paces into the woods on the other side of the stream, then stops. They walked it backwards and then they walked in the stream."

"Good, then we will return to the road and catch them there."

The captain was about to order the men to follow the course

of the stream east, when one of the trackers cleared his throat.

"They didn't go east. They followed the stream west."

"How do you know?"

The tracker gestured impatiently at the water-skin. "We found this a long way upstream, to the West. It hasn't been in the water long. You can see it isn't even soaked through. By tomorrow, it would've sunk to the bottom of the stream. We wouldn't have found it."

If the tracker was looking for praise or reward, he was sorely disappointed. The Captain snapped, "At first light, find the place where they did leave the stream then. They must have climbed out somewhere." To himself, he added, "What is she planning?" He would advise Greystone against marrying a woman with the sense of a squirrel, running all over the forest with a farm boy and a kitchen slave. Her honor would be worthless after being in such company. Still, she had value, at least until Greystone captured her brother and his friends. They were still causing trouble in the Hills, making it hard for the people of Ostara to accept the Claymon. The Lady Katherine might have as much value as a prisoner as a wife, maybe more.

"Make camp," he ordered.

He was dozing in his tent when the trackers disappeared into the forest with their gear. When his aide woke him the next morning and told him the Woods Runners were gone, he assumed they were following his orders. The Claymon picked their way along the course of the stream to the West, waiting for a report. The captain had commanded the forest trackers long enough to know it wouldn't take them long to pick up the trail.

19

A Trace of Smoke

KATHE STOOD AT THE edge of the cliff with her companions and looked off across the sinkhole toward the East. Though the moon outshone them, a few faint stars began to appear in the flawless night sky. No. Not quite flawless. There was a streak of grey smoke along the horizon some distance to their right, carried horizontally by the breeze. It rose above the crooked line of the stream below the sinkhole. It was so far away that, though Kathe, Meg and Gale all saw it, they weren't certain it was real. But if it was, then they knew what it meant. The Claymon had followed them, at least as far as the stream.

Without a word, they turned and made their way together away from the abyss. At first young trees competed for light at the edge of the stream and around the rim of the sink-hole. When Kathe and Meg were once again able to walk side-by-side, Meg slipped her hand into Kathe's and squeezed it. The relief she felt at standing on solid ground after the frightening scramble up the cliff face had been short lived. If the Claymon were following, then they must have tracked them to her parent's farm.

In walking upstream during the day, they had been slowly climbing a range of low hills. The waterfall behind them seemed to be a demarcation of sorts between the oak and beech forest around Springvale and the birch trees, hemlock and pines of the higher mountains.

Although the trees blocked most moon and starlight, and even though some branches scratched them, they also carpeted the ground thickly with needles, easing each step. As they walked further, and the trees grew larger, all the brambly undergrowth disappeared. In the first open clearing, they sat and passed a water-skin. With stumbling fingers, Meg doled out the biscuits she had pilfered from the Springvale kitchen. Then, lulled by the murmur of water and the whispering of the pines, they lay down on the thick carpet of needles and slept.

Only Patrick, after his years in the land of dreams, felt no weariness. Putting aside the fear of pursuit in their exhaustion, his three companions had set no guard, but if one of them had awoken in the night, they would have seen him sitting with his back against a tree. He was mourning the life he might have lived and missing the sword Mabus, searching his memories for some clue or purpose to explain his death and reawakening.

Kathe awoke in the pre-dawn, shivering uncontrollably. The night before, by unspoken agreement, they had hardly paused to eat before sleeping. She had not even dug in her bag for her cloak in the warmth of a summer evening. The relief at simply lying down and closing her eyes had been exquisite. Now her skin shrank from contact with her damp dress. She moved her hands to her belly, which responded by growling loudly.

With a groan, she rolled away from Meg's warmth. They had been lying back to back. Stretching tentatively, she heard a crackling behind her and scented wood smoke. And something else. The perfume of roasting meat.

She sat up carefully, listening to the protests of her spine. Robbed of Kathe's warmth, Meg pulled herself into a ball and slept on. Kathe saw Patrick sitting on his heels, tending a fire over which a rabbit was spitted. Splatters of fat hissed in the flames. Her last thought before sleep had been of the smoke they saw from the cliff-top and of what it might mean. Patrick's small fire seemed to be burning cleanly.

He had taken off his cloak and the silver chain mail, revealing a plain homespun shirt. He could be any wayfarer, but even if Kathe were seeing him for the first time and knew no better, she still would wonder about him. It was something in the way he held himself – in his expression. At the moment, while his hands tended the meat and slowly turned the improvised spit, his attention was beyond the flames.

Her small noises woke him from his reverie. She shuddered again, then stood and hobbled to the fire to kneel opposite him. She held her hands and face towards the warmth, smiling her gratitude. The few hours since their first meeting had passed in near darkness. Now she saw he was younger than she first thought – surely no more than a few years older than Gale. His brown hair showed no thread of silver where it fell over his forehead and curled over the collar of his shirt.

"You are an early riser," she whispered, indicating the roasting meat.

His response was an expression that might have been a smile or a grimace. After a few more minutes of silence, Kathe rose again stiffly and picked up her pack from the heap near the edge of the clearing.

They had not wandered far from the stream. She reached it almost as soon as she lost sight of their camp. In this place it formed a series of deep pools before traveling on to spill over the rim and into the sinkhole. She gratefully stripped off her soiled clothing and plunged into the nearest pool. This was the same stream's water in which she swam so happily the previous afternoon, but this morning she gasped and knew she was bathing in the melted snow and icy spring flow of distant mountains.

She surfaced, spluttering, then quickly freed the little hair remaining in yesterday's braids, allowing it to float upon the water's surface, carried downstream while she worked her fingers through the mass to remove the worst of the tangles.

Then, dancing in the chill, she dried herself with yesterday's dirty underskirt and dug through her pack until she found her second-best dress, as luxurious as sable in its dry warmth. Finally, with hair drying on her shoulders, she retraced her steps to the clearing.

Now everyone was awake. Patrick was off under the pines, but within sight, collecting more dry branches to feed the fire. Gale had taken Patrick's place and hunched over the fire's warmth, slowly rotating the roasting meat. Meg knelt at the edge of the clearing, emptying her bag. She was spreading the blankets to dry and examining her treasures for damage.

Standing among the trees before entering the clearing, Kathe lingered to watch the kitchen girl, her master's son, and the taciturn stranger. Meg might have lost her courage on the night they fled Springvale. And Gale might not have been wakeful and watching. Was it just luck that led them to Patrick?

She closed her eyes, picturing the clearing empty and herself alone.

"No, not alone," she murmured, "I would have still had the animals."

But she might not have thought to fool the Claymon by following the stream, and it had taken all three of them to work the magic in Patrick's cave. She knew she would never have been able to climb the cliff alone, even following Maraba.

"It's ready," Gale croaked, his voice roughened by the night on the ground and the smoke of the fire. Kathe walked forward to join them.

20

The Tale of the Book

Mid-morning found Kathe, Meg and Gale still lying on the scanty grass in the clearing. Patrick stood leaning against a birch tree waiting for them. Clean and well-fed, yet not fully refreshed, the three friends put off the moment when they must begin walking again. They all were ready except Meg, whose possessions were still airing on a blanket away from the smoke of the little fire. The fringes of her mother's red shawl ruffled in the light breeze, and the gilt edges of the book gleamed where she had leaned it against a stone in case a trace of moisture had touched it.

Kathe longed to look into it again. Running her finger across the raised lettering on its cover, she asked, "May I?"

Meg joined her in the shade and lifted the book into Kathe's lap. The two girls sat cross-legged, side by side, as Kathe again turned the fragile pages. The pictures were just as exquisite as she remembered. Here were animals she had never seen, even in the traveling menageries that passed through Ostara. Some seemed fierce, with long claws and frightening stares; others were small and appealing, looking as soft as the manor cats.

Many of the words had been formed with bold strokes. Others were so spidery that she had to bend close to make them out. All were written in the old tongue, the language they had seen on

Patrick's bier. They seemed to describe the habits of the animals and the characteristics of the plants shown on each page.

She ran her finger lightly under the words. "The Griffon is believed to carry small children to its nest high on the inaccessible face of a mountain in order to feed its young. The creature's preferred food is actually small rodents, though it is omnivorous. It is particularly fond of ripe blackberries." She chuckled as she imagined the berry-picking at Springvale interrupted by the creature shown on the page, with the head and wings of an eagle and the powerful hindquarters of a lion.

And here on the reverse was that map again, the one of the island with mountains in its center, encircled by rough waves and currents. Was this where the animals lived? It seemed to be otherwise uninhabited.

The next page was one she had not yet studied. The outline of the island's shape appeared again here, filling the parchment, but instead of natural features like mountains or lakes, the center of the page held a portrait of three women. The youngest, standing in the middle, was a tall young girl with red hair.

Meg looked at her friend with a wrinkled brow. The girl in the picture looked like Kathe. Meg hadn't noticed until this moment, and she had looked at this page many times. For some reason, the resemblance worried her a little.

The three women were shown with linked arms. To one side of the young woman stood an older woman, also slender, but with a touch of silver in her hair, and laugh lines around her eyes and mouth. She was smiling into the young woman's face. The image of this blonde woman with a basket of herbs on one arm seemed to have completely captured Kathe's attention.

The third figure was that of an old woman. She had grey hair and carried a walking staff, but she stood erect, and her eyes were very bright. She looked off into the distance. In fact, it looked as if she was looking right off the page at them.

Kathe didn't say anything about the illustration, but she

looked as if she was fighting back tears. "Patrick," she said slowly, awkwardly using the old words and propping the book up so that he could see it. "Do you know this place?"

He crouched in front of the page and studied it. The language of the book was of his time. Maybe the island had a different name now. One she would recognize from her geography lessons. He shook his head and walked back to the opposite side of the clearing where he resumed his waiting and gazing into the distance.

Reluctantly, Kathe closed the book and handed the heavy volume back to Meg. "Where did you get this?"

Before she answered, Meg wrapped the book snugly in the dry blankets again and began stacking all her things in a neat pile in preparation for their departure.

"It's the most beautiful thing you have ever seen, isn't it?" she said over her shoulder. "I thought so the first time I saw it." Wistfully, she added, "I can't read the words, you know. It must be wonderful to be able to read."

Mentally, Kathe added to the list of things she must teach Meg: swimming, reading...

"It was three summers ago. You know I don't – didn't – like to go far from the Springvale walls, but one morning Cook sent me on an errand. Early that day I found myself on the track leading to old Pammy's cottage. Do you know about her?" Glancing at Kathe, Meg received the expected shake of the head.

"She was the oldest tenant on Lord Stefan's land. I say 'was' because I think she must have died. At least, nobody carried any baskets to her after mid-winter last year. She didn't have any children that I know of. And if she had a husband, he's been gone a long time. All of us at the manor were more than a little scared of her. We heard she was a healer, and you know that can work both ways."

"She never came to the door when we brought her things. We were just to leave the basket on a big stone in the dooryard, knock twice, and then head back the way we came. As far as I know, no one ever had a mind to linger."

"Anyway, when I had walked about halfway to her house that morning, I saw a painted wagon pulled off along the side of the track. I had never seen one like it before, and it was pointed away from Springvale. I thought that was strange because a peddler cannot get any coin if he doesn't come to the places where people have it – to the manor house, I mean. And we would all have known if that wagon had stopped there. I remember there were two brown ponies grazing under an oak tree, and a tall, old man was cooking sausages over a little fire."

"There was no way to avoid him with the hedge growing thick on the other side of the path, so I decided to just walk by without speaking, but he called out and beckoned me over. I didn't know what to do. I knew I shouldn't be talking to strangers, especially strangers who lived in painted wagons." She paused. "He seemed friendly, and I thought it would have been disrespectful not to greet him – and there were those sausages. Breakfast at Springvale was somewhat scanty," She blushed, "Sorry, Lord Gale."

Gale sat up from his doze, "What? Oh. I'm sure it wasn't enough. I'm sorry I never wondered whether it was. And surely you can stop calling me Lord now."

"Yes…Well, I sat on the ground and ate three of those sausages, and I can still taste them. Crisp and brown on the outside, but dripping juice with every bite." She sensed she was losing her audience and left her memories of the sausages behind. "He asked me questions. Where I was coming from, where I was going, all the harmless questions anybody might ask anybody, and after a while I thanked him and went on my way. When I looked back, he was standing in the middle of the track with his hands on his hips, looking after me."

"When I got to Pammy's, I saw her door standing open. Her window was open too, and the curtain was blowing in the breeze. Those who had been there before told me the house was always shut up tight and that it looked as if nobody lived there, so I was surprised. I put the basket on the stone and reached inside to knock on the doorframe, just glancing into the room to see if the old woman was about. I thought, you see, something might be amiss."

"I thought you said you weren't brave," Kathe murmured.

"Oh, well like I said, I was worried about her. Anyway, at first the room looked empty. It was dark after being outside. Then I saw her. She was sitting on a stool by the table, and she looked like she was writing. I could hardly believe my eyes. I mean, even your mother doesn't write, Gale. And here was this poor old woman scratching like the words had been whispered to her by Godde and she had to get them down before she forgot them. Every bit of the table she wasn't using for the writing was covered with bottles and papers."

"'I brought you a basket,' I said quiet like, trying not to startle her. I didn't think she knew I was there. She never raised her eyes from what she was doing. She didn't speak either, but she lifted her hand to show that she had heard me and that I should go."

Gale interrupted, "Pammy did some service for my father when my mother was so ill a few winters ago. He gave her that old cottage and leave to live there as long as she wished. I visited her many times when I wanted to ask her about plants I had found. If people feared her, it was just because she kept to herself. She was always kind to me. Most of the healing lore I have I owe to her."

Meg continued, "I wasn't afraid of her any more after that. She took no more notice of me than of the breeze blowing through her window."

"I began walking home, and after a little while I came to the place where the peddler had been. I could see the marks his wagon wheels made in the deep grass by the side of the road. There were still a few red embers among the grey ashes where he had made his fire. And under the oak tree, near where the ponies had been grazing, a package had been left behind."

Meg paused, looking around the clearing at Kathe, Gale and Patrick to make sure she had their attention. Then she continued. "You can guess what was inside. The wrappings fell to pieces as I undid them. Before I even looked at what it was, I carried it out onto the track and gazed long in both directions. This was foolishness because I had just walked all the way from Pammy's and would have met the peddler if he went that way, and I was headed to Springvale Manor and would surely catch up with him if he was headed there."

"I carried the book into the shade of the tree and sat for a long time just looking at the pictures and touching the leather cover. I remember it even smelled good. Spicy. I tried to remember if the bundle was under the tree when I was there before. I thought maybe the old man had taken it out of his wagon and forgotten it."

Meg's face became dreamy. "And then I fell asleep in the shade of the tree. I had the strangest dream. Some of the animals in the pictures from the book came and talked to me. Of course I couldn't remember anything they said when I woke up because I was so worried about what I had done. I could tell by the sun that the day was heading towards evening."

"By the time I reached the gates, dinnertime was past, and I knew I was in trouble. No one was about when I entered the courtyard, and there was no peddler or wagon in sight, so I left the book on top of one of the wide timbers in the byre and went inside to get what was coming to me. I told Cook I had fallen asleep, but I didn't tell her about the sausages, about looking into Pammy's cottage, or especially about the book."

Meg concluded shyly, "After a while I began to believe the old man left the book there for me to find. I liked thinking he gave it to me on purpose. Though, if it was so, I don't know why he would leave it with a girl who can't even read."

All this time, Patrick had been standing motionless at the edge of the clearing. "This whole business reeks of magic," he said. "I might have slept forever and never known the difference, but now I want to know why I have been awakened. Have you forgotten, or did you never know? There is no such thing as chance."

He continued, "Kathe is more than the child of a minor king whose forbears tried to kill me."

She looked at him, shocked, and he met her eyes steadily.

"And Meg is incorrect when she describes herself as simply an illiterate servant. And you, Gale..." He fixed a speculative gaze upon the slender young man leaning back on his elbows in the grass. "We shall see."

Astonished by this long speech from the taciturn stranger, the others stared at him open mouthed. He awkwardly placed his hand on his hip where Mabus ought to be and asked, almost belligerently, "Are you going to stay here all day?"

21

INTO THE HILLS

GALE HAD COME TO believe that the stream they had followed all the day before, and followed still, flowed down from a range of hills called the Celadrians. Early in the year, a priest lent Gale a precious, sketchy map of the forest and allowed him to keep it for a day. Because such maps were very rare, and despite the notorious inaccuracy of such documents, he copied it and studied its features.

According to the map, these not-quite-mountains lay to their northeast. He proposed that they continue following the stream, allowing it to guide them into the hills. They might have to scramble sometimes, but based on the traveler's description, the hill tops were above the tree line. From up there they might be able to see the corridor of the forest road. Then they could turn north again and more closely parallel the road to the Three Hills. Gale had heard there were old trails, little used and not on the priest's map, from the days when people used to live in the forest. Maybe they could find one of these or, if they had to, they would set off cross-country after they crossed the Celadrians, keeping first the hills and then the road at their right hand.

"I haven't forgotten those Claymon soldiers," he added after outlining this plan, running his fingers through his already tousled hair and remembering the smoke he saw the night before. "If I were the captain, I'd set some of my men to searching Springvale in case Kathe holed up there and send others to find her scent and follow it in case she bolted. The rest I'd send back to Ostara as fast as their horses would carry them. The only thing worse than bringing the bad news that Kathe is gone is taking sweet time to do it."

The harder he thought, the more Gale's forehead wrinkled. "It will take at least five days for them to reach the city. And then more time to make a plan. Men may sleep in the saddle, but horses have to rest."

Meg said, "Two days have already passed. I wonder if the captain noticed you and I were gone too before he sent those men north with his message. If he did, then they'll be more likely to think Kathe is on her way home. I mean, wouldn't they think a girl, or even two girls, would just look for a place to hide nearby? We'd hope the Claymon would give up and go back the way they came. With you along, though, that's different. With a man to lead us, they'd think we might brave the forest. Of course," she said, "that just shows they don't know Kathe."

"Poor Lord Stefan," Kathe interrupted miserably. "They'll have torn Springvale apart looking for me, and he is the scapegoat. He was tricked into harboring me, and this is his thanks! I am sorry."

Gale's face was grim. "Do you think I haven't thought about that? Why the soldiers came and what they wanted doesn't matter now. The Claymon would have come sooner or later, though I'll admit," he said, putting his hand on Kathe's shoulder and forcing a smile to soften his words, "it is because of you that we have caught this malady so suddenly and strongly. Nevertheless, we all have to search for the cure, and we have agreed it lies north." He looked off in that direction. "I have hurt him most – his son disappearing when he most needs me."

While they planned, Patrick obscured traces of their presence.

When the three finally came to an agreement, he picked up the bundle he had made of his cloak and chain mail and led the way.

According to legend, people once lived in and among these trees. There was even a city roofed by the canopies of giant oaks, the storytellers claimed, where hunters and carpenters traded plentiful meat and created beautifully carved wooden furniture. Skins, chests and chairs were carried along the trails out of the forest, and in return came gold and all the produce of the sunlit world.

The legends may have been true, but the forest seemed to have completely forgotten its human inhabitants. Any wounds left by the forest people must have healed long ago. At least Kathe, Meg, Gale and Patrick came across no sign of them as they labored on through the afternoon and the early hours of another summer evening.

At first their walking was easy among large pines, but every hour the terrain became steeper and stonier. The roots of the giants knotted themselves around the rocks and snaked over boulders in search of patchy soil as the four picked their way up hill.

After getting them started and leading for a short time, Patrick fell behind, and after that, the others had to stop often to allow him to catch up. Since they followed no trail except the sound of the stream, it would have been easy for any of them to become lost. Meg was just ahead of Patrick in their single file, and she often looked over her shoulder to see him standing still, looking about as if he was trying to find his bearings.

"And no wonder," she said to herself. "He must sometimes wonder if he is still sleeping and dreaming. Or maybe he thinks he died after all, though I've never heard a priest talk about an afterlife like this."

As the stream still burbled to their right, it seemed Gale must be correct about its source. Now that it had a steeper route to travel, the water had ceased its meandering. It flowed slightly south-west according to the sun, making only small deviations from this course.

After many hours of climbing, Kathe plopped herself down on a flat boulder. The sun slanted through the trees.

"Ever since our last rest, I've been waiting for one of you to admit you're ready to stop for the night," she declared, lowering her bundle to the ground beside her. "I guess it's up to me. This is the only spot I've seen lately with enough flat ground for all of us to lie down, and *I* am tired. Am I the only one?"

Meg gratefully put down her bundle and joined Kathe on the sun-warmed stone. They stretched their legs in front of them and rolled their shoulders to ease the ache from carrying their packs. Patrick didn't say anything but stopped and stood, almost swaying. He was still many paces behind them down the hill. Meg nudged Kathe and indicated the warrior with a tilt of her eyebrows.

"He looks as if he is still only half in this world," Kathe said softly.

"That's what I was thinking," Meg said quietly. I hope there wasn't some next step to breaking that enchantment. Like maybe some words we were supposed to say to seal it. If he falls asleep again, then what are we to do?

Gale wanted to press forward. He had explored the forest as deeply as he could, anchored as he was by his responsibilities to Springvale and especially to the small farmsteaders along the perimeter of the manor's holdings. Those hard-working folk were his friends, and he lived according to their times of planting and harvest. But for the past two days, every single step he had taken was new. He thought he and his companions were the first people to walk here in a very long time – maybe ever. During the afternoon exhilaration had masked his weariness, but now, looking into the tired faces behind him, he reluctantly moved the few steps back down the hill and began to make a camp for the night.

Here, miles west of the forest road and high in the hills, they felt safe in building another small fire. The dry, fallen branches of the pines were ideal fuel. They burned brightly without much smoke. After coals appeared, Meg began to make a stew from the chunk of smoked bacon and Kathe's dried mushrooms.

Patrick briefly awoke from his stupor when he saw these ingredients. "Is there more where that came from?" he said weakly. "If there is, then we'll have visitors tonight for certain now that we're in the hills. We've been sending the invitation all day. Every cave bear and catamount within smelling distance knows there's good eating in this camp tonight."

Meg's face blanched, and she almost dropped the spoon she was using to stir the stew which was beginning to smell wonderful, even to their human noses. After they had eaten, Gale and Patrick took the length of rope and, bundling their remaining provisions into one of the blankets, they dangled them from a branch high above the ground a good distance from the camp.

"Too high for a bear and too low for a cat," Gale said hopefully as the two men walked back toward the fire.

22

A SUMMONS

KATHE STARTLED AWAKE. SHE opened her eyes and allowed them to adjust to the glow of the fire circle, the faint glimmer of stars through the branches, a hazy, cloud-hidden moon. She listened for a repetition of the sound that had awoken her. She thought, or maybe dreamed it had been the scream of a panther. She thought of Maraba. In the dream it had been the big cat's voice she recognized. No, that wasn't right. The big cat had only spoken to her using the quiet words inside her head.

She made out the lumpy, motionless shapes of her companions nearby and listened to their soft snores. Once again, they had decided to set no guard, but she and Gale slept with their knives at hand. Since she was still at the edge of sleep, she closed her eyes.

"Come."

Kathe sat up. Even though Patrick, Gale and Meg probably couldn't hear the summons, she was afraid she would awaken them if she answered it. She touched the rough, healing places on her arm where Maraba's claws had marked her. Putting her blanket aside, she rolled onto her knees and stood.

A wing brushed her cheek.

Kathe tiptoed away from their camp, following Oro further

up the hill. Barefoot, she found it easy to move quietly, nearly silently, in the darkness. Once again she heard the panther scream, only now it was far away. She did not debate with herself the wisdom of leaving camp and companions behind, but as she had done before, she followed the whispered voice and brush of wings. This time Oro did not lead her far. He stopped a short way up the hillside and landed on a large boulder.

Perched before her at eye level as he was instead of above her head in a tree, Oro's true stature became apparent to Kathe. He was the largest bird she had ever seen, except for a golden eagle she had watched circling the mountaintops north of Ostara one day long ago. And at almost three hands tall, not counting his ear tufts, the owl personified dignity.

"Flame Child. You have found companions."

"They have found me."

"It is difficult for us to lead you when there are so many."

Kathe didn't know what to say. Over the past days she had learned the worth of human companions. Maraba had shown her the way to climb next to the waterfall, but still, she would not have made it to the top or be standing here now without her friends. Also, one of Oro's words bothered her. It was 'lead.' She had thought the animals wanted to help her as she made her way home to Ostara. If she understood him correctly, though, the animals had some plan of their own.

"Where is it you wish to lead me?" she asked.

"To where you must go," he replied.

"And where is that?"

"Where you will find what you seek."

She asked from a slightly different angle, "What is it I seek?"

"You should know that better than I do," the owl huffed infuriatingly.

What *did* she seek, except to be reunited with her family, and to help them. Or to mourn them. She shivered even though the night was warm. She just wanted to go home.

"Do you lead me home?" Kathe insisted.

Oro did not answer her. Instead, he hooted softly and then sat silently, swiveling his head from side to side. He was able to look in every direction, including behind him. It was from there, directly in front of Kathe, that she saw the stag appear. She bowed in greeting. His crown of antlers looked as heavy and perfect as it had when she last saw him at the gathering of animals.

The king himself has agreed to lead you," Oro said.

"You are going to lead me home?" she asked, addressing the stag. He could have nuzzled the top of her head without bending his own.

He did not speak. Instead, he walked a few paces up the hillside and rubbed his antlers roughly against a sapling, noisily shaking it. After he returned to stand next to Oro's boulder again, Kathe saw the blemish he had made on the tree's smooth bark.

"There is the first sign," Oro said. *"Search for the next one."* He flexed his wings as if preparing to fly.

"Wait," Kathe pleaded. "Why do you speak only to me? Are you leading me home?"

"Remember," the owl called back as he took flight, *"Never tell the others."*

The words drifted back with an unspoken warning. Never tell Meg, Gale, or Patrick about us, or we will not speak to you again. We will not help you. We will not lead you home. Kathe sighed. Talking about this was exactly what she needed to do. She climbed the few paces up the hill and touched the wounded tree. Sap trickled down the trunk. Then she sat on the ground and leaned against its trunk.

If only her mother were here. She would know what Kathe should do. As happened so often when Kathe closed her eyes and tried to remember a more peaceful time and place, she found herself sitting on her low stool in the solar at home, only this time she was spinning lumpy thread while the swallows wheeled outside the window. As before, she envied their freedom, but now she saw something else. She saw her mother pause in her weaving, turn toward the chittering birds, and smile. And there was another memory. Her mother standing by a makeshift pen in the courtyard, stroking the velvety forehead of a frightened horse that had been running wild in the hills. Kathe swallowed. The animals had talked to her mother, too. She had loved them. Trusted them.

Kathe started back towards the campsite and stopped with a groan. How was she going to convince the others that they should follow the King's trail? She couldn't even tell them about him.

She slipped silently back into the tiny clearing where three bodies still lay motionless by the nearly dead fire. As she sat down and pulled her cloak around her shoulders, she bowed her head, reviewing her conversation with Oro, trying to remember exactly what he had said. When she raised her face, her eyes met Patrick's.

Kathe stretched out on the ground with her back to the warrior. She wondered what Patrick was thinking, then put him firmly out of her mind. She had enough to worry about.

23

THE KING'S TRAIL

KATHE FELT THE SUN warm on her cheek. She was surprised to
have slept again after her encounter with Oro, and even after
she heard the others stirring and moving about the campsite,
she stayed still with her eyes shut. She had not yet decided what
to say to them.

If Gale would step aside and let her lead today, maybe she
wouldn't have to tell her friends anything, provided she could find
all the King's signs herself. Then she pictured Gale's back ahead
of her the whole afternoon before, choosing the easiest way up
the hill, often turning to offer his hand, and she abandoned the
idea. He would see the suggestion as a slight. Men led. Women
followed, or pretended to. Noble girls learned that basic fact at
about the time they learned to walk – maybe even earlier than
serving girls. When Gale accepted her guidance to climb the cliff
it was because he had no other choice.

And what about Patrick? He looked like he should be a leader,
but yesterday he lagged far behind Kathe and Meg almost the
whole day. Sometimes he stared around as if he must memorize
every detail of the terrain around him; at others he turned inward
and didn't even seem to hear when they spoke to him. Men
sometimes followed – to protect those they considered weaker,

137

but Kathe didn't think that was the reason Patrick lagged behind. He was vulnerable, suffering the lingering effects of an enchanted sleep none of them fully understood. And, she remembered, he saw her return to camp last night.

Godde! she hated lies. At last she rolled over and sat up, rubbing her eyes. "What a dream!" she said, a little too loudly.

Meg paused in her task of feeding small sticks to the coals remaining from the night before. She wanted to make some tea. She yawned, "I was too tired to dream last night. What was yours?"

"I dreamed an animal came and talked to me. It was a stag, and it promised to show us the way we ought to go by marking trees with its antlers."

"That was some dream," Gale joked.

"It seemed very real," Kathe said. In fact, I have trouble believing it was only a dream." She winced. Would a half-truth be distant enough to satisfy Oro? "Sometimes my mother had dreams like this. About animals, I mean, and when she did, they always came true."

"Everybody dreams," Gale said, not bothering to comment on her mother's nocturnal history. "You dream you are going on a journey, and an invitation arrives from your uncle; or you dream that you're rich, and you plow up a coin when you're working a field."

"I once had a dream that I would go home again," Meg said. "It took a while for that one to happen, but it did." She handed Kathe a bowl of tea and remembered again the smoke they had seen from the cliff top.

Kathe enjoyed the warmth of the bowl in her hands for a moment and gratefully took a sip before replying. "I've had that kind of wishful dream. Almost every night I dream about being back in Ostara, but my dream last night wasn't like that. Every detail was clear…"

Patrick didn't often speak, but when he did, the rest of them found themselves listening intently. They were surprised that he spoke at all, and it still took extra effort for them to interpret his oddly accented words. "I wonder if this stag is the same one I chased for a summer during my seventeenth year." he said. "He had the habit of running in and out of dreams." Patrick did not smile, but Kathe had the impression he was laughing at her. "If it is, we would be wise to listen to him. When I was alive...I mean, when I was alive before...having a dream was a serious matter. Gale, you talk as if the mind only plays when it is at rest, and that playing is what we call a dream. When I was young, we believed that when we slept, messengers were most likely to speak to us. And when they spoke...well, we did not always listen, but if we did not, it was to our sorrow."

"I don't know anybody who has that kind of dream these days," Gale said dismissively, "except Kathe, I guess, and in her case, it was probably the mushrooms in her soup talking to her, not a stag."

They shared the rest of Gale's cheese and a little more of the bread, doused the fire, and shouldered packs and bundles that, though slightly lighter, seemed heavier than they had the day before. Still hungry, they began walking again, forming the single file that was quickly becoming habit.

They had not climbed very far up the most sensible, least rocky route when Gale stopped abruptly. When the others caught up with him, they found him staring at a fresh wound on a beech sapling. Sap had oozed and was still drying on the silvery bark. The scrape was at eye level.

The King had to bend awkwardly to make it, Kathe thought. Gale was right about one thing. In their own day, dreams had become safe – interesting, funny, or maybe frightening – and once the sleeper awoke, whether with sorrow or relief, they quickly faded. On the night she marked Kathe's arm, Maraba had told her to pay attention to dreams. She said the land of dreams had no boundaries. Perhaps, after all, it made no difference to the animals whether she set her moonlight encounter in the land of dreams or in the waking world. In that case, she had already betrayed their secret

Of her three companions, Patrick now seemed most likely to believe her and to understand how close to the truth she had come. She risked a glance at him. A small smile played around the corners of his usually serious mouth. He turned to look at her, and she felt a shock of camaraderie. The smile faded, but his hazel eyes still held the laughter.

Gale ran his fingers through his curly hair in a gesture Kathe had come to associate with agitated thought.

"It seems we have come across another coincidence," he said. "The question is what should we do with it?"

Kathe didn't say anything. Maybe she had already said too much.

Patrick spoke up again, his voice sounding weaker than it had a few moments before, back at the campsite. "Here we have a woman who dreamed, and here is a sign that her dream may be true. It is partly through ignoring such a message that I ended up sleeping the years away in that cave."

"What sign? Stags scrape. That's what they *do*," Gale argued. "Birds build nests, water flows in the stream bed – and we go north." He had a mulish look on his face.

"Why don't we go along a bit further and see if this stag really is rubbing us a trail?" Meg asked reasonably. She had lost most of her shyness around her master's son.

With all of them looking for it, the next mark was easily found. It was close to the stream and barely out of sight of the last one. This remained the pattern through the morning as the novelty of a magical possibility – that an animal had walked into a dream to guide them – pulled them forward until they reached an alpine zone where the trees diminished, then disappeared.

They paused there to catch their breath and to allow Patrick to catch up. He had fallen silent again after they found the second mark. Life seemed to drain from him as he followed at a distance, and today they were moving faster. The King had marked the easiest route up the hillside. He seemed to have a better understanding of the needs of people than Maraba.

"It looks like the trail ends here," Gale said, gesturing at the steep, rocky hillside above them. "We'll be on top soon."

"It can't end," Kathe said. "He told me he would lead us where we needed to go. All the way. We could have gotten up here by ourselves."

"From now on, I intend to choose my own path," Gale said grumpily. "First you found the cave where we *had to* break an enchantment…"

"That's not fair," Meg said. "We all agreed. And almost the first thing Patrick did after he woke up was save your life."

"And now we *have to* keep following this dream stag," Gale continued, ignoring her.

"Are you saying the signs are chance?" Meg persisted.

"What I'm saying is I will not follow them any further."

Kathe interrupted, "When I saw you with Meg that first night, I wasn't sure what to think. I know relief and happiness were not my first feelings. I thought I would be traveling alone. Yet now I would be sorry to part from you. You have proven your worth again and again. Perhaps our guides appear when we need them most."

"Well, I have no need of a guide, and it seems this one has left us anyway," Gale replied curtly as Patrick finally joined them, laboring for breath.

Patrick closed his eyes and stood as if asleep, swaying slightly – waiting for them to move on. Meg stood protectively near him. He looked as if he might fall and tumble backwards down the hill. Kathe scrambled ahead up the hillside, scanning the stone for a sign left by the King. She soon found what she was looking for.

It must be urgent that they follow this leading. The stag had scraped at a boulder with his hoof, leaving a white mark on the grey stone, one that would fade with rain and a season but that they could easily follow now. She called down the hill.

Gale shaded his eyes against the mid-day sun as he scanned the hillside above him. A halo of light outlined Kathe's form. The strong wind pulled at her hair and clothing. She was waving her arms, obviously wanting them to follow, but the wind snatched her words and carried them away before they reached him.

It reminded him of seeing her across the sinkhole pool after she found the cave, when he and Meg could not hear her voice because of the waterfall's roar. Resignedly, he took Patrick's other arm, and together he and Meg helped the warrior to climb.

24

A Parting

AFTER SOME HARD SCRAMBLING, they finally sat together on the rocky crest of the hill gazing over a landscape laid before them like rumpled bedding. Hill after tree garbed hill spread into the distance. The green seemed to go on forever, though they knew that somewhere beyond the forest lay the Three Hills, sheltering Ostara like an egg in a nest.

The valleys directly below seemed to be a labyrinth carved by streams and boxed by steep slopes. The forest road should have been visible off to the east, but they still could not see that longed for symbol of safety and danger. The canopy of trees in full leaf must have been hiding it.

"It looks as if we can follow the crest of the hill east. It seems to run fairly straight. The closer we get to the road before we descend into that mess, the better," Gale said, gesturing at the scree strewn slope ahead of them with a half-eaten travel cake. "The walking will be easier, or at least more level, for a while."

Patrick had collapsed onto the stony ground and sat with his back against a boulder. He waved away food and seemed too tired or ill to raise his head.

Meg knelt by him. "Patrick...Patrick...what is happening to you?"

Her answer was a single shake of his head.

From where she perched on top of a large rock, Kathe could see the next mark left by the King – and the one after that. She knew Gale must have seen them too. They led down the hill into a valley that seemed to be completely boxed by more hills. Her mouth was dry. She took a long drink from the water skin.

"Each of us has a reason for taking this journey," she said, after a silence. "Meg is here because she is a good friend, and maybe she has also found some reasons of her own. Gale, you came to offer protection to us – but you also want to protect Springvale, or at least divert the Claymon from that place. And Patrick? We dragged him from sleep. He had little choice but to join us."

She said more carefully, "I just want to go home. I don't think I ever really believed I would be much help to my parents or my city by doing so. It is just a homing instinct pure and simple. Yet last night's dream seemed real, and today the leading has proven true. It hints at a purpose I will never understand unless I follow."

"I don't want to part from any of you, but I do not expect you to heed the dream of another," she concluded, almost in tears.

Nobody said anything. It seemed an eternity with the wind suddenly loud in their ears under the blazing mid-day sun. Then Meg stood in front of Kathe just as she had a few days before, during the berrying.

"I said I would go with you, and I will." She turned to face Gale. "And, by your leave or without it, we will take Patrick with us. Kathe found him, remember, so maybe his fate is tied to hers. And he can only go slowly. I know you find such a pace more tiring than speed."

Gale's face paled under his tan. "If this is your choice, I will leave you a blanket and the firestone," he said tightly. Without another word, he began to sort through his pack for things he could spare.

To lighten his own load, the better to move swiftly, Meg thought bitterly.

Kathe slid down from her boulder and put her hand on his arm, but he shrugged away from her touch, stood abruptly, and adjusted his pack straps.

"Thank you for coming with us so far," she said, trailing off, half hoping he would stay to argue in his infuriating way. Then she turned away. She had depended on him too much. Well, she would not beg him to change his mind. She could make no case anyway for a course that ignored both the arguments of reason and the urgencies of war.

The two girls stood with their arms about each other's waists, protectively near Patrick, who still sat slumped at their feet. Kathe wasn't even sure if he knew Gale was leaving. They watched his slender figure diminish as he picked his way along the hill-top until he disappeared from sight. Then they went to work dividing and packing the objects he had left.

Meg saw Kathe brush a tear away, but her own eyes were dry. She had hoped Gale would stay, but she hadn't really expected him to. During her years at Springvale, she had become used to his disappearances, often at the most inconvenient times. He had his own path to follow, and he stuck to it like an arrow, to his parents' distress. They were lucky he had stayed this far. The protection of two runaway servant girls was slow work – especially when there was an army to be fought somewhere to the north.

Kathe picked up Patrick's bundled cloak and mail. It was surprisingly light, but she considered leaving the armor. He was much too weak to need it. In fact, unless they found help soon, she was beginning to doubt whether he would live. He seemed to labor for every breath. She sighed. He had already lost so much. She added his few things to her own bag.

After they helped Patrick to his feet, Kathe and Meg stood on either side of him to support him as they moved forward. With an effort, he came back to himself and gently pushed them away. He looked about for his bundle, but he did not protest when Kathe reassured him that she had added it to her own.

Their destination still looked unpromising from above, but the route down the slope was less steep than it appeared. The King had marked a zigzag path skirting the largest boulders.

Kathe watched ahead for marks and looked back often to make sure Patrick and Meg still followed. She mentally inventoried their dwindling food supply and wondered whether she might snare something to cook for dinner. Meg's face looked worn. They all would need something nourishing to eat at the end of this day.

This wasn't right! This was not how it was supposed to be! She should have been alone, following the forest road, nobody depending on her, not picking her way through these trackless hills with a sleepwalking stranger and Meg, who trusted her too much.

No, not trackless. Here was another clear scrape on stone, and soon they would enter the trees again. Unlike the southern side of the hill, which they had climbed during the morning, the north side had an abrupt tree line defined by rock slides. The King had marked the place where they should enter the forest by making an unusually large scrape.

After hours in the open, the shade was balm on their wind and sun burned skin. Kathe was painfully aware of how little distance they had actually covered during this day. Climbing is hard and time-consuming. At the same time, she didn't know how Patrick had kept going so long. He looked about to faint, so much so that once they were in open forest again among old trees, the two girls took up their places on either side of him, supporting him. He did not shrug them away this time or speak to them, but he leaned on first one, then the other, so that neither of them would have to bear his weight for long.

If not for the worry she carried, Kathe would have had to admit the walking here was easiest since the beginning of their journey. Even without the King's trail to follow, the way was obvious. The ground was smooth and level, with no snaking tree roots to trip them, and there was plenty of room for the three of them to walk abreast. Gale had told them about trails the ancient ones had made. Maybe this was one, though surely with the passing of years the trees should have reclaimed this corridor. She imagined Gale's reaction if he were to see evidence of the ancient forest inhabitants.

But by now Gale was far to the East. Without them slowing him, he might even have reached the road by now.

Here in the deep shade, darkness fell early. They would have to stop soon, make a fire, eat something. Meg still had some bacon, and there were other things her mother had given her. Had Gale left them any rope she could use to hang the remaining food in a tree tonight?

"Oof," Kathe fell heavily, tripping over a large, blocky rock jutting up near the edge of the path. She released Patrick's arm to catch herself. Otherwise she would surely have pulled him down on top of her. On the way down, she jarred her shoulder against the stone.

She didn't move for a few moments. The fall had knocked the breath out of her. She moved her shoulder a little to see if it was badly hurt. It didn't seem to be broken, but it would be bruised and sore.

"Can you move? Oh, what a place to put a rock!" Meg fussed, kneeling by Kathe's prone body. "Where are you hurt?"

"Nothing is broken," Kathe said. "Just give me a moment. Can you find my bundle? I dropped it." She sat up gingerly, testing her ribs with her fingers. They all seemed to be intact.

"Here," Meg put Kathe's bag on top of the stone that had tripped her. It seemed to be perfectly flat. "What would you think of making a camp here tonight? This stone could be put to better use as a chair than a tripping stone, and we can build the fire near it." This domestic chain of thoughts changed abruptly.

"Whe…Kathe…where's Patrick?

Her injury forgotten, Kathe peered ahead into the forest. "There," she pointed. He was some distance ahead, stumbling along the corridor of trees. She heaved herself to her feet with a groan and set off after him with Meg at her heels.

They were so intent on not losing sight of Patrick that at first they didn't notice the rock formations that began to appear on each side of the trail. The huge flat faced cliffs seemed to extend some distance into the forest on either side, yet they weren't solid. Every so often a narrow canyon appeared between the massive sheets of rock.

Kathe could not be as careful as she would have liked in looking for signs, but Patrick seemed to be following the King's path. Even though she did not know where it led, she was desperate not to lose it.

Perhaps because of the cliffs and the openings they created in the forest, more of the light of the clear summer evening was able to reach this place. Kathe and Meg were out of breath trying to catch up with the man who had been leaning on them for the past several hours. Kathe's shoulder throbbed.

She groaned as she watched him scramble up an outcropping along one of the cliffs. What had gotten into him?

When they caught up with him, he was standing on a narrow ledge about half-way up the rock face. Meg gasped, "Patrick! Where are you going? Wait!"

Her voice trailed off when they reached the spot where he started to climb. She heard Kathe's sharp intake of breath. Why hadn't they seen it before? The stones Patrick had climbed. They were steps. The cliffs were walls.

He stood above them in a shaft of sunlight. They could see tears streaming down his face. "Oh, Patrick…"

Then he turned and disappeared into the dark opening behind him.

25

The Forest City

KATHE DROPPED HER BAG next to the wall. When she was running, she had only seen what she expected to see. Now that she was standing still, it was obvious she stood next to a building constructed of smoothly worked stone. It towered above her solidly – as high as the walls of her own home in Ostara. She had only half-believed the stories she heard in her childhood telling of the forest city. None of the storytellers ever seemed to have actually been there. Generations had passed since the old forest paths were busy with people and goods entering and leaving this place. She tried to sense the presence of others but felt only crushing emptiness.

Patrick's city. She was slowly coming to understand that this ruined place must shelter his memories – and maybe the bones of people he loved. Now his city lay open to the sky, slowly disappearing beneath leaves and soil. She shuddered. At least the Three Hills still held a living town! She ran her hand across the smooth surface again, then followed Patrick up the stairs.

Moss thickly coated the steps, and ferns grew in the soil that had formed on them. Their once even surface had become treacherous. Kathe watched her footing closely. She tried to step in the places where Patrick's boots had crushed the tender plants.

Meg reluctantly stayed behind and stood in the middle of the street with her arms tightly crossed, far enough away so she would be able to see Kathe at all times. One by one, her companions had disappeared throughout this day.

Kathe had said that she was just going to have a look through the dark opening at the top of the stairs and then come straight back down, or she would call for Meg to follow, depending on what she found. Meg watched and listened closely while the evening shadows spread toward her down the ancient street.

When Kathe reached the top of the steps and leaned forward through the black opening, Meg choked back a cry. When Kathe stepped through the doorway and disappeared from view, she felt true panic for the first time since leaving Springvale.

"I can be brave," she reminded herself out loud in an effort to calm her racing heart. "Didn't I stand up to Gale, and when they told me the beasts might be after our food last night, I just kept on cooking. But I'm not about to be left alone here!"

It seemed the shadows were reaching toward her more quickly, lured by her fear, flooding the ancient city deep enough to drown her. She hurried to the base of the steps where her practical side took control again. Should she make the two trips necessary to carry her own and Kathe's bags up through the opening lest all their supplies be imperiled, or just hurry after her friend? Before she could decide, Kathe reappeared as suddenly as she had disappeared and almost slid back down the steps.

If she was surprised at Meg's fierce, welcoming hug, she didn't show it, but said, "I can't see Patrick, but I can hear him. He is inside somewhere. If we go now, I think there will be enough light for us to find him."

Without further explanation, she picked up her bag and hurried back up the stairs, waiting for Meg to catch up with her at the top. She said, "The roof has rotted away. It was wooden, and so were the floor joists. But there is a wide stone ledge that once supported them, and we can make our way along that."

"Don't worry," she said, glimpsing Meg's dubious expression. "It's wider than the cliff ledge was."

"The one that collapsed and almost sent Gale tumbling onto the rocks?"

"It has already held Patrick, and anyway, there is not so far to fall here. While lofty, the lower chamber must be half-full of soil and leaves by now. This stair we are climbing leads to the second story, so if we work our way along the edge inside, we must come to another stair leading down within the walls. Or at least, so I believe," She added less certainly.

Meg tested the ledge. It did seem solid. And it really was not much darker than outside. Perhaps they could camp inside after they found Patrick. It would be something to have four strong walls around them. Even without a roof!

Kathe led their way along the ledge running around the perimeter of the building. She had chosen the direction to take by guessing. They did not know which way they should go in order to find a stairway, and the building seemed to be very large. It was now too shadowy to see anything on the faraway other side. They gambled that any stair leading to a lower floor would gain its strength by being built along one of these exterior walls.

Kathe had thought she heard sounds when she first scouted inside the doorway, but now this structure, which must have once been home to many, was eerily silent. They stopped to listen by one of the narrow, vine-covered windows – searching with ears and eyes for a clue telling them which way Patrick might have gone.

Why were there no trees in here? Generations of the surrounding giants must have dropped their seeds and cones into the roofless building. Young trees should have pulled at the foundation with their roots, buckling the stone and toppling the walls. Yet, like the road they had walked, this place seemed to exist under some protection. It looked as if it was waiting for the people to return, to rebuild the roof, relay the floors, clean out the leaves and restart its history.

The stories Kathe had heard never explained why the forest people left their city. Patrick said Ostarans were his enemies. Was it possible that her own people were an earlier version of the Claymon, wreaking havoc far from home? Or did the forest folk die of sickness? Maybe the young people left, abandoning the city to wither until the last of its elders passed away. Kathe couldn't think of any benign reason for the city's emptiness. The big old house felt like a tomb.

She looked back toward the dim opening at the top of the stairway. They could retreat, but there was no sense in doing so. They had no way of knowing when, or where, Patrick might emerge. Surely a house this size must have several exits.

In truth, they did not know whether he would emerge at all. More likely his sudden energy had been spent in carrying him forward to a once familiar place where his strength would seep from him again. It seemed urgent that they find him even though Kathe did not know what she and Meg might do to prevent his weakness from stealing him away forever.

They met no real obstacles as they crept along the narrow ledge, just the detritus of the years and the continuing knowledge that a dangerous fall awaited them should they take a misstep and lose their balance. They had covered two walls and had just turned to begin a third when they found themselves at the top of a wide stair descending into the darkness.

Meg had been staving off her feelings of vertigo; now she sat down on the top step and strained to see down the stairs. She laughed softly, without a trace of hysteria. Where now was the girl who hid within the manor at night and avoided even the shade of the forest's edge? It was an easy choice to descend into this unknown darkness when the only other option was to return outside where, likely, some other danger was waiting for them to return.

She wondered at feeling so peaceful now when she was so scared outside. It must have just been the loneliness then. Now, with Kathe standing beside her, Meg felt more curious than anything else. And afraid for Patrick, of course. They had traveled with him for only two days, but she already would be sorry to part from him. They had not even heard his story yet! And they were responsible for him. They had woken him up, and now he was sick.

She swung her pack around to her lap and dug in its depths until she found the stub of a candle her mother had included in her hurriedly gathered basket.

"Can you lay your hand on the fire stone?" she asked Kathe, her fingers searching for dry moss and small sticks that littered the steps and gathering them together into a little pile.

"Here," said Kathe, holding the flint out toward Meg and not releasing it until she felt her friend's fingers tighten around it.

Meg scraped at a step until she found bare stone, cleared a small space, and put the dry stuff she had collected into it. It took several attempts, but finally a spark caught the edge of the pile. It began to die out almost as soon as it flared, but before it could do so, Meg lit her candle.

It made a comforting circle of light around them, but it also made the shadows beyond that circle even deeper. They counted thirteen steps before they reached the base of the broad stairway. When they did, the place they had reached looked more like a clearing in the woods than the elegant hall it must once have been.

Kathe walked a few paces forward. Assuming more steps were buried under the forest debris, this room must originally have been lofty, even cavernous. The candlelight caught details of murals covering the walls. Closest at hand was a painting of a mighty tree bearing jeweled fruit. It soared higher into the darkness than they could see with their little light. A richly garbed man and woman reclined beneath it, and the man was offering the red-haired woman one of the lovely fruits. The artist had caught an expression of deep tenderness on his face. Kathe reached up and ran her finger over the plastered surface. He looked a little like Patrick.

They moved further along the wall. Here were forest creatures. A rabbit peeked out from beneath the gnarled roots of a beech tree. It had a streak of white under its chin. Kathe took the candle from Meg and held it closer, lifted it high. She took an involuntary breath. There, on the lowest branch, just above her head, sat a painted Oro.

She slowly lowered the candle again and moved it from side to side. When the flame caught a reflection in the painted forest behind the Beech, she stopped. There. It was the King, blending in among the trees. And the sapling next to him was marked with a scrape that looked very fresh.

"I can't believe it," she breathed.

"It is almost as beautiful as the book," said Meg.

They slowly walked along the painted wall. Despite the urgency of finding Patrick, they hesitated. The snows and rains, the persistence of time, should have erased the scenes before them. Yet here was Maraba, smiling her inscrutable cat smile. And here was Oro again! Kathe glanced back into the gloom behind her. If she were to retrace her steps, would she find that he had somehow flown forward from the painted beech tree to this painted oak?

Meg had gone ahead, to the edge of the circle of candle light.

"What's this?" she said, kneeling next to a knee-high, arched opening in the wall.   Kathe lay on her stomach and peered through. She held the candle ahead of her and snaked forward. The light was too dim to see much, but she could tell this was a much smaller space. And here the silence was finally broken. She could not yet see Patrick, but she could hear his labored breathing somewhere ahead of her. She moved a little further forward and sat up on the other side.

As soon as Meg joined her, the two of them began to search. It didn't take long to find him. He lay sprawled next to the far wall, and he was unconscious.

"Patrick...Patrick..." Kathe called urgently, rolling him over with Meg's assistance. His eyes rolled in his head. At least he was alive. She slapped him hard and made him sit up against the wall.

"Oh no, you don't..." she said unreasonably. "You're not going back to sleep here. Not when we have no magic to awaken you." She remembered the feeling of deep peace, of rightness, they had all felt as he returned to life in the cave, and she took his hand and stroked it.

"Patrick...," she called again softly.

She couldn't be sure, but she thought he squeezed her hand. They had to strain to hear his whisper, "I should have died long ago; it is no tragedy to die now, but.... "

"But what?" Meg asked.

"Mabus," he breathed.

"That was what he called his sword, wasn't it?" Meg reminded Kathe.

"Did you think you would find Mabus here? Is that why you ran away? Is it the reason you have given up?" Kathe asked. When he did not answer, she put her arm around him and tipped his head to offer some water from the skin. It trickled from the corners of his mouth.

"Meg, take the candle. See if you can find anything to help us...to help him."

Meg plucked the candle from where they had stuck it in the dirt of the floor. It was getting very short. Soon it would be gone entirely. There was only one more. Perhaps before this one burnt itself out they ought to make a real fire. As she explored the room, she picked up small sticks they could use to start the blaze.

There were even a few large limbs she had to step over. They would be enough to keep the fire going through the night.

Kathe stayed with Patrick, still holding his hand. She lowered his head into her lap. Meg had moved further away with the candle, but Kathe still could see lines of pain etched around Patrick's eyes and at the corners of his mouth.

The stars shone brightly through gaps in the branches overhanging the house. It felt as if she was looking up at them from the bottom of a deep well. These same stars once shone on this city when it was full of warmth and laughter. They shone upon the artists who embellished its walls with marvelous paintings and upon young men like Patrick who went out to fight and die. It all happened so long ago. Her tears trickled down and fell on his face. She wiped them away with her sleeve. Was pity all they could give him?

She watched Meg moving around the walls with her little light. Before long she returned to Kathe and said, "This room seems to have been a chapel. It is shaped like the one at Springvale, and there are little places built into the wall where the statues could stand, but they are empty. If I am right about the room's purpose, the altar would have been right about here," she guessed, moving to stand a few paces away.

"How do you know?"

"There's the most beautiful painting of all on the wall behind you. I have only been in the one other chapel, but I'd expect the altar to be in front of it, with room for a priest to walk around behind it."

Kathe gently lowered Patrick's head to the floor and held her fingers against his throat. When she was certain his heart was still beating, she stood by Meg's side and turned to look at the painting.

It made her dizzy. She had been here before. Here was a circle of trees, with one great oak directly in front of her. Oro perched on the low branch exactly where she had once seen him, and she could swear the wind was ruffling his painted feathers. It must have been a trick of the light or of the artist. Below Oro and all around the walls of the little room, the circle of animals stood watching. They seemed to be waiting for something.

A sense of deep magic rooted Kathe in place. She thought that, if she were to step forward to touch the wall, she would not feel the smooth, miraculously preserved plaster, but the silky feathers and fur of the animals that had led her here.

"All right, so now what?" she said aloud.

She was talking to Oro and the other animals, but it was Meg who answered. "I'd say the first thing to do is start a fire so we can see what we're doing, whatever that turns out to be."

After they started a small blaze in the middle of the room with the last of the candle stub and the sticks Meg had gathered, Kathe thought out loud, "Patrick must have fought in a battle somewhere between here and the cave where we found him."

"So?"

"Well, maybe he was wounded trying to defend this city. Maybe he lost Mabus in the fight."

She paused, feeding another stick to the fire. She glanced towards the base of the wall, where the firelight danced over Patrick's body. From here he looked as if he was merely sleeping.

"I'll bet his fellow soldiers, the ones who lived, searched the battlefield for his body. They would have wanted to return it here for the proper rites. What if they did not find him, but they did find Mabus?"

Meg saw where her thoughts were heading. "They would not have left the sword there. If they couldn't bring Patrick, they would have brought Mabus, at least, back to his family."

"It would have been important to his people because it was his," Kathe said. "They probably would have treated Mabus as a treasure."

"And such treasures are kept in the chapel," Meg finished.

"On the altar," Kathe rose and stood again on the spot in front of the Painting.

"That's where Patrick thought the sword would be. We have to dig."

Under the watchful eyes of the animals in the circle, and under the spell of the story they had spun, Meg and Kathe used the two spoons and their cooking pot to begin their work. If the buried altar was originally waist high, it shouldn't take them long to find the top of it.

Digging was easy in the loose, loamy earth. There were no roots or stones to impede their progress, and now that they had decided what they must do, they worked with energy. Kathe's shoulder ached, and she was hungry, but she kept digging. Even though she knew it was just as likely Mabus had been stolen by Patrick's enemies or had been taken along with everything else in this house when the people left, she kept working. The King must have marked the way here for a reason.

They decided to make the hole a rectangle, the shape of the altar at Springvale. One of them worked at each end. Because the soil was so loose, they soon had to lie on their stomachs to scoop spoonfuls and potfuls of soil onto the pile growing next to the hole. Every few minutes, Kathe or Meg checked on Patrick. It was difficult to find his pulse; they searched with dread each time until they discovered a sign that he still lived. Kathe did not speak the thought, but she could not help reflecting that, if they were wrong about the sword, this pit would likely become his grave.

When they could no longer reach the bottom of the hole, Meg climbed in and began scooping around her feet, first at one end of the oblong, and then at the other. She filled the cooking pot and passed it up to Kathe to empty. By digging such a large hole, they hoped they might find a corner of the altar even if they had chosen the wrong place to dig.

When the hole was about waist deep on Meg, she climbed

out with Kathe's help, and stretched her cramped legs. They had dug so far now that it was pitch dark in the bottom of the hole, and she had had to work blindly.

"Shouldn't we have found it by now?" she asked wearily, brushing her damp curls out of her face, leaving it even dirtier.

"Let me take a turn," Kathe said. "If we don't find something soon, we'll have to give up until morning."

"Can he make it until morning?" Meg asked.

There was no answer for this question. Kathe lowered herself into the darkness and began to dig. One pot of soil. Two, three, four...ten. Her legs ached from kneeling, and when her bruised shoulder hurt too much, she began to dig with her left hand. Eleven.

Twelve. The spoon scraped something hard. She used it to scrape more dirt away from the object and then discarded it so her fingers could discern its shape. It was smooth and flat. She hoped it was the top of the altar – not the floor of the chamber. Taking the spoon again, she began to clear the surface of soil.

Above, Meg could hear the sound of the metal scraping against stone. She found the last precious candle and lit it at the fire. There was room for only one of them down in the hole, but perhaps the light would allow her to see whatever it was Kathe had found. But when she held the candle over the hole and peered down, all she could see was Kathe's back as she leaned over her work.

The spoon scraped against a ridge. It was about as wide as one of her fingers was long, and it seemed to run across the whole, otherwise flat surface. Again, she discarded the spoon and investigated the obstruction with her fingers. First she smoothed the dirt away from the top of it, and then along the edge. She swore and sucked on a dirty finger, tasting blood.

"We've found him," she said.

Why "him" and not "it"? If it came to that, why was this blade sharp enough to cut her when it should have been rusted dull from years of exposure and then burial in the earth? Instead, when she lifted the sword from the hole a few minutes later, the earth fell away from a weapon glowing red and silver in the firelight. She could even see that the blade carried an inscription.

Meg took the sword and helped Kathe out of the hole. They knelt together and examined it more closely. Kathe poured a little of their precious water down the grooved blade and wiped it clean with her sleeve. She traced the letters with her finger as she read haltingly: "Giver of death and of life, bound to one."

"Well, we know who that one is, don't we?" Meg said. "I reckon it's time to reunite the two of them."

26

Not Quite Abandoned

Outside the city's edge, in a small house made not of stone but of thin branches bound in bundles and roofed with faded green thatch, Patch and his son Patchson rested on heaps of soft furs spread on the single room's dirt floor. In the hours since their arrival, Marion, Patch's cheerful wife, had had ample time to cook venison for their evening meal and to add carrots and new potatoes from her garden just outside the door.

The two Woods Runners had been chosen to follow the red-haired girl and her companions until the Ancients told the Runners what to do or maybe until the Northerners needed placating. They had been given the job because they were the most skillful trackers among a whole race of trackers – men who could follow a deer through a swamp, and it was very important that this particular trail not be lost.

From the beginning they had believed themselves lucky to be following the young people instead of reporting back to the Claymon captain. The other Runners would have looked away or at their feet as they recited the agreed upon half-truths. Patch could picture the Captain's face darkening in anger just before he barked out another set of orders. He was a hard man.

"Do you want more meat, M'dear?" Marion looked up from

her knitting with a smile. "I hadn't thought to see you yet, not until the leaves start to fall. It has been a peaceful summer here, and good for growing. We'll have enough potatoes to last until spring, and this fresh venison you brought is a treat. I think you've grown again!"

She reached out to ruffle her son's hair. "I'll be adding a strip of leather to the bottom edge of your pants while you're here." She turned to Patch, "I'm guessing you won't be staying long?"

Patch took his time answering. Two nights before, it hadn't taken any skill to find the quarry's camp. And the next day, too, the four young people had moved slowly and left plenty of signs. The trouble hadn't started until today, and he still didn't know what it meant. First thing that morning, when they had picked up the trace, they saw at once that there was a new trail for the quarry to follow, and worse, it was the stag that was leaving it.

It was easy to see the stag's marks were guiding the young people up and over the crest of the biggest hill, the spine of the Celadrians. The quarry moved slowly. It was easy for Patch and Patchson to get ahead of the group and follow the stag's trace, hiding inside the edge of the forest at the bottom of the far side of the hill and watching until the two girls and the woodworker's apprentice passed into the shade. By then the other boy wasn't with them. That was something else to worry about.

They followed at a distance until the three reached the old city gate, then circled back into the forest to their home and surprised Marion feeding her few chickens.

"I can't say," he finally answered after a comfortable silence during which no answer seemed to be expected. "The ones we're following went into the city."

Marion dropped a stitch.

"They've got that boy with them, the one we've been keeping our eye on all these years."

She put her knitting in her lap and stared at Patch in disbelief.

"Are you going in there?"

"No!" His exclamation came without thought, rising from all the stories he had heard by the fire since he was a little boy. No Runner had willingly gone into the city in his lifetime. They hadn't liked to go there even when it was still peopled, and now there was nothing there for them, nothing except the ghosts and the blank eyes of all those empty buildings. Nothing, that is, until today.

"Not until tomorrow, at least," he amended in his usual, calm tone. "Not at all unless we have to. People can't live in there. They'll have to come out sooner or later, if only to hunt, and the boy and I will pick up their trail then. They're about as careful as a bear that's dizzy after a long sleep."

"Well, then," Marion said, picking up her knitting and repairing her mistake. "Have another bite of venison. It is as tender as if I stewed it for hours instead of making a quick dinner for the two of you."

Patch served another helping for himself and his son and spent the rest of the night in silence. The Runners had agreed to lay low and just keep an eye on the fugitives until there was a sign from the ancients. He thought maybe he had been seeing those signs all day – every time he and Patchson found another marked tree. The animals helped this one and that one. They weren't all as choosy as the legends said, especially in his own generation, but he had never known the stag to help anyone but the Lady and her Consort.

Then, too, there was Patrick. He wasn't sure how many greats ago it was, but his grandfather, another Patch, was one of those who carried the wounded boy away from the field of battle and, finally, to the cave. It was as if the story was from his own experience, it was that vivid. In his own life he had been behind the waterfall too many times to count, and lately he had started taking Patchson, training him in the duty.

Every time they went there, the boy lay still as death, too

deeply asleep to reach. Not even a fleeting expression, reacting to a dream, had been noted by any Runner in all these years. Yet today, with his own eyes, he had seen the boy, stumbling it's true, but awake, returning to the city. It seemed like this is where the Ancients wanted Patrick to be, but why?

Before he fell into a restless sleep with his arm around his warm wife, he decided to send Patchson back to find the other Runners. He had followed the plan as far as he could. He thought maybe it was time to make another.

27

Exploring

Kathe lifted under Patrick's arms, and Meg carried his feet.
Together they struggled to carry him closer to the fire. He had
not spoken since he uttered the sword's name. If he was aware at
all, he should have roused when they moved him. It wasn't easy
even for two strong young women to move a grown man. They
did it awkwardly and lowered him as gently as they could.

"I hope we aren't too late," Kathe said.

She knelt next to Patrick, lifted his right hand and molded it
around the sword's hilt. Its amber stones began to glow dully,
but as soon as she released her grip on his hand, his fingers
slipped away and the glow faded.

Meg crawled forward and unbuckled Patrick's empty scabbard,
which he had been wearing all this time, and slid the sword into
it.

"So he won't cut himself," she explained. Then she laid the
sword and scabbard by his right side and rested his hand on the
hilt. The stones began glowing again, more warmly.

"That's a good sign," she said in a satisfied voice without any
trace of surprise. "Let's eat and then get some sleep. I'm about
done in."

"If I awaken in the night, I'll watch for the glow, and you do

165

the same," said Kathe. "If we don't see it, we'll put his hand back in place. I hope Mabus is giving and not taking tonight." She covered Patrick with his cloak, leaving his sword hand exposed. Before she turned away, she looked up at the painted Oro. "Is this right?"

After all that had happened, she half expected him to answer her, but the owl merely peered down at her gravely. She turned away with a sigh and took the dry biscuit Meg was offering her.

The layers of leaves and soil covering the floor of the chamber were as comfortable as a featherbed to the two exhausted girls. When Kathe awoke, she knew at once that morning was far advanced even though the walls blocked the horizon in all four directions. Sunlight poured over the wall and illuminated the painted forest where Oro still sat perched in his Oak. With the arrival of day, the colors of the mural seemed even purer, but the animals no longer looked as real.

She sat up with a start. She was sure there had been a complete circle of animals the night before. When she first saw the painting, they were positioned in the circle just as she remembered from her first meeting with them. Now there were gaps in the ring. Yes. Maraba was missing. She would have noticed her absence last night. And the stag...

Patrick still lay where they had left him, near the cold fire. He seemed the same, pale and unmoving, but his face was relaxed as it was when he slept in his watery cave. Kathe moved closer to him. She had not woken up even once during the night, but his hand was still upon Mabus's hilt. In fact, she found, giving the scabbard an experimental tug, he now gripped it tightly. The emerald and amber stones continued to glow, or were they just catching the sunlight? She cupped her hands over them and watched light escape upwards between her fingers. No. They were still shining from within – and more strongly than before.

She rinsed their cooking pot. By the time she had built up the fire and boiled water for oatmeal, Meg was awake. Like Kathe, her first thoughts were of Patrick.

"He made it through the night, didn't he, but it looks like it is going to take some time for Mabus to bring him around."

"Mmmhmm," Kathe responded, stirring the pot with their shovel, now returned to the status of spoon. "As long as we're waiting, we might as well explore the city, and then we could do with a rest. We need more water, and maybe we'll find some other useful things. Patrick will be safe enough if we leave him for a short while."

She couldn't explain to Meg why she believed this to be true. It had something to do with the circle of animals looking down upon him where he lay here in the chapel. Even if some of the animals had wandered away on their secret errands, the circle still included a bear and a large, grey wolf with eyes the same color as the stones under Patrick's hand. The wolf was the only animal new to the circle, the only one she hadn't already memorized. She moved closer and studied the animal intently. Well, it shouldn't be difficult to recognize it in the flesh. It had one green eye and one gold.

During their exploration of the ground floor of the house, Meg and Kathe found an overgrown exterior doorway at ground level. It was screened on the outside by a honeysuckle bush that had found root space between the paving stones by the door. They pushed their way outside and gazed up and down the street. At their right hand stood what must have been one of the city gates. Looking the other way, the street climbed a slope. They couldn't see where it ended. Meg tore a strip of cloth from her underskirt and tied it to the bush to mark the entrance. It floated in the light breeze.

The shadows of the night before had fled, and the stones of the city's walls glowed in shades of tawny brown deepening through gold. Flea-bane and Fairy Lace, the flowers of waste spaces, brightened the edges of the street. They knew the original paving stones lay buried, but even so, the streets themselves remained almost empty of plants.

Purple-blue swallows performed like acrobats in the air above them. They flew in and out of the many window openings. Shimmering dragonflies hovered close, then darted away. *Maybe they signal water nearby*, Kathe thought optimistically.

The architecture of the city was solid rather than decorative. Rarely did they come across a toppled wall. The houses were closed looking, as if keeping secrets, but whenever they crawled inside, they found sunny courtyards. It seemed these people hid their treasures inside.

In this part of the city, a few houses had small rooms opening onto the street. Although all wooden parts of the structures had rotted away, the two girls imagined that these were once shops with gaily painted awnings and wares spread on shelves. They soon came to think of the inhabitants as fine craftsmen, judging by a few lasting artifacts they found.

The curve of a pot on a stone shelf in one of these outer rooms caught Meg's eye, and she steadied Kathe as she scrambled in to retrieve it. It was narrow-necked and heavy. It must once have been used to store grain, but when they turned it upside down, it was clear the mice had long ago emptied it. It was beautifully shaped, with a creamy white glaze and a pattern of blue leaves; it lent a human touch to the place, but it was far too heavy to carry with them. The same was true for the silver plates they found leaning against the stone mantelpiece in one particularly fine house and of the carved stone animals which guarded the doorway of another. They looked like a cross between a housecat and a dragon, with the cat's self-satisfied expression and the dragon's scales and wicked looking talons.

"Whew! It's a hot one," Meg said, lowering herself onto the low stone step by one of these creatures and leaning against its cool stone side. "It would take us more than one day to see the whole place, I'll wager."

"We should return to Patrick soon," Kathe said. "I wonder where the people who lived in these houses got their water."

There was plentiful evidence that the city once was well supplied with water. Dry public fountains graced nearly every street corner, albeit at knee level. The stone pool in a bathhouse was further evidence of a plentiful supply. It was now full of debris. All their traveling until they began climbing the hills had been along the stream. Drinking, washing, even swimming had been underappreciated luxuries.

Kathe wondered whether this city, so close to the Celadrian Hills, might have had a supply system similar to the one in Ostara. There, aqueducts led from streams and springs high on the mountains to supply the city below. She studied the next public fountain along the way more closely and looked speculatively at the roofline of the building above it.

"I think I know why these houses are joined to one another." Kathe said.

Meg, who had spent her life in a place where water came from a well, waited for the explanation.

"In Ostara, we built special channels to carry water through the town, but here it looks like they used the buildings themselves." She looked back at the long, straight street behind them. "The city is built on a slight slope. That would also explain why the houses are becoming more elegant. The ones closest to the source would have been claimed by the wealthiest residents who wanted to enjoy the steadiest, coolest supply of water."

Although the stonework here was similar to that of the houses lower down the hill, Meg saw that surfaces were more highly polished. Doorways carried crests and carved mottos. She wished she could read them.

Exterior stairways to the second floor, like the one they had used to enter Patrick's house the night before, were a common feature of buildings in the city. It was easy to find one nearby, and from there, an interior stair carried them to the gaping roof. Although the height frightened them at first, the thick walls were plenty wide enough for walking.

Around them, they saw a warren of similar shells. All the roofs were gone. The city looked like a honey comb abandoned by giant bees. In one of its cells, they hoped, Patrick slept and slowly returned to life. Pockets of green trees rose here and there among the empty buildings, and further away, in every direction, the forest stretched away like a green sea.

"There's the top of the slope," Kathe said, pointing.

Along the street side of the house, they found what they had been looking for. An indented channel like a shallow ditch ran along the top of the wall and continued on to the next house. Like the stairs and ground floors of buildings, it had collected leaves over the years, and small plants grew in it.

The two girls reveled in their view of the city from above. The wall they walked along felt solid and safe, even where it crossed the street far below disguised within a graceful arch. Following this aerial path, they soon reached the city's edge. There, the aqueduct took the form familiar to Kathe and climbed the hill among the trees on a high, arched platform of its own.

The sound of flowing water came from just beyond the forest edge, but the section of stone that would have connected the city to its water source lay broken at the base of the wall.

There was no gate to bar them from leaving the city. They simply climbed down through the interior of the last building and followed the music of water to the end of the street and a little way into the forest. There the aqueduct faithfully continued to supply a trickle of water.

It fell in a thin, steady stream and pooled in a natural depression before flowing away. Kathe and Meg followed the water until it disappeared underground between two boulders, then returned to the aqueduct to bathe in the pool and to fill their two remaining water skins.

"We can easily refill them again whenever we want," Kathe said gratefully, "and once Patrick has recovered, we will leave the city with plenty of water."

Each of them slung one of the heavy skins over her shoulder and, otherwise unburdened, started back. The euphoria of finding the sword and getting a decent night's sleep was wearing off. Maybe Patrick was awake by now and wondering where they had gone.

Meg had memorized their route as she went along, but by the time her reverse recitation brought them to the proper street, their pace had slowed. Both girls were looking for the open-roofed building, so similar to a hundred others they had passed, because it was the one they thought of as home.

"There's the sign I left," Meg panted, pointing to her improvised flag marking the entrance and quickening her pace.

28

DOGS

THEY WERE STILL A few houses away when snarling and growling exploded behind them. It made the hair on the backs of their necks stand on end. They were already running when Kathe risked a quick glance over her shoulder.

What she saw lent wings to her feet. A pack of dogs was chasing them up the street, and gaining rapidly. She had brought her knife, her only weapon, with her on this scouting expedition, but she knew it would be useless unless they cornered her.

Their destination, which had seemed so near only moments before, now seemed impossible to reach. Senses tuned by fear told Kathe the situation was worsening with every step. She could hear Meg panting, but further and further behind her. Her rapid gasps spoke of panic.

The dogs had chosen their prey and now were working together for the kill. Kathe spun around to encourage Meg and saw her friend stumble. The creatures were almost upon her. One more misstep and they would have her.

Kathe yelled as loudly as she could and kept yelling as she ran back up the street towards Meg. She wanted the dogs to think she would tear out their hearts if they came any closer. They had to decide they were chasing the wrong two girls. She drew from an untapped well of anger deep within and poured it all into her voice.

At the sound of her shouting, the dogs hesitated long enough for Meg to drop her water bag and scramble up the same exterior stair they had used the night before when they first entered the house. She crouched at the top and added her voice to Kathe's.

"Come on! You can make it. Run!"

Kathe knew Meg was wrong. Her yelling had startled and distracted the dogs, but now they turned their attention toward the prey in the street instead of the creature that, for all practical purposes, had been treed. They were so close to her that she didn't dare to turn her back in an attempt to reach the stairway.

Instead, she backed against the wall and crouched in a fighting stance as Bard had taught her. She thrust her knife at the animals in the tight half circle whenever any of them lunged forward. It seemed as if she was fighting one grey beast with five snarling mouths. Their lips were pulled back to reveal yellow fangs, and their breath was hot on her face.

Blood spattered her dress. She wondered whether any of it was her own. With each lunge with the knife, she risked a step to her right along the wall, inching toward the safety of the stairway.

An individual separated itself from the snarling entity in front of her. In a swift movement Kathe could not parry, it latched itself onto her left wrist and tried to drag her forward. She screamed and plunged her knife into the dog's neck. It released its grip and fell back behind the others.

She knew it would be a mistake to look at her arm right now. Instead, she held it protectively against her body and waited for the next attack. She knew it would come, and she knew that next time, there might be two, and that would be the end.

She spoke a prayer, hoping her mother and brother might sense it. If she died here, they would never know her fate.

The dog she had wounded did not return, but the others tightened their circle, hackles raised. Four against one, and that one with only one tooth. She tightened her grip on the knife. Meg was still calling and crying, though it sounded as if she was doing it from far away. Kathe crouched more deeply. She was almost at eye level with the beasts now, protecting her abdomen with her knees, still parrying their advance with her good hand.

She was so focused in her effort that when the largest of the dogs yelped and fell back, she thought she was the one who had hurt it. Then a growling deeper and much louder than any she had yet heard, not only in this fight, but in her life, erupted to her left and outside the circle, where she could not see what was making it.

Hearing that sound, she surrendered. The front of her dress was stained deep red from the wound on her wrist, and her breath grew shallow as she tried to combat the tingling heaviness of her body and the buzzing in her ears.

Even as she awaited the final attack, the dogs broke and scattered. She watched them disappear down the street and stood to peer after them. She caught a glimpse of a much larger animal as it whirled and disappeared around the corner. Its tail looked wolfish.

Kathe steadied herself against the wall with her good hand. Two dogs lay dead in the street before her.

29

A Guilty Conscience

SHE PONDERED THIS STRANGE sight. The larger of the two animals, the one that had died by her knife, had swollen teats. The other was a male, and it had an arrow protruding from its side behind its foreleg. An arrow?

Meg was beside her, talking gently, leading her to sit on a low step of the stairway so that she could see what might be done to tend to Kathe's torn arm. Kathe leaned her cheek against the warm stone of the wall and closed her eyes. She wasn't yet ready to look at the injury. The buzzing hadn't left her ears. She heard Meg's sharp intake of breath and low moan of distress.

"They came right out of the stones, I think," she said, "like ghosts, but their teeth were real enough. What are we to do with this tear? If we were back at Springvale, Cook would call the healer for certain for a wound like this."

Kathe still hadn't seen it, but from Meg's reaction, she knew what ought to be done. "It will need a stitch, or maybe more than one," she said. "Didn't your mother give you a bit of clean cloth and some sewing things? Was there a needle?"

"Yes," Meg said, shortly, not wishing to carry that thought any further.

The sound of running footsteps came from around the corner

where the wild dogs had disappeared.

Kathe still held the hasp of her bloody knife in her right hand. Meg pried her fingers away and took it, placing herself between her friend and the sound of footsteps. Unless Patrick had made a miraculous recovery and had come out to look for them, they were about to meet a stranger. And Patrick had no bow.

Meg made a sound surprisingly like a growl herself. With an effort, Kathe stood next to her. There was no hiding place save the marked doorway. Meg dashed forward and pulled her scrap of petticoat from the bush outside the entrance. As far as they knew, Patrick still lay helpless in the open-roofed chapel, Mabus clutched uselessly in his hand.

A lone man rounded the corner with a shout. When he saw them, he stopped and bent over with his hands on his knees, gasping to catch his breath. His bow was still clutched in his right hand.

"I got one more before they disappeared into one of the buildings," he called loudly.

Meg lowered the knife she had been holding before her like a talisman.

"Gale?" she said, as if she didn't believe her eyes.

The buzzing in Kathe's ears was loud again; now the street began to spin. She took a step backward and fell awkwardly onto the steps. She concentrated on just breathing until her dizziness subsided slightly, then opened her eyes to see the faces of Meg and Gale swimming sickeningly above her. She closed her eyes again. She still held her wrist protectively against her abdomen.

Meg gently pulled it away and shook her head over the wound again. She turned and looked up at Gale. Around Springvale, he was known to have a gift for healing, but right now he was looking very worried and something else. What was it? Guilty?

"We have got to get her inside before those creatures come back, and then we must tend to her arm. Collect the water skins,"

Meg ordered, pointing to where they lay in the street.

If Gale was surprised to be taking orders, he didn't show it. Meg draped Kathe's good arm around her shoulder, and Gale supported her on the other side as they made their way into the house.

When they entered the chapel, there was no sign of Patrick. His cloak still lay on the ground near the fire where he had rolled out of it, and their packs were still leaning against the wall. Mabus was gone too.

Meg shook her head irritably. Where was he? Well, she was finished chasing him. There were no signs of a struggle. He obviously left under his own power, and he could come back the same way.

She and Gale helped Kathe into the thin shade along the room's west wall. It was an hour or two past mid-day. Kathe was still shaky, but the shock of the injury, the fight, and Gale's sudden return seemed to be passing. She gingerly moved her arm and looked at the wound for the first time.

"It is time to find that needle, Meg," she said.

This time Gale took her arm and cradled it, examining the jagged edges where the dog had pulled and torn the skin.

"First we must cleanse the wound as well as we can. Since we don't have a basin, we'll sponge it well. Dog bites can be dangerous. Then I'll stitch it."

Meg's sigh of relief was audible.

"We will have to watch carefully as it heals. If you begin to have any fever…" his voice trailed off. Better to deal with that possibility if it arose. "You are likely to carry a scar."

Kathe shrugged. She didn't care about a scar, but she was beginning to be curious about Gale's reappearance.

While Meg rinsed the wound and sponged it with clean cloth

her mother had given, Gale went outside to the near edge of the city to look for elder leaves to pack under the dressing. He was more shaken than he liked to admit. If his arrival had come a few moments later, Kathe would have been killed. At least her hurt would have been more serious. It was bad enough. If he had not left them alone on the mountain the afternoon before, he would have been here to protect them. Was the knowledge he had gained worth the cost?

He heard a shout behind him and turned to see a familiar figure striding down the street. Patrick. He now realized how ill the warrior must have been, and the knowledge added to his guilt. Gale had seen Patrick growing weaker every hour since his awakening, his life running away like the sand of an hourglass, and knowing it, he left anyway.

Now Patrick looked truly alive. In fact, it was as if Gale was seeing him fully in this world for the first time. There had been a shadowy quality about him before, but the darkness that once gathered around him was gone. Now his face was flushed with heat, and his eyes shone in welcome. He stopped next to the two dead dogs in the street and stood quietly, reading the story they told. Gale saw his hand grip the hilt of a sword tightly, and his knuckles whitened. He carried something under his other arm.

He turned to Gale, and when he was closer, he spoke in his usual odd, direct way – without any greeting. The old dialect he used was easy to understand now, just as these ruined walls were easily recognizable as homes and public buildings. "I am looking for Kathe and Meg. Have you seen them?"

Gale jerked his head back towards the entrance in the wall. "They're inside. They went for water and there was trouble. They were attacked."

"Where were you?"

Gale winced. Though he didn't think Patrick intended it that way, the words sounded like an accusation. He realized Patrick did not know Gale ever left them. Well, yesterday the man had looked like a sleepwalker.

"I came too late. I killed one of these. Kathe is hurt. I am going into the forest to find a plant that will help her."

Without another word, Patrick turned on his heel and ducked through the entrance.

Meg was sitting against the west wall listening to her friend's quiet breathing and watching the shadow grow as the passing minutes slowly broadened the shade inside the room. She had rinsed Kathe's wounded arm with water three times and bandaged it loosely, ready for Gale's return. Now she gently stroked the injured girl's hair. Kathe lay facing the wall with her eyes closed, but Meg knew she wasn't asleep.

Patrick climbed through the door on his hands and knees, then stood and quickly crossed the room, sidestepping the pit where the girls had found Mabus. He knelt next to Kathe.

Meg had shed no tears in the time since hearing the first growl in the street behind them, but now she could feel them about to fall.

"They would have gotten me, but Kathe made them turn away. You must have heard her. She sounded dangerous! I'm sure that's what saved me."

Patrick picked up Kathe's bloodied knife from the floor. "It looks like she didn't only *sound* dangerous," he said.

At the sound of his voice, Kathe turned away from the wall and struggled to sit up. Meg tried to help her, but Kathe shook her head. "My arm is my only injured part, Meg. And it doesn't hurt so much now."

"When I woke up alone, with Mabus back in my hand, I couldn't stay here." Patrick explained. "I was filled with restless energy. It is one of the effects of the sword. It likes to be active. I decided to look for you, to show you what had happened – and to thank you."

Meg and Kathe looked at each other in amazement. They too could understand Patrick's odd pattern of speech without difficulty now, but there was a new strength in his voice. Even though his face was full of concern, he seemed to be glowing with an internal flame. His hand went to the hilt of his sword as if to reassure himself that it was really there.

"We went looking for water," Meg said. "We were attacked…"

"I know. I met Gale outside."

"One of the dogs bit Kathe."

Patrick gently took Kathe's hand and rotated her arm, carefully pulling away the loose bandage so he could see the wound. Meg had sponged it clean, and Kathe had kept pressure on it, so most of the bleeding had already stopped. There was a puncture wound near her elbow and a jagged tear closer to her wrist. That was the area that would require Gale's attention with the needle.

Patrick returned Kathe's hand to her lap and turned to the bundle he had brought into the room.

"I have something that will help," he said. "This morning I passed some houses I know well. One was Demeter's, the vintner's. He made the best wine this side of the Celadrians, and he bottled it so well that I have some hope it is still good enough to use on your outside to prevent fever, and maybe even good enough so your inside won't feel so much hurt."

He pulled a bottle out of his bundle. Clumps of earth still clung to it from Demeter's half-buried shop, and something sloshed inside. Meg hurried to get one of their bowls while he worked at the cork. She sniffed. It certainly smelled like wine. She poured a little of the purple liquid into the bowl and tasted it tentatively.

She made a face.

"I don't like wine much," she explained. "I wouldn't be able to tell if it's good or not."

Patrick took the bowl from her and drained it. "It shouldn't be good, but it is. Even tightly corked as it was, the bottle should have been empty after all these years, yet I can still taste the blackberries he used to add to the summer wine. Perhaps it has been preserved like some other things here. He lifted his eyes to gaze at the mural above him.

Kathe scuttled away from the wall until she could look up and see the mural too. Something had been troubling her. She searched the circle of animals until she found him – the wolf. He was sitting just where he had been when they left the room that morning. She remembered feeling grateful that he would be there to watch over Patrick. Yet something was different.

She stood and took a step closer to the painting. This morning the wolf had been sitting with his mouth closed, looking as if he was sniffing the new day's air. Now his mouth hung open in a wolfish grin, and he appeared to be panting, as if he had exerted himself in the heat. And what was that under its paw? She looked more closely. Was that arrow there this morning? Weren't Gale's arrows feathered in black?

"I've seen my share of battle wounds," Patrick said. "Yours doesn't look too bad considering you've been in a dog fight. But you should take advantage of it. Sit down and let us take care of you."

Kathe tried to smile, but it was more like a grimace. She resumed her place against the wall.

"Now, drink this," he demanded, holding out the bowl filled with wine.

When she had drunk it and held it out for him to take, he refilled it instead.

She protested, "Wine makes me sleepy!"

"That's the idea," he replied.

30

What Gale Saw

By the time Gale returned, Kathe was dozing with her head on Meg's shoulder.

"I'm sorry it took me so long. I had almost given up when I finally found an elder bush in a clearing some distance back towards the hills. I couldn't help thinking I had just passed that way. I wished I had filled my pockets then."

Patrick looked at him sharply, eyes narrowing.

"We've washed the wound and doused it in wine," Meg said. "And here is the needle. I held it in the fire and kept it in the bowl ready for you."

She fished the needle out of the bowl of wine, threaded it with a length of the fine linen her mother had provided and handed it to Gale. He turned to his work.

"I had to learn this part of the healer's craft," he said softly, as he began to close the wound. "Accidents are common in the new fields at the edge of the forest."

Meg watched Kathe's face closely. She did not open her eyes or make a sound, but she winced with each stitch – and the knuckles of her good hand whitened as she clutched her skirt.

Patrick looked on approvingly as Gale closed the raw wound with a row of neat stitches.

"Two more," Gale said.

When Kathe's arm was neatly bandaged, Gale sat back on his heels. He busied himself with cleaning the needle, but soon he had to look up and face the three pairs of eyes that were studying him intently.

"Your needlework has counteracted any effect the wine had on me," Kathe said. "I am in the mood for a story, and you're the one who must tell it. And...," she paused and shifted her gaze to Patrick. "You're next."

Gale nodded as if coming to a decision. "You shall have your story, though I do not yet know whether you will think the ending is happy." He sat silently for a few moments, collecting his thoughts.

"After I left you yesterday, I grumbled for the first league. And I did it aloud since there was no longer anyone to hear me. How could you have chosen as you did – to follow a stag down a hill? Common sense, basic intelligence, should have sent you with me along the ridge towards the road. What kind of help could you hope to offer your family by going in the wrong direction and getting lost in a forested maze?"

"After a while, I simmered down, and I began to think it was for the best." He glanced at Patrick. "I was traveling lightly, almost running. Even though the way was rocky, the going seemed easy after the climbing we had done and after matching my pace to yours. I pictured arriving in Ostara in a few days, blending in with the crowd, presenting myself to the leaders of the rebellion as their newest fighter, assuming I could find them.

Meg interjected, "Did you picture their reaction when you told them that you left Kathe on her own?"

He winced. "I know I haven't said it yet, but I am sorry. At once, even as I walked away from you, I was sorry to have left you. And I was sorrier still to return and find you in such trouble."

"Let him finish," Kathe said.

Gale took an audible breath. "I knew it wouldn't take me

long to gain sight of the road if I kept to the hill-tops. As it leaves Springvale, the forest trail runs straight, but it soon begins to curve to the northwest. Since I was heading due East, I knew I would come to it. Before nightfall, I hoped."

"I was looking forward to walking a road. I thought I'd camp out of sight and make myself scarce if I met anyone, but meeting anyone seemed unlikely. Remember, we decided that, even if the Claymon left Springvale as soon as they realized Kathe was gone, it would still have taken them at least a week to reach Ostara. I figured I'd be following the Claymon delegation at a distance, and maybe I could reach Ostara before Peter even decided to send anyone back down the road to Springvale."

"That makes sense," Kathe said. "What happened to change your mind?"

"A little bird," Patrick guessed.

Gale looked startled. "I didn't think of it then, but you are probably right. I reached the pass in late afternoon. The sun was behind me, and I could finally see the line of the road curving away below and into the distance. It wasn't a clear view. More a thinning of the forest, like a half-healed wound. I was looking for the easiest way down the hill when I saw the first flash of red."

No one said anything, but he sensed he had their complete attention. All three of his companions leaned slightly forward.

"All of a sudden my skin crawled. I was standing exposed on that rocky outcrop, and I felt certain eyes were watching me. I flattened myself on the ground behind a pile of boulders and studied the road, trying to read what lay below me." He paused.

"Well?" Meg said.

"There were at least a hundred Claymon soldiers in full battle array, marching south along the road towards Springvale. One hundred soldiers to subdue a manor house and farm!"

"And to search for me," Kathe said soberly. The effects of the two bowls of wine had completely worn off now, and she was feeling unusually alert, though her arm ached miserably.

"As I lay there watching, intent on the movement along the road, I caught the sound of sliding stone close by. It sounded like a few small stones had been sent rolling down the hillside. I inched forward."

"This one wasn't wearing red. In fact, if he had not made that sound, I might not have seen him at all. He blended almost perfectly with the colors of the rocks on the hillside. I watched him ranging across the slope. His eyes were intent on the ground before him."

"You are describing a Woods Runner," Patrick interrupted. "They used to hang around the edges of Pallas, though they never strayed far from the forest. As they once were, they wouldn't have allied themselves freely, but a few have always been mercenaries. The Claymon captain must have sent a dove flying back to Ostara to tell the usurper his prize had run. It is what I would have done. This Lord Peter has wasted little time."

"He is unused to such irritations," Kathe said. "He may not even want to marry me now, but he would never give up what he believes to be his."

"What did you do then?" Meg prompted Gale.

"I didn't move. I barely breathed. I kept watching the tracker as he ranged back and forth across the hillside, methodically searching. I assume he was looking for a sign that we passed that way. No one could have slid down that hill without leaving some trace."

"It's a logical place to come to the road," he admitted ruefully. "If he made one more sweep, I'm sure he would have found me. I watched until he curved down towards the Claymon and out of sight. Then I crawled back the way I came until I thought it safe to stand again, and I began retracing my steps. I made it back to the place we parted by moonlight, but I couldn't see the marks the stag made. I was afraid they had somehow been erased, that

I had been judged unworthy to follow. I dozed a while, but in the morning they were there."

"They were there for you, and there they will remain for anyone who chooses to follow them," Patrick said soberly.

There was a long silence after Gale stopped speaking. He sat with his head bowed.

"I guess that means we'll be leaving," Kathe said.

"Not until tomorrow," Patrick said.

"Gale," Kathe said. "The way I see it, you went off to do some scouting. That might not be what you intended, but that's the way it turned out." *And maybe you were following someone else's plan – like I am.* "And you have returned with important information, and just in time to save me from being torn apart by those dogs. And now you have stitched my arm so that, though it is as heavy as a log, it will surely heal."

Gale looked up and gave her a half smile.

She stretched her legs in front of her, making herself more comfortable. "All right, Patrick. Your turn."

31

Patrick's Memories

Patrick looked confused, as if he couldn't imagine what story she might be wanting.

"Oh come!" she said. "I do not know how many nights I have spent listening to stories of the forest city and its people, but there were many during every winter of my childhood. In my room at home, at the end of my bed, was a little wooden chest. It was given to me by my mother, who was given it by her mother, who was given it by her mother…well, no carvings like it have come out of the forest or anyplace else since forever. The sides of my chest are covered with knots of carved vines, and a flock of birds covers the top. The keyhole is at the center of a flower. I keep all my favorite things in it."

"Like what?" Patrick asked.

"Like an illustrated bestiary, not as lovely as yours, Meg, that my father gave me at Midwinter when I turned fifteen, some flowers I dried, letters…you are trying to distract me."

"Not at all, Lady," Patrick said formally. "I will gladly tell you what I know of Pallas's story…"

"And your own."

"And my own. But remember, I only know some parts of the story. Others I may have dreamed during my long sleep. Other parts I must guess."

"I understand."

"But I will tell it after you have slept and eaten. There are still places I must visit in Pallas before Mabus will allow me to rest."

Kathe opened her mouth to argue with him. She nearly asked for his promise, but something stopped her. Asking someone to promise is one way of saying you don't really trust him. And he was right – she was very tired.

Patrick strode up the streets of Pallas, following nearly the same route Kathe and Meg had taken that morning when they searched for water but without any of their hesitations or side explorations. Before he reached the edge of the forest and the broken aqueduct, he turned west and followed a wide street to where it ended at a wild square. Once, this open space near the city's edge had been a groomed park. Then, sheep kept the grass under ancient Sycamores trimmed close. The giant trees still stood, their branches sweeping the ferns that now grew thickly beneath them.

Even though he couldn't see it yet, he pictured the large house beyond the trees. Though similar in design to others he had passed as he walked through the city, it was set apart in its own walled gardens, and an iron gate guarded its entrance.

It was now easier to walk around the square on the street than to take his old shortcut across the park. As he approached the house, he noticed that even though the gardens surrounding it had grown as wild as the park, they were still beautiful. The breeze carried the scent of the flowers his mother had planted and loved. He halted for a moment, closing his eyes in sudden pain. Lavender, once trimmed in precise globes, now bloomed in a waist high riot along the walk leading to the front door.

Climbing roses covered the entire, sunny façade of the building, clinging to the stonework and hiding the large, gaudy crest carved directly into the stone above the heavy front door.

His otherwise practical father had liked the way the carved owl in the crest peered soberly down at everyone who entered. At one time, this crest carried the only gilding in Pallas. Everyone admired it and tolerated its knowing eyes whenever they entered the house, but they never imitated it. Patrick believed it was a sign of the respect in which they once held his father.

Patrick fought his way through the wilderness of garden to the double doors at the side of the house that once stood wide open at this time of year, bringing the garden indoors on warm summer afternoons. They were open now, but it was because, as everywhere else in the city, the wood had rotted away. Only the heavy hinges that once supported the doors remained. He ducked through the opening.

This house was under no special protection. Like all the others, it was open to the sky. Maybe remnants of the carved chairs and benches, examples of the best work of the city's woodworkers, still lay buried under the debris covering the floors, but no trace remained of the colorful tapestries that once covered the walls in his mother's favorite room. After a moment's hesitation, Patrick crossed the room and bent low to pass through an inner doorway into what had been the spacious central hall. This area of the house always had been open to the roof. The stone balcony that circled the entire space, giving access to the upstairs rooms, still remained. The shields of his ancestors once hung on the walls along this balcony. Mostly made of wood and leather, they had also disappeared.

At the end of this long room, opposite the main entrance to the house, was a broad hearth. It always was ridiculously inefficient at heating the huge hall. That work was done by braziers, which could be moved close to wherever people were talking or working. Still, there always was a fire burning in the hearth fall through spring when he was a boy. The hearth was so deep that he could sit inside it to warm himself when he was a child without being endangered by the flames.

Patrick placed his hand upon Mabus's hilt again. The sword was his connection to the past. In a way, it lived. It was the only living thing left behind in this otherwise dead place. With the sword at his side, the terrible sense of being alone and off balance in a strange time was muted, manageable. He felt whole again, even if the world he once knew was gone.

The last time Patrick stood before this fireplace, he was too short to reach the mantle, but he watched his father closely, so he knew what to do. Now, thanks to the layers of debris laid down over years, he did not have to stretch as his father had. He could look for what he sought with his eyes as well as his fingertips. Still, his fingers did most of the searching along the flawless surface of the stonework.

It had been near the center, he thought. There. One leaf among the thousand carved as a decorative border loosened, turned, and became the pull for a drawer.

The container slid out of its hiding place smoothly on hidden rollers, untouched by time. Patrick pulled the drawer all the way out and placed it on the floor. It was made of the same stone as the mantle itself, and it was even heavier than he expected.

At first, it seemed to be empty, but when he knelt to look more closely, he saw a small, metal tube lying against one side. Protected within the stone for all these years, it still carried a slight luster.

Its top fit tightly. Patrick pried it open without concern for marring it and fished around inside with one finger for the hoped-for message. He caught a corner and gently slid the rolled message from its hiding place. The ink looked as dark and fresh as if his father had written the words yesterday instead of on a dark winter morning who knows how many lifetimes ago. Patrick smoothed the single page across his knee and read it slowly, whispering the words aloud as he did.

"My son. If you are reading this, then all has been lost. One day I will find a way home from the bitter exile I am about to enter. You must be the voice for peace until I return. Restore hope to Pallas. Do not search for me. Beware the one who claims to heal. I cannot write his name here, for I do not know how much power lies in that name. One you love made him welcome in the city. Do not blame her. How could she have understood such duplicity? If only your mother were not so weak now. Too weak for the journey that lies ahead of us..."

The note ended abruptly, as if the last moment arrived earlier than expected. What had his father left unsaid?

Patrick read his father's words a second time. They told him both more and less than he had hoped for when he sought out this old hiding place. Still clutching the letter, he left the drawer on the floor of the chamber and climbed the stair to the stone balcony, then climbed higher still, to the top of the tower at the forest-side corner of the building. Taller than any other structure in Pallas, it had been his father's favorite place. From here he had been able to look out over the forest to the north or back over the entire town.

Patrick leaned against the wall that formed a barrier around the otherwise open space and turned his face to the sun. He had been cold so long that being warm wasn't even a memory. That was probably what that interfering fairy intended – to keep him well chilled, like a side of meat in an ice house. He shivered in the heat of the afternoon and placed his icy hands against the stone.

Why was he back in Pallas now? What led the Three to his bier far too late to prevent the desolation of the city? Too late to save his mortal, fallible, lovable kin? Too late for revenge? He read his father's message a third time. It made no plea for revenge. It spoke only of peace.

The one he loved. Well, love was not the word for what lay between him and Honorus. He knew his parents had been pained by the strained relationship between their two sons. His elder brother was careful to hide his bullying nature behind a veneer of excruciating correctness. Once, Honorus had been bigger and much stronger than he was – it was strange now to think of him as only dust.

No. The person who had opened the gate to the unnamed healer must have been Bethany. Of all the people who once roamed the streets of Pallas, whose faces crowded into his memory as he walked the empty streets, she was the one he longed to see one more time.

Bethany alone had understood when, at fourteen, he moved down to the lower city to live with the man he called uncle, but who wasn't really even a relative. By then, illness so defined his mother that the people began to forget all the vibrant life she once carried and only spoke of her softly, with sad faces. His father's sober nature had descended into humorlessness as he watched his wife waste away. As his parents gradually became more and more preoccupied by illness and grief, Honorus barely took the trouble to hide his cruelty.

While sorrow swirled through the rooms like a fog, Patrick decided he could not pain his parents further by declaring an open battle among their children. Nor could he tolerate his brother's bullying any longer. It seemed Honorus had even begun bullying their father, questioning every decision and treating him as if he was already in his dotage. By this time Patrick was as strong as Honorus and nearly as tall. Without consulting his parents, he apprenticed himself to a merchant woodworker he met in the lower city.

Leonides, despite his legendary skill, lived simply in the oldest house in the most ancient part of Pallas. When he first passed the place, Patrick was fascinated by the intricately carved benches angled invitingly at the doorway. They were as comfortable as they were beautiful, and cunningly joined. Leonides had watched the gawky, tousle-headed boy in his fine clothes running his fingers over the carved surface for a time before he invited him inside. After that, Patrick returned to the house nearly every day, at first just to watch the work in silence, then to fetch and carry, to sweep the floor.

Patrick decided he would never really be missed. Someday, when the merchants and their quarrels passed under the owl's watchful eye, they would be coming to see Honorus instead of his father. He thought that perhaps his brother would change through the years. Maybe in time he would become a good leader for Pallas. Or, if nothing else, maybe Honorus would forget he had a younger brother.

He found the life of working with wood suited him better than training to become the second son of Meier Steele ever could have. He wasn't cut out to be the ambassador to somewhere or other – or Honorus's shadow. Master Leonides was exacting, but kind, generously sharing the secrets that made a length of tree trunk nearly as malleable as clay under his hands, that made the deep grain of the precious wood he chose an essential part of the design of each piece. Patrick was the master's only apprentice, and Leonides treated him as a son.

From the time he made the decision to leave home until the end, his sister Bethany was the only one of his family he ever saw. No, that wasn't quite right. Pallas was a small city, and he passed his father or brother nearly every week in the streets. Sometimes they even met his eye. When this happened, his father would nod, or even smile absently, but Honorus – never. All this time, his mother was far too ill to go beyond her own gardens. He never saw her again after he left home.

She had withdrawn into a world of her own long before he left, but why had he not climbed the hill at least to sit with her, or to carry her out into her beloved garden? He could have done that. The pleasure it would have given her would have been worth the risk of meeting Honorus.

Instead, Bethany was the one who ran down to the lower

city. She didn't seem to know how to walk. A young version of their mother, but glowing with good health, she caused a dip in production in the neighboring workshops every time she visited him.

She honestly admired each piece of furniture he made, and as his apprenticeship passed and he began to receive commissions of his own, she was as proud of him as if she were his mother instead of his sister.

He remembered how, at Midwinter of his twentieth year, when Bethany was seventeen, he made matching jewel boxes for her and for their mother. He lined the three trays inside each box with velvet cloth and carved each woman's initials within the shape of her favorite animal. He never knew how his mother had received hers, didn't even know whether she was well enough to accept it or aware enough to recognize its source, but Bethany's reaction was unexpected. She burst into tears and threw her arms around his neck.

"You're worth two of Honorus," she blurted, and he was stunned into silence. Bethany had never hinted that Honorus bullied her too. Patrick had never considered the possibility. Suddenly it seemed all too likely.

He held her at arms length. "Are you happy?" he asked.

She wiped her eyes with the corner of her apron and told him that she was, and how could it be otherwise with such a fine brother? She ran her hand across the surface of her box, with its carved panther. From his current vantage point, with its unbridgeable view of the past, he wished he had left the comfortable life he had built in Leonides's old house and climbed back up the hill with her one last time to reassure himself that she was telling the truth. As with everything else, it was too late to put that omission to rights.

Kathe's image floated through Patrick's mind. Now there was a girl with problems. She seemed to be running both from and towards an unwanted marriage. Bethany had been of marrying age when he marched away to battle.

He wondered who she might have married if the trouble had not come to Pallas. If Bethany had not opened the gate to the danger, whatever it was, and if Patrick had lived to a content old age. He knew Leonides intended to leave him the house. His own descendents might still inhabit that old place in the lower city where his new companions now slept through the heat of the afternoon.

Patrick had wanted to be just like Leonides, only less alone. He would have become the most famous wood worker Pallas ever produced, and he would have kept a jar of sweets at one end of his workbench for when his nieces and nephews came running into the house. They would have had brown hair and tawny eyes like their mother, and the same light step. He would have watched their hands to see which of them would become his apprentice.

Surely he would have met someone and married too. Patrick sighed. All the characters of his daydream deserted him. They all would have been dust by now even if the trouble, whatever it was, had passed Pallas by. He drank in the deep green of the forest. At least this view was unchanged.

His father must have believed his message would be found within weeks or, at the most, months from the time he hid it. The note even seemed to carry a hope that the exile could be avoided or that it might end quickly, and no one would read the message at all. When his father sat down to write it, eight years had passed since Patrick set foot inside his family home, and it had been ten years since his father showed him the secret drawer above the mantle.

Kathe and the animal guides made it impossible that chance had carried him here now. She wasn't hiding that secret very well. At least not from him. But then he was a citizen of Pallas, and he once had guides of his own. When he last saw the stag, it had led him and the other townsmen to where soldiers massed in a rock-bound valley.

There was a time when he trusted the guidance the animals gave him. He wondered whether the stag knew how his story would end – and if it ever watched from the rocky cliff top above his tomb. When Kathe followed its leading, she had brought him back to Pallas – and to Mabus. She had brought him back to life. And judging from her reaction to the painted animals, she was on speaking terms with several of them.

The warmth from the stones was finally seeping into his bones. It is easy to make a decision when you have only one choice. A city is its people. Empty, it wasn't really a city at all. Pallas was peaceful now, peaceful and empty. Patrick had followed Kathe like a sleepwalker, but now he would continue to follow her by choice.

She seemed intent upon finding the trade route to the Three Hills. Perhaps that old trail still hid some clue to explain the emptying of Pallas, even if only in the seeds of legend the people sowed as they passed. Based on all he had seen so far, his fellow citizens packed their belongings and left without haste or panic. Patrick fingered Mabus and thought of Demeter's summer wine. If this was indeed the way they left, then they forgot to take some of the greatest treasures with them.

32

The Fifth Companion

KATHE WOKE SUDDENLY. THIS was the second time she had napped during an afternoon on this journey. If she ever found herself a safe place again, she thought she would do it every day. Her arm felt better. It still throbbed, but the green salve Gale had smeared on the wound seemed to be helping.

He and Meg still slept deeply, on opposite sides of the chapel, their positions reflecting the tension that had arisen between them. Most of the room was in shade now. It would have been easy for Kathe to slip into a doze again, but something was nagging at her. It was neither a dream nor a talking animal. It was a sound. She lay with her eyes closed, listening deeply. There. A whimper.

She looked sleepily up at the mural again. The wolf seemed to have recovered from his earlier exertion. She thought he looked much more dignified with his mouth closed. As usual, he seemed to be gazing intently at her. Maybe he would seem that way to anyone looking at the painting.

There it was again, that sound. It seemed to be coming from close by. Kathe decided to investigate. She had not forgotten what happened to her the last time she walked Pallas's streets, but she shoved the memory roughly to the back of her mind. It was still a long way home, and she would undoubtedly be badly frightened several more times before the Three Hills came into view.

Someone had cleaned her knife. She slid it into its sheath and, without waking the others, crawled through the chapel doorway and crossed the outer room. At the door, the honeysuckle bush screened her from sight as she shaded her eyes and searched the street in both directions.

No living thing was visible except the swallows diving for insects and a cloud of flies. They were buzzing around the bodies of the dogs she and Gale had killed. They still lay in the open no more than fifteen paces from the doorway. Someone would have to move the animals soon. The task would become more unpleasant with each passing hour.

She heard the whimper again. It came from the direction of the fallen animals. Was it possible one of them was still alive? No. The last coherent thing she had done after the fight was to look at the damage she had done. She would have known.

A detail nagged at her memory. Hadn't one of the dogs, the big female, been nursing? Kathe slipped from behind the bush, and keeping the wall at her back, side-stepped until she had a better view of the two dead animals.

Ah. She couldn't have seen it from behind the honeysuckle, but there it was. A pup nudged at its mother's teats in a confused way. As Kathe watched, it raised its head again and whimpered.

It hadn't noticed her yet. Perhaps two months old, it had the big feet of puppyhood. Those feet predicted a large dog, maybe as big as the mother. Its belly was round, and it had sleek brown hair. Was this the only survivor from a litter?

Kathe took a step forward. The pup noticed her movement and hunched against its dead mother. It growled in a puppyish way, and the hackles rose on the back of its neck, but it did not run away. Maybe it thought its protector was only sleeping.

When she was a few steps away, Kathe knelt in the street

and began to speak soothingly to the young animal, using the crooning voice that comes naturally when one is holding or talking to a baby of any species. In any country, in any language, it is the same.

No person had ever spoken to this pup before. It belonged to a wild pack descended from the pet dogs of Pallas left behind in the exodus, but the animal seemed to recognize the tone. It looked interested. Kathe dug in her pocket for a scrap of stale biscuit. She broke it into two pieces and held one forward. When the pup growled again and backed away, she put it on the ground between them and sat back on her heels.

As she had known it would, curiosity won very quickly over caution. Some of the hunting dogs in her father's kennels were only a little tamer than the pack that had attacked her, and their young had been like this one. "Yer spoilin' 'em," the kennel master used to shout, chasing her away whenever he caught her petting them or giving them treats. Here was an opportunity to put her spoiling experience to good use.

The pup licked and nibbled the bread, then sniffed and found every crumb. It sat back on its haunches expectantly. She now saw its eyes were the same amber color as the stones in Patrick's sword, as the wolf's golden eye, and that the sun caught reflections of red in its brown coat.

This time when she held the piece of biscuit out to the pup, it pranced forward nervously and took it from her fingers. As it chewed the mouthful, she stroked the top of its head gently with a finger; then when it didn't object, she ran her hands over its back and sides.

"You're a handsome one," she crooned. "I think I'll take you home with me. Do you want to join our company?"

She lifted the little animal into her lap and scratched its belly. "Not handsome, I see, but pretty. That's good. It will keep the balance on the female side."

Kathe stood awkwardly, still holding the pup while favoring

her arm. "I'm sorry about your mama," she said in the same
gentling voice, "but I almost was your dinner. This is a much
happier ending to the story, for me, at least. Now what shall I
name you?"

33

A Secret Shared

"KNOTHOLES AND CROSSGRAINS!" PATRICK broke into a trot as he rounded the corner and caught sight of Kathe standing in the street outside Leonides's house. Her back was to him, and she seemed to be struggling with something in her arms.

"I thought you were resting," he called from a distance, scanning the street beyond her. He had believed the wild dogs would not enter his master's old home. He hadn't thought it necessary to warn the others to stay inside.

His voice startled her, and she tightened her grip on the pup, causing it to yelp in protest. She spent a moment soothing it before she turned to greet Patrick.

"This little one woke me up. She was looking for milk, but I think she's old enough to be weaned. Do you agree?"

"Hmmm," he mused, scratching the pup's ears to an enthusiastic response. "Do you really think you need another animal in your life? At least the others look after themselves."

Kathe shot a startled glance into his face and then busied herself with the squirming puppy.

"Let me guess. They made you promise you wouldn't tell. That's what they always do. Well, you haven't told. I guessed."

When Kathe still didn't answer him, Patrick continued. "The

stag is a friend of mine from the old days here in Pallas. When I worked the wood, he helped me to find straight walnut trees in groves that needed thinning. Later, after I picked up the sword, he led me and my comrades into my first and last battle. I'm assuming, since he used to move so easily between this world and the dream world, he must have known he was leading me close to death. He never had much to say, but I'd like to ask him about that."

After a moment he continued, "Some of the people in Pallas would have felt lost without their animal guides. Our most important family advisor was a rather pompous owl."

Kathe stared at him.

"Ah, I see you have met him, too. We need say no more about him or the others now. But I know them, and after all we've been through in the past few days, I'm beginning to think they remember me."

Kathe shifted the puppy's weight, and it licked her chin. Thinking to ease her injured arm, Patrick took the animal from her. It was fat and heavy. Kathe remembered the day her journey began, when Meg guessed her secret. She felt the same kind of relief now.

"Perhaps we can discern their purpose together," she said hesitantly, "I have been following blindly. At first I thought it possible that we found you by chance, but I wonder. Ever since that hour, it seems they have been leading me – first to Pallas and Mabus, and now?" She gestured towards the house, "Do you know anything about the paintings? The animals keep watching me, as if they are waiting to see what I'll do next."

Patrick looked thoughtfully at the familiar façade; he supposed the house now belonged to him. He said wryly, "You don't have to figure it out. Ask them. If you do, then at the most unexpected and inconvenient time one of them will appear with an indecipherable hint for you."

Kathe smiled uncertainly. "I'm not sure I'd have any sense of humor if I arrived back in the Three Hills more than a hundred years after everyone else left. This must be awful for you."

Patrick looked into the distance, "Yes and no. Having Mabus helps. I always thought I'd come back from the battle. I just didn't think it would take this long. And it would be worse if I were alone."

The pup began to whine; Kathe took her back into her arms where she immediately settled down. "Her name is Rowan. I have always liked the feel of the word on my tongue, and it was at about this time of year that I used to go with my mother to collect rowan twigs. We hung them around the doorways of the house. I know it will be my job to protect her at first, but later she will protect us."

She cupped one of the pup's paws in her hand. "Based on the size of these feet, she will be formidable."

There was a rustling, and Meg emerged from behind the honeysuckle bush. The side of her face was creased from sleep. She managed to yawn and look worried at the same time. Gale followed her closely.

"I wish you wouldn't go off like that! When I opened my eyes and you weren't there, I thought I was back at Springvale."

"She rattled my bones shaking me awake," Gale said, "and I wasn't all the way back before she dragged me to my feet."

He didn't sound annoyed. Just amused.

Meg caught sight of Rowan. "Oh, sweet!" she exclaimed and rushed forward to begin the round of scratching and petting (from the human side) and sniffing (from the canine) that makes up a complete introduction.

"Is this the whelp of the bitch that sliced your arm?" Gale said doubtfully.

"The very one," Kathe said lightly. "Gale, meet Rowan. She

will be joining our company."

"That ought to confuse the Claymon! Three become four become four with a dog. Pretty soon it will look as though they are tracking a whole village."

She had never really forgotten, but Gale's words restored the urgency his tale carried.

"We had better take stock of our supplies and pack to leave early in the morning," Kathe said, "If the woods runners are as good as Patrick says they are, it won't be long until they guess we're holing up in Pallas. And, as Gale has said, it won't be easy to cover our tracks when they do. Patrick…it looks as though your story will have to wait."

He nodded. It was just as well. He hadn't decided which combination of truths and half-truths would most satisfy her.

34

HUNTING

THEY MADE A SOUP out of the remaining scraps of food, sharing with Rowan. Starting tomorrow, they would have to hunt and forage in earnest. Gale suggested gutting one of the dogs from the street and cooking the meat even though they had been lying in the sun all afternoon. Kathe said the flies had been busy around the animals, but that wasn't the real reason behind her reluctance. No matter how hungry she was, she didn't want to eat the mother while the pup looked on. But it wasn't reasonable or fair to the others to deny them fresh meat. In the end, when Gale decided the animals were too far gone, she breathed a sigh of relief. He and Patrick dragged the carcasses far down the street so that they would not attract other predators during the night ahead.

Despite her long nap, Meg declared herself still bone weary. "For all I know, we still have days of walking ahead of us." She spread the blanket on the ground and lay down with her back to the group. "Talk if you want. It will be a lullaby to me."

The remaining three sat silently at first, watching night deepen and looking up at the stars emerging above wispy clouds. After a time, Gale asked Patrick a question about the geography of the forest, and soon the two of them were engrossed in discussing the old path to the Three Hills. Kathe listened for a time. Then she rose to her feet.

"I'm not going outside," she said when they looked at her questioningly. "I'm just going to climb the stairs up to where the roof used to be and look over the city in the moonlight." Gale stood as if he would accompany her, but she held out her hand to stop him. "Thank you, but I want to spend a few minutes by myself. I'll be perfectly safe. I trust the two of you to choose the best path for tomorrow. I won't be gone long."

Gale looked at the dark, low opening as she disappeared from sight. "Lady Katherine has secrets," he said.

"We all have secrets," Patrick replied.

"Speak for yourself!" Gale said.

Once she left the small fire, her eyes adjusted quickly to the darkness, and the moon and star light were enough to guide her back up the stairs to the second story of the house and then to the narrower stairway that once led to the building's flat roof. When she reached the top, she settled herself on the edge of the wall and kicked her legs over the side, waiting quietly. The street below was a dark abyss; she tried to imagine torches being carried by revelers returning to their homes – or more likely at this early hour, beginning their round of the city's taverns. There would have been the cry of a child, the barking of dogs.

Long ago, Patrick walked through the rooms of this house every day. She had figured out that he was a woodworker, one of those who made wonderful things from the trees growing around Pallas. How old was he when he last sat at his workbench? Twenty, twenty-three? Then he became a soldier, and now Mabus continued its work of drawing him back into the world. Why? What was Patrick in the here and now? Neither warrior nor carpenter. Something else?

Rowan had taken a strong liking to Meg. When Kathe left the chapel, the pup lay curled in the curve of the girl's belly. It should have been harder to win the pup's trust. Even the offspring of her father's hunting dogs, raised within a busy human compound, were warier of people than this little one. It used to take at least three visits to the kennels to lure them into her lap.

She was about to give up and go inside when she felt the silken brush of feathers against her cheek. Though she had been hoping for it, even expecting it, the touch startled her, and she nearly fell backwards into the building.

"Hey, I can't fly, you know!"

The owl landed on the wall near her and made a noise that sounded suspiciously like a chuckle. Weren't owls supposed to be serious birds? There wasn't enough light to see him as anything more than a shadow, except for the occasional sparkle of starlight reflected in his eyes.

"*Welcome, Flame Child, to the city of Pallas,*" Oro said formally.

"Actually, I've already had my welcome – from a pack of dogs."

"*Yes, we heard about that,*" he clicked his beak in a gesture that might have been irritation or sympathy. "*Many travel with you...a crowd, a hoard.*"

"Three – and now a pup," Kathe corrected.

"*Three is many. It is difficult for the little ones to find and cover every sign after so many. If they miss even one, the silent ones will find it.*"

"The silent ones?" Kathe asked. She remembered something Patrick said earlier in the day. "Do you mean the Woods Runners?"

Oro did not answer. After a surprisingly comfortable silence, he said, "*We are not gods, but in this place we were gods. Do you understand this?*"

Kathe thought for a moment and then said, "I think so. The

people worshipped you. Treated you like gods?"

"They captured us in paint. Small pieces of our spirits still are trapped here, but we have learned how to use the walls as a place to rest. Long ago, people left things inside the edge of the forest. Things we couldn't eat. When we didn't eat these things, the people came back later and ate them themselves."

"How very odd," Kathe murmured, wondering why the owl was telling her all this.

"We were always near, but the people acted as if we were far away. Almost no one really listened when we spoke. A few, Youngest Boy for one, heard our words, and we tried to help them. Even though we aren't gods, we know things."

"I've noticed."

"When we saw the jinx grow into manhood, saw him settle in and grow strong, we told the people who would listen. We said everyone must leave. The jinx could take the stone city, but we didn't want it to have the people. We liked being treated like gods. If the bad one won, then it would want to be the god. You understand?"

"Not exactly. I thought few would listen."

"That is true, but those few were enough. Most people didn't listen to us, but all but a few believed those who did, and nobody wanted to be left all alone here. The few told everyone, and they decided to leave. They followed the leader of the city who had already gone far away. They decided to go just for a short time, until the jinx gave up and went somewhere else."

"So they just loaded up everything they could carry and left the city?" This seemed far-fetched to Kathe. She wondered if the owl was telling her the truth. It would take more than the rumor of evil to send the citizens of Ostara packing

"Yes. We promised we would tell them when it was safe to return. It took a long time, but at last the bad one faded like grey smoke and blew away. We tried to find the people, but they had crossed the water. We forgot to tell them not to do that. And now they no longer remember the way home."

Kathe wondered who Youngest Boy was. Oro talked as if she should know. To him she was Flame Child, so Youngest Boy must have been a real person – one of those who listened to the animals' warning. The animals had led her to Patrick and to Pallas. Was Patrick Youngest Boy? He didn't seem like a boy to her, but then, she didn't feel like a child.

It worried her that the animals hadn't shown any interest in what was happening to her kin within the Three Hills. Now that she thought of it, she couldn't remember them ever acknowledging her desire to return home.

Kathe woke from her thoughts, realizing that Oro was waiting for her to say something. "That's sad," she said, wondering what his story had to do with her.

"Yes, very sad. We have been very lonely."

"We will be ready to leave the city at sunrise."

"That is good. The silent ones have not forgotten this place. They still come here sometimes. When you leave, follow the river in the sky until Maraba tells you to turn away. Tell Youngest Boy to watch closely for her."

Well, that answered one of her questions, at least. "That makes sense," she said. Truthfully, she was relieved that she could follow someone else for a while. "How many days must we travel before we reach the Three Hills?" she asked.

Oro suddenly edged away restlessly. He listened intently, then spread his wings and swooped into the street. It happened so quickly that Kathe could barely follow his motion. A moment later he flew past her carrying something small and frightened in his talons, but he did not return to the wall. She watched Oro flying away to the north – low over the ruined city.

She sighed. Had he left because he saw the chance for a meal or because he did not wish to answer her question? Gingerly, she eased back over the wall and felt for the stairway with her toes.

35

Divided Loyalties

THE GRIZZLED WOODS RUNNER had been waiting next to the door of his house all afternoon. Before his son left the clearing early that morning, they had enlisted the help of the few far-flying birds that were not busy raising second broods. In the morning, Patch helped Marion to cut the remaining venison into thin strips for drying, but now he watched alertly, wanting to be watching when the first of the other Runners appeared. He hoped he wouldn't have to act alone. Even though they lived mostly solitary lives in summer, the Woods Runners gathered in winter, and they depended upon one another in a crisis. He knew he wasn't alone in thinking there had been a lot more trouble since they started scouting for the Claymon.

He wished he knew what was going on inside the city, but it didn't occur to him to go there. There had been a steady scent of smoke all night and into the morning, and the birds would have told him if anybody left.

There had been some news. The two women had found the aquifer pool, but they went right back inside the city. The man who was missing had returned. That was one less worry, not that it made him feel any better. They still had to figure out how they could please both the Ancients and the Claymon, and that wouldn't be easy.

The day was fading when Patchson and five other Runners appeared from the shadows. Marion had already brought two bowls of stew outside so that she could eat with Patch while he waited. Now she went back inside and returned with the whole cooking pot. Without greetings or thanks, the newcomers pulled bowls from their packs and filled them. After Patch had finished his first bowl and while they ate their second, he told them everything he had seen, little as it seemed to be in the telling. Then both silence and darkness fell again over the clearing and the little house.

Finally one of the younger men spoke up, "We won't be able to decide what to do. There aren't enough of us."

Patch feared this was true. More than half of the Runners were hunting and tracking for the Claymon army, either along the forest road or in the Hills. Others, who had disagreed with the alliance and who had no desire for gold, had disappeared into the forest months ago. He doubted they would have come back even if his message reached them. Only this remnant and a few others even knew about the red-haired girl the Northerners wanted to find. Fewer still knew about Patrick's waking. Now the two of them, the runaway girl and the boy the Runners had sworn to protect, traveled together.

A second voice spoke out, "There's nothing we have to decide. We already made our choice when we agreed to scout for the Northerners. Unless we want them as enemies, we have to give them the girl, or bring them to her. The Claymon don't know about the boy – don't even know he exists. The Ancients can have him," the man spat expertly towards the edge of the clearing.

The first Runner spoke again. "Grayn is right. You keep following 'em, Patch. We'll tell the Claymon we know where she is and bring them after you, follow your trail, make enough confusion so the Northerners can take her. Then everything will be easier."

No one spoke again for a long time. Patch couldn't see anything wrong with this plan, yet it made him uneasy. If the Lady had chosen this girl to awaken the apprentice, wasn't there a chance she was under her protection too? No one had seen the Lady in a long time, and that was fine by him. He didn't want to be the one to bring her back angry. At the same time, the Claymon were all too real, and the Runners could only keep the secret so long. If they found out that Patch and the others had known where the girl was almost since she left Springvale – well, they'd stop paying the gold, and chances are they'd make the Runners pay in other ways.

After a time, the silence in the clearing became an agreement. All the Runners except Patch and Patchson melted back into the trees. Marion was last to enter the house for the night, and when she took a last look at the stars, she saw a dark form glide across the clearing and wing away above the trees. *I won't tell Patch about the owl*, she thought. *He has enough on his mind.*

36

ALONG THE AQUEDUCT

DURING THE NIGHT, THICK clouds blanketed the city. The rain they carried smelled like moldering leaves. Even though Fall was still weeks away, this change in the air reminded them of its inevitability. The refugees from Springvale had become so used to the series of sunny days that it came as a surprise and felt like a betrayal to awaken after fitful sleep under wet blankets and cloaks. Patrick found the dampness didn't add much to his own discomfort. His bones were still slowly thawing, and Mabus was a reassuring, warm presence at his side.

Meg tied the blanket she and Kathe had shared to the outside of her pack. She hoped it might dry by nightfall – or at least the dampness would not spread so quickly through her other possessions. "We spend the night inside for a change and wake up soaked to the skin," She muttered grumpily.

"If you ever get a chance to choose between a roof and walls," Gale said in a surly tone, "pick a roof. What good is complaining?"

Like most people, Meg didn't like to have her faults thrown in her face. She and Gale finished preparing for the next stage of the journey in stony silence. There was nothing to eat, and the fire was drenched. The four were ready to go before dawn.

Kathe lingered in the chapel after Gale and Meg crawled through the doorway on pretence of adjusting the shoulder strap on her bundle one more time. She whispered Oro's instructions to Patrick. He nodded.

"You've got to trust them," he said. "Either that, or don't listen at all."

They decided to stop at the aqueduct pool in order to refill their water skins, and it was there Patrick spoke up.

"I've been thinking. I know we talked about using the old trade road, Gale, but during the night I remembered something. You tell us the Woods Runners are tracking for the Claymon, and the Claymon are sure we're heading for the Three Hills, so if they follow us to Pallas, maybe they won't think of the old trail by the aqueduct. The city used to maintain a good path next to it so it could be repaired quickly. It doesn't lead anywhere, really. And until we choose to turn away from it and cut cross-country, there will always be a steady source of water. It will take us north as well as the other, but it does curve slightly away from the forest road."

"After what I saw, that isn't a bad thing," Gale responded.

What a smooth liar, Kathe thought. When it finally came time to hear the tale of Patrick's history and adventures, she wasn't certain she would be able to pick out the true parts. And Oro hadn't told her about the curving road. It seemed as though every path the animals chose headed in a slightly wrong direction.

Patrick also failed to mention the Woods Runners' legendary tracking skills this morning, though she was certain he had not forgotten. So far, they had taken only the simplest measures to cover their tracks. Surely the trackers could follow them without difficulty wherever they might go, despite the efforts of the "little ones."

They followed the aqueduct for two drizzly days. They couldn't lose their way with the ancient structure towering at their left hand, even though the old path was filled with brush. It was easy to see Patrick remembered the route, and even Gale was content to follow a guide who was so familiar with the lay of the land. As Patrick had promised, in certain places it was fairly easy to climb a stone support and push a small section of the aqueduct's stone cover aside in order to reach cool, sweet water.

On the other hand, the rain made walking miserable. They slept fitfully under wet blankets both nights and woke up aching with cold. Though movement warmed them and loosened their joints, the rest they had in Pallas was only a wishful memory by the end of the second day.

In fact, Kathe thought, that rest seemed to make the return to walking even more arduous. They were soon so worn out that it was difficult to be civil to one another, so they mostly trudged in silence. Gale snared two rabbits each day, and they cooked them over smoky fires at night, knowing that anyone nearby would know exactly where they were encamped and what they were having for supper.

Ever since Oro had asked her to learn the animals in the gathering circle, Kathe had become uncomfortable about eating them. Since meat was practically all they had to eat, she thought about the talking animals at every meal. She checked every rabbit Gale shot for the white streak that had identified the rabbit in the circle, but she found a dead creature bears little resemblance to a live one, and white streaks are common among rabbit kind. Then again, she wondered whether just not having met an animal really made eating it acceptable. Were there two kinds of animals: talking and ordinary? And, if so, what made it important not to eat the talking ones?

Walking gave her too much time for thinking. If her companions heard her sigh, they probably thought she was tired or in pain, but sometimes it was because she knew she must eat whatever Gale or Patrick managed to kill. If she didn't, she would soon be too weak to continue walking.

Rowan seemed content to follow, sometimes at Kathe's heels, sometimes at Meg's. It seemed she had forgotten her wild upbringing. Every so often one of the girls would scoop the pup into her arms and carry her until she became too heavy. This was as much to warm the bearer as to rest the pup. She slept between Kathe and Meg at night, against both their backs. For this service alone, they believed, she was a valuable member of the party. Also, she was the only one always in good spirits.

Massive, widely spaced tree trunks formed a colonnade at their right hand. Underfoot, the saturated leaf mould cushioned each step. In this ancient part of the forest, the canopies of huge trees starved the under story of sunlight except along and beneath the aqueduct, where the thick brambles had recently borne a large crop of berries. Deer and Bear had tramped and stripped the canes. The trees sheltered the travelers from some of the wind and wet, but they were in no mood to be thankful as the way gradually steepened and a mixture of rain and sweat trickled between their shoulder blades.

Whenever they stopped to rest, they could hear the gentle murmur of water flowing through the covered aqueduct. It provided a background melody to the percussion of water dripping from leaves and puddling at their feet.

Meg was day-dreaming at mid-morning on the third day when Patrick stopped abruptly. She had been following the brown, water-stained breadth of his back in a kind of forest trance. When she ran into him, she grabbed his arm in order to regain her balance.

He steadied her, glancing over his shoulder at Kathe. "As you know, it has been many years since I have wandered these woods," he said, "but I have found them little changed from the days of my youth. Up ahead, another half-day's journey would carry us to the hillside where the Mother Spring bubbles from the rocks. We could go there and climb the range of nameless hills above the source. From there, for a time, the way would be trackless. I have never been in that part of the forest."

He is lying again, Kathe thought with admiration.

"But with each step, my memory has become clearer. I have just recalled yet another ancient path that skirts the base of those hills, back towards the northeast. If we can trace it, it will connect us with the trade road. That road was once so traveled that time cannot have completely obscured it. Coming upon it from this direction, we will be able to watch for signs of recent use. I have some of the Woods Runners' skills, and I have seen that you are also a skilled tracker, Gale."

Kathe studied Patrick's face. If she had not been watching for the big cat's shadow all morning, fearful that Patrick would miss the sign, she would have believed his story. His brown eyes were guileless, his demeanor relaxed, and the direction he would lead them was appealing, especially since it avoided more climbing. Except he wouldn't be the one leading them, she reminded herself. It would be Maraba.

She had been walking behind the others that morning, slowed by Rowan's antics. The pup kept stopping to explore fascinating scents in the dense undergrowth. These inevitably drew her into the forest where she disappeared behind fallen trees – just long enough to waken a seed of panic in her mistress.

Kathe had finally picked Rowan up, thinking to quicken her pace and catch up with the others, when Maraba boldly appeared at her side. She met the cat's green eyes in shock before turning away to make sure the others hadn't noticed. In that breath, and before Rowan could even whimper, the panther had disappeared. And then, unbelievably soon, she appeared again on a branch arching over the path just ahead of the group.

Kathe gasped. Even though partially screened by leaves, Maraba would have been clearly visible to Meg and Gale if either of them had happened to look up. Luckily, they both were staring at the ground ahead. Now they all stood in a bedraggled circle considering Patrick's suggestion.

"Is that the sun trying to peek through?" Meg asked hopefully just before a sudden gust of wind rattled the leaves, dumping more water into her already streaming hair. A rattle of thunder in the distance answered her.

Meg's comment and the rumbling thunder struck Kathe as funny for some reason. Maybe because it closely mimicked the rumbling of her stomach. She and Meg had been foraging along the way, thinking to collect a few leaves, berries and roots to eat along with rabbit that night, but most of the little they found went directly into their mouths, and Gale had had no luck hunting so far.

Her first journey through the forest when she and Abel came to Springvale now seemed a luxurious holiday even though it was winter then. Their packs had been full of food, and she and Abel were warm and dry every night by a blazing fire.

To her own ears, her laughter sounded loud and inappropriate. The others looked at her, worry in their faces.

"The rain has to stop sometime," Gale said curtly, "and my feet long to walk on a proper road. Let's go."

The party formed a single file again, following Patrick, except this time Gale walked behind Kathe, at the end of the line. Before they moved on, he studied her arm for infection and insisted she drink a little from one of Patrick's precious bottles of wine.

Meg and Gale assumed Patrick was following a path. As far as they could tell, it had disappeared into the forest to all but his eyes. They trusted it was mapped in his memory. Kathe distracted herself from her misery by watching for the tip of a tail, a parting of leaves – the signs that marked Maraba's guidance. Now that the cat was certain she had their attention, she became much more subtle.

38

Ambushed

"**YOU CAN TELL US.** We're lost, aren't we?" Even though Meg attempted a humorous tone, her voice revealed the exhaustion they all felt. With no horizon in the forest, and with twilight only a gradual dimming behind the general grayness, it was impossible to tell even whether they had been heading in the correct compass direction during the hours since they left the aqueduct. As the daylight ebbed, they searched the dim landscape for any pile of rocks that might hide a cave or for a fallen, hollowed tree where they could at least get out of the rain for a few hours.

Gale had managed to shoot one small rabbit and a grey squirrel during the afternoon; it would be a lean meal. Despite her confusion over eating animals, Kathe's mouth watered at the thought of it. It would seem like more if they made it into a stew along with the roots in her pocket. She snuggled Rowan close. The pup sucked on one of her fingers and dozed in her arms, dreaming of milk.

"Lost?" Patrick repeated. "What makes you think that?" He gestured ahead at the forest in the general direction they had been heading. The place he indicated looked exactly as tangled as in every other direction, but Kathe thought she saw two green eyes peering through the undergrowth at them, like two unnaturally green leaves. "The path is clear."

"Maybe to you," Gale said grudgingly. "But with neither sun nor stars to guide you, how do you know you are really going toward the road?"

Patrick's back straightened. The soldier in him had heard a hint of mutiny. He paused before answering. The fat drops falling from the leaves sounded percussive. "I am certain we are on the right path, and we will reach the trade route early tomorrow. Will you follow me that much longer? If we don't find the old road by midday tomorrow, we will make another plan."

And what might that plan be? Kathe wondered.

"The sun has got to appear sooner or later," Meg said. "I have no doubt we will keep ourselves alive until then." She glanced at their dinner dangling by a string from Gale's pack. "We've come too far to give up now. We have got to find out for sure whether this way will lead us anywhere. I can wait one more day. But I tell you, when I see a wide blue sky at last, I am going to just lie back and stare at it. You won't be able to move me."

Kathe wondered what Patrick was thinking. She was sure he had no more idea where Maraba might be leading them than she did. He pretended certainty about their destination, but he was only following a shadow – a shadow, moreover, that had no comprehension of human needs. Maraba probably didn't understand about human hunger or their need for rest any more than their inability to leap up a cliff like a panther.

Was Patrick's trust greater than her own, or was he starting to believe his own lies? She reminded herself that they were following a man who, except for the last few days, had been bound under a deep enchantment. Here were more questions to think about while walking. It was important to her that she understand this enigmatic stranger, but she didn't seem to be making much progress.

In order to shorten the journey the next day, they decided to keep going almost until full darkness. Meg fell back and took

Kathe's cold hand. Even Rowan seemed exhausted. She had lost her interest in play and followed quietly at Kathe's heels. The men ahead of them lost definition and became grainy shadows.

"Be patient, little one. Soon we will stop, and we will share a bit of the coney with you." Kathe stooped to stroke the pup's silky ears.

As she stood up, a branch brushed her face. It felt wrong. She touched the leaves and then bent again to pat the ground. Standing, she peered over her head, searching the few openings in the thick forest cover.

"Stars!" she exclaimed. The others stopped, turned. They must have thought she was raving again.

"Look! Stars!" she repeated, pointing upwards. "The leaves are dry. The ground is dry. Back there," she pointed into the darkness behind her, "it is still wet. Only a few steps away – wet. Now dry!"

She hoped they would get the message. She was too tired to say any more, let alone to figure out what the change might mean.

"Some tracker I am," Patrick said wearily, but with a hint of the amusement Kathe had been missing. "I didn't even notice."

Gale picked a fallen branch from the ground and broke it with a dry snap. "It is almost dark, and this spot is flat enough to sleep. The wood is so dry that it will burn fast. We'll be cooking over coals in no time." He sighed deeply. "Just a little less misery, and already I am nearly content."

Meg and Kathe began gathering tinder and small sticks to start the blaze while Gale skinned and gutted the squirrel and rabbit. Rowan lay near him, watching every move.

Patrick didn't help them. He stood tensed, looking intently into the forest. He had not yet put down his pack. On other nights, when they decided to make camp, he was the one who dragged large branches to break for feeding the fire through the night.

"You couldn't have led us any farther in this darkness," Gale said over his shoulder.

The growing blaze illuminated the small clearing, obscuring all but the brightest stars. Kathe tended the fire while Meg wrung blankets and cloaks and hung them over branches. Kathe paused in her task and looked at Patrick inquiringly. He gave a tiny shake of his head and shrugged. After another moment, he leaned his pack against a tree and began to drag a large fallen branch towards the fire.

Kathe felt in the top of her pack for the cooking pot. She intended to make what she called "forest tea," a more or less bitter concoction of leaves, bark and berries of any plants she knew were not poisonous.

Her mother had often prescribed variety in diet in order to prevent or heal some of her patients' ills. In winter she often sent them back to their villages with baskets of dried or fresh herbs, fruits and vegetables from the glass houses. It was a season when many common people consumed nothing fresh or green at all. When Kathe had asked her about it, worrying there wouldn't be enough of her favorites to last until spring, her mother had replied shortly, "You can't grow a strong tree in poor soil."

In her search for firewood Kathe had noticed a Sassafras bush. The spicy fragrance caught her attention when she bruised a stem. Their hot drink would actually taste good for once. She kept this information to herself as a small surprise. She wanted to see how long it would take for the others to notice the unmistakable scent of the brewing leaves.

She had just poured some water into the pot and nested it into the fresh coals next to the fire when pandemonium erupted. The fire flared as debris fell into it from above. Earsplitting snarls assaulted her ears, both from the branches swinging violently overhead and, even more deeply and loudly, from the direction she thought of as behind them, the path they had walked for so many hours.

There was a split second of paralysis; then every hair on her arms and on the back of her neck stood straight on end. She grabbed Meg's hand, dragging her closer to the fire. In a breath, Gale and Patrick were beside them. Mabus flashed from his scabbard with a metallic scream.

The cacophony swelled. Kathe strained to see what might be hidden in the crashing branches above them. Surely Maraba couldn't be making all that noise by herself! Then a fluid black shape dropped from the tree and, still snarling, advanced towards them. Gone was the teasing, tricky panther that licked Kathe's face and talked of the world of dreams. In her place was a nightmare creature. Maraba looked as if she was ready to devour them all. The bloody, skinned rabbit lying near the fire held no interest for her. Gale and Patrick pushed the women behind them and prepared to fight, but the big cat crouched just out of sword range. Her muscles rippled. As she inched forward, they took an involuntary step back.

They had all seen cats hunt. She was preparing to leap upon them. When next she opened her mouth, the sound that emerged was like nothing any of them had ever heard before. Maraba's nearly human scream tore their breath from their bodies.

"Run!" Patrick yelled, pushing the girls away with his free hand.

Meg stood frozen in place. It wasn't fear that rooted her. It was a strange calm. This was the end. There was no point in running. She waited.

Meg was aware of Kathe dragging on her hand, begging her to come, not understanding the foolishness of running away from something that could move through the forest as smoothly as moonlight. She pulled back, trying to break free.

The animal did not leap towards Meg as she expected but took one more step forward, crouched low, and screamed again. This time the sound drove Meg a step or two towards the edge of the clearing despite her determination.

"She's warning us! Run!" Kathe yelled.

39

BATTLE

AT LAST, MEG UNDERSTOOD. She stumbled as Kathe pulled her towards the safety of the darkness away from the clearing. Shouts mixed with the snarling of animals as men ran into the campsite, their short blades drawn. They must have encircled the camp and waited for their moment. Now they attacked from every direction, including straight towards Kathe and Meg. There was no time to count, but Meg thought there were at least twelve.

Kathe twisted aside, but the soldiers were faster. One of them grabbed her arm and threw her to the ground. Kathe screamed as the man's fingers tightened on her wounded wrist. When she slashed up at him with her knife, he relaxed his grip long enough for her roll away and struggle to her knees. By the time Meg pulled Kathe to her feet, the man was yelling for a comrade to help him.

Now it was Meg who pushed Kathe towards the safety of the darkness beyond the clearing. Someone took hold of her braid, pulling her back. Though she had no weapon, she struggled wildly against her attacker, hitting and scratching. She had seen the blood-red linings of their cloaks; it was the color on the Claymon standard.

Kathe's knife darted again, and Meg's attacker let go of her hair. Two more steps. They had almost reached the cover of the forest. Three men circled, trying to capture, not kill, the girls. The girls also circled, facing the Claymon as if in a desperate contra dance. Kathe's short weapon was no match for a sword. If the Claymon had wanted them dead, they would already have been killed. A battle raged only a few steps away, but the men paid no attention. They had their orders.

A few of the Claymon carried both swords and oil drenched torches. They thrust the ends into the small fire where they ignited with a sound like wind.

It was as if no time at all has passed since Patrick's first battle so long ago, when he fought with John Daine at his back. During the long years, Mabus had never forgotten what he must do. Now Gale stood back-to-back with him, doing the best he could with the battered old knife he had been using to skin the rabbit that was to have been their supper. His bow was strapped uselessly to his pack on the other side of the clearing. He couldn't have used it at this range anyway.

In the split second when the attackers came yelling from the cover of the trees, Patrick and Gale exchanged a look. That single glance carried their agreement. If they had the time or peace to come up with words, they might have said they agreed to fight to gain some time for the girls to get away, but once the blows started coming, this goal was distilled to the simple, primal effort to stay alive.

Patrick quickly felled his first opponent with a thrust to the abdomen. The Claymon were not wearing chain mail. Maybe they didn't expect their victims to put up much of a fight. Or maybe they were counting on surprise to protect them. Maraba had foiled them there. Now she fought nearby, but three soldiers encircled her, swinging their torches in arcs and leaping in to slash at her glossy coat.

Gale's agility made up for the length of his blade. He ducked and dodged his opponent's blows until he could hook one of the man's ankles with his foot. As the Claymon struggled to keep his balance, and with a cry of anguish and triumph, Gale slit the man's throat.

Patrick and Gale would have been overwhelmed at once were it not for the animals fighting alongside them. Maddened by the blazing torches and the scent of blood, a big, grey wolf pulled a soldier down from behind and was itself felled by a Claymon sword. Patrick saw the wolf fall from the corner of his eye, but just as when the Ostaran killed John in that first battle, he could not turn away from his own private fight to help. He howled in anger as he blocked the blows of a seasoned Claymon warrior.

When a fourth soldier joined the group surrounding Meg and Kathe, the men decided to risk Kathe's knife and separate the girls. One targeted Meg, pushing her roughly so that she fell out of the circle. A second advanced on Kathe. When she retreated, a third man attacked her from behind, gripping her elbows and twisting her arms back. Kathe screamed as she dropped her knife, and Meg writhed forward and caught it as it hit the ground. Still kneeling, she began jabbing at the kicking, hose clad legs of the Claymon. Finally, overwhelmed by kicks and covered in the blood of the soldiers, she huddled in a ball and covered her head with her arms.

At the scream of the panther, once so dreaded, she peeked up. The big cat had leaped upon the soldier who was holding Kathe. He never saw the instrument of his death, but Maraba's attack made the other men stop kicking Meg and confront this new foe. Kathe had fallen to the ground close by and was lying on her side.

"The cat has given us another chance," Meg muttered to herself. She stood painfully and helped Kathe to her feet.

Together they covered the few remaining steps to the edge of the clearing. There they crouched behind a fallen tree and tried to see what was happening back at their campsite.

Torch flame danced frantically around the clearing illuminating first the grimacing face of a wounded Claymon, then the flashing of swords as Patrick blocked a blow. Meg clapped her hands over her mouth as the light caught Gale narrowly twisting aside from a sword blow. She swallowed the scream that had been trying to force its way out and felt it at the base of her throat. Its pain rivaled the bruises from Claymon boots.

Close by, Maraba crouched before the party of men that had been trying to capture them. The torchlight caught the panther's eye shine and the gleam of blood on her sides. Tears poured down Kathe's face. When a torchbearer ran over and began swinging the fire in front of the panther, a grey shape separated itself from the melee in the center of the clearing and knocked the man down. In an instant, the wolf stood next to the panther, but another torchbearer appeared. A sword flashed toward the dazzled animals, striking the wolf on its head. Kathe hid her face it her hands. She had never seen or even imagined such horror.

Gale choked on an acrid mixture of burning hair and smoke. He had wounded a second Claymon, but it had been at the cost of his knife, which was wrenched from his hand when the man fell back. Now he used a thick stick from their wood pile to block the blows of still another foe. How many were there! The sword buried itself in the wood, wrenching his shoulders but giving him a crucial moment of control before the next strike. Patrick's sword still rang out behind him. It almost sounded as if it was singing.

He risked a glance towards the edge of the clearing. Good. The girls seemed to have disappeared. He and Patrick would have at least made that small purchase with their lives. Gale was not afraid, but he was sure of two things. He was not finished fighting, and he was going to die. Only the moment of death remained uncertain.

His current opponent's eyes widened, and the man staggered back as if Gale had wounded him. Then he turned and ran. Gale spun around and there, standing in front of Patrick, was the biggest bear he had ever seen. It seemed to tower to twice his height, and its mouth was open in a roar. Its teeth were as long as his fingers. The Claymon who was fighting Patrick still had not seen the bear, though he must have heard it. He continued to strike as if Death was not looming over him.

When the bear swiped the Claymon soldier aside with one enormous paw, Patrick pushed Gale away from the fire and yelled, "They're battle mad! They'll kill us."

Ducking and dodging their attackers, who were now fully occupied with fighting Maraba and her companions, Patrick and Gale dove out of the clearing and into the cover of the woods close to the log where Kathe and Meg were hiding. Reunited, they ran for their lives heedless of direction until the sounds of battle faded. Then they paused, heaving for breath.

When he could speak, Gale's fear made his voice squeak. "What were you about back there? Why didn't you run at once? You almost got yourself killed!"

Kathe felt Meg's fingers tense around her own as the girl's panic shifted to anger. "What's it to you? I wasn't clinging to you was I? For that matter, why didn't *you* run? I know well that your heels have a mind of their own. They used to have *wings* when your mother and father wanted you at home."

Gale gasped.

"And what was I supposed to think," Meg hissed furiously, "when that black demon screamed at us? Hey," she said, her voice going flat. "What made you think it was screaming 'run' anyway?"

"I don't know," Patrick said honestly. "I've never seen her behave that way before."

Out of shocked silence Meg whispered, "You *know* this creature?"

Kathe decided the moment had come to snip this thread of thought before it raveled the fabric of their fellowship any farther. "We don't have time right now to explain, and this is not the place. We aren't far enough away from whatever is happening."

Night stretched around them like a cloak, but they could still hear the clash of the bizarre battle echoing out from the camp. She waited for one breath … then two. At last, as she knew she would, she felt a whisper of wind from familiar wings. "I think you know what we must do," she said to Patrick. "Lead us."

Gale sputtered a protest, but the others were already following Patrick as he began to trace a path through the woods after Oro. Kathe slipped her fingers around Patrick's sword belt, noticing the warmth there and the movements of the muscles in the small of his back. "Well, what did I expect," she muttered to herself. Patrick was becoming more real to her with each passing hour and less a frozen figure from the past.

She noted distantly that her injured arm was bleeding again and ached terribly. She peered back into the darkness but could not even see Meg's face behind her. Still, she knew any Claymon surviving the battle would find it easy to follow the trail they were making now. Meg held tightly to Kathe's sleeve. This meant Gale had to take Meg's hand. Otherwise they would certainly have lost each other in the darkness.

They had gone only a short distance when Kathe gave a cry and pulled back on Patrick, nearly toppling him.

"Rowan," she moaned. She couldn't believe she had forgotten!

His weary voice told her he had already thought of the pup. "There's nothing we can do now. Maybe she hid during the fight. Maybe she'll follow us, or we'll find her tomorrow. We will have to return and at least try to salvage some of our things."

Kathe knew he was right, but she couldn't lay down her guilt at adopting and then abandoning the pup. Rowan must be terrified. Her mother was killed just days ago, and now her new pack had deserted her too.

Meg's hand tightened on Kathe's again in sympathy. Or perhaps she was remembering her own treasure left behind – the wondrous book wrapped in a red shawl, and a golden case shaped like a bee hive.

Their awkward journey lasted deep into the night. Sometimes Kathe was certain she must be asleep and stumbling through a nightmare. During those hours, she didn't bother to wipe away the tears she shed. Her sorrow over losing the pup was the final drop in a cup that now overflowed with all the other losses of the past year.

The tears were still streaming down her face when the trees around them began to thin and the undergrowth became dense, halting their progress. This wasn't just the usual thick growth responding to the light at the edge of a forest like around the cleared areas at Springvale. Instead, a thick barrier rose before them. When they tried to push through it, thorns tore at their clothing and dug maliciously at their faces and hands. It was so thick that Oro was able to sit within a cleft in it waiting for their attention, like a feathered saint in his niche. His intention became clear when, as soon as he was certain they saw him there, he suddenly soared up and out of sight.

40

NEW ALLIES

FIVE WOODS RUNNERS STOOD in a tight group at one side of the clearing, directly opposite and as far as possible from the two Claymon soldiers, the only ones who had survived the battle. Their leader lay face down next to the dead fire, felled by the boy's sword. One of the Northerners sat on the ground and clutched a corner of his cape to his shoulder. His pale face made him seem like a ghost in the half-light just before dawn.

"What are you waiting for?" ordered the uninjured Claymon, taking command. "We have lost hours already. Get after them."

The Runners didn't move.

"I said, Go!" he shouted.

Still, the forest trackers did not obey, but silently watched the soldier expend the last of his energy in kicking a cooking pot as if it were a ball. It went an unsatisfying, short distance. He took a step closer and glared.

"I can't go after them alone, can I?" he said savagely, making a gesture that took in his wounded comrade the dead captain, and his other fallen comrades. It was supposed to be just the four of them alone. A surprise attack." All at once he sounded shocked and vulnerable, like the boy he truly was, "You never warned us.

You should have warned us…"

One of the Runners stepped forward and looked back over his shoulder as if seeking permission from the others.

"We agreed to track the girl for you, and we have done so this far, but we won't go any further. As for the animals, well, we didn't know they were protecting her, and now that we do know, there's nothing more we can do for you."

The Runner was speaking to just one frightened, young soldier, but he knew the boy would carry the message back to the other Claymon. "Tell your next leader that the Woods Runners expect the truth. We had a deal. We believed the Claymon when they told us we were tracking a girl who had run away from what was good for her, but now it seems there is more to it than that. Who is she?" He didn't really expect an answer. The boy didn't even know who the girl was. He had just been following orders.

The speaker and two other Runners turned and disappeared into the forest. Patch and Patchson remained behind. Patch gazed steadily at the young Claymon.

"Well, what about you?" the soldier demanded. "Why don't you run away like the other deserters?"

"We'll track 'em," Patch said. Patchson shot a surprised look at his father.

The soldier did not question the decision but took a long drink from a wineskin before offering it to his companion. It would take this boy a long time to make his way back to the main body of the Claymon force, especially burdened with a wounded comrade. When he spoke again, all his authority was gone.

"Why didn't you fight? When you saw there were too many for us, you should have helped."

"It wouldn't have made any difference." Patch responded levelly. "Besides, the Claymon pay us to track and spy, not to fight." He didn't tell the lad that the Woods Runners had never, in all their history passed down from mother to daughter, from father to son, taken up arms against the animal guides. It was simply impossible to imagine.

The wounded Claymon hadn't spoken in all this time and said not a word while Patch bandaged his shoulder more securely. He guessed this one wouldn't be a burden for long. While Patch was seeing to the wound, the boy opened the two closest packs and dumped their contents onto the ground. He knelt in the dirt, throwing objects over his shoulder. Patch guessed he was looking for something valuable. There wasn't much chance of that! He had seen enough of the young fugitives to know they had barely enough to keep them alive. Out of the corner of his eye, he saw the young soldier slip a large bundle into his own open pack. Well, he didn't begrudge him a souvenir. It would be a miracle if he even found his way back to the other Claymon to tell his tale.

Patchson waited until he was sure the two Claymon were out of earshot before he spoke up. "It doesn't make any sense, Da. We all agreed, even you! The Woods Runners are no allies of the Northerners, not any more."

"You're right. But sometimes a man has got to think for himself. Can five of us really make such a decision? A dozen or more of us Runners are traveling with the Claymon along the road right now, sniffing out anything along the way that might be interesting to their masters. Others are off on errands we don't know about – maybe don't want to know about. If we could tell every one of them what has happened, would they agree with us? Some of them love gold. They'd have a hard time giving that up. Your Ma doesn't care about the things gold buys. She told me when we were home that she'd trade all that gold can buy for a few more days with the three of us together."

"Then why do you want us to keep following them?"

"I said we'd keep tracking. I didn't say we'd keep tracking for the Northerners. The alliance is broken, at least as far as I'm concerned, but we'll keep following the girl and the others. If the Claymon think we're doing it for them, that's good. Maybe we'll learn something we can use to help her. And there's Patrick. I was one of those who looked in on him over all those years when he was in the cave, but what was the danger there? Now he has woken up into a world of trouble, and I'm guessing the Lady still sees him as my responsibility."

Patchson looked at his father in awe. Woods Runners didn't make plans like this on their own. At least not until now.

"If we get the chance," Patch continued, "We'll introduce ourselves to the girl and offer our help, and I'd like to have a talk with the woodworker's apprentice too – one where he does some of the talking, I mean. For now, we'll just keep an eye on 'em."

41

REFUGE

KATHE WAS SURE ALL four of them had seen the Great Horned Owl fly over the hedge and out of sight. She glanced back at Gale. She couldn't see his face, but she knew he was waiting for an explanation. That he was not asking for one worried her.

They released hold on each other and dropped to their bellies. Then they began to worm their way through the hedge towards a brightness they glimpsed, or maybe just suspected, ahead of them. Kathe had suggested that there wouldn't be as many thorns close to the ground, but she had to force herself to wriggle forward against the needles scratching her back and arms. She was sure Patrick's chain mail had been left behind in his bundle back in camp. Too bad for him. At least the ground was dry here. She paused to catch her breath and scented the earth's loamy richness. It was cool against her cheek. When she continued, the thorns seemed fewer, and the passage between the trunks of the bushes a little wider.

When they emerged on the other side, they stood with the stiffness of old men and women and squinted at the sudden brightness of a simple, open night sky. When they could finally tear their attention from this marvel, they saw that the only garments that had resisted the thorns' shredding were Gale's leather jerkin and both men's sturdy leather boots. All their other clothes looked like a mending woman's nightmare. Their arms and faces were streaked with blood, but based on the condition of their clothing, the hedge let them off lightly.

Kathe remembered how it was when they stood on top of the cliff by the waterfall, how they fell into each other's arms from the sheer joy of surviving the climb. Now, after crossing to safety again, they stood aloof from one another, except for Meg, who still clung loyally to Kathe's hand. There were too many secrets between them. If their positions were reversed, Kathe wasn't sure she could be as trusting as the dark haired girl now leaning her head against her shoulder.

What did Meg think of her – of the guides? Did she think Kathe somehow commanded them, had power over them? What would she say if she knew it was the other way around, that Kathe followed almost blindly? She sighed. The truth would have to come with the new day, promise or no promise.

Once their eyes adjusted to the starlight and to the pale glow of the moon, they began to notice more details about their haven. Patrick bent and rubbed his fingers in the springy growth under their feet and sniffed. Kathe scented the herb even though she stood several paces away from him.

"Lemon thyme," they exclaimed in unison.

"Look," Meg whispered.

Far away, but straight ahead of them in the clearing, she had been the first to see a dim light. It was so out of place after all they had been through that they just stared at it dumbly.

"It's shaped like a window," Gale finally said. "It looks like there's a candle in a window over there."

"Impossible," Patrick said, but there was no conviction in his voice.

"We should be careful," Gale said. "It could be a trick. A candle in a window always *looks* friendly, but who knows what hides behind it."

"It could be danger," Patrick said.

"It could be a Woods Runner outpost," Kathe suggested.

"It could be warm beds and a hot meal," Meg said, stepping forward boldly. "That's what it is, I'll wager."

The others trotted to catch up with her. As their feet crushed the plants, a delicious fragrance filled the air.

"Remember how Cook would put a touch of lemon thyme in a sauce? It made the toughest mutton taste like spring lamb," Meg said.

A few moments later, the fragrance changed. Gale practically groaned, "It's basil. After winter, do you remember? The first green salad with a few basil leaves?"

Kathe said wearily, "If you're trying to make me hungry, it's too late."

Her spirit had lifted slightly since entering the clearing. The temperature here was delicious. There was a hint of coolness and moisture in the late summer breeze. The plants beneath their feet were lush enough for sleeping, but the rectangle of light irresistibly lured them.

Trees once again appeared around them, but they were small. They seemed to have been planted in straight rows and circular groves.

"Pears," Meg said, "Ripe ones." She picked one for each of them, explaining that they ought not offend whoever was waiting ahead of them in that house by helping themselves too liberally to his fruit. The sweet, sticky juice trickled down their blood streaked chins as they climbed the small slope in front of the house.

Finally its shape loomed before them. It was no mansion, but neither was it a mere hut. It looked most like a cottage, with two levels. The only window blessed with a candle was the one they had seen at a distance, but now they could see other lights inside. Smoke from its chimney curtained the stars in a small part of the sky.

As they approached, a cat darted forward to greet them, eliciting a curse of surprise from Gale. As it braided itself around their ankles, Kathe found herself close to tears again, but not from sorrow this time. The cat meant home. Its purring was a homey sound. When she bent to stroke it, its silken coat was a tactile reminder of safety. Kathe wanted nothing more than to sit for a whole day by whatever fire was making that streak of smoke, holding this particular cat on her lap.

"I'm hoping you are right in your guess about this place," she told Meg.

"Oh, I am," Meg replied. "I have a feeling."

"You and your feelings," Gale said, but his voice carried some of its old teasing tone. Something between them had eased.

Patrick was silent. When they came to a low hedge of lavender where the stone walk to the front door began, he crushed a stem in his hand and breathed deeply. Then he shook his head as if he was trying to clear it or as if he was having an argument with himself.

He said warily. "One of us should approach the house alone. Even if the person who lives here is not dangerous, he's likely to mistake us for thieves."

It was true. After days of traveling in the rough and rain, it would have been a gross compliment to call them merely bedraggled. Blood still oozed from the deep scratches on their arms and faces, and they carried nothing at all with them. Kathe had to admit she would think twice before inviting such rough looking characters into her house. Her mother, she thought wryly, would have thrown the door wide even as she called over her shoulder for supplies.

"All right," she said. "Who, then?"

Gale shifted uneasily. "Since you and Patrick have been keeping some important facts to yourselves, maybe you know where we are and who might be behind that door." He stood defensively next to Meg.

"I'll go," Kathe said, smoothing her tattered dress and tangling her fingers in her hair.

"No, Gale's right," Patrick said quietly. "You are a stranger here, and new to the ways of the guides, but I ought to know this place."

"Do you?"

"It is impossible…" he said, his voice trailing off as he started towards the house.

Kathe, Gale and Meg, stepped to one side of the path. Just before he came to the door, Patrick paused under an arch leaning slightly under the weight of summer roses. Their scent mingled with that of the lavender. The sweetness permeated the shadows where the three waited. Patrick cupped one blossom in his hand and stood very still.

He had just raised his fist to knock when the door flew open and an old woman stood haloed in the opening. Patrick stared into her face, then stumbled back over the low stoop. When the woman whispered a few words, Patrick leaned forward to gently cup her chin, and he looked into her face just as he had looked at the rose a moment before. Then the three saw him enfold this tiny person in an embrace, lifting her feet from the threshold as he buried his face in her shoulder.

"It looks like he trusts her," Gale said.

He would have left the shadows then, but Kathe held his arm. "It's a reunion. Remember how it was when Meg met her mother?"

"Who is she?" Meg asked. "Maybe it's his grandmother."

They waited patiently until the two figures in the spill of lamplight separated. After another whispered exchange, Patrick called them.

"Come on. Meet my little sister, Bethany."

42

IN BETHANY'S HOUSE

"THIS STORY JUST GETS stranger," Gale muttered.

Now that they were closer, Kathe could tell the woman wasn't as old as she first seemed. She might have seen sixty years. It was hard to tell. There were lines around her eyes, but her blue eyes were bright, and her generous mouth curved in a welcoming smile. Her figure was plump in the way a good cook's is plump, and she stood straight, giving an impression of strength.

"I always told my brother he should make some friends," she said. "I am glad to see he has finally taken my advice."

Gale lagged behind the two girls. Meg dragged him forward by the hand, and they followed Patrick and Bethany into one of the most welcoming rooms any of them had ever seen. A collection of pewter glowed on the mantle above the stone fireplace. Colorful rugs warmed wide floor boards. In one corner, a stairway led to the upper story, promising sleep. Near the fireplace, a round table was set for five, and something bubbled and sizzled in a pot over the flames. It smelled wonderful.

The lady of the house stood waiting expectantly. Someone had to take responsibility for the introductions even though she seemed to know exactly who they were and had even been expecting them. Kathe looked around the room with curiosity, but her face was drawn. Her arm was hurting again. Patrick had fallen silent after his ebullient reunion with his sister. Meg stepped forward, "I'm Meg, just Meg. This is Gale, son of Lord Stefan of Springvale and his gentle wife Irene, and this," she said, "Is Lady Katherine Elder of the Three Hills."

"Ah," said their hostess in a warm, quiet voice. "Welcome Meg, and welcome to you Katherine. We have met before, though you will not remember it."

"We have?"

"It's Pammy, Old Pammy," Gale blurted. In the moment of awkward silence after his outburst, he recovered his composure and said more politely. "You seem familiar, ma'am. You remind me of one who cured my mother of an illness and taught me plant lore."

"Yes, welcome Gale. I have been waiting for you. I have been waiting for all of you for such a long time." She turned a radiant smile upon Patrick, and he gathered her into his arms again. "I've missed you so," she told him.

Without further delay, Bethany led Kathe to one of the benches by the fire. The others looked on as Bethany unwrapped her arm, probed it gently and examined it close to the light. Kathe's skin was smeared greenish brown from the herbs Gale had applied, and her arm carried some new bruises, but the stitches had held, and the edges of the wound looked pink and healthy.

"You remembered what I taught you, I see."

"Forgive me," Gale said, "but you seemed so much …older when last I visited you."

"I expect you will have many questions," she said. The room fell into silence as each of them pondered this understatement. Before they could open their mouths to begin asking, however, she continued, "I will answer them all. But before that, baths, breakfast, and sleep."

Kathe nearly groaned out loud at the thought of immersing herself in warm water. She and Meg followed Bethany up the stairs and into a tiny bedroom just large enough for two beds and a large tub of steaming water. Fresh clothing had been neatly arranged across each bed.

"These gowns were mine when I was a young girl. They are very old, but they were made by a gifted seamstress, and the cloth has held up well. I think they will fit you."

Kathe fingered the supple, sturdy looking fabric. "Thank you, Ma'am."

Meg looked down at her own tattered clothing. She wouldn't like to see Cook's face if she saw the best servant's tunic now!

Kathe tested the water with her fingertips. She looked up in surprise. "The temperature is perfect. How did you know we would arrive before it cooled?"

"Questions, questions. Is that really the question you most wish to ask? And is the answer to any of your questions as important as the bath right now?"

Kathe had to admit the answer to that question was no.

"I will show the men their room. When you are finished, come downstairs. Breakfast will be ready then."

Kathe figured it must have been long after midnight when they came to Bethany's house. By the time each girl had taken her turn in the deep tub of water that somehow retained its warmth, the stars had long since turned towards morning. Patrick and Gale were already clean and downstairs by the fire again by the time Meg and Kathe had dried themselves with big rough towels and had found the wide-toothed comb their hostess had left on the small table by the window.

They untangled each other's hair and took turns with the silver mirror that matched the comb. Kathe wasn't sure whether Lady Irene owned such a precious object. Meg didn't think so. Kathe had not seen her own image in a year, and Meg had never seen her own face. She thought it did not look right, somehow. Large, dark brown eyes stared back at her. They looked bruised. She fingered the black hair curling around the heart-shaped face.

If she ever thought about how she looked, and it wasn't often, she had hoped she looked like her mother. She guessed that was right. This is probably how her mother's face looked when she was a young woman.

The clothes fit well, as far as they could tell. The style was new to them, wrapping around to form a fitted bodice, with three metal clips at the side. Someone had embroidered flowers and vines along the edges that crossed in front and formed the V shaped necklines. The hems brushed the tops of their bare feet even though Meg was a hands breadth shorter than Kathe, and they could have sworn that their hostess was shorter than either of them. In fact, the two garments were identical, except for color. Kathe chose the deep green gown, leaving Meg the one she liked best, which was dark blue.

At last, clean, dressed, and unconscious of how much time had passed since they entered the bedroom, they hurried down the stairs, leaving their damp hair to finish drying over their shoulders. They found Gale slumped awkwardly in a corner of the settee, fast asleep. The cat lay across his lap. Patrick and his sister stood by the candlelit window in quiet conversation.

Bethany turned to them as they entered the room. "It was thoughtful of you to give us some time alone. After all these years, our meeting came as quite a shock to poor Patrick, though I have been hoping for it since late last winter when I became aware that you were traveling to Springvale, my dear."

How had Patrick's sister known she and Abel were making their way to Springvale? Ah, that was one Kathe could answer herself. The animals must have told her. But their hostess couldn't have foreseen Kathe's decision to run home, couldn't have known she and her companions would stumble upon Patrick's watery cave – or that they would figure out how to awaken him – could she?

Bethany was regarding her with an enigmatic expression. "Breakfast is ready," she said. She blew out the candle on the windowsill, and a square of pale light appeared on the floor in front of the window. The sky was brightening with dawn.

Meg nudged Gale awake and settled onto the settee next to him. Patrick and Kathe sat on a bench on the other side of the fire, and Bethany took the chair at the end of the table. She took Patrick's hand and bowed her head for a moment. The others did the same. It had been days since any of them had paused to be thankful before a meal, though they certainly had felt thankful enough for anything Gale managed to shoot.

Breakfast was plentiful and delicious. There was warm bread with butter and honey, an egg pie from one of the hearth ovens, sausages sizzling on a platter, and from the kettle, stewed fruit – apples and some of the ripe pears from Bethany's orchard.

Soon the combination of the warm bath, a full stomach, and their apparent safety made them all very drowsy. Kathe thought Patrick was the only one who truly belonged here. It was as if the rest of them had traveled back through time to meet him at his proper age. His damp hair curled against the snowy collar of his open-collared shirt. He seemed younger to her than at any time since they first met. Perhaps it was because he now had been given a context, however unlikely. He had both place and family. She knew Patrick had been sleeping during those missing years. What had his sister been doing?

No one asked anything during the meal. They were too tired. Or maybe they knew the answers would be too complicated to understand in their present state. Eventually, as the light grew in the room, and they pushed their plates away one by one, Kathe felt something like contentment. It would be all right. They would rest for a few hours, and then they would sort it all out.

Their hostess rose and began to scrape the plates. Kathe slid out from her place on the bench to help with the clearing of the table, but Bethany motioned her to a cushioned chair by the window.

"You have already helped more than you know. We will share

many more meals, and later we will share the work. For now, you are guests. The same goes for you, Meg."

Kathe wasn't sure she understood the implications of Bethany's words. How long did she think they were going to stay? She sighed and waited for the moment when she could climb the stairs again to that cozy bedroom. Surely it must be coming soon. She would draw the curtains to shut out the day, and when she woke up, there would be time for all the answers and explanations before they set off again.

Before sitting down at table, Patrick had unbuckled Mabus for the first time since recovering the sword, but it was leaning close at hand. His hand closed around the hilt as a scratching at the door brought him to his feet. The grey cat leapt across the table, upsetting a cup, and disappeared up the stairs in a blur.

The scratching persisted as Bethany hurried to the door. "Thank goodness," she said. "I was afraid I was going to have to send you all up to bed before he got here."

Patrick placed a restraining hand on her arm. She looked back at him questioningly. Then firmness crept into her face and voice. "Trust me, brother. I am no longer the girl you knew. Do you think the thorns let you pass because you were clever?" She spoke slowly, enunciating each word. "They let you through because I told them they must. The scratches you bear are the signs of their reluctance."

He dropped his hand as though it had been burned but stayed just behind her when she threw the door open.

Their visitor leaped over the threshold. Meg cried out as a huge grey wolf headed straight towards the chair by the window where Kathe was sitting. He appeared to have something in his mouth. As Gale struggled to climb over the bench, Bethany stepped in front of Patrick. He had instinctively raised Mabus and would have beheaded the creature.

"Think!" she commanded. She stayed in front of him until he lowered the sword to his side again.

After her first cry of surprise, Kathe wasn't shrinking back in her chair. In fact, she had fallen forward to kneel in front of the visitor who had dropped a wriggling bundle in her lap. The bundle was trying to lick her face.

"Lupe chose Kathe to be his pup's new mother," Bethany said softly. "He was very concerned when they were separated."

Patrick watched in amazement as the big wolf allowed Kathe to scratch him under the chin as she thanked him over and over for returning Rowan.

"They never let me do that," he muttered.

"If you will excuse me," Gale croaked, "I need to sleep." He disappeared up the curve of the stairway.

Meg rose from the table and stood next to their hostess. She would have liked to have welcomed Rowan too, but she was afraid of the wolf. He turned his enormous head at her as if he could read her thoughts. There were streaks of blood on his face and muzzle and along his side. One ear had been nearly sliced off.

"He is hurt!" she exclaimed.

"He has been in battle," Bethany said sadly.

She put the dish of sausages on the floor and half-filled a bucket of water. She took Rowan from Kathe and held the pup up, examining her for injury.

"Dirty and tired. Otherwise unharmed."

Meg took Kathe's arm. "This all feels like a dream. And around here, it might be important to be able to tell the difference. Let's go to bed."

43

IN THE ORCHARD

KATHE WOKE SQUINTING AGAINST a vivid sunrise leaking through the cracks in the shutters. Red and purple tinted the whitewashed walls of the room. Sunrise? No. It must be sunset. She had slept the day away. Her first night in a real bed since fleeing her own bedroom in Ostara had been a day.

She stretched luxuriously, smoothing her hands against the softness of well-worn linen. Then she propped herself on her elbows to investigate a heaviness across her knees. It was Rowan. The pup instantly raised its head, ears alert. She seemed to be saying, "It's about time." Without waiting for more encouragement, Rowan wriggled up towards Kathe's face.

Kathe discovered that she wore a soft, loose, nightgown. Where had that come from? The clothing she had been wearing at breakfast hung on a hook in the corner of the room along with a soft, web-like shawl. Meg was still asleep, so Kathe dressed quietly and slipped from the room and down the stairs.

The house was deserted, but there were signs of cooking. A bowl of vegetables was on the table, chopped and ready to be added to the pot of broth hanging over the fire. Someone, presumably Bethany, had covered bread and a bowl of soft cheese with a towel and left them on the table. Kathe helped herself and stood near the window, sharing pieces with Rowan and silently chewing, washing the bread down with a mug of warm goat's milk. The grey cat lay curled peacefully on a cushion in the chair by the door.

In between returning for mouthfuls, Rowan explored. After a couple of minutes of snooping in corners and under the table, the pup noticed the cat. In her eagerness to see this strange creature more closely, she knocked over a low work table next to the chair and then, frightened by the noise, she hurried to the safety of her mistress's side.

Kathe knelt on the floor and began collecting the bright silks, needles, and thimbles that had fallen out of a wooden box. Its clasp had come loose when it tumbled to the floor. She replaced everything neatly in the container and held it up in front of the window to see whether it had been damaged.

It was cunningly made, with smooth, curved corners and an oiled finish. Kathe heard the clasp click into place as she gently closed the lid. A shape stood up from the top in relief. Kathe ran her fingertips across the satiny finish and held it in the rosy light. A face she knew stared out. Maraba. With a guilty look around the room, she lifted the lid again. The items inside were all ordinary tools of a well-to-do housewife, but on closer examination, she saw that someone had carved a graceful "P" on the front inside edge of the cover.

She closed the box thoughtfully and placed it in the center of the little table again. As she did, she caught sight of their hostess outside. She was in her orchard picking pears into a basket slung over her shoulder. The sun glinted on her silvery hair.

Kathe slipped outdoors. She could finally see the extent of the clearing. It wasn't as large as it had seemed the night before. In fact, by day this open space in the forest looked less like a small farm than a large garden. A few goats gamboled in a wooden enclosure. A cow and a half-grown calf grazed placidly near an open shed. Fences kept them from eating all the cabbages and carrots and the pole beans that climbed in a riot towards the sky in the vegetable garden. She didn't understand why the grass within the animals' pens looked so fresh and green. By this time in the year, surely the ground in such small spaces should have been trampled to dust.

The orchard where Bethany harvested pears was also smaller than it had seemed the night before, but in addition to pears, Kathe could see there would soon be apples. And earlier in the summer there must have been cherries. A few spiny fruits Kathe did not recognize still hung withered in the upper branches of an unfamiliar tree.

It was an ordinary scene, even comforting – a woman taking advantage of the last daylight. Nearby, a house with a fire and a cat. Preparations for supper underway. Kathe looked more closely. A flock of sparrows pecked in the grass around Bethany's feet. More perched in the branches of the pear tree, fluttered around her hands, and two sat on her shoulder as if they contemplated making a nest in her hair.

"Can I help you?" Kathe asked quietly. She was trying not to startle Bethany, who seemed intent on her task.

Without turning, the woman replied, "Can you help me? Oh, my dear, you have no idea what you are asking!"

She chuckled and faced Kathe. "Oh, you mean with the harvest. Certainly. Take a basket." She indicated a second wicker container that had been left leaning against the trunk of a tree.

Kathe began picking the firm, green fruit, enjoying the slanting light, choosing the moment to ask her first question. In the end, Bethany broke the silence.

"The chapters of the story that hold all four of you, I will save for when we are all together again. It began long before you were born, and for all I know, it will continue long after your grandchildren tell it to their grandchildren. I have lived long enough to know most stories are never really finished."

She flashed a sideways smile at Kathe. "It is all so tangled that

I am having some trouble separating the strand that is Kathe's alone. Still, I will try to do it, and you will see how it is plied with my own."

She ducked under the heavy branches of the tree, sat with her back against the trunk and patted a spot nearby, inviting Kathe to join her.

"As you know, I am Patrick's little sister. I was very lonely after he left our house to begin his apprenticeship."

Seeing Kathe's questioning look, she said, "Oh, he has not told you about himself? That doesn't surprise me. Patrick was always the quiet one in our family."

"From the time we were very small, Patrick bore the taunts and abuse of our elder brother, Honorus. We say he had a cruel streak. He would have called it a strong sense of duty. With our mother sick and our father preoccupied by her health and the work of running the city, he took it upon himself to discipline his brother. It's what finally drove Patrick from the house. He was drawn by Leonides welcome and by his promise of teaching, but it was Honorus that drove him. After Patrick left, Honorus turned his attention to me. By the time I was sixteen, I could barely remember what it felt like to be happy or free, or a time when my mother was not an invalid. As her health failed, my father became unwilling to leave her side. Honorus must have been about twenty-four then, and almost all the council business fell to him." The sunset was behind Bethany, and she gazed up into the cobalt sky as if she were looking into the past, sorting out the details she needed to share to make the story complete.

"From an early age, I was always free to come and go; children were much indulged in Pallas during my girlhood. As often as I could, I went to the school. It met two days each week under very old trees in the square in front of our house. As you saw, we were great builders in stone, but it was our tradition to school children outdoors. If the weather was foul, everyone just stayed home."

"Girls weren't supposed to join in the classes, but the teachers tolerated me so long as I sat silently at the edge of the shade. Some of the teachers were citizens of Pallas and taught the skills of craft and business for which we were famous, but others came from far beyond the forest to teach history and geography, languages, even the folk stories of places beyond the forest. After Patrick left, Honorus convinced my parents that I already had too much education. He told them it was time I stayed home to keep our mother company and to learn how to manage a household."

Kathe grimaced in sympathy.

"Honorus often told me that, when it came time for him to take our father's place, it would not be as the leader of a council. He would be a prince. And when he was, he would see that I made a suitable alliance. We forest people never had thought of extending our influence in any way except by trading the beautiful things we made in our city. Whenever Honorus talked about it, he would reach out his arms as if his reach already extended far beyond the forest."

Bethany paused, "I see by the wrinkle between your brows that you do not see how you fit into this story. Be patient, my dear, and you will see how our two lives have been knotted together."

"While Honorus plotted and planned to rule other cities, other cities had their eyes on Pallas. Perhaps word of my father's weakness and my brother's ambition spread outside the forest. It may have seemed an opportune time for an attack. Or it may have just been our wealth. We were hardworking people and had been well-rewarded for our skill." She paused before continuing. "A few months after Patrick made my little work-box, it happened. The animals told us, and the Woods Runners confirmed it. Soldiers had circled around the city and were preparing to attack us in a valley on our side of the hills. They were soldiers from the Three Hills, Kathe." She spoke flatly now, purposely ridding the words of any feeling, "Patrick went out to meet them. He died, or so we thought."

"I don't remember reading about that battle in any of the history books," Kathe interrupted. Rowan had become bored with chasing the birds and lay curled in her lap, eyes half closed.

"Though they seemed an army to us, the soldiers from the Ostara were only a patrol, really. Our men managed to chase them away, and the battle became little more than a hiccough in history. Let's see. Where was I? Ah. Many years later I learned that Patrick lived, in a sense, but when I heard the news of his death that autumn, I mourned him bitterly. And anger grew – that my parents seemed to have forgotten him – that Honorus mocked his sacrifice."

She sighed in frustration. "This story is even longer than I remembered. Perhaps there is another way." She placed both her hands on Kathe's shoulders, looked intently into the girl's face and continued, "A few months before the battle, a wanderer came to Pallas..."

The green leaves of the orchard swirled above Kathe in a sudden wind, and when it had passed, she found herself standing beside a street in the living city of Pallas with her back against a wall. Inviting benches framed the doorway beside her. The city glowed as warmly as she remembered, but now there were people in the streets. Women passed her, walking proudly erect. Some of them carried baskets on their heads or small, ornate packs on their backs. Others tightly held the hands of small children. Men stood talking in groups of three or four or walked and chatted alongside the women. Colorful awnings protected the open rooms she and Meg had believed to be shops. Business was brisk.

Kathe stared wildly in every direction. The orchard was

completely gone, and though there were many sounds – smells too – the gentle rhythm of Bethany's voice had disappeared.

A man stepped through the doorway and sat down on the bench closest to her, stretching his legs out in front of him and leaning against the sun-warmed wall. She gasped. It was Patrick, but Patrick without a trace of worry around his mouth, without the guarded eyes. Suddenly weak legged, Kathe sank onto the bench beside him. She could feel its solidness beneath her, but Patrick did not seem to notice her hand when she grasped his arm or to hear her when she urgently spoke his name.

Kathe closed her eyes and shook her head, hoping to clear this image and return to the orchard, but when she opened them, nothing had changed. What was she supposed to do? Was this Bethany's way of showing her a way to help? He had not gone into battle yet. Was there something she could do to save him?

Disorientation and panic made her suddenly nauseous. If she saved him, she would never meet him. His cave/tomb, assuming she ever found it, would be empty. Without Patrick, maybe Gale would have died when the ledge crumbled. Maybe the woods runners would have already caught them. She leaned against Patrick, breathing deeply, trying to regain her balance. The roughness of his homespun shirt and the warmth of his shoulder grounded her.

The dizziness was beginning to subside when she opened her eyes to see a woman about her own age running down the street toward them. This person stopped in front of the dozing Patrick and, with a mischievous expression in her blue eyes, she leaned forward and tickled him under the arms. Kathe found that, though he could not see or feel her, his elbow could send her crashing against the far end of the bench.

"What are you about, imp?" he asked good-humoredly.

"Father sent me to the city gate to watch for a visitor. You haven't seen a healer pass by here, have you? I guess he'd be wearing a long, grey cloak, and I'll bet he has a long grey beard to match."

"No, but I just came outside. Sit and I'll watch with you."

Kathe stood hastily, not knowing what would happen if this young, glowing Bethany were to sit on her lap.

"A message came this morning heralding his arrival; father has been waiting for weeks. The healer's gifts are rumored to be the greatest of this generation. Perhaps he will be able to do something for mother. Ease her suffering, at least."

Patrick became grave, "Is she worse?"

"Well, it has been a bad summer."

An unspoken rebuke lay between them. Kathe could see it as if it had wings and hovered in the air. Patrick turned away, and Bethany sat twisting the material of her skirt between her fingers.

"There's nothing you could do even if you were there, you know," she said finally.

He slipped his arm around her. "I am not so much a coward that I cannot pay a visit at least. I will come soon."

Bethany took his hand and squeezed it. "Ah, I think this must be our healer. He isn't quite what I expected."

A tall figure had just passed through the wooden gate and stood at the end of the street surveying his surroundings. There was no hint of haste or worry in his demeanor. He did wear the grey cloak, but instead of a grey head, he had unruly black hair. Grey eyes gazed calmly from a lean face. He looked too young to have attained his reputation.

Bethany released Patrick's hand and walked swiftly towards the stranger. By now many of the shopkeepers and customers in the square were also observing the interaction between the council head's pretty daughter and the stranger in healer's robes. Patrick could tell the man was aware of their interest even though he acknowledged no one until his grave face relaxed into a smile after Bethany bowed in greeting and spoke.

Patrick and Kathe couldn't hear what she was saying. Bethany gestured up the street in the general direction of her home and collared a young boy who was ambling past. She extracted a coin from her purse and pressed it into the lad's hand, at the same time indicating the visitor's small bag. Together, Bethany and the healer began to climb up the street with the boy trailing behind carrying a leather bag that, based on the lad's struggles, seemed to be much heavier than it looked.

Though still apparently relaxed in his seat on the bench, Kathe could see wariness in Patrick's face. It was an expression she had come to recognize in the more worn Patrick – the one who was her trusted companion. He watched the little group until they disappeared out of sight and then rose abruptly and went back into the house. She almost turned to follow him inside, but after a moment's reflection, she trotted up the street instead.

44

BACK AT THE CAMPSITE

PATRICK AND GALE AWOKE early in the afternoon. Actually, Gale woke first, but since he made no effort to be quiet, he and Patrick descended the stairs together and found Bethany sitting quietly by the window, sewing.

When they shared their plan to return to the camp and retrieve their gear if they could, she gave them a second breakfast. Then Bethany led them to the hedge and showed them the best place to pass through the thorns. Neither man mentioned waking Kathe or Meg even though both knew the girls would want to come along. The truth is, they didn't know what they would find and wanted to spare their companions more horror if they could.

It was easy to retrace their trail. Following Oro the night before, it felt as if they walked for hours to reach Bethany's house, but today it was only mid-afternoon when they reached the clearing. Along the way, they found three places where they had circled in the darkness before heading off in a new direction. Oro must have been trying to confuse the trail, leading the exhausted party a roundabout way.

The Claymon, assuming they had not all been killed, should have been able to follow them to Bethany's easily, especially with the help of the Woods Runners. There had been so much chaos in the clearing during the battle that Gale and Patrick could not agree about how many soldiers there had been, but they both thought at least five were still alive when they fled the clearing.

Gale kicked at the ashes of the fire with the toe of his boot, sending up a cloud of ash and revealing a glowing coal underneath. It burst briefly into flame. He and Patrick had approached the campsite cautiously, but it was deserted. Deserted by all but the dead, that is.

Four Claymon had fallen near the edge of the clearing where the girls had taken up their stand, and three others lay near the fire. They were all tall and light-skinned. Gale recognized their uniforms from the day when he had hidden, looking down on the road, afraid the Northerners would discover him. He found none of the slight, green-cloaked Woods Runners.

Gale stared down at the man he had killed in battle, wondering how he was supposed to feel. He had never killed anyone before. Even though he was going to Ostara, he never really thought about being in a fight or killing. He wondered who the man was and whether his family would ever find out what happened to him. If the Claymon had not come to Springvale, he would have hoped never to have to kill again. As it was, he didn't waste hope on something so unlikely. He guessed what he felt was sick, but also glad to be alive.

Nearby, another soldier lay on his back. His throat was torn, but the body was otherwise undisturbed. Gale wondered why no one had buried the bodies. A she-wolf lay in the clearing too, her mouth frozen in a rigid snarl. A knife protruded from her side. There was no sign of the big cat except among the confused prints in the soft earth.

Patrick parted branches and entered the clearing. "I found two more bodies," he said, "and an animal must have taken a bad wound, judging by all the hair and blood. No body, though."

"And look at this," he called. He had retrieved his own pack, which held his chain mail and his share of the other supplies. He had been inside the edge of the woods the night before when he took it off to help with the fire, and it was just as he left it. "Must be they found whatever they were looking for before they got to this."

Gale's bundle was intact too; even his bow was undamaged. However, Kathe's bundle had been dumped. Its contents lay scattered across one side of the clearing. Meg's had been torn apart. It looked as though someone had tugged at the knot securing her bag, and when it didn't open readily, they had ripped it, or maybe slashed at it with a knife, then turned everything out onto the ground. Whoever did it was working in a hurry. They had dug through her things, throwing aside whatever they didn't want.

Patrick and Gale worked together silently to pile the women's few belongings. The wet blanket and cloak Meg had been trying to dry lay filthy, trampled on the ground. The cooking pot had been kicked away from the fire. It bore a dent in one side, but they could still use it. Patrick dumped out a little liquid remaining in it and sniffed a leaf he picked from the interior. "Sassafras," he murmured thoughtfully. He discarded a spoon that had been flattened between a rock and a booted heel.

Gale untangled Meg's precious scarlet cloth from a thorn bush. Gale had watched her folding and treasuring it away each night of their journey. Sometimes she had fingered its edge to calm herself or to help sleep to come. Now it had one small tear. Gale carefully smoothed and rolled it before putting it in his pack. He searched through everything else on the ground and found the golden beehive hidden in leaf litter as if it had tried to worm itself out of sight. The book was gone.

"Patrick, look here," he called. "It looks as if two men left this way. They didn't even bother to be careful. They must have been in a hurry to get away. I guess we have the animals to thank for that."

"Can you blame the Claymon for bolting?"

"I can understand why they decided not to follow us to Bethany's without more help, but why would they take the book?" Gale asked. "Kathe's bundle was emptied too, but nothing else is missing as far as I can tell."

Patrick recalled Bethany's words just before they wormed their way through the thorns, "Whatever has been lost may be replaced. Except the book. We will have need of it soon." He didn't question her about the book's importance then. Now he wished he had.

"They were careless, maybe in shock. They knew they had to report back quickly. And one of them was wounded. See his uneven stride?" Patrick followed the footprints a short distance into the woods before returning to the clearing. "That will slow them both down."

"If the Claymon are looking for them to return with Kathe, they won't want to return empty handed," Gale said.

Patrick stared off in the direction the Claymon had gone. "Books are as precious as gold. Even more precious. I'm guessing the two Northerners took the book because it was the only valuable thing they saw here."

"What about the animals? Couldn't they have taken it?" Gale spoke slowly, as if trying out a new idea."

"The animals might have seen it when we had it out to look at the pictures, but none of them have much interest in the things we carry -- except the Jackdaw. He likes to steal scraps of metal to brighten his nest. And Oro collects words. He's the owl who guided us."

Patrick continued thoughtfully, "It doesn't surprise me that Beth knew we had the book. She's tighter with the creatures than my old master, Leonides, was. With all the reports they brought her, she knew we were coming before we did."

Gale saw where he was heading. "She's strange, all right…as strange as you, but it's clear she'd not attack us, and she didn't steal the book, either. She wanted us to find it and bring it back. Is there any chance the animals told the Claymon about Meg's book?"

Patrick didn't seem to notice Gale's insult. He settled himself on his heels by the pile of gear. "You have reminded me of a story from when I was young, and an apprentice woodworker. A rich Claymon lord once sent slaves to Pallas to have chairs made for his house. It was a journey of almost a month, but they boasted that their master must have the best and brought their own cart and oxen to haul them home. They were the largest, heaviest chairs I ever made and the most ornate – by the time they left, I made certain they were the most uncomfortable, too."

"Why is that?"

"I was young, and I guess I didn't like being told over and over how they were doing me a favor by letting me craft a place for their master to rest his royal rump. Leonides thought it was a good idea to take the commission, but he left the job to me. Every day the Claymon watched me while I was working, and an old friend of mine, a Raven, used to stop by the window to visit. I passed the time in crafting insults for the Claymon while I made the chairs. When I shared them with Raven, he was very appreciative. In fact, when I called them puddling ice peckers, he made a lot of noise and flapped around the room."

"So?"

"It scared the Claymon. I could see they didn't know we were talking to each other, had no ideas animals *could* talk or see the humor in a joke. They thought Raven was just a pet."

The two men finished collecting what could be saved of their belongings in silence. Everything stowed easily into their two undamaged packs. Gale understood the point of Patrick's story at once. The Claymon couldn't have known about the book, because they were deaf to the animals, and Bethany knew, but didn't steal it. It must have been taken as plunder, pure and simple.

The two stood staring at the gap in the underbrush through which the two Claymon had passed. Then they looked at each other.

"Are you thinking what I'm thinking?" Gale asked.

Patrick knelt again and began removing the girls' things from his pack, piling them neatly under a thick bush. After a moment, Gale crawled in beside him and added a few more objects to the collection.

"They won't begrudge us the cloak and blanket, but I doubt we'll have so much time on our hands that we'll want to take up knitting," he said, placing Meg's needles and wool on top.

"I could only find one of Kathe's shoes," Patrick said. "It will be of little use to her, but even less to us. What's this?" He dangled the golden hive by its short length of chain. Gale had put it onto the pile to leave behind.

"It held a seed that woke you." Gale recalled the radiance of the pearl as it performed its intricate dance over Patrick's sleeping body. His words felt inadequate. Patrick contemplated the hive for a long time and then stowed it in the bottom of his own pack.

When they finally straightened and turned around, Gale smothered an oath. Maraba was lying at her ease at the entrance to their intended path, licking a paw. It took several long moments for him to remember this creature had warned them the night before. *Warned us by nearly scaring us out of our skins*, he thought.

The big cat stretched lazily and rose to her haunches. Her glossy sides were marred by cuts crusted with blood, but she looked strong and self-contained. After his first, instinctive reaction, even Gale couldn't help being pleased to see her. Maybe she wanted his help. If so, he would have to find the courage to approach her. It was the least he could do after what she had done for them.

"What is she saying?" he asked.

"Nothing yet," Patrick responded shortly.

Maraba twisted in an impossible, cat-like way and licked her sleek shoulders, first one side, then the other. Finally she fixed her green eyes upon Patrick. *"You are planning to follow the fighters, yes?"*

"Yes."

She arranged her face into what could only be called a grin and boasted. *"I thought so. I am getting better at guessing what you will do next."*

"If we follow this path, what will we find?" he asked

"Tell Shaky Knees to close his eyes and listen with his skin. I want him to hear what I have to say."

Patrick repeated Maraba's words to Gale, including the name she had given him.

"Shaky Knees, eh? Is that to be my name from now on, or can I earn another? And what does she mean – listen with my skin?"

"First you have to make yourself quiet inside, forget being afraid, forget whatever it is you plan to do next. It's hard to explain, but I really do hear them through my skin and bones. It sort of echoes up to my brain. It gets easier. After a while you learn to listen whenever animals are around. You can even learn to call them."

"Why would I want to do that?" Gale said sulkily, but in contradiction to his words, he rested his pack by his feet and closed his eyes. *Here I am*, he thought.

A strange, tickling sensation began on the palms of his hands and spread up his arms. He could not make out any words, but it was pleasant, and he held his hands forward toward Maraba as toward a fire, hoping to increase the sensation. When the words finally came, his concentration broke. He had to begin again.

"This doesn't come easily to you does it? No. Not as it does to Youngest Boy and Flame Child. Yet you are willing to try. That is something."

Gale opened his eyes experimentally to find Maraba staring at him intensely. He snapped them shut again.

"This is the first time I have talked to two. It is against the law, but then, the law is already broken. You were not supposed to see us at all, Shaky Knees, but since we were sworn to protect all of you – and the book too – we were forced to choose. We are not used to choosing, or guessing. We chose to protect you. The book is gone."

"Where has it gone? Who has it?"

Gale heard Patrick's words the same way he heard Maraba's, a slightly rougher vibration, a deeper echo.

"Not the silent ones."

"Who then?"

"Not the Men from the snow."

"Who?"

"I cannot tell. It is a secret."

"I have never known animals to keep secrets," Patrick said.

"Like breaking the laws, it is something new. Some of the animals call Running Girl friend."

"Running Girl is what they call my sister," Patrick told Gale. The two men waited for Maraba to continue.

"Some are friends with another. But all animals are friends with each other. Even when we eat each other, we are still friends. And we keep each other's secrets."

"Ah. And if we follow this trail will we find this other?"

"I cannot tell."

Gale was getting better at this kind of listening. He was almost sure he picked up a trace of sulkiness in Maraba's last comment.

"Can you do this at least? Go to my sister and tell her where we have gone. We will follow the trail and try to return Meg's book."

"It is not her book."

"Then whose?"

"I cannot tell."

Gale heard irritated movement next to him. He opened his eyes and, following Patrick's lead, shouldered his pack. Without a farewell, Patrick turned abruptly and began to follow the Claymon's trail. Gale followed.

From behind them a few more words came. Gale felt them as warmth on the back of his legs. *I think that is what people call rude,* Maraba said.

45

IN THE DREAM WORLD

AT FIRST IT WAS hard for Kathe to keep Bethany and the healer in sight as they climbed the crowded streets of Pallas, but after a while, some of the stonework along the way began to look familiar. She decided they must be following almost the same route she and Meg took when they searched for water. Was that really only a few days ago, or had she somehow flown back in time more than a hundred years? Then, they had climbed the shell of one of these houses to use it as their aerial path. If she were to try that today, she would be trespassing.

The barriers between past, present and future had blurred. Kathe felt hollow, as if she had been kept awake for a whole night. Still, she kept following the fresh, young Bethany – a girl with exactly the same eyes and smile as the grandmotherly woman who sent her here.

Except for her bare feet, Kathe saw she was dressed much like all the other young women of the city. It wouldn't have mattered if she were still wearing her ragged dress, though. No one in Pallas could see her or feel her when she bumped against them. In the street's traffic, she was finding it tricky to stay out of the way of people who were not aware of her presence.

If Oro was telling the truth, then on this warm, late summer afternoon, all these people were still going about their daily work and pleasures, enjoying the sunshine, thinking of the animals as gods in the forest – if they thought of them at all. Yet they soon would abandon everything they had built and pass through their city's gate never to return. Why?

The man adjusted his stride to match the shorter girl's. As they walked, and the city's architecture became more elegant, the two stopped occasionally so Bethany could point out an especially venerable tree at the edge of a park or the fine carving above one of the fountains where water flowed and sparkled.

Kathe caught up with them as they paused at one of these fountains and dipped her hands into the cool water, splashing her face. She had been keeping her distance, following these two as if they were Bard and one of his friends, up to some mischief and trying to exclude her – except Bethany and the healer couldn't see her.

One thing was certain. Today this man had entered a living city, and not long after his arrival, the forest city was terribly damaged, even emptied. Bethany wouldn't have shown her these events if they weren't important. The girl interrupted a lively description of Palladian stone sculpting techniques and glanced over her shoulder with a slight smile. For an instant, Kathe thought Bethany was looking right at her. Her spine prickled as the sensation washed over her.

She flattened herself against the wall on the other side of the flowing water. One ear heard only the water bubbling in the pipes within the wall. The other strained to catch what Bethany was saying. "My mother has been ill…many years. She has not left the house, even on a litter, since I was a little girl. Unless you traffic in miracles, you will be able to do little for her. But hope is a great healer even if it must work all alone."

Kathe could not see the healer's face or hear his murmured response. The two continued along the street. The crowds of people thinned as they walked along. There were few shops in this part of the city. Based on the delicious aromas wafting from the doorways they passed, the supper hour was fast approaching.

Kathe shrugged off the feeling that Bethany had seen her, but she allowed a little more distance to grow before following again. Bethany might not have had magic when she was a girl, probably didn't, in fact, but something had happened to her later. And whatever it was had something to do with this lanky man with the kind face who had just bent to listen to her with such seeming respect and interest.

The pair finally entered a grand house. It was at the end of a street. Any windows in the back part of this house would overlook the forest, while the front faced a large public square. She sat down next to one of the Sycamores at the edge of this park and pondered her next move. It seemed her legs could still grow tired, even if she was just traveling in spirit or in a dream.

This was the largest tree of its kind Kathe had ever seen. Its greenish grey branches arched down gracefully, almost making a room inside. A *school-room*? Squinting, she peered through the leaves at the house. Unlike any of the other buildings she had seen in Pallas, this one stood apart in its own grounds. It was symmetrical except for a tower jutting upward from one of the rear corners. A kitchen maid in a bright white apron was collecting ingredients for dinner beyond a low wall that ran along the front of the property. She sang as she picked leaves from a globe shaped plant – Sage maybe? And what could that purple next to the walk be but Lavender?

Kathe struggled to her feet amid a storm of falling leaves. The breeze had shifted into a sharp wind and blew a swirl of yellow and gold around her feet. She glanced up the massive trunk again. She could have sworn there had been nothing but green there when she looked a few moments before, but now she could see patches of pale blue sky. The remaining leaves rattled in the increasingly cold breeze. She wrapped her arms around herself, then bent to pick up a piece of shed bark. She rubbed it reflectively between her fingers, scenting its spiciness.

Kathe walked up to the front door and tested the latch. It was locked. When she knocked, the same fresh-faced maid who had been collecting the herbs in sunshine opened the door to an autumn squall, looked around in confusion, and shut it again firmly. Kathe waited a few breaths and knocked again. This time she entered with a gust of wind before the maid could close the door.

A wide hall stretched before her. It should have been, maybe once was, welcoming. Her father's house had included such a generous room just inside its front door. It was the haunt of musicians practicing their instruments; noisy with the chatter of tradesmen and visitors waiting to see the master or mistress of the house; and further peopled by servants stopping in their work to flirt and gossip.

In contrast, this space was chill, empty, and nearly dark. A large fireplace at the far end of the room gaped neglected and cold. A little warmth and light came from a single brazier near the door. Kathe moved a few steps nearer to it to warm herself.

The servant who had unwittingly allowed Kathe into the house slammed the door and locked it, then wrapped her woolen shawl more tightly around her shoulders and hurried toward a door at the opposite end of the room. As she crossed the room, she muttered something about young busybodies, or she might have said she was too busy for such nonsense. Kathe couldn't hear clearly in this huge space. It swallowed voices as if it was hungry.

At least the maid had been able to hear her knock. The people who lived here would probably be able to tell if she tipped a chair or spilled the soup at dinner too. It would be an inefficient way to communicate, though. If she could find materials, maybe she could write a message, but what would it say? She sighed. She was only a visitor to the past, little more than a ghost. This was Bethany's way of telling her a story. Kathe still didn't understand how she and her family fit into it, but she did know she had to learn all she could about the people who lived here.

Darkness was falling too quickly beyond the two windows framing the heavy door. Squares of pale light fell through the glass and spread around her feet, then faded as if someone standing outside turned down the flame of an oil lamp. Even though she believed the changing season and the fading light were just more tricks of time, Kathe felt afraid. Well, not afraid exactly. More lonely. And maybe it was the loneliness that accounted for the heaviness. Her legs felt heavier than at the end of a long day of travel.

She had become used to moving in darkness, but until this moment in her journey, a friend had always been an arm's length away, or even closer. Each time she awoke in the night, Meg's and more lately, Rowan's warmth reassured her. Gale had exhausted his supply of jokes in the first two days of the journey, but there always was talk. He liked to share what he knew of forest plants and lore and to point out every new wonder he noticed along the way. Even when they walked in silence, his mercurial moods made it seem as if she had three or four companions instead of just two. Even the puzzle of Patrick's cave was solved by talking, she remembered. Darkness had been falling then, too.

Patrick. Even after regaining his sword, Patrick never said much, but she had come to treasure every word and expression that crossed his mobile face. When she sat down on the bench outside his workshop an hour or a season ago, she wanted him to turn and give her one of his half smiles. Then she would have been able to tell him everything, and he would have helped her to understand what she should do. She trusted his guidance more than the animals', but something told her that, like Patrick, they weren't here anymore.

She sighed. She had always intended to travel alone. There's no denying it would have been simpler. She should have been more than halfway home to the Three Hills by now. Surely if she had stayed off the road, but close to it, she could have evaded the Claymon patrols. *But what about the Runners?* she asked herself. *And what exactly did you intend to do when you reached Ostara? Knock on the door of home, kick Peter out, sound a trumpet to call everything back to the way it used to be?*

To her right, a door swung open, pushed by a chilly breeze that made the brazier flame dance. Candle light flickered in the draft and spilled out into the corner of the hall where she stood slowly freezing. Although she still believed in her invisibility, she looked for her shadow behind her and stepped to one side of the doorway before she peeked inside.

It seemed to be a small library. Wind rattled the windows and swirled the ashes on the cold hearth. A man sat at a table in the center of the room. His head was bent so close to the flames of the candles that it was a wonder his hair didn't catch on fire.

It wasn't the healer. This was a young man too, but he had sandy hair, meticulously cut and brushed. His shirt was white. Metallic threads in his brocade vest glinted in the candlelight. He was reading, and judging by his grimace, the material was either unpleasant or difficult to understand.

Kathe slipped into the room, tiptoed closer. When she was still a few steps away, she leaned forward and rested her hands on the edge of the table, resisting the urge to reach forward and run her fingertips along the silky surface of the page he was studying.

How could this be? Who could this be? It was impossible, but here was Meg's book, opened to the very page that had so fascinated Kathe the first time she looked into it. The fantastic animals flew, swam, and ran around the margin just as she remembered, encircling the map of the island.

The man looked up, frowned. Now Kathe guessed who

he must be. She had met both his brother and his sister; the family resemblance was clear. Bethany had disliked this person. Honorus? Maybe the story she had been told colored her vision and caused his face to look so cruel to her now. She shivered, wondering whether he sensed her presence. He got up abruptly, bumping her elbow, and firmly shut the door, turning the key and dropping it onto the table.

Although she was insubstantial enough to avoid notice, Kathe was not really a ghost with the freedom to ease through solid stone or wood. She supposed she could just stand near the door until he opened it again, but she believed she had to learn what she could quickly and return to the orchard.

She felt a faint touch of the warmth she left behind there and caught the scent of ripe fruit. She knew the other Bethany was waiting, anchoring her. Nevertheless, the heaviness in her body was growing. It was almost like dozing off. But if she fell asleep here and slept deeply enough, she might never awaken.

Her bare feet made no sound on the stone floor of the room. She moved to one side of the table to look more closely at the books stacked near the man's elbow. They were all bound in smooth, fawn brown leather, but no titles or decorations showed on the covers. Scraps of parchment with spidery notes fringed out from the pages. Honorus fished another large scrap from his pocket and began to scrawl.

Or draw. In curiosity, Kathe circled the table so she could look over his shoulder. He was sketching a copy of the map, dipping his quill into a well of black ink and adding its most obvious features. He whispered the words on the page, closing his eyes as if committing them to memory.

Kathe leaned closer. She had only opened the book a few times, but when she did, the pictures had so entranced her that she did not notice the tiny script written along the lower page edge, where it would not interfere with the decoration. Honorus didn't bother to sketch the pictures, but he wrote the island's name clearly across the egg-shaped land – Niue.

She jumped back when Honorus sat up and rubbed his neck. Kathe realized she had been standing there so long that he might have felt her breath. The wind rattled the window more loudly. It sounded as if rain was beating against the glass. She took another look at the page, noting a harbor at the more pointed, southern end of the island and a large mountain, or maybe a small mountain range, in the center. Then she silently loosened the window latch so that the next gust would blow it open.

The chill from the stone floor had already turned her bare feet to ice. Now it was climbing her legs. She stood first on one foot, then the other, trying to warm herself. This dress must have been sewn for summer weather. Finally, as she had hoped, the window flew wide, but as it did, one pane shattered, and any papers not anchored in a book flew off the table and whirled around the room.

It the ensuing storm of cursing, it was easy for Kathe to dodge the furious Honorus, borrow the door key from the table, unlock the door and return it without notice. If Honorus wondered how the door could blow open a second time after he had been so careful to lock it – well, it was very wild weather that night.

46

WINTER TO SPRING

KATHE STAYED IN THE shadows next to the door until Honorus closed it again, with a slam this time. The brazier in the great room still glowed dully, but the room felt even colder than before she went into the library. She started towards the fireplace and the opening through which the maid had disappeared.

She had walked only a few steps when a second door opened opposite the library where she assumed Honorus still was engaged in his secretive studies, but further along the room – closer to the fireplace. Again she glimpsed candlelight.

When an old man emerged, Kathe guessed it must be Bethany and Patrick's father. If so, he looked as if he carried a heavy load of trouble on his stooped shoulders. Kathe watched him walk slowly across the room and stop in front of the fireplace.

It was too dim to see clearly, and he carried no light. He seemed to be feeling his way along the wall above the hearth. The click of the catch securing the secret place was tiny, but it echoed through the otherwise silent hall. The man looked nervously over his shoulder before sliding a long, narrow drawer from the compartment. It only took a moment for him to pull something small from his pocket, slip it into the drawer and slide it shut again. Then, with another furtive look around – strange wariness to exhibit in one's own home – he made his way back to the side chamber.

Kathe followed him. She didn't know what else to do. She had never been good at finding and opening secret hiding places even when it had been a rainy-day game for her and Bard at home in Ostara. In those days, the game always was his idea, and he was the one who always turned up with treasures in the end.

This new room was much more comfortable and welcoming than the library had been. Icy pellets battered windows and glass doors opening to the garden, but no draft entered here. Bright, woven hangings covered the walls. In summer, with the doors opened wide, this space would be almost a pavilion. Kathe gratefully noted a bright fire in the small hearth. Its warmth was barely noticeable at the door, but its crackling drew her like a moth.

A child lay on a small bed next to the fire. Its face was turned to the red and gold flames. It watched them with unblinking blue eyes. It seemed to barely breathe, but the small body was so bundled in covers that Kathe couldn't really tell. When the man poured a glass of wine, the child turned, and Kathe saw it was a grown woman lying swaddled like an infant in the firelight. Her face was a page of fine parchment wreathed in the loose grey silk of her hair. The content of that page was suffering, but she smiled.

"My dear, are you back so soon?" she called softly. "What did Patrick say? Will he come with us?"

The old man hurried to her bedside. He took her hand in both of his own as if trying to warm it.

"You should be asleep," he said brusquely. "Tomorrow will be long, and the night is half gone."

"I may not survive tomorrow," she replied calmly, "but I had hoped to see my youngest son once more."

"Don't say such things! You are stronger than you think!"

"Yes, I am," she reassured him. "Haven't I proven it again

and again? So why do you keep secrets? You have been hiding something since before the first snow. Tell me."

The man seemed to weigh her words. He rose abruptly to stand by the fire with his back to his wife. Kathe moved so that she could see his face. It was expressionless.

"You heard the trumpets when our militia marched from the city. I told you how that battle was won and of Patrick's brave part in it. The servants kept you well supplied with gossip, I know. I couldn't prevent that, but I did threaten to turn them out if they said a word to you about him."

"What about Patrick?"

"He marched with the men of Pallas and fought bravely." Silence grew in the room like a malignancy. "He did not return."

She groaned as if she had received a physical blow. He knelt by the bed, taking both her hands this time.

"I did not tell you then because there was hope. Later, I searched for words but could not find them. They could not find his body. You know he would never have left his sword behind willingly. His friends returned it to Leonides. They had seen Patrick wounded, and after the battle they found the place where his blood stained the ground, but he was gone. There was no trail for them to follow."

"How is that possible? How was that hope?" she asked in a whisper.

Her husband did not answer. Instead, he began folding clothes that were piled on a nearby chair and stowing them in one of the three trunks in the center of the room. All their lids were gaping open.

"Marta can do that, or call Bethany," the woman said. "Come and sit with me." Her eyes were shining with tears.

"Marta is gone," the man replied. "As are all the others. Only Ann remains to do all the work of the house, and if she had not come here as an orphan – if she had anywhere to go – she would have left us too."

"I almost convinced myself that the quiet in this house was just the blanketing of the snow. I have little to do but think, and I admit I sometimes imagine phantoms, yet it seems you have hidden more from me than I could have dreamed," she said.

He sat on the chair by her bed again, his head in his hands. His wife propped herself into a sitting position with an effort and stroked his hair.

"I should have sent the healer away months ago," he said after a long silence, "but you are stronger than before he came – you know you are."

He lifted his head and his eyes reflected the firelight. From where Kathe was standing, he looked slightly mad.

The woman twisted the edge of her bed-sheet between her thin fingers. "I don't understand."

"Honorus says the people hate the healer. Some of them think he is keeping me prisoner. Honorus told me others believe I am holed up in the house plotting to become more than leader of the council. The people think the stranger is lending me powers I can use to become a king."

"How could they think such things? They are our friends. They chose you."

"Yes, they chose me to be the council head, but that was long ago. Perhaps I have kept myself too much to myself – and to you, my dear, these past few years. Yet there was no objection when I sent Honorus to take my seat at the council table. I left everything to him, and from the start the people looked to him for guidance despite his youth. You know I don't often go out into the city these days, but when I do, I can see it is true. People go out of their way to avoid me."

"I finally cornered Brian Mar the day before yesterday, and he told me in as few words as he could that I'm a stranger to him now. He told me that when I speak, it is with the healer's words, except he called him a mage. He couldn't wait to get away from me! A few of our old friends look on me with pity. Pity! They still trust Honorus completely, but they all believe I am under the stranger's spell."

"What foolishness!" she exclaimed in a choked voice. "And after more than a year, Gerard is no stranger."

"I do not know how to counter this. Honorus says the people are meeting. Some of them are even arming themselves against me."

She laughed. It was an ugly sound. "Arming themselves against an old man and a sick woman, with a daughter and a maid servant for protection!"

Honorus said you and I should look for refuge in the north. He says exile will be better than waiting here for the people to break down our door. He told me that even if I sent the healer away now, it would be too late. Honorus says he will send for us in the spring, when he has convinced the people of their error."

"Honorus says all this. And it is Honorus who will convince the people," she repeated thoughtfully. "So, our visit to my sister and her husband will be much longer than the month you planned. I wondered why you chose to travel in this bitter weather."

"We are not going to your sister," he said, kneeling next to one of the trunks and lifting a pile of blankets into it. "Honorus has found a safer refuge for us. And he has arranged for an armed escort to accompany us. We will winter there, and you will grow stronger. Bethany will stay in Pallas to look after the house until our return."

Kathe saw the woman's eyes widen. Her hands tightened on the sheet as if she would tear it. "You believe it is true! You think Gerard is evil, that he seeks power through you, that he makes you do and say as he bids!"

"Do you have another explanation for our troubles?" he asked bitterly.

"If that is your belief, then how can you leave Bethany here, alone in the house with only her brother and the one you fear to protect her?"

"Honorus has told me, and I have watched her. It is true. She is already his."

The woman turned away from him so that her face was towards the fire once more, but Kathe could tell she was no longer seeing the flames. Tears coursed silently down her face and dropped onto the coverlet. Surely those were for Patrick, but there was another emotion below the sorrow. What was it? Fear? No. Anger, deep and smoldering, hotter than the coals spilling from the hearth.

The woman closed her eyes, but Kathe knew she wasn't sleeping. After a time, the maid made the first of several trips into the room with more things to fill the trunks, including enough food to last several days. When the old man left to help with the carrying, Kathe walked out of the room close behind them. She didn't bother to keep to the shadows, and she resisted the temptation to seize the old man's shoulders and shake him until his brain rattled. It wouldn't do any good.

It wasn't the old man's fault that he was weak and fearful, was it? He must have been much different long ago, when he was young and the city elected him to lead the council. Kathe tried to think of reasons a healer would wish to control Pallas, and if he did, why he would choose such an unlikely way to reach his goal.

One thing she could say about Peter, the Claymon general. When he wanted the Hills he simply took them. The minimum amount of spying, a smattering of street fighting, and then he was planning his elaborate coronation. She hadn't stayed around for that last step, but she knew that was how it was.

It didn't make sense. Bethany's father admitted the healer had helped his wife, even though she still looked as if she would blow away in the first March wind. At first the healer had been a welcome, even honored guest in this house. And Kathe knew the nature of his work required the freedom of travel. If Kathe had understood correctly, the man had been here for more than a year. Who then was the prisoner? Kathe thought she scented treachery. The stink was familiar from the months before Ostara's capture.

She decided to follow the old man and the maidservant. Maybe she could learn where they intended to go after leaving Pallas. She was almost certain Patrick was ignorant about his family's fate, or that of the other citizens of Pallas.

Kathe thought of the child-woman in the room behind her. Her body might be weak, but there was nothing watered-down about her spirit. Kathe had sensed her grief and anger washing out, filling the room like a storm wave. She thought Patrick's mother was stronger in important ways than his father. Had she survived the winter journey she was about to begin?

As the man and maid disappeared from sight, Kathe's eyes caught a white brightness crossing the open balcony running across the end of the room above the fireplace, connecting the two halves of the upper story. It looked insubstantial at first, like a cloud of mist, but as she watched, the shape resolved itself into that of a girl in a white nightgown. Her hair was loose down her back, almost to her waist. She carried a candle. She stopped in front of a door and tapped gently. Kathe dashed up the steps and managed to slip into the room with Bethany before the door closed.

Kathe halted abruptly just inside the door, and watched young Bethany take two steps forward into the healer's arms. He rested his chin on the top of her head while she stood there for several breaths with her face buried in his shirt. He gently held her shoulders before pushing her to arm's length and searched her face in the candlelight. His expression was earnest – even grave.

Kathe leaned against the wall, watching this latest scene. This dreams of hers really was beginning to feel like a play, a mystery in which time passed and things happened in between the action she saw on stage – unseen events she must surmise. One thing stayed constant, though. She was bone tired of being here. It was time for the climax of this story. If it didn't come soon, she might start throwing things, even though that would communicate nothing but her own frustration.

She noticed gratefully that the floor of this room was cool, rather than icy. The windows stood open to catch the breeze. Ah. It must now be one of the first clement nights of spring. Kathe inhaled the delicious smell of damp earth and growing things. Rain dripped from the trees outside the window, and a candle augmented the pearly light of early morning.

"It is done," the healer said. "The last wagon left at dawn. The city is empty except for one old stone mason on his death bed and his wife who refused to leave him."

"And a few hungry cats," Bethany added, trying to speak lightly. But the tremor in her voice betrayed her.

The healer brushed a strand of hair from her face. "It was the only way. A city is only its people. Let Honorus rule this emptiness if he wants to. The people will be safe."

"Unless he brings them back."

"He cannot do that," the healer said firmly. "I would have shared knowledge freely with both of you, but he chose to steal the gift instead. Today he must suspect I reserved some secrets for myself."

He paused, then continued brusquely, "There's no denying your brother's talent. I have learned to respect his ability to create chaos. While you devoted yourself to learning how to ease the hurts of the body, Honorus became skilled in creating doubt and sickness in the minds of the citizens of Pallas. Nevertheless, he has made the mistake of underestimating me. He may have memorized everything in my books, but there are lessons which have never been written, and more that were written but are concealed between the lines."

"Honorus has never been able to hear the animal guides. The people wouldn't have left if the animals didn't tell them to, and we're the ones who gave the animals the idea" Bethany said. "I hope we were right in urging this exodus."

"I think we were. Honorus was already encouraging the citizens to arm themselves. If, as he boasted, he really intended to form them into an army, then we needed time to find a way to stop him."

Don't worry," he continued, "The people will use the map you made to find the island, but they are the only ones it will guide to safe harbor. That same map, in the hands of one seeking power or intending harm, will only be a guide to endless wandering."

"I'd feel better if I didn't have to draw it from memory. I tried to match it with the original one, in the library, but the door is always locked. And when I asked Honorus if I could look at it, he just turned away."

"Don't look at me that way," she continued after a short silence. "We were in the street surrounded by many."

"Still, it was a risk. Like me, your brother hides some of his power. Because of his early cruelty, it has been easy for Honorus to explore the dark edges of magic."

Bethany changed the subject. "The people of Pallas left a trail a blind man could follow.

"That is why I will remain here until the traces of their passage have faded. It won't take as long as you think," he said, seeing her face. "I already sense a stirring next to the path. Nature sends vines to stitch the wound, rain to salve it. I hold some power over that corridor." Honorus looked into Bethany's eyes as if to emphasize his words. "If I have to, I'll stay until the city is forgotten, and its craftsmen have become legend. Honorus knows he cannot defeat me, and he will not dare to leave me here to my mischief, as he would say. I will recover the Book – all my books, and…"

Bethany interrupted, "And I will go into the world – continue the work you were doing before you became entangled in the webs strung by this family of mine."

The healer lowered himself into the straight wooden chair by his work-table. His back was toward her. He stared out the window. Bethany knelt next to him.

"It doesn't take a mind reader to know you were about to tell me to follow the others before the trail disappears. If I were to leave now, I could probably catch up with them in a day or two."

She laid two fingers across his mouth as if to seal it. "And I know your reasons. If I followed your suggestion, I would be able to care for my mother and father, assuming they are alive, and across the water on this island refuge, I would be safe."

"Only I may not find them there. Honorus made the map for my parents, remember. We do not know for certain where he sent them. Even if I do find them on the island, the people will not trust me. I have been tainted by you." She laughed softly.

"On the other hand, if I stay here, Honorus will find a way to use me against you." She sighed. "You know he will. So you must do without peace of mind."

"Do you remember that first day as we walked through the streets? I said hope was a great healer?"

Kathe suddenly was aware of the great silence and emptiness outside where the city should have been waking.

"And I told you, 'without it, all my remedies are only water.'"

"Yes, well, distrust prevents healing. Like an infection, it would keep me from doing any good for my mother. I doubt if even my father would let me near her."

"Where will you go, then?" he said unwillingly.

She went to the window and leaned on the sill, drawing a deep breath before turning towards him and continuing in a businesslike way. "I intend to dress, pack as much as I can carry or as little as I need and leave today when the sun is highest. I will bang on the library door on my way out of the house and invite my maggot-brained brother to watch me go. I'll follow the path the people took, and since Honorus has never bothered to talk to the animals, he will most likely think I have followed them. He will then heartily wish me ill and turn back to your books."

"But where do you intend to go?" he repeated stubbornly.

"Does it matter?"

"I may wish to…that is – I may need to communicate with you."

"Why? To ask my opinion? If so, it will be the first time." She sighed. "I'm sorry. I didn't mean that the way it sounded. It's just I can't imagine anything happening that you cannot handle, especially now that the people are gone. And if you are determined to stay in Pallas until Honorus is no longer a threat, well, I will likely be an old woman or in my grave before your work is done."

"Please, Beth."

She sighed, took his hand and said gently, "When I come to the River Dove, two days journey by our map, if I remember rightly, I will turn east and follow the water until I reach…well, my plans become a little vague at that point, to tell you the truth. I picture myself in some small manor, where a daughter runs wild in the fields ready to learn the skills you taught me. If I meet anyone along the way in need, I will practice the gift…and I suppose that is the story of the rest of my life,"

The healer was shuffling papers on his table as if it was important work he must do that moment. Bethany touched his shoulder, and he turned into her awkward kiss. She traced the angle of his jaw with her finger and whispered, "Goodbye." Then she was gone, leaving the door wide open.

"Goodbye," the man echoed, looking a decade older than the young healer Kathe had followed from the city gate to this house. Kathe watched him lower his head onto his folded arms, and then she followed Bethany.

47

BOOT PRINTS

The sunlight slanted down through the leaves, warming Gale's shoulders. A light breeze ruffled his hair, cooling him. After the rainy days he had spent following Patrick since leaving Pallas, this was a stroll in a meadow. Only he hadn't been following Patrick before, he reminded himself; he'd been following the big, black cat.

With a full belly and limbs that had rested in a bed, he felt renewed. Their destination was unknown, and the terrain unfamiliar, but he could still allow a good portion of his attention to wander. A child would have had no difficulty keeping to this trail the Claymon soldiers had left.

Gale and Patrick believed only two men had survived the battle at the campsite and passed this way, but if that were so, then they had walked so carelessly they might as well have been school friends strolling to a favorite picnic spot.

As usual, Patrick traveled silently, his eyes ceaselessly searching the ground ahead. Gale was content to follow. He sensed something new behind Patrick's silence this afternoon. For one thing, he obviously wasn't used to playing word games with the animals. The few times Patrick had spoken of the talking animals in Gale's presence, it was obvious he believed he could depend on them, that the animals were incapable of lying. He had shown no hesitation in following the stag's signs leading into the hills, and last night, after his initial alarm, he accepted the wolf's unexpected delivery of Rowan. But back in the clearing, even Gale had been able to tell Maraba was dancing around Patrick's questions.

Between the new rules Maraba laid down and his reunion with his long-lost little sister who had somehow turned into his much older sister, Patrick had plenty to think about.

For that matter, Gale had much to occupy his own mind. For example, there was the business of understanding animal talk. Despite his early reluctance, he was eagerly awaiting another opportunity to test his new skills. He wondered if Maraba was around here now. Maybe she was following them for a while before carrying their message to Bethany.

He tried to make himself move more quietly, ignoring as best he could the stream of thoughts and impressions always flowing through his active mind. When he did, he heard more animals, but only the usual unintelligible chatter of squirrels and bird song. He walked for a distance with his hands held open before him, trying to pick up the warm sensation he felt when Maraba talked to him. Nothing.

Meanwhile, other thoughts constantly clamored at the edge of his consciousness, demanding his attention. Before long, he gave up his effort to keep them out. A few moments later, Maraba could have been pacing at his side, and he wouldn't have noticed her. He was lost in a daydream about what would happen when the girls woke up in Bethany's house and found him and Patrick gone.

Gale was sure that, sooner or later, Maraba would keep her promise and go to Bethany. He imagined Meg's expression when she learned he and Patrick had decided to go after her book. Was it Meg's? Surely she had as good a claim as Bethany after carrying it so far and keeping it safe for so long.

With a pang of remorse, he remembered her face on the day he left her on the hill top. She had looked surprised and hurt, as if he had broken some long-standing trust, though surely he had not. Worse was the resignation that quickly replaced her first, unguarded expression. Later, when he returned to the city, she was angry, even after he shot the dog that attacked Kathe. Come to think of it, that was also when she started giving him orders.

Maybe knowing that he was going to some trouble to retrieve her book would help even out her moods. She ought to appreciate the sacrifice he was making, especially since it meant yet another detour away from Ostara. That's where his true duty lay.

Even in a day-dream, this assertion was nearly too much. He snorted, causing Patrick to glance back over his shoulder. It was only in a daydream that he could really take on the Claymon Army, thereby returning Springvale to its proper state of bee murmuring drowsiness. In reality, he expected to be counting every basket of the harvest and reporting to a Claymon overlord for the rest of his life, if his father hadn't already disowned him. His impatience to reach the Hills was fading the closer he came to them.

Turning back from these uncomfortable thoughts and returning to his daydream, he firmly pictured himself crawling through the thorn hedge in a day or two, hugging the precious bundle under his body, and how pleased Meg would be to see him – or it. She would be standing in the cottage doorway, and when she saw him, she'd come running.

The image of Meg racing toward him with her black curls flying behind her shattered as Gale pitched forward, landing on his hands and knees. The root that had tripped him was still looped over his boot toe. Patrick stood a few paces ahead with a thoughtful expression on his face. He offered a hand and pulled Gale to his feet.

"Come look at this," he said.

Gale brushed himself off, catching a finger in a new hole in the sturdy fabric of his trousers. He thought of his mother first weaving, then sewing the garment, never imagining how much abuse he would give her good cloth. He forced himself to pay attention to what Patrick was saying.

"Do you see anything unusual?"

Gale looked behind them, then ahead. He could see where the trail continued, but on either side the forest maintained its chaotic uniformity. The only unusual thing here was a large boulder almost blocking their path. It thrust up from the earth like an island. Red and green lichen covered it. In fact, Gale saw that the ground under his feet was thinly cloaked in lichen and moss. The bones of the earth were close to the surface here. Still, that wasn't really unusual. He shook his head and sat down on the rock, nursing his scraped knee.

"I think the men we are following stood here for a time." Patrick continued. "One of them sat on the rock just about where you are sitting." He dropped to a crouch. "Look at how this lichen has been disturbed where he kicked his feet against it. It's tough. If they just passed over this place, we wouldn't see a mark."

"So, they stopped to rest."

"I think they stopped because someone was waiting for them here. This is the first big boulder we have passed, and you probably noticed we have been climbing slightly. Ahead of us, the trail descends again. This seems to be a landmark – a big boulder on top of a hill. By the way, if we continue the way we're going, we will reach the Forest Road sometime tomorrow."

"The road? Are you sure?"

"They could change their direction later, but by the sun, I'd say that's where they are going. It makes sense, doesn't it? Isn't that where you expected they would go?"

Gale fell silent at this news. He was remembering his last view of the road, crawling with Claymon soldiers.

Patrick continued searching the ground. "Look. Here's someone new."

During the past few hours Gale had become familiar with the prints made by the worn boots of the Claymon soldiers. Here, in the thin layer of soft soil that had accumulated along the lower edge of the rock, he saw a new shape. It was another boot print, but long and narrow.

He looked more closely at the forest edge behind him. Patrick was right. There were signs. Someone had passed that way, and not too long ago. Whoever it was had been moving more cautiously than the Woods Runners, and he had been alone, but after so many days of reading the land, the page detailing his visit was clear.

"So, what now?" He asked.

"It would be easier to follow the soldiers, and I have questions I'd like to ask them, but I'm almost certain they don't have the book any more," Patrick said.

"What makes you say that?"

"If Maraba told us the truth, then the animals were charged with protecting us, but last night they had to choose between keeping us safe or saving the book. They chose us. She also said that some of the animals are friendly with another person, not Bethany. Maraba as much as told me this person has the book now."

Gale knew Patrick was building a case for following this subtle trail and the solitary traveler who had met the Runners at this spot. He waited silently for the rest of the argument. It wasn't long in coming.

Patrick pulled a small piece of parchment out of an inside pocket of his leather vest and handed it to Gale. "My father left this message hidden in Pallas. He said my sister had welcomed someone into our house, someone dangerous, and that person forced my father and mother into exile. I think I know who it was."

Gale scanned the note. He raised his eyes when Patrick paused.

"In the year before the end, my father invited a healer into the household. He invited him, but Bethany was the one who welcomed him – warmly, according to the gossip of the town. I knew my father's library, and Meg's book was not in it when I was at home. The healer, Gerard, came carrying a heavy bag – full of books, I wager. I can't guess why it came into Meg's hands, but I saw how much Beth wants it, and if she wants it, chances are the healer wants it too. I think this footprint belongs to him."

"But," Gale sputtered. "That all happened more than a hundred years ago." He shut his mouth and kicked at the ground, doing further damage to the lichen, realizing how stupid his remark was considering the man standing before him and all he himself had experienced in the past days. "All right. So we follow this healer, magician – whatever he is. What will we do when we catch up with him?"

"That depends on the reception we receive, doesn't it?"

48

GERARD

THE HEALER HAD LEFT a subtle trail. Patrick and Gale lost it twice in the next hour and had to back track in order to pick it up again. At twilight, they feared they would miss the slight signs of passage, so they sat down on the ground near a clear boot print and shared the food Bethany had packed for them. When she pressed it on them, they had thought it far too much to carry to simply scout the battle site. They believed they would return to her house by evening for another of her good, hot meals. Maybe she anticipated this journey. Or, more likely, her long life had taught her to expect surprises.

Gale opened his eyes and groaned to see the grey light of early morning. They had made no fire the night before, just stretched out on the ground, rolling themselves in their cloaks. Patrick still slept nearby. His deep, regular breathing was the only sound. The birds hadn't even started singing yet. Well, good for Patrick. It had been a while since the man truly slept.

Even at Bethany's house, though her beds were soft and warm, Gale had awoken in the night to hear Patrick murmuring. He couldn't understand the slurred words of the old tongue, but he was sure they recalled trouble. On the mornings since leaving Pallas, they had come to depend on Patrick's restlessness. He had been the one scavenging breakfast or scouting the trail before any of the rest of them awoke.

Nevertheless, it was for him to wake up now. The healer's trail had been difficult enough to follow yesterday. It would be doubly hard today. Gale groaned again, flexing a stiff neck and shrugging his shoulders. He must have hardly moved in the night.

Then he froze.

He felt something move under his cloak. Tipping his neck slightly, he saw movement among the wrinkles and folds. An instinct he didn't even know he possessed told him what it was. It had never happened to him, but a few of the farmers at Springvale had told him of times when they fell asleep in the field, thinking to make an early start on their work the next day, and a serpent crawled inside their blankets for the warmth there. Usually the result was only a bad scare for both farmer and snake, and a story to tell later on, but he knew of three times when a man had been bitten, and of one who died.

"Patrick," he whispered.

There was no response.

"Patrick," he whispered again, a little louder.

This time Gale looked into Patrick's face and saw he was as alert as if he had not ever been sleeping.

With his one free hand, Gale pointed at his chest, where the form of the coiled snake was clearly visible under the cloth. Gale's first movements, and now his barely controlled tension, had disturbed the creature. It shifted and began to uncoil. Gale could see the head, lifting the cloak slightly, moving up his body towards his face.

"Jump up and back. Drop the cloak. Mabus will get it." Patrick whispered.

Gale nodded, took as deep a breath as he dared, then leapt

to his feet. The viper dropped, but it became tangled under the cloak. So did Gale's feet. In the next instant, he kicked his way loose and jumped back, but by then the snake had wriggled free. It rose to strike.

Mabus fell with a whistle and sliced through its body into the earth, but too late. Gale staggered away from the wriggling halves of the dying creature. It was longer than his arm. How had its weight gone unnoticed? He must have been sleeping the sleep of the dead. He sat down heavily on the ground and enlarged the tear in his leggings.

He and Patrick stared at the two neat puncture wounds. A single drop of blood welled from each.

"A strong man may survive the bite of a viper," Patrick said.

"I used to think I was strong," Gale said. His face had paled even though the poison had not yet begun its work.

"I am certain you are. Still, it is a good thing we are on the heels of a healer. Shall we do what we can to better your odds?"

Gale nodded, uncertain of Patrick's meaning, then gasped in pain as the warrior used the tip of Kathe's knife to make a shallow cut between the two puncture wounds. Warm blood trickled down his leg. Tossing the knife aside, Patrick removed his belt and bound Gale's leg above the knee.

"Some of the poison may flow out with the blood, and the belt will slow the rest from spreading through your body," Patrick said without apology.

When Gale opened his eyes again, he found Patrick had rummaged a spare shirt from one of their packs and was using one sleeve of it as a compress. There was no purpose in letting the wound continue to bleed longer. He soaked another piece of the garment in water and wrung it over Gale's face and into his mouth.

Then for a time, since there was nothing else to be done, the two did nothing. They sat quietly, knowing that if Gale moved, the venom would do its work more quickly. They also knew that if they did not move, he might die here. Despite the old belief in bleeding, Patrick long ago had lost a boyhood friend, a fine, strong lad, to the bite of a viper smaller than the one that had bitten Gale.

Patrick emptied his bundle onto the ground and hurriedly sorted through it, putting everything that seemed useful into Gale's larger pack. Luckily, it had not been full. He held his chain mail before him and almost set it aside before shoving it into the top. He lashed Mabus to the outside with a piece of rope.

He offered Gale another swallow of water and loosened the belt slightly above his knee. Then he shouldered everything and reached a hand down to the injured man.

"We must move. Do you understand?"

Gale nodded. He felt cold and feverish at the same time. Patrick seemed to be speaking to him from far away. Still, he watched himself reaching up to take the offered hand, and he allowed himself to be pulled to his feet.

Since Gale was almost a head taller, Patrick pulled one of his arms across his shoulder and held his wrist firmly. Hunched under the weight, with his eyes searching for the next sign of the healer, he began to move forward.

It was a miracle he did not lose the trail at once. His tracking was limited to what he could see on the ground ahead and to his limited peripheral vision. As the sun rose toward mid-morning and Gale's breathing became labored, Patrick finally admitted he had been seeing signs where there were none. He hadn't found a booted print in almost an hour, but in his methodical searching to regain the trail, he had twice seen the imprint of his own boots with Gale's, almost dragging, alongside them.

He kicked away fallen branches and laid his companion on the soft loam under an oak. A finger at the weak pulse in his throat reinforced what Patrick already knew. Gale was strong, but the poison was stronger. Death would soon take him.

Maybe he should leave Gale here with one of the water skins and some food and go on alone. If he did, this offering would only assuage his own conscience. Gale was too weak to eat or drink without help. Then, assuming he could find the healer's trail again, he would follow it, somehow force the man to come back with him and help.

Or he could stay here. Be with Gale at the end, protect him until it was time to bury him. Then go back to Bethany's alone, without the book.

His little sister had somehow overtaken him, grown old and wise. No such wisdom had descended upon him during his wasted years of enchanted sleep. Wisdom is a gift for the living.

The memory of Kathe's words intruded into his thoughts. What was it she said? *Maybe we can figure out their purpose together.* She had been speaking of the animals when she said that, but she had mirrored his relief in finding someone to talk to. He had known he could trust her almost from the beginning. He imagined her stubbornly molding his fingers around Mabus's hilt in Pallas. He wished her here now.

He wished it though he knew even her stubbornness could not save Gale. The youth lay tightly curled on his side, as if protecting his belly. His curly hair was drenched in sweat, but his skin felt cold and clammy. Patrick covered him with one of the cloaks and leaned back against the tree.

He unstrapped Mabus from the outside of the pack and laid it next to his outstretched legs, tracing the shape of the hilt with a finger. Patrick no longer depended on the sword for life itself, but its presence still comforted him.

Another hour passed. Now it was hard to tell whether Gale was breathing at all. Patrick watched him hopelessly. After they stopped, Patrick had offered water, but the second time he did so, it just dribbled from the corners of Gale's mouth. Patrick didn't think he swallowed any of it. He tucked the cloak more closely around the dying man. Well, at least the choice was made. As far as he knew, the book had only brought trouble to those who carried it. Surely he already had enough of that.

Patrick was still sitting with his face in his hands when an enormous hound loped out of the woods. He cursed and struggled as its rough tongue washed his face and the arms he flung up to protect himself.

Less than a minute later, a man entered the clearing. "Violet, come," a deep voice commanded. The hound immediately ceased its greeting and obeyed.

Patrick struggled to his feet, Mabus in his hand. The black hound sat peacefully at its master's side with its long red tongue lolling from the side of its mouth. Patrick wiped his sleeve across his face and grimaced. The healer's black hair had turned nearly white, but he still stood tall and erect.

"I hope you will forgive my dog," he said, as if they had just chanced to meet on a city street, "but I find she helps to shorten the initial awkwardness of greeting. I am Gerard. I expect you know that."

Patrick still stood dumb, glaring at the healer, trying to reconcile this man with the demon he had been expecting. Gerard had become the enemy in his mind, the one who destroyed Pallas and sent his parents into exile. Patrick had even cast Gerard as the architect of the battle in which he, himself, took the wound that should have brought his death. How could he reconcile this image with the man standing before him, still in grey robes and wearing the kindly expression he now remembered – with an adoring dog at his side?

He felt Death's icy presence behind him and he turned away from Gerard to kneel by Gale's side. When he took his friend's hand in his own, there was no response. The healer had come too late.

49

Following Bethany

Kathe sat in a chair by the cold fireplace and waited for Bethany to pack her bag and come down the stairs. When she first entered this central hall, carried by the winds of late autumn, it was achingly cold. Now sweat trickled between her shoulder blades and the stifling heat of a closed house at high summer made her sleepy.

Even though she knew she shouldn't, she shut her eyes and leaned against the high arm of the chair. She had just stayed awake through a night that lasted almost two years. After all she had seen, she wanted to sleep. Maybe she could escape the dream for a little while that way.

She rested a hand at the base of her throat on a tiny, cool patch of skin. It was the only place where she still felt any connection to the woman who had sent her here – a faint throbbing below her own pulse.

When she awoke, her eyes were gritty and crusted. Based on the way her neck ached, she must have slept longer than she had planned. This chair was most uncomfortable. Bethany would be leaving the city soon. Unless Kathe had already missed her. Panic brought her to her feet. Sunlight streamed through the windows around the door, and Kathe noticed something strange. Somebody had left the door open. A few dried leaves skittered across the stone floor in eddies of sultry air.

More leaves had collected in the hearth and in the corners of the room. A thick layer of dust lay on everything. Kathe ran toward the open door. She had almost reached it when she stepped on a piece of broken glass. She hopped backwards, noticing too late that every pane in the windows around the door had been shattered. Fist-sized stones littered the floor among the shards.

For the first time the place felt absolutely dead. She sensed no one lingering in this house now – except her. She picked her way through the shards and pushed frantically through to the wilderness of the garden. The roses that once framed the door now almost obscured it. Their thorns tore at her face and arms.

When she finally stood knee deep in lavender where the walk should have been, Kathe tried to still herself enough to search for the link to Bethany. It was still there in her throat, but weaker – much weaker than it was before she fell asleep. She tried to picture her body, left behind lying in the soft grass of the orchard under the pear tree, but she could no longer do it.

She tried to remember all she had seen and heard just before she fell asleep. What had Bethany said about her plan? Kathe had been eavesdropping intently, but she had been as aware of the tension between Beth and the healer as she was of the words they spoke. If she remembered rightly, Beth was going to leave through the city gate and follow the trail of the people as far as the River Dove, then East. There was nothing more to observe in this empty city. Kathe would have to do the same.

She wondered whether any trace of the trail would remain for her to follow. If not, then how would she know which way to go, or how to find the river? She remembered the name from one of her geography lessons; as usual, she hadn't been paying much attention. Well, at least there was no hunger in this endless dream even if she could grow bone weary and hurt herself.

Something feathered erupted from the tangle of roses behind her. Kathe shrieked in surprise as it flew over her shoulder, brushed her neck, and landed on the gatepost. As soon as she recognized Oro, she rushed forward and stood close to him, fighting the impulse to give the big owl a hug.

"Running Girl said you may sleep a long time, but you slept longer than long. I almost gave up," he said.

Kathe reached a tentative finger and stroked the silky feathers of the bird's wing. He didn't move away.

"Is this dream almost finished?" she asked plaintively. "Do you know the way back to the orchard?"

"The dream will be finished when you wake up under the fruit tree. Not when you wake up in this dead rookery. Running Girl says I must show you something, and we must hurry. If you don't see it soon, she may lose you, and then you will stay here dreaming always. I like the other world better. I eat there." The owl yawned hugely.

"Show me," Kathe blurted, adding, "please," to show how glad she was he had come. She tasted bile when he told her she might be lost here forever, a solitary ghost in this desolate place.

Oro did not answer. He flew ahead of her through the park she remembered, past the still flourishing Sycamores and down through the city streets to the gate. He didn't bother to make sure she was keeping up. He seemed to trust that she would know where to go.

He was already sitting above the opening preening himself when she caught up and sagged against the wall, panting. Before she could catch her breath, however, he flew again – out into the forest.

Fearing she would lose him, Kathe followed, ignoring the stitch in her side and the pain of her injured foot. He could fly much faster than she could run, but she found she could run faster in this dream than she ever could in what the owl called the "other world." Now that they were outside the gate, she found she could trust him not to lose her. He never stopped long enough to really rest, though, not even when the day turned to afternoon and then to night. When full darkness fell, Oro stayed closer, guiding her as he had on the night they first met, when he took her to meet the animals.

It must have been nearly morning when Kathe stumbled into the shallows of the river. She paused there with her hands resting on her thighs, digging her toes into the mud and relishing the coolness on her battered feet while Oro flew on to the east. When it became clear she was not following, he returned to perch on a branch nearby, tsk-tsking in owl talk.

"You can scold all you want," she gasped. "I may be able to live in the dream world without food or rest, but I remember both those things, and I miss them."

"Are you going to stop here, then?" Oro responded. *"If you are, I'll go back to the other world and catch a juicy mouse for my breakfast. I'll tell Running Girl you would rather stand in the water than see."*

"Can't you tell me where we are going?" Kathe asked.

The owl remained silent.

"I'm coming," she sighed, taking his silence as her answer. "It's just that when you fly, you don't have to touch the earth. You don't get bruised and scratched and stubbed like I do."

Oro floated down to a lower branch.

"Is this your first dream? When you wake up, you will carry no mark. The memory of me and the water you are in and of everything you have seen will fade away like the dawn. If you are not very careful, you may lose it all. That would be too bad, wouldn't it, after all you have been through?"

Kathe nodded mutely and stepped out of the river. The bottom of her foot was swollen. She probed the angry, red edges of the wound. She hoped Oro was right about what would happen if she woke up. When she woke up, she told herself firmly. When.

It was easier to run along the bank of the river, and where there were sand bars, Oro slowed enough so Kathe could walk in the shallow water. It sparkled just like the rivers in the other world, but here, in addition to little minnows that came to nibble her toes, she attracted a procession of larger fish. Catfish, salmon, and trout swam solemnly next to her and followed behind until she was leading a stately procession. When the water became too deep for her, and she had to return to running along the bank, she could still see their shadows pacing her.

It must have been about mid-day when the forest abruptly ended and gave way to fields and pastures. Oro became more impatient. The bright light hurt his owl eyes, and there were few places to perch. Finally, he landed on the ground in front of her.

"If this were my dream, I'd put more trees in it," he said grumpily. *"You can find her now. Keep following the river, and when you come to a big nesting place, stop."*

Kathe did not want him to leave. She squatted in front of him. "What do you mean 'a big nesting place'? What if I can't find it? Who is 'her'?"

"A big nesting place," he answered, shortly. *"Where the man and woman raise their owlets. It is around the river bend. I have to leave now. This dream is no place for an owl."*

Kathe watched him fly away, back toward the forest. Before he reached the trees, his shape became indistinct, as if seen through a frosted window, and then she couldn't see him at all.

"This is no place for me, either," she said sadly to herself, but she continued plodding towards the bend in the river. Some dirt had worked its way deep into the cut on her foot. She should probably have stopped again to wash it in the river, but she wanted to see this last thing she must see, and maybe then she would be allowed to go home.

As she rounded the wide curve in the riverbank, the roof of a house came into view beyond the trees of a park. Kathe walked more quickly. This had to be the nesting place Oro told her about. As she drew closer, she could see a cluster of buildings set on a hill. The solid shape of the main house reminded her of Springvale manor house except there was no wall here. A straight graveled road started at the front of the house and ran down to a little dock jutting into the river. Several small boats were tied there. They were painted bright blue and gently swayed with the current.

Her foot was too sore to bear walking on the gravel of the road, so she picked her way along the grassy edge as she slowly made her way towards the house. Smoke curled from three chimneys, and a flag lifted in the breeze. It was yellow and blue, the same shade as the boats on the river.

When she came to the lawn, Kathe stopped and looked up again. The building was made of stone in the shape of a U, but it didn't look cold as stone houses often do. Instead, it looked open, even welcoming. The breeze picked up suddenly, and the sound of the snapping flag drew her attention upward again. She saw its design for the first time and drew a sharp breath.

She knew this standard. All her life it had flown beneath the green dragon of the Three Hills in Ostara. Its river of stars often appeared in her mother's weaving, and little wonder. It was the emblem of her family.

Even though she never had been here, she now knew where she must be. Like Pallas, this place no longer existed in the other world. Or rather, it no longer carried life as it did here, with its door inviting her to enter, tempting her with the fragrance of food and the murmur of voices.

Fire had consumed the house and killed both grandparents

before she was born. As far as she knew, her mother visited the shell of this place only once after that tragedy. She was pregnant, and the sight of her childhood home blackened and lifeless had caused her such distress that the babe came too soon and lived only a day. By the time Kathe was born, her mother was able to speak of her grandparents and to describe this place with love, but never without an undertone of sadness.

But always there were the stars, embroidered on her coverlet; adorning the wall of the hall in vibrant silk; flying in the breeze over their house. When she was young, her parents' marriage had seemed perfect to her, the union of the fire dragon and the water reflected stars.

During all her years in Ostara, Kathe had never asked to visit her mother's old home. Once she learned to ride, Bard would have taken her; she was sure her parents would have had no objection. It was little more than a day's journey from home. But she was never interested. Or perhaps she was reluctant to spend too much time thinking of the grandparents who would have loved her and of her sister, another victim of the fire. She knew that men had come from a nearby village to work the land. They pulled down the walls of the house and used the stone to build their walls and barns. There was no monument to her grandmother and grandfather in the other world.

Kathe dragged herself up the wide, shallow steps and through the front door. She stood in a narrow passageway open at each end. A breeze played through the house.

The voices she had heard weren't from inside. Instead, they were coming through the house, channeled to her by this hallway. When she reached the end of the passage, she stood framed in the doorway, looking over a sunken garden. Below her, a woman of middle age and a little girl were playing with a ball, kicking it back and forth. Their laughter drifted up to her along with the warm scents of growing herbs.

Kathe watched the ball roll under a bush. The little girl raced to retrieve it, her long, blonde hair flying behind her. When she returned, she carried a stem broken from the plant, and she showed it to the woman, who knelt down and, tracing the delicate leaves with a tip of her finger, began to talk seriously, but of course, much too quietly for Kathe to hear.

The girl listened intently, with her eyes first on the plant and then on the woman's face, but after a few moments, she looked away as if she had heard something. She glanced up towards the house and tugged urgently at the woman's sleeve. She pointed.

Kathe thought, *She is pointing at me.*

She looked over her shoulder to see whether someone had come down the passage behind her. None of the people in Pallas had been able to see her, only Oro. The woman stood up and gazed in Kathe's direction as if she was waiting for something. She took the little girl's hand.

Because she didn't know what else to do, Kathe painfully began climbing down the steps into the garden. When she was halfway, she sat on the steps and bumped the rest of the way down. Her attention was all on descending without falling, but when she finally reached the expanse of lawn at the bottom, she looked up.

The woman and girl were crossing the lawn to meet her. Kathe thought they were smiling, but looking through tears, she couldn't be sure. She brushed them away impatiently and dragged herself to her feet.

"It is time for you to go home at last, my dear," the woman said gently. "But first there is someone I want you to meet."

Kathe tore her attention away from Bethany's voice, Bethany's vivid blue eyes, to the child standing beside her.

She was wearing a sleeveless summer shift, rather dirty from playing outside. Her nose was freckled, and she had a scab on one knee. She looked familiar, like seeing her own face in a mirror. Kathe knew who this must be before she spoke.

"I am Ellen," she said politely, "and this is Beth. She's

teaching me to be a healer, just like she taught my mama and grandmama."

Bethany stroked the child's hair, but she looked directly into Kathe's face when she said, "She has a quick mind and a powerful gift. Just like you."

At least, Kathe thought that was what Bethany said. She was already falling.

50

Rough Waters

Gale dreamt he was sailing in a boat. As he struggled towards consciousness, the craft swayed from side to side and bumped over choppy seas. In this dream, he was neither captain nor crew – just cargo trussed in a hold. He tried to open his eyes, but the rocking movement made this too difficult. Despite his best intentions, he kept drifting back into sleep. His mouth was dry. When he tried to swallow, there was a bitter taste.

Gale had never been on a boat, but he had always enjoyed listening to stories about them. So he knew the sounds here in the hold should be the creaking of wood and the splash of the sea against the hull. Instead, the clatter of tin ware against the walls of the little room jarred his nerves as the vessel jolted forward. He noticed that the craft often lurched, as if it was in danger of capsizing. Were they going through a storm? Bright sunlight throbbing beyond his closed eyelids belied this theory.

He remembered following the trail of the stranger with Patrick, but he couldn't remember finding the man. He recalled only pain and confusion. He forced his eyes open and shuddered. Now he remembered. The viper bit him; Patrick cut the wound, trying to save him. Did it work?

Well, of course it must have. Otherwise he wouldn't be riding in this boat now. He struggled to an upright position, leaning against the inside of the hull, but he quickly rolled back to the thick pillows on the bed. The deep featherbed cushioned him from the worst of the movement, but when he leaned against any hard surface, bursts of blinding light erupted from behind his eyes. He gasped and leaned over the side of the bed where he found a bucket at the ready, as if someone knew how he would feel when he woke up.

The snake had struck on his thigh, just above the knee. He gingerly pushed the blankets away from his leg. He didn't expect to see the punctures. He knew they had been obscured by the small cut Patrick made. But he couldn't see the wound at all. Someone had dressed it with a bandage. He dipped his fingers in the ointment smeared around the edges and sniffed – Heal All and at least one other herb, but he didn't recognize it.

He pressed his hands to his eyes, trying to quiet the ferocious ache behind them, then looked around the hold for a jug of water. His throat burned, and he longed to rinse his mouth. He now saw that the little room where he lay was only two steps from side to side, but it was a whole house in miniature. Cupboards had been built above, below and opposite his long, narrow bed. A grey, woolen cloak hung from a peg by the door and swayed with the motion of the boat. Bundles of plants dried along the peaked roofline. He didn't see any water, though.

Wait a minute. A boat wouldn't have a peaked roof, would it, or a door? Gale swung his legs over the edge of the bed. He had to close his eyes and hold his head again, but when the pain subsided, he saw trees crawling slowly past the small, round windows. He looked over his shoulder and out the other side of the vessel. More trees.

Not a boat, then. A wagon. A wagon like a little house, he thought stupidly. He staggered, hunched, to the back door. There wasn't enough space to stand without bumping his head. Kneeling there, he could see a road winding away behind the wagon. When it hit another hole, his shoulder crashed against the unforgiving wood of the doorframe. He crawled back to the bucket to be sick again, and when he sat up against the side of the bed, he saw a small window slide open above him, in the front of the wagon. He had an impression of a face looking down at him before the opening slid shut with a snap. Then the vehicle turned, slowed and stopped.

Gale struggled to pull himself to his feet again but decided it would be more dignified to greet his visitor sitting on the edge of the bed than crouched over. He wondered if the role he was playing was passenger or prisoner. In addition to patient, that is.

He spotted a water skin hanging in the shadowy corner above the bed and recognized it as one Kathe had carried from Springvale. He took a long drink. The water was cool and fresh. He was wiping his mouth with the back of his arm when the door swung open with a squeak.

"We didn't expect to see you for another day, at least," said the stranger as he angled his body to enter the room, sitting on his heels in front of Gale and reaching up to place a practiced hand on his forehead. "How do you feel?"

Gale didn't respond. He was finding it very difficult to remember how to turn his thoughts into spoken words. He instinctively leaned away from the stranger's touch, grimacing as the movement triggered another blinding flash of pain, and he felt the nausea rise again. He had no choice but to allow his visitor to steady his shoulders as he made use of the bucket for a third time. Afterwards, he felt better. Whoever this person was, he didn't seem to mean any harm, at least not right now.

"If you can stand, there is someone waiting outside to see you. I'm afraid there is barely room for one in my little home, let alone three."

Gale looked around again, this time noticing the table folded against the wall, just large enough for one and the single mug dangling from a hook in the ceiling. *I would have expected someone shorter to live here,* he thought.

"I'll try," Gale said.

"He's coming out." the stranger called.

The door opened again, and this time a familiar, tousled head entered the tiny space. Patrick's face was wearing a grin Gale had never seen before. "Welcome back to the land of the living," he said.

51

The Story of Pallas

PATRICK AND THE HEALER had driven through tall grass, stopping the wagon a short distance from the road. From his seat among the roots of a venerable beech tree, Gale could see it close by. From all he had seen and been told, the forest road was little more than a foot path for most of its length, but the route looked well-traveled here – plenty wide enough for the wagon. Did that mean they were getting close to Ostara?

Gale watched Patrick going about his usual business of fire-building and waited with unusual lethargy for someone to tell him what was going on. *So this is what it feels like to be patient,"* he thought. *"The patient has no choice but to be patient."* Gale had little experience being ill. Seeing Patrick had allayed his fear that he might be a captive, but it really made no difference if he was. An attempt to run away would look like a joke. He was as limp as a vine. In fact, if he had tendrils, he would use them to keep himself from sliding any further from his upright position among the slippery tree roots.

When the fire was well ablaze, Patrick left it to sit by Gale. "The first thing you need to know is if anyone shows up, I'm going to move you into the bushes." He gestured behind the tree with his thumb. "And there won't be time to ask your leave."

Gale raised his eyebrows but didn't say anything. Patrick asked the stranger, "Did the snake steal his voice? Believe me, it isn't like him to be quiet for so long."

"Give him time. Give him time," the man said good-naturedly.

"Gerard here," Patrick said to Gale, "turned out not to be quite what I expected."

"What did he turn out to be?" Gale croaked.

"He speaks!" Patrick joked. "Gerard is a traveling healer and sometimes magician, with an unexpected tie to Pallas."

"Maybe I lost my voice, but you seem to have gained yours," Gale said sullenly, and indeed, something had changed about Patrick. It wasn't just the lilt in his voice. It was as if he had been carrying a heavy weight before, and now he had put it down. "It would help if you made more sense."

"Fair enough," Patrick said more seriously. "Goddes, though, it's good to see you sitting there with that sulky expression on your face. I never thought I'd see it again. I'll tell you the story. Let me know if I leave anything out he needs to know."

This last was addressed to the healer who had settled onto his heels nearby. It seemed to be his favorite position.

"The day you were bitten was…let's see," he looked over at Gerard, who held up three fingers, "three days ago. You grew weaker every hour until I dared drag you no farther. Gerard showed up soon after I had given up on you; by then you had half slipped away. He…well, lets just say he knows a few more tricks than I do when it comes to dealing with a viper bite."

"Between the two of us, we got you back to the wagon, and we've been watching you ever since, though of course you wouldn't remember anything about that."

"I remember we were supposed to be following someone dangerous," Gale said, taking a side-long glance at Gerard, "and that we were supposed to get Meg's, er…Bethany's er…something back for her, and that we hadn't figured out how we were going to do that, and then the snake bit me."

"Yes it did," Gerard broke in soberly, "and if I'm not mistaken, you have a bad headache. Don't worry about wrapping your mind around the whole story. Just take it in, and I promise you it will make better sense later."

"What about your father's letter?" Gale asked Patrick with a suspicious glance at Gerard. "Have you shown that to him?"

"I have," said Patrick. "Not immediately, but after I rode with him for a while. After it began to seem you might survive. As it turns out, I made some assumptions that were wrong. The truth is both better and worse than I feared, but at least it is the truth. I can feel it here," he said, touching the center of his chest, "and here," he continued, tightening his grip on Mabus. "If I seem different, it probably is because I finally understand why I am here and what I have to do, even though I know it won't be easy. Breakfast is nearly ready, Gerard. Why don't you take up the tale?"

When Patrick stirred the pot, Gale caught a nutty whiff and suddenly was ravenous. What was cooking? Oatmeal? How long had it been since he had eaten anything?

"I don't know anything about why the people left Pallas," Gale said, dragging his attention away from the cooking pot. "You might have to start earlier in the story than you think."

The healer studied him and seemed to come to a decision. "I'll start with the day I walked through the gate, summoned by Patrick's father, and met his sister waiting there." The healer was still facing Gale, but for a moment his eyes were faraway, as if he stood again on the street in Pallas, watching a girl approaching him with a light step and outstretched hands.

"She wasn't aware of her own power, not yet, but I couldn't keep from loving her as soon as she spoke to me."

"To make a long story short," Patrick called softly over his shoulder, "Gerard is my brother-in-law."

Gale looked at the healer with renewed interest. Bethany was married to this man? Well, he did look to be about her age, but what age was that? Other than having an unusual number of smile lines around his eyes, Gerard didn't seem any older than Gale's father, Stefan.

Gerard continued in a matter-of-fact voice, "As soon as I discovered Bethany's gift, I encouraged her to work with me to help her mother – Patrick's mother. I don't think that good lady would ever have been completely well, but she was growing stronger, and as Patrick has said, I had decided it was time to marry. But such hopes take time to bear fruit. In the end, I stayed much longer than I ever intended. I even stayed after Bethany had learned enough to take over her mother's care herself. Since I was stubborn…"

"Still are," Patrick said, good humouredly.

"As I was saying," Gerard continued, without rancor, "I was determined to stay in Pallas, and since there was little work for me there, I took it upon myself to educate Bethany and her brother, Honorus. I knew she had a second brother; she often spoke of him, but I never met Patrick. In the beginning, he wasn't living in his father's house. Later, Bethany and I believed him dead. By then, the changes had started."

"What changes?" Gale asked, eyeing the thick porridge Patrick was ladling into bowls.

"I told you I sensed a strong gift for healing in Bethany, and I was right about that. She soon surpassed me. I rely heavily on plants, but that girl – she can heal with a touch. I thought I saw something similar in Honorus, but I was wrong. I have spent my life since then trying to correct that error."

Patrick placed a warm bowl of porridge in Gale's lap and tried to feed him a spoonful.

"Do I look so weak?" Gale protested indignantly. "I can feed myself." He held his hand out for the spoon and lifted it shakily to his mouth. Only a little bit landed on the front of his shirt.

Gerard and Patrick exchanged a look, and that's how Gale

knew there had been other meals when one or the other of them had fed him.

"Gerard is too harsh on himself," Patrick said. "He didn't have the benefit of knowing my brother through childhood, as I did. I'm sure Honorus showed his courteous side, at least at first. He always had good manners when he decided they would serve him."

"He learned quickly. I will give him that," Gerard said. "He took all my books, committed them to memory, destroyed some of them, then turned their contents to purposes I never could have imagined. These were books of healing! Except for one, the one I had to get back."

"Bethany's book," Gale guessed, now wishing he had not been so hasty in refusing Patrick's help. He doubted whether he had the dexterity to move another spoonful of porridge to his mouth. Gerard sensed his dilemma and poured the mixture into an earthen mug he could hold with both hands and drink without spilling.

"So it really was your book," Gale said. "But in that case, how did Meg get it? Why does Bethany want it?" he asked after taking a sip.

"You have probably guessed that the peddler who shared his sausages with Meg one morning long ago was me. On that day I was eager to see my wife, the woman Meg called Old Pammy. But I had a problem."

"What was that?" Gale asked.

"The book – always and forever the book. Bethany knew as well as I did that if we were ever to restore Pallas, the answers all lay within its pages. If I had taken it with me to her cottage, she would have asked to look at it. She wanted to bring the people back to the city as much as I did, but it would have been too dangerous for her to try. It still would be."

"Couldn't you have just hidden it in the wagon – said you didn't have it?"

Gerard sighed. "You don't know Bethany very well, do you? Or me, for that matter. No. The book had to really be lost, and I found the answer in Meg's honest face. I knew she would care for the book, but no one would ever guess she had it. It would be safe with her for a time."

"Who has it now?"

"I have it again," Gerard said shortly. "And this time it will stay with me until the wrong is made right." He held his hand up to stop Patrick from speaking. "I have to do what I can. I had nothing to do with the attack on your camp, would have prevented it if I could; afterwards a friend of mine, a wolf, told me where I could find the book."

"Gerard is a man of few words, but I am one of even fewer," Patrick said. "This story has run on too long. Let me see if I can finish it. My brother used what he learned from Gerard, plus the city's native distrust of strangers – especially healers – to create a lie. In it, Gerard was chief villain and my father his dupe or accomplice, depending on who you talked to. Once the people were convinced, he began to squeeze. He used the Ostaran raiding party to convince them that they needed a stronger leader. A few months later he sent my parents into exile."

"Bethany and I saw it all, but we were helpless to stop him." Gerard interrupted. "We remained prisoners in her house while Honorus spread his lies and began to build an army. The city's craftsmen learned to make weapons instead of furniture and stonework. Once his father was gone, Honorus intended to create a new threat, one from outside, He would send Pallas to war. The people believed anything he told them, even that they could only save themselves by killing. His true purpose was to grow powerful. He didn't care how much sorrow he spread before him."

"Then why did everyone go away?" Gale asked irritably. "I've been trying to think of any reason all the people in Springvale would up and leave, but I can't.

"I can hardly believe it myself," Gerard replied. "At first we tried to tell the people. Beth and I went out into the streets more than once, but they stopped their ears when I tried to speak to them for fear my words might be enchanted, and they saw Bethany as just another of my conquests. All the animals agreed that we should send the people after Bethany's father and mother into exile until we could find a way to deal with Honorus, but it was difficult. It took all the persuasive powers of the ancient guides and of the few women and men who could still hear their voices.

The animals have wonderful imaginations. They told the people I was preparing to bring a plague on the city. Everyone who didn't die would go mad. They said I had poisoned the mother spring and that the tainted water was even then flowing through the aqueduct toward the city. They told the people they would only have to leave the city for a short time, and that my destruction was sure. The animals would see to it, but it was essential that the city be emptied for the final battle when fire would rain from the sky and biting insects would swarm through the streets. Apparently this was more plausible than leaving because of Honorus and his vicious greed. The citizens of Pallas believed I was the real threat until the end. They probably still believe it"

Now that he had eaten, Gale discovered he could hardly keep his eyes open. His head felt a little better, though. He felt as if he had just been given a history lesson that didn't have much to do with him, but something in it jarred.

"What do you mean, 'still believe it,'?" he asked. "All of this happened a long time ago. Those people are dust by now."

"I don't think he'll be awake much longer, and we should go," Patrick said, "but I think he should know where he's going before we tuck him into bed again."

"Where are we going?" Gale asked, still not much caring.

"To Ostara, my friend," said Patrick. "There, we'll sell this wagon, or if we're lucky, we'll trade it for horses and supplies. Then, if you choose to join us, we'll cross the White Mountains and make our way to the Isle of Niue, where if the book is to be believed, the people of Pallas live still."

"You were right," Gale told Gerard, using the tree to rise to his feet and leaning on Patrick as they made their way back to the wagon. "I cannot fit my mind around this."

"Sleep, lad," the healer said soothingly.

52

AWAKE

HER HEAD FELL BACK towards the stone steps and the sky began to spin, but Kathe knew she was not really falling. Instead, she was rising, lifted by unseen hands. They supported her under her arms, at the base of her spine, behind her knees. As she slowly spiraled upward, her limbs instinctively tried to swim through air as thick as water, straining for a surface, but a voice whispered, "Slow." The hands held her back, insistently guiding her progress. When she struggled against them, thrashing her arms and legs, they tightened.

She could now see the translucent line binding her to Bethany and the present, as fine as a strand of spider's silk. One end caught in her throat like a hook at the end of a fishing line. Her eye followed it up until it disappeared into brightness. It looked so frail, and Oro said it might not hold. What would happen if it snapped? Would she then become no more than a fish swimming through this watery ether between the dream world and the waking world? Kathe tugged one hand loose from the invisible guide and held it at her throat protectively, willing strength into the bond.

Even though the pulse of connection was still there, the line sang between her fingers and pulled a cry from her throat as it tugged and frayed. Bethany must be weary after keeping watch all this time. Somewhere above, the old woman strained to reel her in.

Just before it snapped, the line's song rose to a shriek. Kathe sensed a sickening drop behind her. The hands fell away, but as they did, she caught a glimpse of leaves, backlit by sun. Kathe twisted upright and swam as hard as she could. She was a little girl racing Bard. She was almost catching him. Up. Up.

When an arm reached for her, she grasped it, gave one more mighty kick, then lay gulping the sweet air in the orchard. She bolted upright and sat choking under the pear tree, one of her hands clinging to Bethany's, the other clutching a fistful of grass. Then she jumped to her feet and spun around, reacquainting herself with her clean, unbruised body, surprised she wasn't dripping wet. Rowan had been sleeping, but now she woke and danced around her mistress, thinking she wanted to play.

You're back," Bethany said dully, as if she didn't really believe it.

Kathe saw her own exhaustion reflected in the healer's haggard face. During all the years she had spent exploring the past, the sun had barely dipped below the trees here.

"I shouldn't have sent you so far. I should have prepared you," Bethany apologized.

Kathe didn't respond. She couldn't. It was just as Oro had predicted. Now that she stood in the orchard again on her two uninjured feet, all she saw and heard in Pallas and in her grandparents' garden started to fade. She opened her mouth to speak, then shook her head and raced to the house. She flung herself into the chair by Bethany's writing table and spilled ink into a little dish where pigment had begun to dry. She rummaged for a quill among the papers lying there, dipped it into the fluid and began to write furiously on the first scrap that came to hand.

Bethany came into the house a few minutes later carrying

two baskets of pears. She set them on the floor next to the door. Except for her tired eyes and a wrinkle of worry on her forehead, her demeanor said nothing unusual had happened outside. She stood looking over Kathe's shoulder for a moment but did not disturb her, only lay a fresh sheet of parchment to one side for her to use when she finished filling the margins of a letter Bethany had been writing to Gerard. Then she lit two candles on the low shelf above the writing table.

When Meg awoke, Bethany met her at the base of the stairs and whispered, "Kathe has had a dream, and she wants to make sure she doesn't forget it." Then she put some bread and cheese on a plate, filled a mug, and led the girl outside to the low stone wall that enclosed the kitchen garden. They sat there together in companionable silence, looking down the sloping meadow at deer grazing near the edge of the woods and watching the first stars appear.

Meg wondered when Kathe would finish writing and come outside so that they could finally badger Bethany into answering some questions. Or would they have to wait for Gale and Patrick to wake up? She had listened at their door but didn't hear a sound from the room.

When it was nearly full dark, one of the shadows along the wall disengaged itself and padded close enough for them to see moonlight reflected in its eyes. Maraba's sudden appearance startled Meg, who lost her balance and fell backwards off the wall into the garden. A bushy patch of mint cushioned her fall. She lay on her back for a moment wondering if she really had seen what she thought she saw. Well, of course she had. There was nothing wrong with her eyes, and hadn't she seen the very same apparition before?

She heard Bethany's low laugh and words of greeting. Meg knelt and peeked over the stone wall.

"Maraba says she won't eat you even though you invited her to do so when you last met. She has brought a message from

Patrick. Seat yourself." Bethany patted the stone Meg had vacated so abruptly.

Meg stood, and slowly swung first one leg and then the other over the wall. She smoothed her skirt and tried to assume an air of dignity, but she had the feeling the big cat was laughing at her.

"Well, what is the message, my friend? Is Patrick going to be late for supper?"

Bethany leaned slightly forward as if she was listening intently, and Meg saw the smile fade from her face. "How dare he! The old fool!" Her fists clenched in her lap. "How dare he leave me out of it!"

The old woman jumped to her feet as if she had just remembered somewhere she must go without delay, and she paced a few steps forward, sidestepping the panther. She stood staring towards the edge of the clearing, her shoulders rigid. Standing that way, engulfed in emotion, Bethany looked younger. Meg thought she should go to her, but she didn't want to walk by the panther. It was staring at her and didn't seem to mean any harm, but old beliefs die slowly.

What message had the animal brought that so affected their gentle, good humored, hostess? Was there a way to find out? Meg took a deep breath and forced herself to look directly into the panther's face. Kathe and Bethany could understand animal talk. So apparently could Patrick. Could she? She squinted up her face, scowling.

"*You're too tight. The words won't fit.*" The low rumbly whisper echoed at the very edge of her hearing. Well, not exactly her hearing. It went deeper than that – somewhere near the base of her skull. It was like a gentle tickling on her hair, as if someone was teasing her with a piece of grass. She closed her eyes so she couldn't see Maraba and tried to relax.

"*That's the way. That's better.*" The words came slightly clearer this time. "*You are friend to Flame Child. I knew you would hear me better than Shaky Knees."*

"Who is Shaky Knees?" she asked aloud.

The cat ignored the question. She seemed unconcerned by the effect of her message on Bethany. She licked one paw and flexed her claws.

"You are the one who respects me. I think I will call you Careful. And you don't have to use your mouth."

Meg was confused for a moment, then thought hard. "What did you tell Bethany to upset her so?"

"Don't try so hard," the big cat said, wincing. *"I told her the two males are following the other."*

"The other what?"

"The other old one, the one who took something she wants from those who took it from you."

"And what was that?"

The big cat made a motion that in a person would have been called shrugging. Meg was beginning to understand that answers were not going to come easily just because she was learning how to hear the animals. But at least she *was* learning. She shivered with delight and discovered her fear of Maraba had disappeared, though the respect remained. She was sure that would never leave.

Bethany seemed to be winning whatever internal struggle she was waging. When she returned to the wall and sat next to her again, Meg could see she had calmed herself, though there was a new steeliness in her expression.

"Please forgive my outburst, my dear," she said. "I just suffered a shock and a disappointment."

"The panther told me Patrick is not coming back right away, and neither is Gale," Meg said. "Is that a problem? Is that why you called him an old fool?"

Bethany looked from Meg to Maraba before answering. "Patrick isn't the old fool," she said. "But here comes Kathe. It will take all three of us to find a way to smooth this latest wrinkle."

Kathe stood in the doorway. She was holding several pieces of parchment covered with dark lines of writing. It must have been quite a dream. Meg thought she looked both very tired and extremely pleased with herself.

"Come join us, dear one." Bethany called.

"I can barely see you," Kathe said. "Why don't we go inside?"

"We will. But first you may like to greet and thank a friend of yours. She saved your life last night."

Kathe stood next to the wall squinting into the darkness. When her eyes had adjusted well enough to see Maraba, she scrambled over and knelt next to the big cat, kissed its head and hugged it. Maraba looked up and caught Meg's eye. Her expression seemed to be saying *See what I mean?* Meg couldn't help laughing.

Kathe caught the sound and smiled up at her. "Goddes! It is good to be back."

"Back?" Meg said. "Where have you been?"

"Come," said Bethany. "I'll pour some tea. Farewell, Beautiful," she said, but the panther was already melting back into the shadows.

"Goodbye, Careful. Don't let her do anything crazy." The panther's voice tickled Meg one more time before it disappeared. She followed Kathe and Bethany into the house.

"I heard that," Bethany said. Some of the humor had returned to her voice. "It is like Gerard to warn the guides to guard against my 'craziness.' After all this time he still doesn't understand that everything we do seems crazy to the animals."

"Who is Gerard? And what did he take from you?" Meg asked. She stirred the coals into life with an iron poker and added a log to the fire.

Kathe sat silently at the table. Her excitement at seeing Maraba again had drained away, and she stared down at her hands.

Bethany forced her to hold a cup of tea and tipped her chin up. After looking into Kathe's face, she took a jar from the mantle and sprinkled a pinch of leaves into the steaming cup. As they sank into the hot liquid, the scent of peppermint filled the air.

"Gerard is my mate," Bethany said. "You've seen him, though not met him, Kathe."

"The grey-cloaked healer with the kind eyes," Kathe said softly.

"Yes." Bethany paused. "He has taken the book."

"Ah." sighed Kathe.

"My book!" Meg said indignantly.

"You may lay some claim to it," Bethany said, "Though it was Gerard's when I met him, and his master's before that. He was in peddler's guise when he put it into your care. And even that, I now see, was to keep it from me."

"But why?" Meg asked.

"That book hides knowledge we can use to bring the people of Pallas home, but even if we can decipher the message, the way is perilous." Bethany paused, a faraway look in her eyes. "Death has his own maps, and the island of Niue doesn't appear on them. He has never blighted its shores."

Kathe listened intently. Was it possible the frail, lovely lady of Pallas and her husband still lived in this island refuge? And all the people, the young women and couples who had passed her in the street – still living?

"That's not possible." Meg said skeptically.

"Neither are talking animals, sleeping warriors – or me, for that matter. I should have been dead long ago. And that is the problem at the heart of Gerard's scheming. We have both lived long as healers, devoted to life. Whenever we use our gift, it pours out on whoever or whatever we are trying to mend, but a little shower of it blows back upon us – a little extra life. I could appear to you as a young woman, but of all the ages I have lived, this is the most comfortable."

"Why doesn't Gerard bring the book here then instead of stealing it?" Meg persisted. She was smarting from the loss.

"As I said, that is the problem. We think the people of Pallas have lived on an island, frozen in time all these years, but we believe that place will have the opposite effect on old ones like Gerard and me who have outstayed a human lifetime here. If we go to the island, we will have to stay there. Otherwise, our own lives are likely to end at last." Bethany studied the dancing flames. "Gerard can't imagine a world without me any more than I can imagine one without him."

"Will he go there alone, then?" Meg asked.

"Not if I know Patrick and Gale," Kathe said with a sigh.

"Why does Gerard have to go there at all?" Meg persisted, passing over Kathe's remark. "If this island is such a paradise, why not leave the people there forever?"

"Life without death," Bethany mused. "Think of it. Imagine a sprouted seed that never buds or becomes a flower. Babes that never learn to walk. Children who never shoot up into gangling youth and go courting. No new babies. No grandchildren. No comfortable old age. Worse. To be trapped in a frail, ancient body with no hope of release."

"Oh," Meg said, aghast.

"Perhaps they have become used to such an existence, but they must at least be given the choice. Gerard and I have always agreed about that, at least."

The tea seemed to be reviving Kathe. She invited Rowan into her lap and stroked her.

"Why now? Why not long ago?" Meg asked.

"You never knew my eldest brother Honorus. Nor were you privy to Kathe's dream. You could read her parchment. I imagine that would explain a great deal."

"I can't read."

Bethany looked at her intently before continuing, "Ah. Well, the pages will lie on the desk until you can. In the meantime, I will try to answer your question without creating more."

She paused, collecting her thoughts. "For a time after the people left Pallas, my brother Honorus kept the book close and squatted in our old house like a toad on a rock. He still planned to become the Prince of Pallas and to extend his reach beyond the forest. To do this, he had to first find the people of Pallas and bring them home. He threw away what was left of his youth in searching for them. The book relinquished many of its secrets, but the map to Niue was as fluid as water. Every time he looked at it, which was every day, the island lay in a different compass direction. Gerard became accustomed to hearing his howls of rage echoing up from the library."

"As he promised, Gerard stayed close by to watch Honorus. He passed the time by learning all he could from the animals. They were his companions during those years, they and his first hound, adopted from the dogs left behind in the city. At the same time, he was always watchful for an opportunity to recover the book. In time, all his others could be all be copied from memory, or purchased from merchants. The book containing the map to Niue is irreplaceable. Its content changes as the world changes. If a discovery is made on the other side of the world, a new page may appear, or a new plant may be added to a border. The book also changes depending upon its reader. Honorus found that some pages were glued together, and he could not separate them without destroying them."

Meg bit her lip in concentration as she listened to Bethany's incredible story. She knew the book was beautiful and guessed it was valuable, but it almost sounded alive!

Bethany continued, "The Runners kept Honorus supplied with food. He traded everything of value from first our house and then other houses in the city to pay them."

Kathe interrupted, "So how did you get it?"

"One day Honorus simply disappeared. He left the library door wide open and the book lying on the table. He may have finally given up. Or, maybe he decided to leave it to Gerard – and to me—to find Niue. That way he could get what he wanted without having to seek the answers himself. He must be dead by now. Honorus was no healer, quite the opposite, so he would have lived a mortal life."

"At first Gerard and I worked together to find the solution to the puzzle, but to be truthful, we didn't work too hard at first. During those years we built this house, and it is the only time in our marriage when we lived as husband and wife. We were happy, but when Gerard had learned enough to see that the rescue of the people might mean the end of me, he took the book and left. Now we rarely meet, and when we do, he never has it with him."

"He may have finally found a way to know for certain when the book is showing the truth, or maybe he just decided to take it back when he learned Meg had lost it in the battle. In either case, he seems to believe the time has come to go to Niue at last."

"But what about Patrick?" Kathe blurted. "He is an old one, too. What will happen to him if he goes to the island?"

"I don't know," Bethany said. "He never figured in our plans. Do you believe you could stop him from going there?"

There was silence.

"What are we going to do?" Kathe and Meg said at almost the same moment.

"That's the question, isn't it? We could hare after them. Of course, the animals, poor things, would feel duty bound to tell them, and then they would move more quickly and maybe more carelessly. Or…"

Meg refilled her mug from the teapot.

"Or what?" Kathe demanded.

"Or we can play our parts as they are written. After Gerard left me, I was very lonely. I decided to return to my old wandering life. For many years I didn't even write letters to him. I tried to put him out of my mind, though that was impossible. Then, about seventy years ago, I was walking along the River Dove in the same area where I first began my journeying after I left Pallas, and I came upon a manor house."

Meg noticed Kathe was sitting very still. Her eyes were pinned upon Bethany's face.

"It was newly built of worked stone. When I saw it, I knew a longing for Pallas and a homesickness I had not felt in many years. As I approached the door, it opened exactly as if someone had been waiting for me, and a little girl stepped out. That was your great- grandmother, Kathe. She was about ten years old, and when she walked down the step and took my hand, I knew I would be staying. I had never felt the healing gift so strongly in any other person. Untaught as she was, it flowed through her fingers and into me. She healed me, Kathe, or at least she started. Her daughter, your grandmother, finished. And now you have stumbled into my clearing, and it seems likely you will be the greatest of the four."

There had been tears shining in Kathe's eyes when Bethany spoke of her Grandmother, but now her mouth dropped open in disbelief.

"I have no gift at all," she said. "Mother tried."

"You have the gifts of courage, friendship, a kinship with the creatures of the forest. They love you, Kathe. That isn't true for everyone. And other gifts lie sleeping, waiting to be coaxed into wakefulness. The gift of healing is only one of them. I can't tell what else is there until we begin."

"Begin?"

"Begin your training. And yours, Meg. You already are skilled in loyalty and determination. It is time for you to learn how to read. You too are ready to bloom. Unless the men have the good sense to winter in Ostara, they will be journeying north into the teeth of winter. By the time they reach the sea, they will be met by ice and the storms of early winter. In order to reach the island, they will have to find a seaworthy vessel and learn to sail her themselves. I happen to know Patrick and Gerard have never set foot on the deck of a ship. Has Gale?"

Meg shook her head.

"Some things are hard to learn from books. Our pursuit now would have little effect upon the two feckless young men and one fey old one now hurrying north. The course I will suggest may seem easier, but it is really much more difficult, and ultimately more dangerous." She looked first at one girl, then the other. "If you stay here, I promise that, by early spring, you will both have learned much. You will be better able to face the trouble in Ostara, Kathe, or if you choose, you may come with me to find Gerard and to seek Niue. When he and I leave this world, it will be together," she concluded firmly.

Bethany busied herself around the kitchen, latched the door for the night and pulled the window shut.

"Tell me," Kathe said. "Do you know whether my mother still lives?"

Bethany stared out through the glass into the darkness. "I am not certain, but I believe she does. I think I will know when her spirit leaves this world. The last time I saw her was when she visited years ago and brought you, Kathe. She was so besotted with you that she feared she was seeing a gift where there was none. She wanted to know for sure."

"You are thinking you should go to her, but there is a way to send the message that you are safe here, with me, and learning all you can to help your people…and mine." she finished so softly that Kathe and Meg could hardly hear her.

For long minutes there was no sound but the snoring of the pup and the crackling of the fire. Kathe gently put Rowan on the floor, stood and took Bethany's arm. Standing together, they might have stepped off the page of the book where three women walked arm in arm. *Where is the blond woman to stand on the other side of Kathe? She should be here,* Meg thought.

Kathe's voice interrupted her thoughts, "This is not what I

expected on that day you caught me daydreaming when I should have been picking berries, friend. Yet Bethany has laid out the choice clearly. I want to go to Ostara even though I know my return would likely only make more trouble there. Patrick and Gale are our friends. I want to follow them at once to tell them how angry we are that they left us, and I want to meet Bethany's Gerard. My heart tells me I can keep them all safe even though my head counters that it isn't true. So what do you say? I am leaving it up to you this time."

Meg doubted whether Gale had ever been on a boat, let alone sailed one. She remembered the night he insisted on going with her to meet Kathe under the lightening struck tree at Springvale. Then he was Lord Gale, her master's son. Now he was just Gale, someone else entirely.

Meg wasn't the same person who stepped into the forest beyond the lightening struck tree, either. She remembered her mother's embrace; the way it felt to hold Kathe's hand and Gale's when Patrick awoke; the terror of climbing the cliff and of running from the dogs in ancient Pallas. She took her time, tracing her way day by day through her memory until she reached this moment in the warmth of Bethany's kitchen.

Bethany and Kathe watched her patiently. They really seemed to be waiting for her to make a decision. The panther had called her Careful; she considered each choice until one felt right.

Finally, she spoke, "Bethany is right about you, Kathe. You must become a healer, like your mother. Through winter, we will be seeds under the snow, and in the spring we will be ready to leave this place. At least we will have talked through enough long nights to know what we must do. I think we should stay here. And," she added, "I do have a powerful wish to read."

53

WAITING

PATCH STOOD OUTSIDE THE door of his house to watch the first snowflakes swirl into the clearing and settle on his wife's garden. The dry leaves of the frosted plants rattled in the wind. Inside, Maron waited, snug under a heap of pelts next to the central fire. This winter, for the first time, Patchson slept away from home, in a hut with the other young men. For a Woods Runner, this was part of becoming an adult. The tween house was not far, but Patch missed him.

Woods Runner men were supposed to be silent loners, roving in the forest from spring through fall, but Patch was getting older. He would have been happy to stay at home year round with his wife. Maybe that's what he would do next spring – stay here with the old men and the women, help Maron in the garden, choose a boy and start teaching him how to track.

Patch was getting cold. He didn't know what he was waiting for. No animal would stop by to talk on a night like this. The old owl glided through the clearing as soon as he came outside, and it landed on a low pine branch, but it didn't speak, only hunched down and hid its head under its wing.

He was just about to go inside and warm his feet by the fire before crawling into bed when he saw movement. He squinted to make out the shape, then waited as Patchson emerged from the snowstorm.

"Call's sons came back today from the Claymon camp with as many bottles as they could carry. It's too noisy to sleep in the tween house tonight. Can I stay with you and Ma?"

"Fine by me," Patch said.

Patchson put a hand on his father's arm to keep him from going into the house. "I thought we could talk. Make some plans for spring. Now that the boy from the cave has taken a different road from the red-haired woman, we'll have to decide who to follow, unless we work alone, follow both, and use the animals for sending messages to each other."

"I thought you'd be on your own by next spring, collecting skins to trade for a bride come fall, or maybe tracking for the Claymon like some of the others," Patch said.

Months before, he and Patchson had followed Patrick and his companion from the battle site. It was the two Woods Runners who found the healer and sent him to where Patrick's companion lay poisoned by the viper. When the peddler's wagon turned north toward Ostara carrying all three men, the trackers returned to Running Girl's farm and made their camp in the forest until a crow told them that Kathe and Meg looked to be settled until spring. By then Patch had convinced himself that he had done his duty by the Lady, but it seemed his son had other ideas.

"Patrick and the two other men were heading north when we saw them last," Patchson said. "You've never said. Do you know where they are going?"

"No," snow was now collecting on Patch's fur slippers. Without being aware of it, he made the sign to ward off evil in the direction of the city wall.

"They'll have to hole up somewhere for winter. Some of the other Runners traveled far this season, to Ostara and beyond. They say no one can cross the mountains north of the Three Hills after snow comes, and it comes much sooner there than it does here," his son said.

"So, you're thinking we should pick up their trail in the spring," Patch said. He had not yet talked to his son about his idea of staying at home, and neither of them had told anyone about the whereabouts of the girl from Ostara.

"I was thinking the same as you, that the boy from Pallas woke up for a reason, though only the Lady knows what that reason is. I know the Woods Runners always lived outside the walls of Pallas, and our dealings with the city folk were mostly limited to trade," Patchson paused, and his father waited patiently for him to continue. "Still, Runners from Great Grandda on down have been keeping watch over that boy. He's our responsibility. His friend would have died if we hadn't found the healer in time. Suppose they need us again!"

When Patch didn't answer, Patchson continued.

"And what about that girl, the one the Claymon wanted us to find for them? We followed her long enough to know she won't stay put on that farm forever. She might need us too. We haven't had any word from the Lady yet, and until we do, you said we have to look after the girl, and Patrick too."

Patchson was right. Patch looked around the clearing, reluctantly letting go of his dream of drowsing away the seasons in the company of his wife. Lifting the curtain of skin which was the door of his house, Patch gestured his son forward into the warmth.

"Spring will come, and everything will begin to flow again. We'll spend one more summer together, my boy," he said softly.